A TOWN CALLED NOWHERE

BY

MARIA HARLAND

**'OH WHAT A TANGLED WEB WE WEAVE
WHEN FIRST WE PRACTICE TO DECEIVE'**

*From the verse Marmion;
A Tale of Flodden Field by Walter Scott 1808*

Dedicated to the memory of

Jean Cooper

(12/01/46 - 25/04/03)

who taught me that life is not a dress rehearsal. Also special thanks to my amazing wife Liz and wonderful daughters Katie, Claire and Ami for their help, support, love, and for encouraging me to pursue my dream of writing a novel.

PROLOGUE

'Write our story,' said Jean.
'Write our story,' she said.
'Write the story of us.'

She had asked me more than once to write our story during that all too short month before she left me. That last desperate month when even reason lost all reason...

I know she did not choose to leave me, so why did I blame her for going? I knew that it did not make sense, but then again not a lot did make sense during that time. My emotions were all over the place. I would plead with her to give up and be free from the pain but the next moment I would beg her to fight. Fight for that last breath, that last moment of consciousness to spend with me. Grieving, like death I now understand, can be both selfish and selfless. It is only now with the passage of time that I can confess that I was terrified of inhabiting a world without her in it. She defined me and I had no idea who I would be without her. The thought of not being close to her, not being able to touch her, hear her, see her, filled me with dread. I was overwhelmed with grief yet desperately trying to hide my feelings. In my own clumsy way I suppose I was trying to protect her. If I voiced what was happening, it would become true. My worst nightmare would begin. Death the greedy impatient mistress was tiring of waiting in the wings.

Jeans' leaving; her dying, was like our falling in love. It was out of our control, out of my hands, and out of hers. Her life, like a speeding train, gaining momentum until it reached the inevitable cliff edge.

We talked those last few weeks.

We talked of things which people only talk about when there is nothing to hide and no reason to hold back.

We cried those last few weeks.

We cried until there were no tears left to cry. Each morning I would wake with my arms wrapped about her and wonder if the next *morning I would wake alone. I could not, I would not, contemplate a world without her in it.*

How could I?

She was my world.

'*Write our story.' said Jean.*

'*Write our story. Not in a trashy magazine, someone at the hospital did that for her boyfriend when he died. It was tacky. Don't do tacky Louisa. Write a proper novel, with proper people. Write about me. Write about Lucy. Write about us. Write a happy ending. Make me special.'*

I stopped her then, holding her face in my hands as I gazed into those wonderful green grey eyes. We lay there, very still, unspoken words whirling above us, a vortex of questions, promises, declarations. As we lay looking deeply into each other's eyes, I remembered once reading that the eyes were the window to ones' soul. Perhaps if I stared long enough, I could reach her soul, take it, save it, protect it, and covet it forever. All these thoughts raced through my mind and it was a while before I could trust my voice to speak.

'*You are special, my darling,' I said struggling to fight back my tears. 'I promise to write our story and I promise that in our story we will live happily ever after.'*

'*Just like in a fairytale?' she asked.*

'*Yes just like in a fairytale.'*

I pulled her towards me then, slowly, gently, so as not to jolt her pain-racked body and I tenderly kissed my fairytale princess. Enrobed in that kiss was the promise to write our story. My fairytale princess would live happily ever after forever and ever in our story.

Well this is it, I've written our book Jean, and yes it has a happy ending.

I kept my promise Jean.

Enjoy your book.

Enjoy your happy ending...

A TOWN CALLED NOWHERE

And so Jean our story begins;

Allow me first to introduce you to Sooty. Sooty lives in a town far far away from Jean. Sooty lives in a town called Nowhere. Sooty it must be said had not always lived in Nowhere, although it often felt as if she had. So familiar were the streets, smells and sounds of the sleepy market town. It was the place she now referred to as home. Old adages ring true, home is where the heart is, and it was in Nowhere that she first lost her heart, oh so many years ago.

The first time Sooty had visited the sleepy market town she had been a young pigtailed schoolgirl on an end of term trip. She and her fellow students had marvelled as the school coach manoeuvred through the archway of the narrow tower on the outskirts of the main town. Staring out of the coach window to their left they had seen a meandering street of quaint bow fronted shops fronted by a slope of uneven cobbles. There was a sweet shop, its jars a kaleidoscope of candy reflecting and winking in the sunlight. A butcher's, a baker's, probably even a candlestick maker's. Why not, the whole town had a nursery rhyme feel to it. Sooty had almost expected 'Little Bow Peep' to cross the street. Nowhere's fairytale castle stood high on a hill flanking the historic town. A meandering river wound around its base crossed by an ancient stone bridge. Sooty sat munching her sandwiches and sipping her lukewarm lemonade on the banks of that very river watched over by stone knights high on the castle ramparts. Her surroundings so startlingly different from those she had left behind earlier that morning. Sootys home town of Newcastle, a grey cheerless blot on the landscape where desperation and despondency were reluctant bedfellows. If towns were paintings L.S. Lowry would have painted Newcastle; all grey and industrial populated by matchstick men and matchstick cats and dogs. By contrast Nowhere with its chocolate box views and endless landscapes would be classic Constable. Alas she mused, towns were not paintings and nursery rhymes were just words in books, and nonsense words at that. She was brought abruptly back to reality by the teacher instructing her young wards to pack up their sandwich boxes and head back to the coach.

A short while later, as Sooty was jostled back upon the coach, her toes smarting in her Sunday best buckled shoes', she silently vowed that one day she would live in Nowhere. She crossed her fingers and wished really hard, as hard as she had ever wished for anything ever before. One day she would walk the cobbled streets and stare from her window at the endless landscapes and far away green felted hills crowned by the majestic castle. She would rewrite her past to fit into her new future. That Nowhere was her future she had no doubt.

So it came to be that Sooty achieved her dream, albeit through methods she would prefer not to dwell on. Yes, Sooty had now lived in Nowhere for such a long time that even the stalwart locals could little remember a time when she had not walked their streets, graced their homes and taught their ever increasing broods of children. Sooty had gained her air of respectability; she belonged. She had wiped the slate of her past clean, ingratiated herself. She had chaired charity committees and sung off-key in the church choir. Basically, she was now a fully-fledged member of the community, a privilege she coveted, often pinching herself in disbelief at her good fortune.

EARL GREY AND THE ARCHERS

The day began like any other. A steaming mug of coffee, a round of toast spread thickly with marmalade, a quick scan of the local newspapers, then a casually dressed stroll to the post office. Sooty it must be said, was not a greatly attractive woman. She had never had the blonde hair or hourglass figure that classically beautiful women seem to have, but despite this she did possess a certain presence which was accentuated by her height. Sooty turned heads, she held herself well, not stooping apologetically as some tall women have a habit of doing. Her voice too, was authoritative, instilled with confidence. When Sooty spoke no one interrupted, to the contrary people stopped what they were doing, turned and listened. Her correctly pronounced vowels echoed her years of elocution lessons and her accent was now impossible to define,

Back to today. Sooty strolled purposely towards the post office, her intention being to purchase a belated birthday card for her mother. As she meandered up the street browsing in the shop window of the local ladies' outfitters, she glanced across at the Bistro that stood awkwardly on the corner of the street. Rumours had been circulating that the business had been taken over, and that the new owners were not locals. Sooty had also overheard that the two ladies were of a particular persuasion. Rumour-mongering was a favourite pastime of many a rural town. It had been remarked that, if no gossip was readily available, then some would be manufactured. Nothing surprised Sooty any more. She knew now to expect the unexpected. Giving in to curiosity she slowed her pace and crossed the road. Approaching the Bistro she bent over to peer into the large glass shop window. The window had been sprayed with '*Windolene*' from the other side to deter exactly this, but where one stroke met another a gap had formed; the perfect spy hole. Cupping her face in her hands in an attempt to block out the sunlight, Sooty peered in. It took a while for her eyes to become accustomed to the unfamiliar darkness. But when she did she could see that the Bistro interior was in a state of disarray. Cardboard boxes lay strewn everywhere, a tool box, paint cans, newspapers and crumpled carrier bags.

Two coffee mugs, one lipstick-rimmed, sat on the table closest to the door, along with what looked like the remains of a sandwich. Sooty tried hard to focus upon the area between the stairwell and the bar, and, as she did, a figure appeared at the doorway leading to the kitchen. But before she had a chance to form any opinion about the figure, Sooty was grabbed from behind by a very familiar pair of tanned freckled arms.

'Oh Lennie,' she gasped, when she recovered from her shock and recognised the arms. 'You did give me such a fright.'

'It's what a nosy parker deserves,' replied a smiling Lennie.

'I was just going to the house for a cup of tea. Where were you going before your curiosity got the better of you?'

'Only to the post office to buy my mum a card, but I can go later. Come on, I'll walk back to the house with you, I could do with a cuppa.'

The house in Gloucester Court was a short stroll from the Bistro, about halfway between it and the castle that had so enthralled Sooty as a young girl. It was set back from the street, accessed by an arched doorway squeezed between another house and an Italian Restaurant. This narrow dark corridor led to a large sun kissed courtyard garden. Sooty had chosen the house from a romantic notion that the corridor led to a secret garden, but a more cynical friend, who fancied herself as an amateur psychiatrist had a different interpretation. Sooty had, according to the friend, chosen the house purely because it was hidden from the street. Just as Sooty chose to hide her true sexuality from the populace of Nowhere, so she had chosen a house that hid its true frontage and presented a false facade.

'Psychodribble and psychodrabble' said Lennie who did not suffer fools lightly.

Although it must also be noted that Lennie had never had any time for the friend in question, due to an earlier dalliance the friend had once shared with Sooty.

Her cleaning lady Maggie was locking the front door as they approached the house.

'Oh, hello Miss T, I was just leaving,' she said, stating the obvious. 'The kettle's still warm, I had a quick brew. The ironing's done and I've changed the bed in the spare room.'

'Thanks, Maggie,' Sooty replied. 'You're a gem. See you on Tuesday then.'

Sooty opened the door and led the way into the house. Lennie followed, closing the outside world behind her. She spoke almost before Maggie was out of earshot. Most unlike Lennie to be so careless thought Sooty to herself.

'Have you heard the rumours about the Bistro?'

'What rumours?' said Sooty, although she knew exactly what Lennie was alluding to. Sometimes it gave her a warped sense of pleasure to hear Lennie struggle to explain things in detail.

'The rumours,' Lennie repeated. 'Oh, you are exasperating, Sooty, the rumours that the new owners are of a particular persuasion.'

Lennie had an old fashioned turn of phrase, which Sooty had once found endearing but which now infuriated her.

'Do you mean they're gay, Lennie?' Sooty intoned, her voice louder and coarser than she had intended.

'You know exactly what I mean, Susan,' Lennie barked back, using Sooty's full name to register her annoyance.

Realising she had been unfair, Sooty playfully slapped Lennie's behind to lighten the mood. A gesture which at the beginning of their relationship would have had Lennie panting for more and racing Sooty upstairs for a quick fumble beneath the sheets. Now, the gesture only served to further annoy Lennie as she bustled into the kitchen.

'There is a time and a place, Susan,' she reprimanded.

'If only there were,' Sooty muttered under her breath, but not too quietly; she wanted Lennie to hear.

'Let's not quarrel,' Lennie cajoled. 'Come on Sooty Sue, the kettle's still warm. Why don't I make us a nice pot of Earl Grey and we can sit together and listen to the Archers?'

Sooty was still in a contrary mood. She wanted to argue, she wanted to feel the blood rise in her cheeks, to feel her pulse quicken. She wanted Lennie to fight back, to argue, to shout, then to lie and stroke her hair as she used to do in the early days when the best part of an argument would be the tender making up.

Lennie, however, had no compulsion to argue anymore. The fire of passion had left her belly. She had her garden, her endless cups of tea, her cats, and her blasted Archers. It was only Sooty who wanted, who needed, who craved more. So Sooty had her indiscretions, her moments, her lady-friends, as Lennie politely called them. Sooty felt her passion stir as each new relationship entered the honeymoon period, only to feel it inevitably ebb away as it ended. Sooty, they said, was married. Sooty, they said, was married in mind if not in body.

She was conjoined by the superglue of habit and companionship. No one could ever destroy the bed-dead relationship. And so we leave Sooty and Lennie for the moment, each silently harbouring her own thoughts, companionably listening to the Archers and sipping their Earl Grey.

JOHNSON AND SONS, ANTIQUE EMPORIUM, NOWHERE

Elsewhere in Nowhere, high up in the eaves of his warren of an antique shop sat George Johnson. He was methodically tapping the keys of his calculator. Suddenly he sneezed. He sneezed loudly, so loudly that his secretary, who was in the adjoining office texting her lover, jumped in her seat. George, unaware of the commotion he had caused in the other room, produced a monogrammed handkerchief from his left breast pocket and blew his nose loudly twice, as was his manner. Then, pressing the intercom on his desk, he summoned Yvonne, his secretary, into the office.

'Yvonne, a favour,' he began, giving her a wide smile, which he thought made him seem friendly and approachable but had been cruelly described by his wife as a creepy, ingratiating leer.

'Would you pop down to the travel agent and collect my plane ticket and then en- route nip to the cleaners for my white linen suit? I've mislaid the collection tab but I'm sure it'll be fine, just say it's mine.'

George had a great sense of self-importance. A big fish in a little pond, he believed that the mere mention of his name could move mountains. In a way, it was probably true. He came from old money, and, whilst not the sharpest tool in the box, he had managed to charm and cajole his way through life. George had his great grandfather, Harold Johnson, to thank for his notoriety and big fish status. Harold had been Nowhere's first Town Mayor way back when, and upon his untimely death his son had commissioned a visiting Italian stonemason to design and erect a fountain and drinking font in the town's market place. The Johnson memorial fountain still stood, although subsequent events had somewhat marred its presence.

It was claimed by town historians that the fatal epidemic which swept through Nowhere in the late 1800's had originated from the water in the font. The terrible illness, which wiped out vast areas of Nowhere, had directly benefited George's paternal grandfather, Harold's son, who, as the local undertaker and carpenter, had seen a dramatic increase in trade. More cynical citizens of Nowhere had remarked upon this coincidence at the time, only to be silenced by thinly veiled threats.

George had political ambitions of his own, or rather Lillian, his pushy wife, had. A Machiavellian puppeteer with George as her chief puppet, Lillian rather fancied herself as Lady Mayor, dressed in robes and mayoral chains, lording it over the Women Turning Fifty coffee mornings. With this ambition in mind, Lillian had sent George hotfoot to the local optician's only the previous week to be fitted with disposable contact lenses. How George longed for his tortoiseshell framed spectacles in their velveteen case, and how George's eyes itched and watered. But George was the first to concede that Lillian was not an easy woman to disagree with, and often compliance was the easiest option. At least, thought George, he had his brief jaunt to Venice to look forward to. George thoroughly enjoyed his career as an antiques dealer, and through his friend, the Earl, he had a wide and diverse range of wealthy clients. George was only too happy to source a specific item for a specific client, especially if the search entailed an all expenses trip abroad. This thought reminded George that he had a haircut booked at '*Hair Today*' at two thirty. He must make haste. Pausing only to collect his distinctive brass-tipped walking stick and overcoat, George left the office.

HAIR TODAY, GONE TOMORROW

Raymond of 'Hair Today, Gone Tomorrow', was preening himself in the salon mirror as George crossed the street. Mortified at finding a stray grey hair, he hastily retreated to the gents' to pluck out the offending follicle. Smoothing his eyebrow with a dampened fingertip, Raymond glanced down at his wristwatch. Oops, he thought, better get outside. It was time for his next client.

His next client, George was waiting, tip-tapping his walking stick rhythmically upon the salon's tiled floor, much to the annoyance of the other customers and salon staff.

Raymond presented himself in front of George.

'Hello to you, Mr Johnson, and how are you today?'

'Never better, Raymond, and you?' replied George, rolling the R of Raymond in a way which he thought made him sound cosmopolitan.

'All the better, for seeing you Georgie,' Raymond whispered as he bent to fasten the towel around George's neck. Producing a metal comb with a flourish from his hip pocket, somewhat like a magician producing a rabbit from a hat, Raymond parted George's fringe.

'Do you want the usual short back and sides?' Raymond enquired, tilting his head to the side as he asked the question.

'Yes please, I'm too top heavy with this unruly mop. I'm off on a wee jaunt tomorrow, hoping to top up the tan.'

'And will the lovely Mrs Johnson be joining you?'

'Unfortunately not as she had other commitments, wouldn't you know.'

'What a shame. Still, I'm sure you won't be short of company, a well-travelled man like yourself.'

'A little bird told me you were on holiday yourself fairly soon, Raymond.'

'Now that would be telling, Mr Johnson.'

Ten minutes later Raymond stretched behind the chair to reach a small rectangular mirror, which he positioned behind George's head. George peered at his reflection in the mirror and nodded.

'Very nice, Raymond, thank you so much. I've said it before but I will say it again: you are wasted in a provincial hairdresser's like this, a talent such as yours should be exploited.'

'Flattery will get you everywhere,' Raymond whispered into his clients' ear.

'I very much hope so, dear boy,' George replied as he pressed a coin into Raymond's palm.

'A little bird tells me that your love life is as complicated as ever? teased Raymond's next client who was Georges' wife, Lillian Johnson.

'Ask me no secrets, Mrs Johnson, a true gentleman never tells.'

Lillian's face dropped, she had been hoping to glean some noteworthy gossip to pass on to her friends at Women Turning Fifty group she chaired. Realising that her expression had changed and fearing that his tip for the haircut would be similarly diminished Raymond hastily changed the topic of conversation.

'May I say you are looking particularly attractive today Mrs Johnson. I do declare that you look younger every time I see you. I am convinced that husband of yours has hung a Dorian Gray style portrait of you in your attic.'

It took a while for Lillian to comprehend the reference to Oscar Wilde's play but once she did she laughed girlishly.

'Oh Raymond,' she said flicking her hair theatrically.

'You are a very naughty young man, but you do such a lot for a woman's confidence.'

Raymond winked at Lillian's reflection in the mirror secure in the knowledge that the tip would reflect his flattery.

AN UNBURDENING OF GRIEF

Jean sat ninety miles away, far south of Nowhere, in a suburb of Leeds. She sat by a long picture window gazing out at her rabbit Fudge, as he raced across the lawn, spooked by the neighbour's cat. The cat had been lurking in the hedgerow, crouched, poised, waiting for birds. Two squirrels climbing the tree at the crest of the hill which framed Jean's garden stopped, freeze-framed by the commotion below. Jean sat quietly watching, motionless, without expression. Suddenly, unbidden, tears began to stream down Jean's face. She cried as she had never cried before. When her mother had died, leaving Jean an orphan at only 14 years of age, Jean had cried. All those years ago when Lucy had first been diagnosed, and Jean had struggled to come to terms with the fact that she and Lucy would never grow old together, Jean had cried. But those tears had been controlled; they were a blessed release, an unburdening of grief. The tears she cried now were different. They were desolate, alone, devoid of all hope.

Just a short while ago Jean had said goodbye to Lucy, and, with her, goodbye to a part of herself. Oh, people had offered the usual platitudes:

'She's out of pain.'

'She's in a better place.'

'She would want you to carry on, to be brave.'

All words, well meant, but merely words. Words wouldn't keep Jean company when she woke in the early hours of the morning, alone and afraid. Words wouldn't make Jean a cup of sweet milky tea and hold her until the terrors subsided and sleep overtook her. Words wouldn't be there to laugh, soothe and encourage. Words were silent without Lucy to give them voice. Words were merely audible sounds. They were just words.

The two squirrels hopped from tree to tree. Fudge the rabbit sat contentedly munching on a juicy plant, and Midge, the neighbour's cat, bored with stalking birds in Jean's garden, sidled across the lawn to number 23 to tease the excitable spaniel that lived there.

And Jean?

Jean cried on.

THE CHARRED REMAINS OF DINNER

Back in Nowhere, Bob the taxi driver pulled into the drive of 9 Moss Side Drive. Tuning in the intercom in his cab he rang the switchboard at the office to check his bookings. An early fare to the airport: Mr Johnson the antique dealer at 6am before the usual school runs. Best try to have an early night. Climbing somewhat gingerly from his minicab, constricted by the sheer nylon pantyhose concealed under his stay press slacks, Bob made his way into the house.

'Honey, I'm home,' he shouted to his wife. 'Have you shrunk the kids?'

It was their private joke. How it had made Yvonne laugh the first time he'd said it. Now he feared it irritated her, but old habits die hard. Glancing quickly into the lounge, he saw that Yvonne's young charges were no longer there. She supplemented the income from her part-time job with old man Johnson by looking after some of the local school kids, collecting them from school and entertaining them until their parents got home from work. Yvonne quite enjoyed it, and she said it ensured that their own brood were never short of playmates. Hearing noises from the kitchen, Bob popped his head around the door.

'Hi honey, just phoned the office, early pick-up in the morning. I'm taking your boss to the airport.'

'Don't talk to me about that bloody man,' replied Yvonne, her voice somewhat muffled, as she was removing Bob's dinner from the darkest recesses of the oven.

'The bloody man's had me running all over Nowhere today, preparing for his bloody trip. What that wife of his does all day escapes me. I've felt more like a glorified servant than a bloody secretary.'

Sensing that his wife was not in the best of moods, Bob made to beat a hasty, well-practised retreat.

'Where are you buggering off to? I've just got your bloody dinner from the oven.'

Bob turned quickly and retracing his steps made his way to the table. Surveying the burnt, dried out plate of food his wife presented before him, Bob nearly made the cardinal sin of asking for the ketchup, a grave mistake he had once made, only to instantly regret it as the plate had hurtled through the air. For such a slight woman, Yvonne had a very powerful throw. At this thought, Bob took knife and fork in hand and prepared to do battle with the charred remains of his dinner.

Yvonne, meanwhile, stomped out of the kitchen into to the hall to answer the telephone, trying to keep her voice even as she realised that the call was from her lover Clive.

'Oh hello Clive, yes that's fine. I will be straight home after the school run so drop off the bag then.'

'You sound so sexy.'

'Yes that's fine too,' Yvonne replied, aware that Bob could hear her side of the conversation from his vantage point by the oven.

'I take it that Bob's ear wigging.'

'Yes that's right. Thanks for calling to let me know, see you tomorrow.'

Yvonne was now desperate to hang up the telephone.

'Go on blow me a kiss...I dare you.' Clive goaded.

'Goodbye then,' said Yvonne hanging up.

Yvonne was irritated by Clive's laissez-faire attitude, sometimes it almost seemed to her as if he wanted Bob to find out about their affair. Smoothing her apron she made her way back into the kitchen.

'That was Clive on the phone,' she said.

'I know darling I heard,' Bob replied not looking up from his dinner plate.

'Be an angel and pop the kettle on my throats drier than the Sahara.'

GREENHOUSE BISTRO

Elsewhere in Nowhere the two new proprietors of the Bistro were weary. It was starting to grow dark outside, and they had reached the stage of exhaustion at which even forming a lucid sentence took sublime effort and dexterity. Eventually, after nearly losing her balance while climbing down from hanging yet another painting, Louisa turned to Joey.

'Let's stop for tea before we burn out completely.'

Joey sighed deeply before replying. 'But Louisa, we've got such a lot more to do.'

Collapsing into the nearest chair, Louisa said, 'Will ten minutes make such a difference? I don't think so.'

A few minutes later, a rather out of breath Joey also conceded defeat and slouched opposite her partner on the other side of the table. Both girls gazed out of the large restaurant window, lost in their own private thoughts, each hoping the other would offer to make the long trek into the kitchen to switch on the kettle.

Louisa and Joey had been a couple for just over a year, both coming out of long-term relationships and hardly believing their luck in finding each other so quickly. In the early days, they had an empathy that had eluded their past relationships. It was this empathy that persuaded them to move in together so early in their relationship. In retrospect, they would probably both concur that they had moved in too quickly, not giving themselves time and space to really make the decision. But as they joked to a mutual friend, they were real life examples of the classic lesbian joke;-

What do lesbians do on their second date?

Move in together!

They found in each other, in those early days, a soul mate, a confidante. This was especially important to Louisa, coming as she did from such a troubled childhood. Louisa thrived on the security that Joey offered her. Joey had made her feel safe in a way that no one else ever had, anticipating her emotional needs in a sensitive caring way.

Louisa had not experienced the most secure of childhoods. Born in Scotland in the early sixties to a bright, young, successful, moneyed couple, she was the eldest of three daughters. Her parents had both married within their social circle, a Scottish society wedding. Her father was the successful young doctor, the son of a well-respected surgeon, her mother a lady who lunched, pampering herself until the right beau came a-calling. They had been so happy, so young, so in love, the envy of all their peers. Somewhere along the line, her father's gambling had become a problem, and her mother had turned to alcohol to numb the pain of a life so ordinary. The girls' childhood was spent being ferried between maiden aunts and when the patience of the maiden aunts wore thin the girls bore time in the local orphanage.

On one such occasion, after the girls' mother had been committed to the local infirmary to have her stomach pumped yet again, the three girls were taken to a different orphanage. It was a Catholic orphanage, run by an order of nuns from the nearby Convent of St. Therese. They were driven there by their paternal grandfather, a fierce, scary, moustached man who communicated with his grandchildren in a series of guttural grunts. The three girls, collectively aged between 5 and 13, huddled together on the long leather back seat of the Bentley, wide-eyed, holding hands. As the Gothic looking building with the black iron railings came into view, Caro, the youngest sibling let out a squeal of pure terror and soaked her knickers. The Bentley engine purred to a halt at the entrance to the orphanage. Their grandfather sighed in exasperation as the urine formed a puddle and slowly dripped from the leather seat onto the floor of the car. They were greeted at the door by an expressionless nun, who glanced at Caro's wet backside, pursed her lemon lips and ushered the girls into the cold entrance hall. Their grandfather drove off without a backward glance. He had an important operation to do that afternoon, and had no time for such tomfoolery.

The following day the girls were escorted along with the rest of the children to the local park to play on the swings. Recreation was an important part of the orphanage's day, as it gave the nuns a chance for silent prayer in the chapel without being distracted by their boisterous wards. The day was fresh and crisp but bitterly cold, and Louisa shivered in her thin anorak as she pushed Caro on the swings. Her other sister, Anne Marie, called for Louisa to watch her as she leapt from the other swing, legs outstretched. Louisa watched Anne Marie, giving her the obligatory hand clap and congratulatory smile, then turned back to push

Caro, but as she did, she slipped clumsily on the frosty leaves underfoot. The heavy wooden swing hit her squarely on the chin, knocking her backwards and, more worryingly, rendering her unconscious.

Louisa could remember nothing of subsequent events save that she had woken up in a strange hospital bed. She lay in that bed for one long week, being a brave little girl, fighting back the tears as the other children on the ward were visited by their parents. Louisa would deliberately not look towards the ward door as visiting time arrived, but she would nevertheless cross her fingers beneath the bedclothes hoping against hope her mother or father would come and visit her. Sometimes a kindly nurse would come and sit beside her and chatter to Louisa in an attempt to try and lighten the little girl's spirits. It was becoming obvious to the nursing staff that Louisa's parents would never visit. They were angered by the fact that Louisa's grandfather, the fierce Mr Scott, was often seen parking his Bentley in the hospital grounds, and her father, young Dr Scott, would visit patients in the very next ward. When the doctors eventually decided to allow Louisa to go home, she was so happy she thought she would burst. But as there was no one to collect her and, because the nuns at the orphanage did not possess a car, she had to wait until early evening for an ambulance to take her home.

So it came about that Louisa arrived back at the dark, austere orphanage very late that night. All the other children were tucked up asleep in bed so Sister 'Lemon Lips' shone a torch to guide her to the bed wedged between Caro and Anne Marie. Immediately the nun saw that she had reached her bed she turned away and Louisa was left in darkness. It was not until she drew back the sheets that the stench of urine hit her nostrils. Her bed was wet through, the mattress so sodden that placing a hand upon it left an imprint. Louisa heard Caro weeping into her pillow and it quickly dawned on her that to avoid punishment her sister had swopped beds. Louisa was so happy to be back in the midst of her family that even this did not alter her joyful mood. Quickly stripping off her outer clothes she climbed into bed beside Caro, falling asleep almost before her head hit the pillow.

The girls were to spend many months at the orphanage, and although the place never felt like home, it at least became bearable because they were together, a family unit of sorts. Throughout their time there the girls formed a great dislike for one nun in particular,

Sister Loreto, the stern lemon lipped nun who they had first met on that dreadful night when their grandfather had dropped them off so unceremoniously at the entrance to the orphanage. For some reason Sister *'Lemon Lips'* took a particular dislike to Louisa and would seize upon any opportunity to chastise the child. One such incident preyed upon Louisa's mind, although, as she grew up, she embellished the story, normally to dinner guests, and in a strange way it became almost her party piece followed as it was by its more titillating anecdote.

Louisa would take her place at the head of the table and relay her story.

'My sisters and I were playing in the orphanage grounds. *'Lemon Lips'* believed that children should play out whatever the weather. We would have to run around in ice and snow, and 'woe betide' the child who stopped to catch their breath and lean against a wall to escape the bitter Scottish wind. But, as children do, we soon discovered that there was a place that *'Lemon Lips'* could not spy us from her designated position at the orphanage door. So when she was not looking we would run one at a time and hide behind the gardener's shed. Once there we would congregate and chat, jumping up and down on the spot to keep the feeling in our feet and hands. Well, on this particular day I had been holding court and showing off. At school that morning one of the day children had handed a piece of paper around the classroom. The paper contained the rudest rhyme that I had ever heard and I gathered a group around me to listen as I recited it. Performing the actions for my open mouthed audience, I pointed at the various parts of my anatomy when saying the appropriate words.

It was at this point that Louisa would usually struggle to her feet, wine glass in hand to add more drama to her story.

'*Milk milk'* she would say gesturing towards her breasts.

'*Lemonade'* she would add, pointing at the crotch of her jeans.

'*Around the corner, chocolate cake'* she would finish pointing at her bottom.

Once the raucous laughter had died down Louisa would again take her seat to return to her story.

'Well, the other children were mouths agape. You have to remember this was the sixties. They encouraged me to repeat the rhyme, with some of the braver children mimicking the actions. So intent was I in repeating the rhyme that I was blissfully unaware that the expressions on my audiences' faces had gone from being enthralled, to blind panic. An icy chill filled the already freezing air. Caro even went so far as to shriek out loud before wetting her knickers. I felt a tap on my shoulder and slowly turned. 'Lemon Lips' frosty gaze met mine. Wordlessly she grabbed me by my ponytail and dragged me to her office. Knowing my fate, I was determined to show her no fear. It became almost a battle of wills. I knew she wanted to break me and would beat me relentlessly until she did. I must have been a strong determined little bugger, typical Aries traits, because as she caned me I remember looking her deliberately in the eyes. My hand was turning red, ugly wheals were appearing on the palms. I knew if I apologised it would stop, but I would not form the words, my pride would not allow me. I believe she would still be caning me today if there had not been a knock at the door. A young novice nun, named Bernadette entered the room having being alerted to my punishment by the other children.

Well the young novice nun was taken aback upon seeing the state of my hand and witnessing the ferocity of the cane strokes. However she calmly said 'Sister Loreto, I think you have punished this young lady enough'. Upon hearing the soft tones of Bernadette, 'Lemon Lips' seemed to come to her senses. The cane dropped noisily to the ground. 'Lemon Lips' followed its downward path, falling to her knees in silent prayer, hands tightly clasped and eyes closed.

Bernadette took me by the arm and led me gently to the bedroom, where she sat me on the bed and held me as I sobbed. I think it was at that moment that I fell hopelessly in love with her. Although at such a tender age I didn't recognise it for what it was'

Louisa would stop her story at this stage and pour herself another glass of wine. One of the diners would inevitably ask Louisa if Bernadette and she had become lovers when she was so young. Louisa would shake her head and say,

'Heavens above no, I was just thirteen. No, it was much, much later, when I was about thirty and we met quite by chance. I was working for an estate agent's in Glasgow at the time, and a well-dressed woman walked in looking for a flat to rent. As I beckoned her over to my desk, something about her deportment felt familiar and I felt a chill run up my spine. My palms began to itch, and when I stretched out my hand to shake hers it was like an electric shock running through it but I still didn't recognise her completely until I heard her speak.

For years and years I had dreamt her voice, waking at night trying to recollect where I had heard that voice. I felt that the voice haunted me, triggering feelings, which once I tried to analyse them would slip annoyingly from my grasp. Bernadette, I have to say, had the kindest, most gentle voice I have ever heard, it caressed the eardrums. Her voice could soothe tempered angels and calm troubled storms. A voice like a pink marshmallow, its melting sweetness and softness intoxicated me. I was powerless, spiralling helplessly in its wake, mesmerised by its tone and pitch.

I remember staring at her for a while, willing her to recognise me, the young girl she had held and comforted on that dreadful day. I then made a point of introducing myself to her, substituting my married name for my maiden name in the hope that she would remember me. After a few moments, the name must have triggered a memory, for she blinked as if to clear her mind before repeating my name, over and over, so quietly only I could hear. *Louisa, Louisa*, she repeated as if it were a mantra. But before we had a chance to talk properly and reminisce, another well-dressed lady walked in the door and made her way across the office towards us. She placed a hand upon Bernadette's shoulder. She did this in such a proprietary manner, that it made the nature of their relationship immediately apparent to all but the least observant. Lucy, as I later realised the woman was called, took over the conversation and the matter in hand. She prompted me to search out the list of flats they wished to view, make the necessary phone calls to landlords, and in no time at all they had left the office. I think I was shell shocked for the remainder of the day, going through the motions on autopilot.'

'It was my job to lock the office at night. I was the keeper of the keys, a more important job than it actually sounded. It was dusk, I remember, and I struggled to set the alarm and pull down the heavy metal shutters. I was uncomfortably aware that I was being watched. From the corner of my eye I could see a figure in the doorway of the shop next door. I felt vulnerable and wary until I heard a voice gently calling my name. Bernadette emerged from the shadows, thankfully alone, with arms outstretched. My heart missed a beat, and I knew then why my marriage was a marriage no more. I had searched for that voice forever and on that day I found it. I ran, overjoyed, from the proverbial heterosexual closet, unfortunately trampling on poor John, my husband, in the process. But that, as all good storytellers will tell you, is another story altogether.'

Louisa would stop again at this point as if to collect her thoughts. She would continue when encouraged to do so, but her eyes would have a faraway look, not entirely attributable to the amount of alcohol she had drank.

'Bernadette and I became lovers that very night. I returned to the office and from a drawer in my desk I took the keys to a house nearby. The owner was on holiday abroad and had entrusted the keys to the estate agent, so any prospective buyers could be shown the property. I knew I was risking instant dismissal if found out, but so strong was my compulsion to be with Bernadette that all my fears fell to the wayside. I smoked in those days, and when we reached the house and closed the front door behind us, I used my lighter to light the way into the bedroom. Once we reached the bedroom, I was suddenly shy, so Bernadette took the lead all the while speaking softly to me as she slowly removed my clothes. When she reached my underwear, she raised her eyes questioningly. I nodded assent. I had lost the power of speech. Very gently she reached behind me to remove my bra, cupping my breasts in each hand as the bra dropped to the floor. And so my initiation began.

Bernadette took me to places I never knew existed, a foreign land of which I had heard but never visited. Although the language was alien to me, the contours of her body were roads I travelled with confidence and with almost a sense of déjà vu. Her soft skin and silken touch made me feel more alive than I had felt in all my thirty years. But the night had a dreamlike ethereal quality about it, almost too perfect to be replicated. We talked into the early hours of the morning, time being inconsequential and of no substance. It was then that she told me of Lucy's illness, the cancer which was slowly eroding her life. There was never any question of us meeting again. I knew neither of us could cope with the duplicities of an affair. To have such a relationship would cheapen the purity of our feelings. We would only have one perfect night, a night when time stood still and the world stopped revolving.

As we said goodbye the next morning, I said goodbye to my old life too. Bernadette made me promise to continue my search, not to settle for anything less than true love. She made me promise, made me clutch a tiny silver cross she wore around her neck as I made the promise. For although her love for Lucy had forced her leave her vocation, she had not divorced the man she married when she took her holy orders. She still believed, had her faith. She had not abandoned it, but embraced it in a different way. The man she had married, she said, would understand. He was gentle and forgiving. Had he not given his life for us on that cross?

At this stage in the story, Louisa would cross to wherever Joey was in the room, and kiss her gently on the lips. She felt that Joey needed reassurance of her love, needed to feel that she was not second best, a consolation prize. Taking her lover's hand in hers, Louisa would conclude her party piece. Louisa and Joey's dinner parties were legendary. Wine flowed, emotions were raw, but people never forgot the food or the ambience of the hosts. Friends who had been to the dinner parties previously would bring a bottle of *Blue Nun* and smirk as they placed it to chill in the fridge.

THE POINTLESS ATTACK

The girls sat quietly, gazing out of the Bistro window. Joey even commented on how quiet the street was at this hour. The occasional car drove past but apart from that nothing. The normally bustling Public House 'The Brits' which was opposite the restaurant had yet to open its doors, its staff were standing at the bar chatting about their weekend plans whilst polishing glasses and waiting for happy hour to begin. The only person on the street, an elderly lady, stood illuminated by the streetlight in-front of the bar, obviously waiting for her friend, who had just come into view and who was trudging slowly down the hill with the aid of a walking stick.

Suddenly, as if out of nowhere, and with a speed which made both girls gasp aloud, there appeared a youth of about twenty years. Like a battering ram to a castle portcullis, he did not slow his speed or try to divert his direction, instead he ran full force into the old lady, knocking her heavily to her knees. The handbag which she had been clasping in her left hand flew through the air with a similar force, its contents scattering upon the cobbles. Assuming they were witnessing a very violent mugging the girls expected the youth to make a grab for the old lady's purse and speed away. But worse was to follow for after regaining his balance the lad began to throw punches at her face. With clenched fists he struck her again and again before finally concluding with a well aimed kick to her ribs. In the time it took this whole event to unfold, which seemed to be played out in slow motion but in real time was only moments, the two girls had raced to the door to go to the old lady's aid. Seeing the Bistro door open, the youth ran off down the street. Joey, who witnessed his hasty departure, rushed across the street, whilst Louisa hurried back into the Bistro to ring the police.

AFTER THE ATTACK

Sometime later, the old lady and her friend were sitting in the Bistro sipping warm milky tea. They were both visibly shaken and seemed suddenly so very small and timid.

'Thanks so much my dear...' said the old lady, wincing as she sipped the hot drink with lips that were already swelling and dark.

Louisa had also requested an ambulance, being unsure of the extent of the old lady's injuries, and Joey was standing at the doorway waiting for the arrival of it and the police car. Both vehicles arrived simultaneously, sirens loudly blaring. They screeched to a halt in front of the Bistro. An older policeman quickly alighted from the police car and was first to approach the doorway. He crossed the room towards the old ladies with an expression of grave concern upon his face. It was obvious from his manner that he knew both of them personally. He turned to ask the ambulance men to hang on for a few minutes and knelt by the injured lady, taking her hand in his and gently reassuring her, as one would a child.

'Ah, Maggie, you have been in the wars! Did you see who did this to you?'

'It was that boy Robbie who used to live in the flat above me, he just started kicking and hitting me Inspector Dodd,' said Maggie before bursting into tears.

After talking quietly to Maggie for a few minutes, the Inspector left her side to request that the paramedics take her to the hospital to be checked over for broken bones. He would follow later with her friend in the police car.

Another policeman entered the Bistro, he was very young, and from the air of nervous excitement he exuded very new to the job. He hastily pulled a note book from his uniform pocket and earnestly began to question the old lady's friend. He then made to cross the room with the obvious intention of interviewing Joey and Louisa. Stopping him in his tracks, the older policeman pulled rank and asked that he first go outside to check the scene of the crime for any clues. Looking slightly bemused, but knowing better than to question his superior's authority, the young policeman left the building followed closely by the old lady's friend. Once they were out of earshot, the older policeman motioned for Louisa and Joey to sit down. Almost without prompting, Louisa started to tell him what she had seen. But before she had a chance to utter more than a few words the policeman put a finger to his lips and said.

'Sorry to interrupt my dear, but to clarify, you're telling me that it was very dark. You heard a commotion in the street but could see nothing.'

Confused, Louisa said 'no officer, we saw it all very clearly, it was....'

Interrupting again, the policeman repeated his last sentence, this time speaking very slowly accentuating each word carefully 'So you're telling me, it was very dark and you saw nothing.'

Joey was first to decipher his proposition and said, 'Well.... it was pretty dark I suppose.'

Upon hearing this, the policeman nodded sagely. Motioning his head in the direction of the young policeman on the street he said,

'Please remember to tell this to the eager young pup outside because as you two ladies are new to the area you are both quite conspicuous and it would be all too easy in a small community such as this is to find out where you live and to do some serious damage to yourselves or the business. Let me reassure you that we know the thug who carried out this attack. He used to live in the flat below Maggie and she has positively identified him. Apparently she once lodged a complaint about the loud music he was playing in the early hours of the morning and ever since he has held a nasty little grudge against her. My colleagues are picking him up in the police van as we speak. Even with witnesses the best we can hope for in court is a rap on the knuckles. But I have an uncanny hunch he will try to resist arrest, and trip up as they help him into the van, if you catch my drift.'

Both girls nodded, suddenly understanding. Delayed shock had set in. It was strange but watching violence on the television screen and in movies anaesthetised it. Seeing it played out in the real world was sickeningly different and Louisa especially was beginning to look traumatised.

Realising this, the policeman took the decision to ask the girls to visit the station the following morning to give statements, as neither were in a fit state to string a sensible sentence together. Staying behind, he helped them to lock and alarm the Bistro doors then personally drove them home in the police car after arranging for a colleague to drive Maggie's friend to the hospital.

That night as Joey and Louisa lay in the darkness of their bedroom enveloped in each other's arms they replayed the night's events again and again, trying to make sense of it. But it seemed the more they talked the more pointless the attack seemed. After all what motivation could there ever be to terrorise a defenceless old lady?

9 MOSS SIDE DRIVE

Bob the taxi driver was washing up in the kitchen of 9 Moss Side Drive. His caked on dinner took some shifting from the surface of the plate. Normally he would have left it to soak, but Yvonne's mood, which he presumed was pre-menstrual, prompted him to try and leave the kitchen spick and span to avoid any potential domestic row.

Yvonne was sprawled out on the sofa in the lounge. She was sipping a vodka and orange, relaxing, couch potato-like in front of some nightly soap. The children could be heard through the ceiling above pounding from room to room, squabbling over some toy. Yvonne was of the opinion that as long as she could hear them they would come to no harm, but silence was ominous as it usually meant that they were up to some mischief or other.

In the hallway the telephone rang. Bob dried his hands on the tea towel and trundled from the kitchen to answer the call. He was off duty tonight but perhaps one of the other taxi drivers had rung in sick and there was a rush job on. Yvonne could hear from the tone of his voice that the call was not connected to work, and left the comfort of the lounge to make to his side.

'Ok, I'm on my way. You sit tight and I'll be there straight away.' Bob said into the handset before replacing the receiver and turning to Yvonne and saying.

'That was Flo, your Aunt's friend speaking on the telephone. It seems that they are both at the hospital as Maggie has been attacked. She is bruised and battered, but no serious damage, thank God. I said I'd go straight there to collect them both. Shall I bring them here to stay tonight? They sound really shaken.'

'Of course the poor dears.' said Yvonne. 'I'll make up the beds in the spare room. I better ring Sooty too, she'll want to know.'

Sooty and Lennie were enjoying a casserole they had prepared earlier that day in their slow cooker when the telephone rang. Their appetite's swiftly disappeared after speaking to Yvonne.

'Give us five minutes and we are on our way,' said Sooty.

They were both very fond of Maggie, particularly Sooty, who had employed her as a cleaner for close to thirty years.

When Sooty had first moved into Gloucester Court, Maggie had come along with the purchase of the house. A human *'fixture and fitting'*. The vendor, an elderly vet, thought highly of Maggie, and it was an unspoken term of the sale that Sooty carry on her employ. Sooty, then a young teacher full of liberal values, found the concept of employing someone to clean her house jarred with her left wing beliefs. After a few difficult months of trying and failing to come to terms with the idea, she gently suggested to Maggie that she did not really need the services of a cleaner. She was, she explained, considerably younger and more physically able than the previous occupant of Gloucester Court and on her teacher's salary she was hard pushed to even meet her mortgage repayments. So Maggie had left her employ, leaving Sooty with a clear conscience as she declared that she had found a new job almost immediately. Unfortunately Sooty's feeling of vindication came to an abrupt end when she realised a few weeks later that Maggie's new job was as a toilet attendant in the public lavatories which had just opened in the town's bustling market place. A feeling of terrible guilt at once overcame Sooty and she rang Maggie to plead with the older lady to return to Gloucester Court. She even went so far as to empty some clean laundered clothes from her drawer into the laundry basket to back up her claim that she couldn't keep up to date with the housework. So Maggie returned to Gloucester Court where she had worked ever since. Although now, as she was well past the age of retirement, her duties were mainly to keep the cat company whilst Sooty was at work.

So we return to 9 Moss Side Drive, and three ladies awaiting the return of Bob from the hospital. Yvonne had gone into the kitchen to make cups of tea and Sooty and Lennie were sitting on the couch in the lounge. Sooty let her gaze take in the decor of the room and her eyes lit almost immediately upon a small watercolour on the wall above the fireplace. Nudging Lennie she got to her feet and crossed the room to look at it properly. Yes it was definitely an Elizabeth Blackadder and by the looks of it an original, or the best print that Sooty had ever seen. At that moment Yvonne came back into the room. Sooty flushed at been caught out snooping.

'Sorry for being a sticky beak Yvonne, I was admiring this wonderful watercolour. Is it an original?'

Yvonne smiled and giggled. 'Well yes, I suppose it is in a way.'

'How did you manage to get your hands on a Blackadder? Her watercolours command quite a price now, I understand.'

Again Yvonne giggled. 'Sorry for teasing you.' she said to Sooty. 'It is an original in that I painted it. It's not a copy of anything she has painted, just in her style.'

'Well, it's very good,' said Sooty, still admiring Yvonne's handiwork.

'I've got hundreds more paintings in the attic.' Yvonne added. 'It's something of a hobby of mine, I suppose, it calms me down when the kids are being particularly disruptive.'

'Well you've certainly been hiding your light under a bushel.' said Sooty. 'That's quite a talent you have there. I'm surprised that neither Bob nor Maggie has ever mentioned it to me.'

Yvonne brushed the remark away. 'Bob often tells his friends that I'm an artist, then laughs as he follows it up by saying 'I mean a piss artist.'

At this comment Lennie was prompted to join in the conversation and barked her disgust by adding, 'That man can be so crude.'

It was at that very moment that Bob came into the room, flanked by Maggie and Flo. All three looked tired and drained. There had been paperwork to fill in at the hospital and the doctor on duty had been reluctant to send Maggie home at all. But Bob had managed to convince the Registrar that Maggie would be well looked after and if there were any problems, however minor, he would bring her straight back to the Infirmary. Sooty, Lennie and Yvonne were all visibly taken aback by the appearance of the two old ladies, and after hugging them gently Yvonne took them straight upstairs to the spare bedroom. There would be plenty of time to talk tomorrow, but for the moment her main concern was that they both get some much needed rest. Sooty promised to ring first thing the following morning and Yvonne reassured her that if Maggie were to take a turn for the worse she would contact her immediately.

The two ladies drove back to Sooty's house in Gloucester Court, where Lennie had left her car.

'I really must make a point of popping into the Bistro during my lunch break tomorrow.' said Sooty. 'From what Bob told us those girls were very kind to Maggie and Flo, and I would really like to thank them personally.'

'It will give you a perfect excuse to sticky beak again' said Lennie wryly.

'That's the last thing on my mind really Lennie you really do have this terrible opinion of me sometimes.'

'Methinks the lady doth protest too much.' quoted Lennie.

Smiling, Sooty leaned across and squeezed Lennie's hand.

'Methinks the lady doth know me too well.' She conceded adding 'Are you sure you don't want to spend the night at Gloucester Court Lennie? I'm sure the cats could survive without you for one night, and it's very late for you to be driving home alone.'

But Lennie would not change her mind, and after a brief somewhat chaste kiss she climbed into her car and drove off promising to ring Sooty as soon as she got safely back to her own house.

GLOUCESTER COURT...THE BED DEAD RELATIONSHIP

In the early days of their relationship Sooty and Lennie had lived together at Gloucester Court. Their lives an odyssey of cosy nights in watching old movies, curtains drawn, happy and content in each other's company. They would bathe by flickering candlelight then make slow lazy love on the hearth rug in front of a roaring fire. Fingers stroking, slow controlled motions, the bringing of pleasure being pleasure enough, followed by luxurious lie-ins, cupped together like spoons. It had been a real life. It had been a good life. It had been a shared life.

Neither woman could pinpoint at what stage it all went wrong, but it was as if a wall appeared between them and all the talking in the world couldn't knock it down. They had tried many times, each getting more frustrated at every attempt. It was during one of these times that Sooty had first strayed, not intending to have an affair but succumbing none-the-less. Lennie and she were in a rut, their sex life all but over, content to cuddle and nothing more, partners from habit not by choice. So when a new trainee teacher had started at the school and Sooty was chosen to show her the ropes, the inevitable happened. Sooty fell head over heels in love. Mary was so unlike Lennie in every way. She wore her femininity as a beacon, stockings and too tight sweaters being the tools of her trade. She teased and titillated, promised then revoked, bragged of exploits with men then one drunken night professed to having fallen in love with Sooty. It was on this night that Sooty confessed to Lennie that she couldn't live a lie. Lennie's heart ached, an emptiness in the very pit of her stomach, a hunger for what had been and what could never be again. She still loved Sooty, but something changed forever that night. Their love was now tainted by the deception and infidelity.

Yet despite this she found herself comforting Sooty when the next day Mary proclaimed that it had been the drink talking. Mary announced that she was leaving for Bradford at the end of term. An old boyfriend had been in touch, her first love, Sooty had been an alcohol fuelled mistake. A heartbroken Sooty pleaded with Lennie to forgive, forget, move on, and Lennie agreed to try. So they trundled on for a few more years, neither particularly happy but neither particularly unhappy. When Lennie's elderly aunt died, leaving her a healthy inheritance, they talked of what to spend the money on, managing to persuade themselves that the sensible idea would be to transform the cash into bricks and mortar. So Lennie set about buying herself a cottage by the beach. Sooty remortgaged Gloucester Court, releasing some equity for Lennie to add to her inheritance, and they prepared to live apart. They failed to convince each other that it would only be temporary and that ultimately Lennie would rent out her home to holidaymakers.

Sooty, for her part, now coveted the independence of living alone. It afforded her opportunities for covert indiscretions and Lennie the opportunity to turn a blind eye. What of the alternative? They both agreed that it was inconceivable to contemplate breaking-up, they were closer than siblings, tied more tightly than blood relations.

So we leave Sooty and Lennie on this very dramatic night, two ladies happier apart than together but conversely happier together than apart.

NEWCASTLE INTERNATIONAL AIRPORT

The following morning broke to brilliant sunshine, George remarked upon this as he was driven to the airport in Bob's taxi. Old man Johnson was his usual talkative self, obviously looking forward to his brief vacation abroad. Having grilled Bob on the events of the previous evening, (news travelled fast as a bushfire in a small community such as Nowhere), he prattled on for the rest of the journey about various places he had visited in the past. The phrase 'suffering from verbal diarrhoea' struck Bob as an apt description for George that morning.

They arrived at the airport with half an hour to spare. Bob steered the taxi into the rank in front of the airport's main entrance and climbed from the driving seat to lift the cases from the boot. George thanked him profusely and confirmed the time he would need Bob to collect him the following week. There was a standing joke in the office that George never tipped, and this morning was no exception. The old adage 'the more money they had the meaner they were' rang true in the case of George Johnson. Glancing into the terminal as he drove off in the minicab, Bob thought he saw a familiar face. He could have sworn it was Raymond, Yvonne's younger brother. But glancing back the figure had gone and George was once again standing alone in the check-in queue.

Perhaps it had been Raymond, Bob told himself, why only the previous week when they had met by chance in 'The Brits' Raymond had been telling Bob of his planned holiday to Spain, choosing to keep 'mum' about the identity of the lady friend he was taking. Bob had presumed it to be the married woman he was rumoured to be having an affair with. He really was quite a ladies' man, Yvonne's kid brother, but Bob supposed he had quite a few opportunities to chat up married women in his line of work.

THE BRITS PUBLIC HOUSE – MARS BARS AND PINEAPPLE RINGS

Meanwhile, at 'The Brits' public house, Clive the publican was chivvying his son Adam to hurry his breakfast. He had a large order expected from the brewery and would like to be back in the bar in time to oversee its arrival. His pot man was lax at checking every crate for breakages or short date codes. Clive had been stung in the past with a Danish lager that had only one month remaining on it and it had meant a special promotion with loss of potential profits as he had no choice but to flog it during the happy hour: damage limitation. He didn't want that happening again things were quiet enough in the pub trade as it was.

'Adam, are you still not dressed? For heaven's sake, any longer and you'll be walking to bloody school.' he yelled up the stairs in the direction of the bathroom.

When Adam appeared, looking frighteningly young and vulnerable in his new school uniform, Clive felt a pang of guilt for his irritability. He ruffled his son's hair as Adam scuttled past him towards the car.

'Dad, remember the bag for Yvonne's, Mum said to remind you.'

'It's already in the boot, Ads. Put your seat belt on, there's a good lad.'

As he pulled out of the side street, Clive's car cell phone rang. Peering at the screen Clive could see it was his ex-wife, Rhonda. He passed the phone over his shoulder to Adam in the back seat.

'You take the call, son your mum will want to say hi.'

Clive grimaced as he heard Adam speaking to Rhonda. God, he could hear every word even above the loud roar of the car engine. The woman had a loud grating American accent which pissed the hell out of Clive whenever he heard it. Why he had ever been attracted to a brash, large-hipped American broad escaped him. He often wished the broad-in-stature broad had remained abroad. The only good thing to come out of the disastrous union was Adam, the son they both adored and constantly argued over. Feeling his aggravation increase, Clive comforted himself with thoughts of Yvonne. Sweet pliable Yvonne, who would comfort him, stroke his fragile male ego and listen attentively as he launched into his latest tirade on Rhonda and the unfairness of the courts in awarding joint parental access. The fact that Rhonda thought of Yvonne as a personal friend made the thrill of netting 'Bob the taxi's' wife all the more tangible. Clive had recognised that Bob bored her to tears when he had first been introduced to them as a couple. He had cast a few compliments her way, dangled his legendary sexual prowess as bait, then swept her off her feet and reeled her into his arms. To be honest had it not been for the factor of getting one over on Rhonda and future goading, Clive would have dispensed of Yvonne long ago. Her body lithe, receptive, full but surprisingly firm despite the children, was the additional pulling point. But her conversation was monotonous, wearisome and constantly repetitive. After sex Clive wanted to cut and run but sexual etiquette dictated otherwise. For Clive the thrill had always been the chase, and with Yvonne it was a case of been there, done it and fumbled beneath the t-shirt. Mind you, he reflected, *why look a gift horse in the mouth*. Yvonne was always up for it, nothing fazed her sexually, and what red-blooded man would not have enjoyed the pineapple rings episode. Yes he had dined out on that fruity exploit many a time. Put that whole Rolling Stone Mars Bar urban myth in the shade, he reckoned. With this thought, Clive allowed his mind to wander to later that morning when he would drop Adam's bag off at Yvonne's, as per Rhonda's instructions. Perhaps Yvonne would be wearing her prim '*mumsy*' floral skirt. Clive decided to ring her and plead with her to forget the knickers. Now that thought was a turn-on.

YVONNE IS ACCOMMODATING

Back at 9 Moss Side Drive, Bob had just returned from dropping off old man Johnson, and was popping out again to do his usual taxi school run. Yvonne rewarded him with a wry smile as he laughingly told her of George's usual failure to tip. She had just taken Maggie and Flo a cup of tea in bed, to find them both lay on their backs snoring like *hippos* so she made the decision to leave them to sleep on. Yvonne herded the children into an orderly queue for the short trek to the school gates. As she left the house she suddenly remembered the telephone message from Clive. Oh bugger, she had completely forgotten his plans to drop off Adam's bag. She would try to catch him on the way back from the school run and advise caution.

Unfortunately Yvonne did not get the chance to speak to Clive because a friend fell into step with her on the walk home. They only parted company as Yvonne turned the corner into Moss Side Drive. Looking up the street, Yvonne was relieved to see that Bob's car was not there, but dismayed to see Clive striding up the drive towards the front door. Yvonne ran to catch him up before he rang the doorbell and woke Auntie Maggie and Flo.

'Hang on,' Yvonne called from the gate 'I'm here. Give me a minute to find my keys.' She said this as she rummaged in her cavernous handbag.

She opened the door and motioned for Clive to follow her into the porch. My God, thought Clive, she did look good and so sexy in her prim and proper school run outfit. Yvonne barely had the door closed before Clive had her pinioned up against the porch wall, his free hand straight up her skirt.

'And what are these?' he muttered huskily, as his fingers twanged the elastic of her panties. Expertly he wrenched her undies from her hips until they were half mast at her knees.

'Now that's better, much better,' said Clive, his hands clasping her buttocks.

At these words Yvonne came to her senses.

'Sorry darling, long story but I have house guests and Bob could be back at any minute.'

Clive reluctantly removed his hands. Pouting like a belligerent child he took Yvonne's hand and placed it upon his bulging trouser crotch.

'Now tell me you're not pleased to see me sweetheart.'

'I promise to ring you later and explain,' Yvonne cajoled 'Bob could be back at any minute.'

As if hearing his cue from backstage Bob's keys rattled in the lock behind Yvonne. Jumping apart they hastily rearranged their clothes. Clive lifting Adam's overnight bag into the air to hand to Yvonne just as Bob opened the front door.

'Oh hello Bob,' said Clive. 'I'm just dropping off Adam's bag as per my dear ex-wife's instructions.'

Then, turning to address Yvonne, he said 'Thanks for being so accommodating. Rhonda's collecting Adam this afternoon, so I'll see you both later this week.'

Yvonne struggled to regain her composure whilst walking into the kitchen, turning her head en route to enquire if Bob would like a cup of tea.

'What did Clive mean by accommodating?' Bob asked her a little later, as they were having their mid morning cuppa.

Yvonne shrugged in what she hoped was a nonchalant manner.

'Beats me,' she said. 'I never know what you bloody men mean half the time.'

In an effort to change the subject she raised her eyes towards the ceiling. 'I think I can hear Maggie and Flo up and about,' she said.

They had gone from being *snoring hippos* to *plodding elephants*, for two such frail elderly ladies they certainly made a lot of noise.

'Maggie asked if it was possible for you to drop them both off at home when you have a spare minute between jobs darling.'

Getting up from the table, Bob made his way into the hallway and called up the stairs. 'Ladies, your carriage awaits.'

Bob popped his head back into the kitchen and looking Yvonne directly in the eyes, he added. 'It seems Yvonne, I too can be accommodating.'

Choosing not to read the hidden meaning in this statement, Yvonne stooped to pick up the wicker basket and pegs from beside the washing machine. 'I'm hanging out the washing. Let me know when you're ready to go.'

As she stood in the garden, arms full of soggy clothing she reprimanded herself for being so foolhardy. Bob was not a stupid man, and Clive had been careless and arrogant. Whilst risk was exciting, she knew the score with Clive, she was a notch on his bedpost, an ego boost. Her motives for the affair were in a way as straightforward as his. Uncomplicated sex, thrilling, and naughty, just the tonic to relieve the tedium of married life. Delving into the basket to look for her new black underwear, Yvonne was exasperated to see that it was missing. She was sure she had included it in the black wash she had done earlier that morning. If she didn't know better she would swear they had a poltergeist, things were frequently going missing only to turn up in the very place she had last looked. It was most perplexing and bloody annoying.

Sitting at the kitchen table sipping his now lukewarm mug of tea, Bob leant back in the chair enjoying the feeling of tautness as the tight black lace panties rubbed against his hips and groin. A quick blast of the hair dryer earlier that morning had taken the dampness out of the silk material, and Yvonne would never miss them. Like most women she had so much underwear.

HIGH UP IN THE CLOUDS

High up above Nowhere amongst the clouds, Raymond and George were settling down to enjoy the flight. George stretched his hand out into the aisle to catch the attention of the high heeled trolley dolly.

'A drink to relax you, dear boy?' he enquired of Raymond.

They had joked before boarding the plane of joining the elite 'mile high club', but George had just visited the tiny toilet and returned to tell Raymond that he had neither the physical agility nor the contortionist skills to become a member. Raymond pouted sulkily before breaking into a smile and explaining to George that he was a paid-up member anyway and it was very over-rated. It had taken a while for George to realise that the younger man was teasing him.

'Oh the look on your face, Georgie darling.' said Raymond. 'Now where is that hostess, I'm gagging.'

'For a drink?' said George, winking and joining in with the frivolity.

'Yes, that as well.' said Raymond, returning the wink.

George reclined his chair and drink in hand started to read excerpts from his Venetian guide book out loud to Raymond. Quite enjoying the experience of hearing his own voice pronounce difficult Italian words. The artist Turner, he read, described Venice as *a city of rose and white, rising out of an emerald sea against a sky of sapphire blue*. George was about to read an excerpt about Byron when he glanced to his left and realised from Raymond's posture and steady breathing that he had, in fact, fallen asleep. Suppressing a surge of irritation, he reminded himself that the purpose of this trip was recreational rather than educational, and if the poor boy slept now it meant he would have all the more energy to entertain later on. Oh the joys of exploring Venice and the joys of exploring Raymond: a perfect combination for a perfect holiday. Letting the book fall to his lap George drained his glass and allowed his own eyelids to droop too.

UPPER WORTLEY, LEEDS – FAR BENEATH THE CLOUDS

Far below the clouds sat Jean. She had reached a state of apathy, had tired of answering the door to well meaning friends. The curtains were tightly closed and she sat quietly, alone, in the darkness.

Suddenly the telephone rang. It rang and rang and rang.......

Surely whoever was calling would assume she was out and try again later.

But no, the blasted contraption continued to ring. Jean put her hands over her ears but still it rang. Then it stopped as abruptly as it had started. Jean relaxed once again into her chair, lulled into a false sense of security. All too soon the incessant trilling began again. Whoever was on the line was determined if nothing else, Jean was irritated and vexed, why could people not just leave her alone. Bloody annoying do-gooders telling her they knew how she felt. How could they know, how dare they presume to know.

Still the ringing went on. Jean sighed heavily and picked up the receiver.

'Hello honey,' said the disembodied voice. 'Are you ok, my love? We have been so worried about you.'

Jean chose not to answer, but the voice continued undeterred.

'You don't need to speak, Jean, I'm just ringing to tell you that Lennie and I are driving down to Leeds tonight. We both think you need some time away so have a bag packed. I've arranged for Linda to look after the animals, and look in on the house, so there's nothing for you to worry about.'

At this statement Jean found voice and began to protest, but Sooty interrupted her indignant response.

'For once Jean, let someone look after you, don't be so dammed independent. We are your friends, and we love you.'

Jeans' anger drained away with these words. 'I'm so sorry....' she started.

'I just feel so...' Jean struggled to find the word.

Sooty waited patiently. When it was obvious that Jean was not going to finish her sentence, she said.

'Honey, I am so sorry I've upset you, please say you will come'

Jean replied with just one word 'Ok' then hung up.

Coming off the telephone she felt her apathy diminish, not completely but slightly, and it gave her enough energy to go upstairs to the bedroom and start to pack a suitcase.

ADMIRING SOOTY'S CHEST

Later on that day found Sooty crouched at the door of the soon to be opened Bistro. Through the etched glass she could see figures darting to and fro behind the bar area. Knocking at the door had elicited no response so Sooty resorted to bending down and calling through the letterbox.

'*Hello!*' she called, '*hello can anyone hear me?*'

Sooty was just drawing breath to call again when suddenly without warning the door flew open. Struggling to her feet Sooty was hopelessly aware that she was revealing a considerable amount of cleavage in her flimsy tee shirt top. After straightening up and smoothing down her top Sooty extended her hand to greet the new owner of the Bistro.

'Hello.' said Sooty as the girl's hand met her own.

My god thought Sooty, not exactly your typical gay woman. If my 'gaydar' were not so in tune I would be very confused. Despite herself she could hear Lennie's lecturing voice in her mind:- 'Oh Sooty, you are so exasperating, when will you grow up and stop falling in love with everyone you meet. Beware your foolish heart.' Willing herself to appear cool and confident, Sooty said. 'I'm not in the habit of shouting in letterboxes but I could think of no other way to attract your attention. I'm a friend of Maggie. I just called around to thank you in person for the kindness you showed her last night.'

'It's very kind of you to take the trouble to call in.' said the girl, tilting her head slightly so Sooty could take in the chaos of the dining area. 'As you can see the Bistro's still pretty much a building site, but do come in and meet my partner Joey.'

Upon hearing her name, the aforementioned Joey popped her head from behind the doorway.

'Hi, it's lovely to meet you,' she said as Louisa introduced them.

'Do come in and have a coffee, it will give us the perfect excuse to take a break.'

Sooty quickly noted that Joey and Louisa were chalk and cheese, opposites in height, girth and complexion. Louisa so open and friendly, her partner so guarded.

Louisa gave Sooty a quick tour of the Bistro, whilst Joey sat at a table waiting for the other two to join her. Then they all chatted for a few minutes before Louisa screwed up her eyes and rubbed at her temples.

'Are you ok Louisa?' enquired her concerned partner.

Louisa shot her a pained expression. 'I'm fine, sorry to make a fuss but I've got a humdinger of a headache brewing.'

Turning to Joey she said, 'would you make us all a coffee darling and I'll just pop to the chemist for some tablets.'

Sensing an opportunity to repay the girls' kindness of the previous night, and to hopefully spend some time alone with Louisa, Sooty, interjected. 'Don't waste your money on painkillers, my dear. I have got boxes of them at home. My mother, before she went into the residential home, stockpiled them. You are more than welcome to a box or two. I just live around the corner, behind the Italian restaurant in Castle Street.'

My God, thought Sooty as they walked along the street, this girl is gorgeous. Auburn hair, amazing blue eyes and full red lips: if I had a type she would be it. Aware of the older woman's proximity, Louisa felt slightly uncomfortable. Sooty's arm dangled by her side as she walked and their hands kept bumping against each other. It implied a familiarity that they did not yet share.

When they reached Gloucester Court Sooty unlocked the door and motioned for Louisa to enter before her.

'Ladies first.' she said gallantly, with a wave of her hand.

'I always thought it was age before beauty?' Louisa quipped.

'Beauty is in the eye of the beholder, my dear.' replied Sooty, checking herself for being so obviously flirtatious.

The front door led onto a porch and a long narrow hallway with the stairway leading off to the right. The doors were all closed and there was a marked contrast between the bright sunlight and the dark shadowy hall. Louisa's eyes took a while to adjust and she stumbled slightly falling back against Sooty, who automatically held out her arms to break her fall.

'Whoops!' said Louisa 'I forgot to tell you I'm incredibly clumsy.'

'No problem.' said Sooty, and it wasn't. It was wonderful, and unrehearsed, and incredibly sexy. Wow, she thought, talk about fate. Louisa felt delicious, smelt delicious, and those scarlet red lips would no doubt taste delicious. Sooty was smitten, in love with the prospect of falling in love again. Reluctantly releasing Louisa from her arms Sooty said 'I'm tripping up all the time, although usually over the cat. She only has three legs and tends not to move out of my way quickly enough.'

Louisa smiled shyly not quite sure if Sooty was serious or not.

'I suppose I'd better let you go. Anyone walking in would think I was trying to seduce you.' Never a truer word said in jest, she thought to herself. Even in the semi-darkness Sooty could see Louisa's face beginning to colour. The girl was blushing, how very endearing. Sooty released Louisa from her embrace, suddenly aware that she may have misread the signals and mistaken friendliness for flirtation. After all, the girl was obviously in a long term relationship. On the other hand, thought Sooty, so was she. Best bide her time and find out, but there was no denying that Louisa would be so easy to fall in love with.

'Excuse me my dear' said Sooty as she stretched behind Louisa to switch on the hall light.

From Louisa's pained expression it was plain to see she was still troubled by the headache.

'Still sore?' enquired Sooty.

Louisa nodded in reply.

'Why don't I go upstairs to find these tablets? Would you like to come upstairs with me? I have the most amazing views of the castle from the study window.'

Louisa followed Sooty up the narrow stairs which opened onto a landing area lit by a round skylight. Straight ahead she could see what she presumed to be Sootys' bedroom. The door was ajar and a three legged ginger cat lounged lazily on a tapestry covered armchair. There was a large double bed in the centre of the room and an old pine dressing table under the window which Louisa assumed overlooked the courtyard. The window was dressed with swathes of luxurious velvet and the bed had a crimson silk throw embroidered with a golden thread. The sheer unashamed decadence of the room enthralled Louisa. A boudoir decorated like a French brothel. Very unlike the type of bedroom Louisa expected Sooty to have had. Even after their short acquaintance she had perceived Sooty to be a practical 'let's call a spade a spade' sort of woman. It just showed how wrong first impressions could be. A voice came from the room to Louisa's left and she followed the direction of the voice into the study. Sooty was on her knees bent over an old pine chest hunting for the boxes of tablets. Upon hearing Louisa come into the room she pointed towards the window on the other side of the room saying, 'Go over and look out of the window my dear, on a clear day you can see not only the castle but also the Folly beyond on the Crag.'

As instructed Louisa went across to admire the view.

'This is amazing,' said Louisa. 'It's like a picture postcard. You do have a lovely home.'

'Thank you,' said Sooty. 'I'm glad you like my house. I saw you admiring my chest earlier.'

Louisa was at a loss at what to say. For the second time that day she felt the heat rise in her cheeks. When Sooty had been at the Bistro doorway earlier on Louisa had stared at her partially exposed cleavage, but she didn't think that Sooty had noticed. How embarrassing to be caught out like a leering adolescent. How could she ever look Sooty in the eye again? Sooty paused a few moments for maximum effect before continuing. She was well aware of Louisa misinterpreting her words. That had been her intention. If anything it was proof that their attraction was mutual.

'It's a very old chest. It belonged to a relative of a friend of mine. He was a seafaring man I believe.'

It took a while for Louisa to catch up with the conversation. She had totally mistaken the context of Sooty's earlier remark. Or had she? Was the much more 'worldly wise' Sooty dangling her on a string? Playing her? Deliberately choosing her words for their double entendre?

'My friend Lawrence is in that photograph on the corkboard behind you.' Sooty continued. 'It was his uncle that the chest belonged to. Lawrence is not a keen sailor although he enjoys cruising of a different nature.'

Louisa crossed the room to look at the photographs. But her eyes did not dwell on the photograph of Lawrence. Instead they were burned by the image of a younger Sooty and another woman in an old black and white image.

'The other woman in that picture is my partner Lennie,' said Sooty, noticing that Louisa staring intently at the photograph.

Louisa continued to stare closely at the photograph. She visibly shivered as she concentrated her vision upon Lennie's distinctive steel grey eyes. Oh my God, it couldn't be...could it? Unaware of her discomfort, Sooty continued searching in the chest.

'At last,' said a jubilant Sooty, holding the box of painkillers aloft.

'I'll go downstairs and get you a glass of water. Let's see if we can get rid of this headache of yours.'

Louisa stood rooted to the spot for a short while longer, transported to another time many years ago.

A cold, lonely, unhappy time...

Forcing herself to look away from the photograph she made her way downstairs while desperately trying to remind herself that she was no longer a young, insecure child, but an adult and a dammed successful one at that. Despite her best efforts the child within her couldn't let it lie. Long buried feelings and thoughts of revenge were gnawing their way to the surface.

The table in the kitchen of Gloucester Court was stripped pine with a warm yellow hue. There was a pine dresser in the corner of the room, filled to the brim with brightly patterned plates and knick knacks. A cosy plump floral sofa sat opposite, positioned by a large bookcase haphazardly stacked with an array of cookbooks and paperbacks. From the kitchen window behind the rather imposing Aga cooker Louisa could see a sprawling cottage garden carpeted with a lush lawn and bordered by an abundance of daffodils and forget-me-nots. In the distance Louisa could make out a small greenhouse and what looked like a pagoda swaddled in ivy.

'Your garden is quite charming,' commented Louisa.

'If you had seen it when I first moved in you would not have said that,' Sooty replied. 'It was a mass of overgrown weeds and bushes. Lennie and I had our work cut out making it halfway decent.'

'So have you lived here long?' enquired Louisa.

She was trying to ascertain the current relationship between the two women. From earlier comments Sooty had made she knew they were long-time partners so it seemed strange that they did not live together.

'I've lived here since I left teacher training college. Lennie lived here for a while but she now lives about five miles away in Newton-by-the-sea.'

'Oh so you don't live together then?' said Louisa, aware that she was being nosy and wishing she had thought before asking the question. But it was as if she was compelled to know and as she asked the first seed of a plan began to germinate.

'It's a long story,' said Sooty. 'And I promise to bore you with it you it another time. But now I really must be getting back to school, or I shall have to give myself a detention.'

'There will be another time, won't there?' Sooty added.

'I'd like to think there will be and I hope you didn't think I was being a busybody earlier,' said Louisa, worried that she had been too inquisitive.

'On the contrary,' said Sooty, stretching her hand to touch Louisa's, and squeezing her fingers as if to emphasise her point. 'I have so enjoyed meeting you and I have a feeling we will become very close friends.'

And so we leave Sooty and Louisa exchanging glances which speak volumes.

BARNACLE BEACH COTTAGE – LET THE ORANGE BLEED THE BLUE

Whilst Sooty was engaging in her mild flirtation with Louisa at Gloucester Court, Lennie sat in her own study at Barnacle Beach Cottage, the cottage that she had bought with the legacy from her old aunt. With her leather chair positioned at the captain's desk she could see the distant seashore and the waves creeping across the sands. Further away still the ancient ruin of Dunstanburgh castle, majestic in its state of disrepair breaking the horizon with its wind-worn turrets.

The fax machine in front of Lennie suddenly came to life, its noisy whirring indicating that a fax was on its way. The paper snaked to the ground as Lennie fumbled to retrieve it.

Dear Lennie,

Random thoughts…..

I really enjoyed our chat last night as it seems to me that we are really getting to know each other at last. It has made me realise how successful this Lonely Hearts process of finding a partner might be. You're so right when you say that we will know such a lot about each other before we actually meet – how exciting to get that perspective first!!!

Lots more of course to share, but it's a great foundation to a first meeting.

With affection…….Tracey xxxxxx

Lennie carefully tore the message from the fax machine then carried the printed sheet across the room to the sofa bed. Settling amongst the cushions she studied the message more intently, poring over each and every word. She was filled with a sense of adventure, of being alive again. Despite herself she also felt guilty and furtive. It was true that she was only planning to do what Sooty had done so many times in the past, but still it felt deceptive. She had answered the Lonely Hearts advert on a whim, never expecting it to go this far.

Sooty's indiscretions had long been a painful part of her life. Lennie could name every time, every betrayal. Her coping mechanism had been to bury her head in the sand and wait for the affairs to blow over. Now it seemed the roles were reversed. Idly she wondered if Sooty had a clue about her secret fraternisation. Personally she doubted it. Sooty was too self-obsessed to notice Lennie's change of mood. Too self-obsessed to care....

After following this train of thought for a while, Lennie returned to the captain's desk in order to compose her reply.

She wrote...

Hi Tracey,

My thoughts regarding your last fax.....

I am also enjoying getting to know you. I have great expectations for our much discussed weekend and am desperately trying to keep my feet on the ground.

I feel as if we have so much to find out about each other, and I am so excited at the prospect of getting to know more about you. Upon waking this morning, the sun shone brighter, the birds were chirpier. Let's be spontaneous, and romantic. Let's allow the orange of our rainbow to bleed the blue.

xxxxxxx Leonora

Lennie quickly pressed send and watched as the message winged its way to a fax machine in Wetherby, near York.

Lennie replaced the receiver, grabbed her handbag from behind the chair and prepared to leave the cottage. Sooty and she were journeying to Leeds to collect their good friend Jean. If they left now they would miss the worst of the rush hour traffic. She quickly rang Sooty from the house phone to say she was on her way then she raced out to the car and turning on the engine put her trusty Metro into first gear. Sooty was waiting by the entrance to Gloucester Court as Lennie pulled alongside the kerb she hopped swiftly into the passenger seat and the two ladies set off on the three hour journey to Leeds.

UPPER WORTLEY, LEEDS –
THE UNWIELDY COUCH

Jean sat perched uncomfortably upon the arm of the unwieldy couch in the lounge of the house she had once shared with Lucy. It was a large brown monstrosity of a couch, with inlaid wooden arms and turned round feet. Jean hated the couch with a passion. She had hated the couch the day she and Lucy put the down payment on it, but Lucy had loved it and would not shift one inch. So Jean had agreed under protest, trying in vain to explain to Lucy how uncomfortable it would be, and how impractical for their tiny modern house. That she had been proved right was of little comfort then or now.

They had bought the couch during the year of Lucy's final diagnosis. That final devastating diagnosis which had deprived them of even the very last vestiges of hope. They had bought lots of things during that year. Lots of things that they had always wanted to own but never got around to saving up for. Jean indulged Lucy's every whim, granted her every wish. There was only one thing that money could not buy and that was the only thing that Lucy truly wished for. The precious gift of time...

Even the God Jean prayed to so fervently when Lucy had first been diagnosed had abandoned hope in Lucy during that last year, prompting Jean to reject the very faith which would have sustained her through those last terrible months. Jean had tired of praying to a God she no longer believed could hear. The rosary beads, once so familiar, so comforting, were lying under a sheaf of papers in a sideboard drawer. Her God had abandoned her in her hour of need, why should she honour and worship him now?

RHONDA SPILLS THE BEANS

Back in Nowhere, Bob was having a well earned night off work. He was settled in the armchair sipping from a nice can of chilled lager. He sat randomly pressing the buttons of the remote control. That was another thing that annoyed Yvonne about her husband. The fact that he would never check the listings in the newspaper, instead choosing to randomly dip in and out of programmes. It really annoyed her.

Upstairs Yvonne was putting the final touches to her makeup. She searched in vain for her favourite cherry red lipstick, cursing when she couldn't find it in the dressing table drawer. Bloody kids, she said to herself. If Becky were still awake she would have checked her bedroom. But it was not worth the hassle. Let sleeping kids lie. Oh well, a slightly darker red would have to do. She glanced at the clock as she slipped on her high heels. Walking towards the bedroom door her stiletto heel caught on the edge of the carpet. 'Bugger! Cheap bloody shoes!' she grumbled. Downstairs, she popped a kiss on the top of Bob's head. *Keep up the dutiful wife role...keep things normal* she thought. For whose benefit remains to be seen.

'I should be home about midnight.' she reminded him. 'We will probably end up at Rhonda's flat for a drink after the meal'

'Ok darling have a good night.' said Bob absentmindedly, not really listening as he was concentrating on a programme he had just tuned into.

When Yvonne arrived at *Don Vito's*, Rhonda and the others were already seated at the table. Seeing Yvonne, Rhonda stood up and waved her over to the table shouting, 'Better catch up girl, we're onto our second bottle of red.'

'What are we celebrating?' said Yvonne as she squeezed her way onto the rustic bench, knocking her head on the empty wine bottles hung from the ceiling as she did so and causing the other girls to giggle uncontrollably.

'Let's raise our glasses to liberation and freedom from bloody ex-husbands.' said Rhonda once the laughing had died down.

The others raised their glasses in salute. Yvonne followed suit, although she still hadn't quite worked out what they were celebrating. Rhonda leant across the table towards Yvonne. 'Hey babe, don't look so confused, I'll fill you in later,' she said in a slurred voice. 'Now where's that sexy Italian waiter? We need more wine.'

Six bottles of wine, five garlic breads, two pizzas, three portions of pasta, numerous 'one for the road's, and six exclamations of 'I really shouldn't but the desserts look so 'moreish' later - the girls were winding their way up the high street towards Rhonda's trendy apartment in the old cotton mills. As the tipsy group passed by the open door of *The Brits* public house Rhonda made a V sign gesture in the direction of Clive's landlord sign.

'The laugh's on me buster.' she said after they were out of earshot of the open door.

This caused her group of buddies to collapse against the wall in helpless giggles once again. Linking Yvonne's arm Rhonda pulled her back slightly from the rest of the group. Yvonne sobered up almost immediately. She had dreaded this happening. Someone had seen her and Clive together and came to the obvious solution. Oh my God how could she wriggle her way out of this one. It was something of a relief when Rhonda said.

'Yvonne, I think it's only fair I tell you this, as the other girls know. I promised my parents not to breathe a word, but I know how much you care about Adam. Don't look so worried, babe, it's not bad, in fact it's the best news ever for Adam and I. My parents have pulled some strings in America and we are flying out there next weekend.'

Yvonne must have looked confused because Rhonda continued. 'Don't you understand what this means Yvonne? I need never see or hear from Clive again. If he thinks he can fight me for custody, he has another thing coming. As far as I am concerned it's goodbye pain in the ass, hello new life

Oh my God well she didn't see this coming. It would destroy Clive and Adam. What of Adam? He doted on both his parents, the poor boy would be devastated.

'Is that really fair on Adam?' Yvonne said hesitatingly well aware what Rhonda's reaction to her question would be.

'*Fair?*' growled Rhonda true to form. 'Is it fair that bloody Clive is dragging me and my son through the courts? Trying to prove I'm an unfit mum. Do you call that fair, Yvonne?

Yvonne couldn't answer.

'Look, I am trusting you with this Yvonne. You're my friend that's why I've told you. You must promise not to say anything to anyone, especially Clive.'

Yvonne mumbled her assent. I'm much too intoxicated to rationalise this tonight, she told herself. I will think it through tomorrow with a clear head. Work out where my loyalties lie. Oh my God, what a night this was turning out to be.

THE HIRSUTE LADY

Whilst this furore was taking place, a drama of a very different nature was unfolding at Yvonne's house.

A tall, rather hirsute lady stood admiring herself in the long bedroom mirror. She was wearing cherry red lipstick, false black spiderlike eyelashes and far too much blusher. Her padded bra contained a wad of cotton wool and her stocking clad feet were squeezed into height defying stiletto shoes. The heels were so high she struggled to gain her balance. She readjusted the crotch area of the black lace panties, so the telltale bulge wasn't so visible when seen in profile. Then she liberally sprayed perfume on her wrists and behind her ears. She deeply inhaled the potent erotic aroma and as she did a bulge once again protruded from the tight pencil skirt she was wearing. Sitting on the edge of the bed facing the mirror, the lady lifted the skirt to remove the annoying bulge from her black lace panties. A look of pleasure crossed her face as she ran a long pink false fingernail along the underside of the quivering penis.

....

It was late in the evening as Sooty and Lennie drove slowly along the main street of Nowhere. Jean sat silently in the back of Lennie's car. She had barely spoken a word during the long journey. The other two had kept up a steady stream of chit chat trying to bring Jean into the conversation but Jean sat poker faced on the back seat. She answered questions politely but without adding anything to the required yes or no's. Both women were very concerned about Jean's handling of the situation. She had seemed to cope with Lucy's illness in such a brave, positive way, but now it was as if she had given up. Hopefully a change of scene would help the grieving process and do Jean so much better than moping about in a house full of memories.

'Oh look,' said Sooty pointing out of the passenger window 'there's Louisa and Joey leaving the Bistro.'

Both Lennie and Jean peered out of the windows, but the girls were walking in the shadows, their faces clouded by darkness.

'Oh, it's a shame you couldn't see them,' said Sooty. 'Never mind I shall take you in to meet them over the weekend.'

'They are both rather sweet,' she concluded.

Lennie raised her eyebrows but said nothing. She had known Sooty so long and she was so transparent. Doubtless she had fallen in lust again, but who was Lennie to judge she had been replaying Tracey's last message in her mind ever since they turned off the motorway.

YVONNE NURSES A HANGOVER

Yvonne had not slept well as the problem of Rhonda's declaration the previous night had preyed upon her mind. Also the large amounts of red wine she had consumed at Rhonda's apartment had made regular guest appearances throughout the night. Bob had been up and about early, waking Yvonne as he plundered the pockets of his jackets searching for his blasted car keys. Yvonne bit back a sarcastic comment to the effect of 'if you put them on the key rack when you came in, you wouldn't waste an hour every day looking for the bloody things'. The words formed on her lips but she held them back. She really couldn't be bothered to row that morning. Eventually Bob found the keys and leant over his wife to kiss her good morning.

'Hello sleepyhead,' he said. 'How's the hangover? Would you like a cup of black coffee, or are you planning to chat to God on the big white telephone again?'

Earlier he had insisted on calling her 'Heave-on' rather than Yvonne and it had taken all of her energy to tell him to bugger off.

Yvonne sniffed the air in the bedroom. That's strange she thought to herself: the room still smelled of her very expensive, 'knock 'em dead' perfume. She wished Becky would stop coming into her room and spraying her little freckled wrists with the stuff. She would have to find a new hiding place for it at the back of the wardrobe. But she reminded herself that was the least of her problems that morning. Once the cup of coffee worked its caffeine magic she would have to focus on more pressing matters.

A VERY SMUG PUBLICAN

Clive the publican was whistling as he bottled up. A casual onlooker would wonder what he had to be so cheerful about, the job was very labour-intensive and his bottle man had called in sick. Clive had received a solicitor's letter that morning, and the good news was that his case for joint custody of Adam was almost in the bag. The court date had been set, and it was almost worth the ludicrous amount of money it would cost to see Rhonda's face as he presented his case. Her conviction for possessing drugs, that dated back to her days as a student would be his jewel in the crown. Whilst he would have preferred to have sole custody of Adam, Clive was a realist, and at least this would ensure the conniving bitch wouldn't be able to whisk Adam off abroad if the whim were to take her.

DANIELI HOTEL, VENICE

In Venice, dawn was breaking, its orange rays shimmering across the murky waters of the canals. The Danieli Hotel where George and Raymond were staying was renowned to be one of the best in the city due to the proximity of the Bridge of Sighs. It was said that Ruskin, Wagner and Proust had all once stayed there. A hotel of its calibre was not cheap, but when George travelled he believed in luxury and indulging in the very best. After all he reasoned his well heeled clients could afford it. George lay on his side, his head resting comfortably in the crook of his arm. He lay still, gazing at Raymond's profile which was highlighted by the sunshine streaming through the gap where the shutters met. Raymond's eyelashes flickered slightly as if he were aware of the intensity of George's gaze......Raymond was beautiful with a straight proud Roman nose, chiselled cheekbones and almond shaped eyes. His lips were full and moist, curling slightly downward at the corners to give him an almost arrogant countenance. The fine covering of soft down which led from his cheekbones to the cleft in his chin and a brown mole on his left cheekbone strangely enhanced his features.

From beneath the snow white cotton sheets George could see a tantalizing glimpse of blonde chest hair. George stretched his free arm across the bed and carefully raised the sheet, gently pushing it away from Raymond's torso. Raymond stirred slightly as if aware of the change in body temperature. He altered his position in the bed then settled back into his peaceful slumber. George continued to gaze and appreciate. He appreciated fine porcelain, well-crafted furniture, meticulously decorated Venetian glass in the same way he appreciated the perfection of Raymond's well-honed body. Raymond stirred again, his hands reaching to scratch at his scrotum, his flaccid penis becoming engorged and emerging rigid from the shock of pubic hair. George stared fascinated, willing himself not to breathe loudly or to move for fear of breaking the reverie.

But it was too late for Raymond turned his head. 'Good morning Mr Voyeur' said Raymond in a sleepy voice as he stretched full length on his back. His arms wound behind his head and he purred in a feline fashion as George bent downwards towards him, lips smacking in anticipation.

GLOUCESTER COURT AND
THE THREE LEGGED CAT

Jean woke late at Gloucester Court. She hadn't slept at all well during the night as the trip had worn her out both mentally and physically. She struggled out of bed to visit the toilet, trying not to wake the three legged ginger cat who had settled comfortably upon her legs in the early hours of the morning. Its purring had been a distraction for Jean, one which she was grateful for, as her night had been filled with her terrible loss. Lucy's face swam into her vision, whenever she closed her eyes, her voice echoing in Jeans ears as the silence of the night descended. Whilst remembering was wonderful, an overwhelming grief would strike her anew when she fully awoke and realised the other side of the bed was empty.

From her vantage point in the kitchen Sooty could hear her friend moving around upstairs so she lifted the kettle from the black metal trivet and put it back on the Aga to boil. Rest and recuperation were the order of the day. Jean needed time to cope with her loss and that meant no visitors today just peace and tranquillity. Once the kettle had boiled and the tea brewed Sooty carefully arranged it on the tray with the sugar bowl and milk jug then made to climb the stairs, checking first that the blasted cat was not anywhere in the vicinity. If she had a pound for every time she had tripped over the cat, she would be a rich woman indeed.

BARNACLE BEACH COTTAGE – THE POSTMAN ALWAYS KNOCKS TWICE

Lennie was in the kitchen sipping her second cup of Earl Grey as she heard the front gate of Barnacle Beach Cottage groan upon its rusty old hinges. The letterbox in the hallway was prised open and there was a resounding thud as the post hit the carpet. Prolonging the moment, Lennie finished her cup of tea before walking into the hallway to collect her post. At first it seemed there were only brown envelopes, but hidden amongst them she glimpsed a long pale cream one. Racing back to the kitchen table she sat down and tore it open. As she had hoped it was from Tracey.

Mon 1.58 am The Hilton, Nottingham

Dearest Leonora, I'm up at a crazy hour this morning. I cannot sleep. I'm rested but cannot sleep – just now. So I thought I'd write to let you know that I am filled with excitement at the thought of the possibilities of us. I feel warm when I speak with you, soothed almost. A gentle understanding prevails in your voice.

Maybe we are aligned right now.

Maybe our time is now?

With love,

Tracey xxxxxx

Lennie sat quietly upon her chair, aware of her own rapid heartbeat and her spasmodic breathing. Tracey and she had yet to meet, but already she was seduced by her language of love. Never had she found the English language, the mother tongue to be so emotive, so compelling.

At that moment the telephone rang; Lennie knew even before she picked up the receiver that it would be Tracey.

And it was......

Whilst Lennie was speaking to Tracey, her partner Sooty was also on the telephone. She was speaking to Louisa and arranging to meet the next day in a small cafe on the beach front, called appropriately enough *The Rendezvous Cafe*. It was unspoken between the two ladies that they would meet alone without their respective partners. And so the deceit began. Neither woman would enter the covert relationship with a lack of forethought but Louisa had a special agenda which even she was hiding from herself. Would she have entered headlong into a tryst if she had not a score to settle? A score which had festered for many a year.

CATCH 22

Later on that day Yvonne was still feeling decidedly worse for wear. But her head was slowly clearing and with it came the reaLouisation that she was in a no-win situation. A classic 'Catch 22'. She could tell Clive of Rhonda's plan and break the sisterhood code. Or not say anything and watch him be destroyed by perhaps never seeing his son again. Normally in situations such as this Yvonne would ask her best friend for advice, but as her best friend was Bob, her husband, this seemed a tad inappropriate. Stuck between a rock and a hard place, but thinking a sexual relationship perhaps tipped the loyalty scales, Yvonne texted Clive and arranged to meet that lunchtime at *The Rendezvous Café* on the beach front.

Clive, upon receiving the request to meet, flattered himself that Yvonne could not get enough of him. Sex in the sand dunes was very *'From Here to Eternity'*. Better have a quick shower - he was very hot and sweaty from the bottling up.

THE RENDEZVOUS CAFÈ – PEACH MELBAS AND COKE FLOATS

The Rendezvous Café had on more than one occasion been described as a time capsule. Its fifties décor belonged to another era. It was not quite retro enough to be trendy, but amongst its regular patrons it held a charm all its own. Its' ice creams were the air filled synthetic whipped type topped with florescent red *'monkeys' blood'* or a chocolate flake, and it still served banana splits, peach melbas and coke floats. The 'knickerbocker Glories' with their tinned mixed fruit were a mountainous calorie filled cherry topped treat and the hot chocolate with whipped cream and marshmallows had tempted many to fall off the dieting wagon.

The owner Louigi, or Gino as he was more commonly known, was Italian. He was a big bear of a man, who despite living in England since leaving the Italian Navy in the fifties still retained a strong native accent. Gino spoke often of his homeland, and Lecce, the village in which he had been born.

'Mangiare, your tiny appetites insult my cooking,' he would say to regulars who visited the Café.

Patting his ever expanding girth he would add. 'See this is the belly of a happy man. There are two things a man needs to be content with life, good food and the love of a good woman.'

This statement always amused his regulars who had met his wife Adrienne because she was a tiny woman with a permanently pained expression who despite her lack of height ruled her husband with a rod of iron. Gino had just put a fresh percolator of coffee on to the heated stand behind the counter when Yvonne and Clive walked through the front door of the café. The couple were deep in conversation. Clive looked angry and Yvonne slightly tearful.

'Sit there while I order coffee' said Clive, pointing to a corner booth away from the rest of the customers.

'Two strong coffees,' please Gino.'

'Strong coffee so early in the day Clive?' said Gino in his familiar way so popular with regulars.

'I know it's early in the day Gino, but trust me, I need it,' said Clive wryly.

Yvonne sat waiting anxiously. She had taken a paper handkerchief from her handbag, and was folding and unfolding it whilst staring into the distance. She looked up as Clive sat down opposite her in the booth.

'I still can't believe the brass neck of that woman.' said Clive in a vexed voice. 'To think she could get away with this hair brained scheme of buggering off abroad with my son. I'm going to take her to the cleaners for this.'

Yvonne flinched at his angry outburst. This was a side of Clive she had never seen. 'Clive you promised not to go overboard about this, my job is on the line if this gets out.' Yvonne said quietly, with a note of panic in her voice. 'You did promise to keep me out of it' she repeated for the umpteenth time.

Clive was irritated by Yvonne's self-motivated manner. But although angry he realised that to nail Rhonda he needed her support. It was incredibly naive of her to imagine he could keep her out of this revelation once he told the courts of Rhonda's plan, but if she chose to believe it could be so, it was in his interest to keep her sweet. Clive stretched across the table and took Yvonne's hands in his. He had reached the stage where he didn't care who read what into their relationship. As far as he was concerned the whole town could gossip of their affair. It would only enhance his reputation as a Casanova. Yvonne's marriage, such as it was, no longer concerned him. His only interest was in thwarting Rhonda's plan to abscond with his son and to drag her through the courts for custody. Clive realised that he must convince Yvonne the secret was safe in his hands. To this end, he changed the tone of the conversation, and, winking at his lover, suggested it was a lovely day for a walk in the dunes. Making love was the last thing on Yvonne's mind: her libido had unsurprisingly taken a nose dive. How she wished she had thought this whole situation through properly. How the hell had she expected Clive to react. Had she really expected him to act rationally?

How would she react in a similar situation? How would Bob?

When they reached the sand dunes Clive pushed her roughly to the ground. The sand chaffed at her naked thighs as he raised her skirt to her waist level. Yvonne looked up at Clive but she no longer recognised the man behind the eyes. She gasped as Clive pulled the crotch of her knickers aside. Bruising her tender flesh, he tunnelled inside her. Clive raised himself up on his forearms.

Thrusting...grinding...pushing.

She felt violated. It was as if he were exorcizing a demon, an evil spirit. *An act of passion devoid of all passion*, he had channelled his frustrated anger and crammed it inside of her. Despite her discomfort she forced herself to raise her hips to meet his.

Thrust for thrust...grind for grind...push for push

This would usually excite him. But to no avail. Clive carried on, thrusting, grinding, and pushing. Finally, thankfully, he stopped and rolled over onto his side, his penis still erect, still hard. Hiding himself, sheltering from her gaze he rearranged his manhood and zipped up his trousers as his erection slowly subsided.

Yvonne lay huddled amongst the rough grass of the dune, unsure of what to say, unsure of what to do. Throughout the entire lovemaking episode, they had shared neither a kiss nor word of endearment. Eventually Clive stood up and helped her to her feet then they walked towards the car. Who was this man she asked herself. How could they have shared such intimacy but remain strangers?

Oh my god, what had she done? They climbed into the car and Clive dropped her off as usual on the outskirts of town. Clive watching dispassionately as she walked from the car. As soon as she turned the corner and was out of sight he picked up his car cell phone and made a call to his solicitor. Rhonda and he were due up in court the following day to each argue their case for sole custody, the AmClivean bitch would have one hell of a surprise when Clive's solicitor dropped this little bombshell.

Yvonne raced towards the sanctuary of her house and once inside closed the door firmly behind her, in a subconscious attempt to make the problems go away.

She had not anticipated that Clive's reaction to Rhonda's plans would be quite so extreme. If she had thought it through with an sober head she would have handled it differently, perhaps not telling him of Rhonda's plans but suggesting them as a possibility to look out for. But hindsight was a wonderful thing and now the damage was done and Yvonne had a feeling the trouble was only just beginning.

THE NAKED CHEF

In the Greenhouse Bistro Joey and Louisa were having a very busy day. Opening night was getting closer and closer and the jobs they had lined up to do were all turning out to be more complicated than initially anticipated. The chef they had taken such care choosing had rung to say that he no longer felt he could accept the job.

Better offer... better job... better prospects.

Sorry for letting the girls down at the last moment, but could he be candid and say he felt ill at ease accepting the position in the first place. He came from a farming family and to work in a vegetarian restaurant would always be a conflict of interests. The girls mulled over the chef predicament all afternoon. It was too late in the day to hire someone and expect them to construct a menu from thin air.

'We really don't want to delay the opening.' Louisa said for what seemed the millionth time that afternoon.

'I wonder how sexy you would look in chef's whites.' said Joey in an effort to lift the mood. 'Don't panic sweetheart, I'm only joking.' she said when she saw Louisa's expression of blind panic.

They sat quietly for a while, each trying to find a solution to the problem. 'Yeah, but joking apart, Joey, I do bake a mean nut cutlet.' said Louisa.

'But cooking for six is slightly different to cooking for forty six.' Joey countered.

'If you think I am up to the job, I'm willing to try. What's the worst that can happen?' Louisa replied.

'Being sued for an outbreak of food poisoning?'

'Your faith in my culinary talents astounds me, sweetheart.'

'Sorry darling, but are you serious? Do you really want to do this?' Joey was finding it hard to hide her astonishment.

'Well there's only one way to find out. We did say that we wanted to be hands on and as the saying goes nothing ventured, nothing gained.'

'Tell you what,' said Joey, fired up by Louisa's enthusiasm. 'When we get home later you can practice at being the Naked Chef.'

VENICE - MARCO POLO AIRPORT

George and Raymond were preparing to board the plane back to Newcastle Airport. Although the break had been short they were both tanned and mellow. The trip had been a success, plenty of sun, sex and vintage Venetian wine.

'Back to Hetroland,' said Raymond with an air of despondency. 'Nowhere the haven of respectability.'

'Until our next little spree abroad' reminded George looking intently at his younger lover. 'I'm thinking Barcelona, Prague or Rome. Have you any preference, dear boy?'

'I hear Barcelona is quite *'Gaudi,'* said Raymond, smiling at his own joke.

'Very witty,' said George, in a somewhat condescending tone. 'I like to think I have taught you all you know.'

'Oh I think I have taught you quite a few things too.' Raymond countered alluding to their lovemaking.

'Touché, dear boy, I do confer you are a very competent teacher.'

'And you a willing pupil.' Raymond conceded.

'Come along now our flight is ready to board,' said George striding off towards the Departure Gate.

MAGGIE THE HERMIT

Since the attack, Maggie had become something of a hermit, afraid of her own shadow. Sudden noises startled her; looking out in the street at night she imagined sinister shadows lurking and watching, waiting to pounce. Her curtains to her flat were permanently drawn and she was surviving on a diet of tinned food.

The previous day, Maggie had had a visit from Inspector Dodd the policeman who had been first on the scene after the mugging. He had made no bones about the fact that he was disillusioned by the law which he was paid to uphold. Not least because he had the hard task of telling her that the youth who had attacked her on that night had been charged with the crime but was now out on bail. He added, in what he hoped was a reassuring manner, that whilst the police could not protect her every hour of every day, they would install a panic button in her lounge, and extra locks on her front and back door. This did little to allay her fears. To the contrary it served only to convince Maggie that she was in danger of further attacks and hence magnify her fear.

Her employer Sooty had been on the telephone earlier that morning to confirm that Maggie was still coming to Gloucester Court for her tea. She would be around to collect Maggie in the car at 4.30pm. It would do her grieving friend Jean good to have a change of company, and Lennie was travelling to Richmond that afternoon to spend the night with some old friends.

There was a knock at Maggie's front door. Such was her shock that the cup of tea she had been nursing on her lap slid off the saucer and onto the hearth rug. Struggling to her feet she opened the curtains a crack and peered from the first floor window of the flat out onto the street. She could see no-one. The street was empty bar a black cat sniffing at a lamp post. She was about to let the curtain drop when a familiar figure emerged from beneath the canopy of the porch. The diminutive form of her old friend Flo waved up towards the window. Clutching her handbag to her chest, she gestured to Maggie to open the front door. The exertion of climbing the bank had tired her out and she was gasping for breath and in dire need of a cup of tea.

BARNACLE BEACH COTTAGE

Lennie had a small dilemma preying upon her mind. Tracey had phoned her the previous evening with a very tempting proposition. She had suggested that Lennie drive to Wetherby and stay as a guest in her house the following night. All above board, she hastened to add, no preconceived ideas or expectations, but it would give them the chance to get to know each other properly and their planned weekend tryst seemed so far away. Now, in the cold light of day, Lennie was fretful. What if Tracey took one look at her and didn't find her attractive? What if she found Tracey unattractive? The whole prospect of the meeting terrified her.

She sat at the kitchen table staring out at the sea. The tide was in and the horizon seemed so very far away, unchartered waters, dark and mysterious. When had she become so complacent? This timid scared mouse of a woman wasn't her. She had been cautious for a long time, and where had it got her? Absolutely nowhere. Inwardly she giggled at her own unintentional play on words and reminded herself that for a very long time Nowhere was exactly where she had wanted to be. Getting up from the table, with a renewed vigour and a spring in her step, she picked up the telephone to ring Tracey to tell her that she was on her way.

NOWHERE MAGISTRATES COURT

Clive and his solicitor sat opposite Rhonda and her solicitor, the opposing teams trying hard to look both confident and nonchalant at the same time. Clive could barely suppress his smug expression but to create the element of surprise he deliberately didn't glance in Rhonda's direction. At last, the Clerk of Courts appeared in the doorway of the waiting area to usher them in before the Magistrate.

'Let the battle begin', whispered Clive to his solicitor, only to be hushed by the Clerk of Courts who took his role very seriously indeed.

THE START OF THE AFFAIR

Gino was rushed off his feet in *The Rendezvous Café* as the morning which was initially chilly was bright and sunny. Dog walkers had long since staked their claim over the stretch of beach in front of the promenade where the café stood. Dogs were only allowed on the beach out of season and on a day like today they took full advantage of the date. Walkers wrapped up in their autumn woollies would stride purposefully along the sands throwing sticks and collecting shells. After their healthy exercise they would inevitably stop at *The Rendezvous* for a hot chocolate topped with whipped cream, telling themselves' they had earned it after their long walks. Huddled in a corner booth Sooty and Louisa sat chatting. Joey was a stranger to the concept of walking being a pleasurable pastime, so Louisa always took their cocker spaniel Jasper for his daily constitutional. Louisa was in the process of telling Sooty that it provided the perfect excuse to meet, whenever and wherever. It was unspoken between them that they were embarking upon an affair. It was just left to set the ground rules.

'Lennie is away visiting old friends in Richmond tonight.' Sooty began, 'It would have been the perfect opportunity to meet but I have an old friend staying at the house and Maggie is coming to tea.'

'It would be difficult for me to get away at such short notice anyway.' Louisa replied.

'Joey and I are still frantically setting up the Bistro for opening night.'

'I don't suppose there is any way you could find an excuse to pop across to Gloucester Court tomorrow, is there? Sooty enquired.

Louisa thought about it for a few moments before replying, 'Well I could slip away to walk Jasper, I suppose.'

'Super it's a date,' said Sooty. 'My friend is going on a retreat tomorrow and I'm taking the day off work to meet and greet Royalty. I'll be home from twelve onwards.'

'Royalty?' enquired Louisa. 'You're teasing me again. Is this your friend Lawrence the Queen of the desert?'

Sooty smiled. 'Have you not read the local paper? The Italian restaurant on Castle Street was opened with a Grant from an Enterprise Trust and its Patron is visiting the place tomorrow. As my courtyard adjoins theirs they have asked if I would like to meet him too. All whitewash of course, the real reason he is here is to join in the big hunt at the castle. I admit I hesitated over the suggestion at first but I am hoping to have a quiet word with him about the morals of hunting.'

'Oh I completely forgot, I think Joey mentioned it last week.' Louisa could have kicked herself for sounding so out of touch.

'Anyway' said Sooty placing a hand upon Louisa's to emphasise her point. 'What do you think of my proposition?

'Well,' said Louisa after recovering her composure 'How can I possibly turn down such an offer? It's practically a Royal Command.'

NOWHERE MANOR – THE PRIVATE EYE

In a large Manor house on the outskirts of Nowhere, Lillian, the wife of George Johnson the antiques dealer sat tapping her perfectly manicured nails upon the dining table. Lillian was growing more vexed by the moment. The blasted private detective was late, and tardiness was a trait which really irritated her. Lillian was contemplating giving up on the whole idea when she heard car tyres rumble onto the gravel drive. Getting up and straightening her skirt she made her way into the hallway to open the front door. Lillian was slightly taken aback as a young woman in her late twenties clambered from behind the wheel of a dusty wreck of a car. What had the blasted man at the Agency been thinking of? The girl looked barely out of High School. Liz noticed the expression on Lillian's face, she was used to it. Looking young would be an asset in her golden years but it was one 'pain in the ass' constantly having to prove she was up to the job. Striding confidently from her car she introduced herself to Lillian and followed her into the house. Pulling an A4 file from her brown leather briefcase Liz perched on the edge of the dining room chair, making a point of listening attentively as Lillian described the job in hand.

'First of all my dear, may I say I am not one of these emotional woman who will be devastated when she finds out her husband has been playing away from home. To the contrary this proof is merely the icing on the cake to ensure my divorce settlement is substantial enough to keep me in the manner to which I have become accustomed. My husband George is a wily old fox. I have no doubt at all that he is having an affair. The question is with whom? I suspect his secretary Yvonne, but as I have said he has covered his tracks well so it will be a hard and laborious task to catch him out. To this end, as I explained to your boss, I know this will be an expensive exercise but the result will, I am assured, be worth it, and one must speculate to accumulate. I have prepared a file of photographs etcetera, which I hope will be helpful to you, and here's my telephone number on which I may be contacted at any time.' Lillian handed a slip of paper to Liz.

'Now' she continued 'if you care to look over the photographs I shall go into the kitchen and ask my housekeeper to prepare us morning tea.'

Liz sat silently through Lillian's long and protracted speech. This type of work always provided a bit of excitement in what was surprisingly quite a mundane and humdrum job. Despite the fact that it was so often dramatised on the TV and in cheap detective novels, most of her bread and butter work was based upon fraudulent Insurance Claims.

There was Mr Smith claiming his car accident has rendered him impotent and unable to satisfy his wife, caught on camera making love to a large breasted neighbour; or Mrs Jones claiming her fall at work had damaged her hip so it made driving impossible, caught on camera collecting the kids for the school run in her flashy four by four.

But it was conversely true that sometimes just sometimes a job would come along which made the other jobs fade into insignificance. A job which required brain work, necessary deception and hopefully if it could be stretched out, a sizable income at the end of it. This job had the makings of just that, and the client, Lillian, had obviously done her homework. In the file she had provided all the information necessary to make a start. Although the details on the secretary were pretty sketchy, at least Liz had an address and photograph of the woman so that was a good start as any.

Studying the photograph of George, Liz suppressed a shudder. The man gave her the creeps. His vanity and old money confidence oozed from the image. Putting the two photographs of George Johnson and his secretary Yvonne side by side on the table top they seemed unlikely lovers and bedfellows. But it was true that money and social standing were powerful aphrodisiacs. One only had to look at the many attractively challenged politicians who managed to bag the beautiful brunette or bleached blonde. How many of these would be given a second glance if not for their positions of power?

Liz looked up as Lillian came back into the dining room followed by her housekeeper. She was carrying a tray set out with a vast array of tasty cakes and fancies. Liz settled back in her chair as the housekeeper poured the tea. Yes, she thought to herself, this job had the makings of being very lucrative indeed. The only downside would be that expanding the time she spent on the investigation might prove to have a similar effect upon her waistline.

CLIVE USES THE L WORD

Yvonne was just clearing up from lunch when she received a call from a very irate Rhonda.

'You are not going to bloody believe this Yvonne.' Rhonda's voice reverberated down the receiver.

'Whatever is the matter Rhonda? Has something happened to Adam?' Yvonne replied, sticking to her plan of playing dumb and denying everything. With a sinking feeling she knew, she just knew, that bloody Clive had dropped her right in it. Rhonda continued still in a shrill voice. 'That bloody man has only gone and told the court that I'm planning to flee the country with Adam. Claims he has proof, claims you told him. He even said that you would be prepared to swear that I'd told you.'

Yvonne was horrified, *Bugger! Bugger! How do I get out of this one?*

'Rhonda, I'm sure you know that is utter rubbish.' Yvonne said, injecting indignation into her voice. 'Why would I tell Clive anything? The bloody man is grasping at straws. Someone must have overheard us talking in the street the other night and told him. I can't understand why he is saying it's me. Probably to make is seem more credible. He and I barely speak when he collects Adam from the house. I can't abide the bloody man and nor for that matter can Bob.'

'Oh honey, you haven't heard the best of it yet. He only went and told the court you were having an affair with him and it was pillow talk.'

'Well that proves he's lying.' Yvonne blustered. 'For a start I'm married and secondly you're my friend.'

'I know that honey and I said as much to the magistrate. I just need to know how Clive got this bloody information.'

Yvonne had broken out into a cold sweat and was at a loss at what to say in reply.

'I mean to say,' Rhonda continued. 'Clive likes his women with more *'upstairs'*, you and him it would be laughable if it wasn't so bloody serious.'

Yvonne grasped at this statement like a drowning man. 'I know,' she interjected 'I'm not exactly his type am I? I think most of my bust slid down onto my hips when I had the kids.' Yvonne had to mentally tell herself to stop babbling as it was making her sound guilty.

Rhonda was very quiet....Oh god thought Yvonne had she gone too far. Desperate to recover the situation Yvonne blurted. 'Look Rhonda, I'm going to have to shoot out and get the kids now. Let's talk more about this after I've have a chance to chat to Bob. Try not to worry. As far as I'm concerned you and I never had that conversation the other night, and I'll swear it in a court of law if necessary.'

Yvonne was shaking as she hung up the telephone. She was convinced she had managed to fool Rhonda, but Bob would be a different kettle of fish. Lying to a friend was different to lying to her husband. Bob could read her like a book. What had she done? Had she risked her marriage for a *'bit on the side'*, a *'roll in the hay?'* All of a sudden the telephone began to ring again. Yvonne stared at it for a while before picking it up, hesitatingly, gingerly like a hot potato. She was convinced it would be Rhonda again and momentarily relieved to hear a male voice.

'Yvonne is that you?'

Yvonne went rapidly from being grateful that it wasn't Rhonda to being incensed that it was Clive. The bloody nerve of the man, obviously he had hoped to pip Rhonda to the post and speak to her first.

'Yvonne?' Clive spoke again, this time with more of a sense of urgency.

Still Yvonne didn't answer. Let him sweat it out, he deserved it.

'Yvonne, I know you're there. I've just passed Bob in the taxi. Listen to me sweetie and I'll try and explain. You may be getting a call from Rhonda, but don't panic, I'll explain what you need to say to her, my solicitor has advised me how best to handle this.'

Yvonne was furious, the bloody cheek of the man, first he chose to drop her in it and then he expected her to help him out.

'I haven't got a clue what you are talking about.' Yvonne said in a very hard clipped voice. 'I would thank you not to contact me again.'

Damn thought Clive, Rhonda must have got to Yvonne first. 'Yvonne, don't do this to me darling.' He pleaded. 'I need you to back me up on this one. We could make a go of things, me, you and the kids. We could be one big happy family. I love you sweetheart.'

Empty promises, the L word, Clive was sure that would do the trick. To Clive's astonishment, the line went dead. Clive tried the number again and again before realising that Yvonne had probably unplugged the telephone at the wall socket. Every time he tried his call was diverted straight to the answer machine. Shit, if only he had kept any of her letters. Trying his own answer machine for the message she had left him the previous week, he was gutted to find that it had automatically erased itself after seven days. At a loss at what to do next Clive drew a whisky from the optic behind the bar, which was something that he would not normally do, but desperate times called for desperate measures. Clive had gone from euphoria to deepest despair in the space of a few hours. If he couldn't prove Rhonda's intentions he hadn't a leg to stand on in court.

Meanwhile, at 9 Moss Side Drive, Yvonne was calmly erasing all messages from Clive. She then deleted his name and number from her telephone book. Let him try and pin this one on her. She had known the risks before embarking upon the relationship and she had been uncharacteristically careful and secretive. As far as she was concerned there was nothing linking Clive and she, so furtive had she been in her movements. Yes, Bob had alluded to Clive in his 'accommodating' statement the other day but she was certain that she could convince him nothing had been going on. Bob loved her, she just needed to keep her cool and admit to nothing. Surely if she played the dutiful wife she would be able to ride this one out? Coming so close to being found out she was desperate to hang on to her marriage. If I get through this, she told herself, I will never risk my marriage again.

ANGEL OF THE NORTH

Lennie was sipping coffee in a service station near Richmond. She was on her way to Wetherby to visit Tracey and spend the night at her house. She sipped hesitantly at the tiny cup of strong black espresso, it was not normally a drink she would choose but she needed it to shock her jangling nerves back into a normal rhythm. The traffic that afternoon had been gridlocked and the iconic Angel of the North had dwarfed her almost stationary car for the better part of an hour. Tracey had rung her earlier on in the day to say she had managed to juggle her work schedule and would be at home awaiting her arrival.

Now as she sat draining her cup of coffee Lennie wondered whether to buy a bunch of flowers or would they imply a preconceived perception of romance. The flowers on offer in the shop were varied in type, the only common denominator being that they were all ridiculously overpriced. Deciding against the red rose combo Lennie eventually settled on a much more organic looking bunch. She wanted to convey to Tracey that she had good taste in a subtle way. After paying for the flowers Lennie made her way back to her car, and putting it into gear, prepared for the rest of her journey.

THE OLD CHAPEL – WETHERBY

Tracey lived in an old chapel. Developers had halved the building to provide two separate living spaces. Cleverly, they had left the defining features of the chapel in place. The large stained glass picture windows cast rainbow shadows upon the wide oak floorboards of the lounge. A mezzanine bedroom was accessed by the original pulpit staircase with an elaborately turned mahogany balustrade. As this was the only bedroom it was surprisingly large with a triple aspect and it led onto a walk-in dressing room. It was here that Tracey had made up the camp bed for her guest. Tracey fervently hoped that the spare bed would not be used but prepared it to create the illusion that she took nothing for granted.

The beamed ceiling in the bedroom was exposed and when lying in bed she would stare up at the ceiling and imagine herself in a grandiose cathedral. In her darker moments Tracey had been known to refer to the ceiling as a dark coffin lid closing her in. Tracey was prone to dark moments, and when they hit her, as they frequently did, nothing could alleviate her sense of utter despair. An ex-girlfriend had once said to mutual friends that the problem with Tracey was that she had forgotten the simple pleasures of life. She inhabited her own little world where anything and everything she craved was affordable. Her own insular world which took the joy out of looking forward to anything from a holiday abroad to a new car. Her friends would fancy a weekend break and book a hotel in the Lake District. Tracey would fancy a weekend break and catch a plane for a weekend shopping in New York. Her friends thought they were adventurous booking a week in Tunisia. Tracey would plan a trip to Nepal to explore the Himalayas, alone. She was easily bored and constantly needed the sugar rush of something new and exciting. She had been in many relationships but none had lasted as she was constantly seeking something else. Nothing seemed to penetrate her, emotions seemed to slide off her surface as water on a ducks back. Tracey was a wordsmith, an art critic, a food connoisseur, something of a culture vulture but an empty vessel emotionally. Perhaps that was why her previous relationships had floundered; when the excitement wore off and real life intervened, Tracey would bail. Despite past experiences Tracey had a yearning to be loved, but she was unsure if she could muster up the emotions to love in return. Romancing from a distance had appealed to her sense of adventure but now Lennie was travelling to be with her she felt the familiar desolation overtake her. The building started to close in on her and the 'black dog' was nipping at her ankles. Desperate not to give in to the familiar feelings Tracey quickly changed into her leathers and collected her helmet from the cupboard above the stairwell. Time to burn some rubber, she thought to herself as she climbed astride the vintage Harley, her latest toy.

HELLS ANGELS AND GODS ANGEL

With the aid of a map Lennie had eventually found her way onto the main road approaching the Yorkshire town. A signpost directed her to Wetherby and she indicated left to approach the suburb where Tracey lived.

Suddenly a motorbike cut in front of her car, causing her to brake violently and jolt forward in her seat.

'Damn fool.' she yelled, although the car windows were shut so she was swearing to no-one but herself and the biker was just a blur in the distance. That had been a close call and mentally she made a sign of the cross. Peering straight ahead she could make out a building that appeared to be a chapel. The red bricked building had a tiny churchlike sphere and arched stained glass windows. As she approached the building, Lennie remembered that Tracey had said she drove a Land-rover so she pulled in behind a rust coloured four wheeled vehicle convinced she had arrived at her destination. She was just collecting her thoughts and building up the courage to leave the safe sanctuary of her car when a motorbike pulled alongside her. Lennie recognised the bike as the one that had cut in front of her car a few minutes earlier. The rider, still astride the bike, motioned to her to wind down her window. With a gasp of exasperation Lennie did just this, formulating in her mind the ticking off she intended to give him for his bloody dangerous riding. It was only as the rider pulled off the helmet and shook her hair free that Lennie realised it was a woman. A damned attractive one at that thought Lennie despite herself. This observation was most unlike Lennie. Sooty's eye for a pretty girl must be rubbing off. Reminding herself that she was still cross, she blanked the bikers smile.

'Lennie I presume,' said the biker, apparently undeterred by Lennie's scowl.

'Excuse me,' replied Lennie in her haughtiest voice 'have we met?'

'I'm sorry I must apologise, I can be something of a boy racer at times. I hope I haven't ruined our first meeting.'

Lennie gasped as it dawned on her that the gorgeous woman must be Tracey. Well if nothing else it proved her fear that she wouldn't find Tracey attractive was completely unfounded. The woman had the most amazing lion's mane of deep brown silky hair and a smoky voice which made Lennie's breath catch in her throat. Desperate to rescue the situation Lennie composed herself and returned Tracey's welcoming smile.

'Let's start again shall we,' she said 'You certainly know how to make a memorable entrance.'

'Am I forgiven?' Tracey said in a crestfallen voice.

'Of course you are,' said Lennie before adding with a frivolity she did not feel 'after all it's not every day I nearly crash into a new friend.'

Tracey alighted from her bike and, after wheeling it into the garden, took a door key from the breast pocket of her leather jacket.

'Follow me,' she said, opening the double arched chapel doors, 'and watch the step in the hallway, my friends call it the step where angels fear to tread.'

'I imagine you have whole host of ecclesiastical puns,' said Lennie stepping carefully over the raised slate tile and causing her overnight bag to jam painfully against her hip.

'Masses and masses,' said Tracey before adding 'pardon the pun. My friends never tire of telling me the old joke about the nuns in the shower.'

'I know just the one you mean.' Lennie said.

'I bet you hear the one, 'I used to be a nun but broke the habit, quite a lot too.'

'Yes that's quite a popular one too.' Tracey conceded turning to smile into Lennie's eyes.

'Actually,' continued Lennie, 'this seems the perfect opportunity to tell you that I did used to be a nun but as the joke states, I broke the habit.'

Tracey went very quiet before saying 'Are you serious?'

'Deadly, swear to God.' said Lennie, miming a sign of the cross on her chest. It never ceased to amaze her, the reaction this declaration inevitably had on people.

'You are really serious?' Tracey repeated again. It was more of a statement than a question.

'Tell you what,' said Lennie, 'pour me a nice drink and I'll tell you all about how I was defrocked.'

JOHNSON AND SONS, ANTIQUE EMPORIUM AND A VERY INTERESTING HAIRCUT

Liz the Private Investigator was on a mission. She had to convince George Johnson that she was a fellow Antiques Dealer, so that afternoon she had visited the public toilets in Nowhere market place and set about the task of deception.

First of all she had changed into the smart businesslike suit she kept for such occasions in the boot of her car. Then tying back her hair and applying a mask of thick foundation she completed the effect with bright red lipstick. Finally giving herself the quick once over in the mirror, she decided that yes, she looked the part. Now it just remained for her persuade wily George. Luckily Liz knew the basics of antiques of a certain period, she just needed to steer the conversation to Art Deco pottery and she could blag with the best of them. Drop in a few well known potters' names, such as Susie Cooper and Charlotte Rhead, and she would hopefully be home and dry.

George Johnsons Antique Emporium was on the main street of Nowhere, leading up a slight incline towards the entrance to the castle. Its excellent position gained George many customers, from Nouveau Riche Americans to well heeled Europeans and latterly members of the R.......F........ The various Earls and Lords who visited George could be assured of his discretion. Many a Country Estate, opened to the public and claiming to display antique works of art and furniture, was in fact furnished by George and his band of contacts abroad. They could reproduce almost anything with such precision that it would fool all including an antique expert. This side of his business he kept apart from the day to day bread and butter Antique Emporium.

The building that the Antique business was housed in was Edwardian and was a rabbit warren of four sales floors with a damp dingy bargain basement. Cunning George insisted that the shop was always dusty and unkempt. Heaven help the eager young assistant who decided to while away a few quiet hours polishing the silver or arranging the china, because George had cleverly hit upon the idea that everyone loved to feel that they were getting a bargain. He worked upon the principle that he would keep his prices high but his stock displayed in such a way that it appeared to be the '*bargain of the century*'. It never ceased to amaze him at the way some customers were prepared to crawl on all fours into cobweb clad corners when they thought they spied a valuable item. Greed seemed to take over, and this was the policy on which George's business thrived.

Liz stood at the entrance of the Emporium. She browsed the shelves for a few moments, picking up a vase and making a point of checking the markings on the base. Sensing a sale, an assistant sidled across and enquired if Liz required any assistance. This was just what Liz had hoped would happen, and following her plan she made a point of engaging the assistant. It had been a quiet afternoon and the assistant was glad of the distraction. Through carefully loaded questions Liz ascertained that George had an office at the back of the building, but neither he nor his secretary was at work that afternoon. The secretary apparently only worked three mornings a week and the boss was getting a haircut at the hairdressers up the street. Liz made an appointment to see George the next day, making a great play of having to check her personal organiser to see if she could make morning or afternoon. She then asked the assistant if she could recommend a good hairdresser as she was staying in the town for a few days and in desperate need of a haircut. As she had hoped, the assistant recommended the very hairdresser that George was visiting.

'His name is Raymond,' said the assistant, 'our Mr Johnson is always singing his praises.'

This was too easy thought Liz as she hurried out of the shop, just feed the right questions to people and they inevitably offered the right information. Following the directions given by the assistant Liz easily found her way towards '*Hair Today, Gone Tomorrow*.' The hairdressers was on the opposite side of the street and in her haste to cross the street Liz misjudged the speed of the oncoming traffic resulting in nearly being knocked over by a jet black Rolls Royce. From her position so close to the side windows of the car Liz could see through the tinted windows and make out the shadow of a man on the back seat. The man had a very familiar profile, with a marked lack of a chin and prominent jug ears. Liz let her gaze follow the direction of the car as it sped away along the street towards the castle, then she continued to cross the road albeit with a great deal more care this time. After crossing safely onto the pavement she took stock and asked herself the question, was that figure in the back of the car who she thought it was. It couldn't be. Or could it?

Telling herself to not be so bloody stupid and to concentrate on the job in hand she strode purposefully into the hairdressing salon, exuding what she hoped was an air of quiet confidence. Putting on her very best upper class voice, she enquired if it would be any way possible for her to have a haircut without an appointment. The gum chewing receptionist with gravity defying hair shouted across the crowded salon.

'Raymond, lady here asks if we can fit her in for a quick trim?' she trilled.

Glancing across the room towards Liz and the receptionist, Raymond replied.

'Yes no problem, I'm nearly finished with Mr Johnson.'

'I should very much hope not, dear boy.' said George quietly, almost in a stage whisper.

Raymond grinned at George's reflection in the mirror. George returned the gesture with a rather obvious wink. Liz's 'gaydar' went into overdrive upon witnessing this brief exchange. My God, she thought, could it be possible that this job was about to get even more interesting? Unless she was very much mistaken, Raymond was a gay boy, and her antenna was indicating that George was of the same persuasion. My God, forget Hebden Bridge, forget Brighton; these market towns were veritable dens of iniquity.

THE POSTCARD FROM GREECE

At 9 Moss Side Drive, Yvonne had just finished clearing up after preparing the tea. Rather in the manner of *'let the good man eat a hearty meal before breaking the bad news,'* she had prepared Bob his favourite food. Ignoring for once the plaintive pleas of the children for mashed potato and pizza, she had prepared Bobs favourite curry. By halving the mixture before adding the curry powder she hoped to appease the children too with a mild slightly spicy stew. Yvonne had still not decided how to broach the subject to Bob, and planned to gauge his mood before embarking upon any lengthy explanations about her day. Hearing the front door slam, she stood waiting by the oven for Bob to come into the kitchen.

'Hi honey, fancy a coffee? she called into the hallway.

'Thanks love, but after the day I've had I think a lager might be more appropriate,' Bob replied. 'I've spent the last hour at the cop shop talking to our friend PC Plod as it seems they've let that young thug out on bail. Your Aunt Maggie is in a right state. I've tried to get the cops to bend the rules and arrest him again but apparently that's the law. One of his drug dealing friends has put up the bail and he's out of the nick scot free until the trial. As I said to our friend PC Plod, Dickens had it right when he had Mr Bumble proclaim *'the law is an ass.'*

'Sit down honey and I'll get you a lager. I've made your favourite curry for tea. I must have sensed you were having a bad day.'

Well, thought Yvonne to herself. No way am I risking telling him anything tonight. In the words of Scarlett O'Hara in *Gone With the Wind, 'fiddle-de-de, I'll think about that tomorrow.'* She was in the process of pouring the lager into the glass when she had a flash of recollection which brought about a feeling of pure panic. She suddenly remembered the postcard she had sent Clive when she had been on holiday with Bob and the girls earlier that year. Desperately she tried to recall what she had written on the card. As it slowly came flooding back, her blood ran cold. Bloody hell, if he had kept it, the game was up. It was all the evidence Clive would need to prove how he had heard about Rhonda's little plan. How could she have been so stupid? She had broken the most basic of rules and left a paper trail. What had she been thinking of? There was no way she could leave it, she had to get the bloody thing back, but how?

THE FEMALE OF THE SPECIES IS MORE DEADLY THAN THE MALE

Liz was sitting in a booth in *The Brits* pub, slowly sipping a half pint of the local ale. The publican was a slimy slug, he had tried to hit upon her the second she walked in. She had met his type before, all mouth and trousers, but surprisingly loose tongued once she had fluttered her eyelashes at him. She had gleaned very little from Raymond apart from the very interesting fact that Yvonne was his sister. This was the explanation he used to describe how he was so friendly with George Johnson. He certainly did not wear his sexuality on his sleeve. But small towns had a habit of forcing people to hide in the closet and bolt the door. But she had also found out that Yvonne was a childminder and one of the children she looked after was the son of the owner of the local pub. Liz was used to men flirting with her. She was not a typical baby dyke more an aptly named lipstick lesbian. Liz enjoyed being a woman and the *accoutrements* of her sex. She wore her makeup, the aforementioned lipstick, high heels and short skirts with pride unlike the stereotypical lesbian portrayed in the gutter press.

'Of all the bars in the world I'm so glad you chose to visit mine,' crooned Clive. Liz grimaced inwardly. That was surely one of the worst chat-up lines she had ever heard. She was about to reply in the slinky deep voice which she knew would turn Clive on, when they were interrupted by a woman who had just barged into the bar. Clive's expression registered annoyance as he looked across at the woman, but despite this he hastily moved along the bar to speak to her. Liz found herself out of earshot and quickly moved her drink to an empty table opposite where they were standing. Bloody hell, this was a turn up for the books. Unless Liz was very much mistaken the woman was Yvonne, she recognised her from the photograph that Lillian had given her. The plot thickened and this was turning out to be a very interesting case.

The woman spoke first. 'I'm sorry.' She said 'It was insensitive of me to not guess how you must be feeling.'

When Clive didn't reply she continued in a more conciliatory manner. 'I've been thinking of what you said earlier about me, you, the girls and Adam. I want that too, I just panicked before.'

Clive was taken aback. Yvonne had seemed so angry earlier, he could hardly believe his luck that she had changed her mind. Using the 'L' word must have worked, he told himself. Women were so predictable.

'Why don't we go upstairs and talk this through properly.' he said, ever the opportunist.

'Oh darling, I would love to.' Yvonne said instantly understanding the proposition.

'Shall I go ahead and slip into something comfortable whilst you sort out the bar staff to cover?

Clive replied by patting her behind. He did this in full view of the customers on purpose, just in case Yvonne changed her bloody mind again this was the proof he needed that they were having an affair. His customers would be tripping over themselves to pass this little gem onto Bob and Rhonda. Yvonne had to stop herself recoiling from his touch. I'm here for one thing and one thing only she told herself as she raced up the stairs to Clive's flat. Wasting no time she quickly checked the drawers in the kitchen and lounge. Finding nothing she made her way into Clive's bedroom. Perhaps Clive hadn't kept the postcard. Why would he? They hadn't exactly been love's young dream had they? She had almost given up hope of finding the postcard when it suddenly caught her eye. It was propped up against a photo frame on the chest of drawers. She rushed across the room and deftly stuffed it into her handbag, hardly believing her luck at having found it. Just at that moment she heard Clive coming into the hallway of the flat. Looking wildly around the room she noticed that in her haste to grab the postcard she had left the bedside drawers ajar. She did not have time to roll across the bed and close it so instead she arranged herself provocatively on the bed. A few seconds later Clive came into the room.

'Oh there you are.' He said. 'I wondered where you had got to.' Glancing towards the open drawers his expression changed. 'What were you looking for in the drawers Yvonne?' he asked, trying to keep the note of suspicion from his voice.

Yvonne was momentarily at a loss at what to say. Trying to keep the note of alarm from her voice she composed herself to reply. 'I was looking for the condoms of course.' She said, as if it was obvious. 'Is that not where you normally keep them?'

Thank God, the ruse worked and Clive's manner changed. He might have guessed. Yvonne was always *'up for it'*. It was so refreshing to be with a woman who enjoyed sex as much as she did.

'Great minds think alike.' Clive said, producing a pack of three from his trouser pocket. 'That's why I've been so long I had to pop into the gents on my way up here.' He pushed her back onto to bed and as his hand snaked up her jumper he skilfully unclipped her bra clasp. 'Just enough' he murmured as he cupped her breast 'any more would be a waste.'

Bugger thought Yvonne. How can I get out of this one? God this skulduggery lark was exhausting. Oh for an easy life, warm slippers and a cup of tea. Yet despite herself she could feel herself becoming aroused. Clive was running his tongue across her nipple and it was very erotic. Reminding herself that she was here for a purpose she blurted out. 'Let me pay a quick visit to the loo first.'

'Ok, but be quick darling.' Clive panted as he unzipped his straining jeans.

'Why not get into bed and wait for me.' Said Yvonne, hoping that with any luck Clive would turn his back to get undressed and give her the opportunity to grab her handbag and leave. Clive did just this and she raced from the room, through the hallway and carefully opening the front door of the flat ran down the stairs.

Clive lay on his back waiting. He waited and waited. What the hell was she doing in there? Having a bath? As he waited his eyes darted around the room. He had a feeling something was missing from the top of the drawers. Now what was it? Mentally he made a checklist of what he normally kept on there then with a sickening feeling he realised a postcard was missing. Very slowly it dawned on him the significance of the postcard. Of course, it explained everything, he'd been duped. It was the oldest trick in the book. He knew even before checking the bathroom that Yvonne would be long gone. That bloody postcard had been sitting on the drawers for so long he had forgotten all about it. To think he'd had the proof in his hands all the time and hadn't realised it. Who was it said that the female of the species is more deadly than the male. Mata Hari had nothing on Yvonne, she had played a blinder.

THE OLD CHAPEL – LENNIE FINDS HER MISSING LIBIDO

Lennie sat curled up on the sofa. Tracey sat cross-legged on the floor by her feet. They were well into their second bottle of red wine and both quite tipsy. Lennie realised that if she were to stretch out her hand she could stroke Tracey's hair, but she felt that the time was not yet right, although the atmosphere was electric with unspoken desire. As she poured the last dregs of the bottle into Lennie's glass Tracey spilt a few drops onto her wrist.

Tracey blushed. 'I'm sorry' she said 'Wine always makes me clumsy. Let me get a cloth to wipe it up.'

'There's no need it's only.......' Lennie started to say, but Tracey was already on her feet and going into the kitchen for a tea towel. When she returned Tracey wrapped the cloth loosely around Lennie's wrist and rubbed very gently.

'Oohh, that made me tingle all over.' Lennie said, without really thinking what she was saying.

'All over?' Tracey mimicked in a teasing voice.

Oh my goodness, thought Lennie, have I misread the signs? Have I been presumptuous? It had been so long since she had been in this situation she was at a loss at what to do next. Luckily Tracey had no such insecurities and she skilfully drew Lennie into an embrace. Their lips met and as they melted into one another the tension disappeared from the room.

'We could, of course, continue this conversation upstairs,' said Tracey as they finally broke off from the kiss.

By way of an answer Lennie stood up. 'Lead the way,' she said, suddenly confident, her libido doing somersaults. 'I don't think I shall be sleeping in the dressing room after all.'

NOWHERE MANOR – THE WINDSOR KNOT

Lillian sat in the drawing room of Nowhere Manor sipping a sweet sherry whilst flicking through a copy of *Horse and Hound*. She could hear George pottering around in the bedroom above. If he thought he was going out again he had another thing coming. It was one thing his having an affair but another to flaunt it in such a cavalier way. She heard his footsteps in the hallway and had worked herself up into to quite a tizzy when he eventually popped his head around the door.

'I'm just nipping out again darling.' He said. 'Don't wait up as I may be late.'

'Glad to have had the pleasure of your company, albeit for such a short space of time.' Lillian replied in a sarcastic voice.

'No need to be so tetchy, my dear.' George intoned. 'I would much prefer to spend the night in the company of my darling wife but this is for our benefit. You were the one pushing me to go for this blasted job of Mayor. As I told you, I must be seen in the right places to oil the necessary palms. Tonight I am attending at the special request of the Earl, even you must be impressed when you remember who is staying at the castle tonight.' At this Lillian perked up considerably. Oh my giddy aunt, she thought to herself. Quickly dropping her magazine to the floor, she beckoned George to her chair as she hastily stood up.

'My dear man, you only had to say. Now stay still while I re-do your tie. I think a Windsor knot would be more appropriate tonight, don't you?'

THE MORNING AFTER
THE NIGHT BEFORE

The next day dawned, a slight ground frost giving the streets a sparkling picture postcard feel. Lennie awoke and gazed across the bed towards Tracey. Tracey's hair was spread out upon the pillow, her breasts tantalisingly discernible under the duvet. They had made love into the early hours of the morning, Lennie discovering a desire and appetite she thought she had lost a long time ago. She carefully crawled from the bed and taking her vanity case from the suitcase silently tiptoed down the narrow stairs towards the bathroom.

The powerful jets of hot water felt like a thousand tiny kisses as they bounced of her breasts. Pouring some shampoo from the bottle beside the shower cubicle she lathered her hair, wincing slightly as it stung her eyes. She visibly jumped as she heard a voice from outside the cubicle.

'Mind if I join you?' said the voice.

Lennie swung the door of the shower cubicle open and rubbed her eyes with the back of her hand. As her vision cleared she saw 'a vision'. Tracey stood there, her hands positioned confidently upon her hips, her burnished skin glowing and achingly just out of reach. A shock of dark silky pubic hair formed almost a heart shape as it curled tantalisingly from between her thighs.

'That's a request I don't hear every day,' Lennie answered, breathless in anticipation.

'We can role play if you wish,' said Tracey as she squeezed in the cubicle her hot breath upon Lennie's shoulder 'we could pretend we are two nuns sharing a shower.'

'I suppose I should ask you *where's the soap?*' in that case.' Lennie said, joining in the fun.

'Yes, it does rather, doesn't it,' Tracey replied as she ran her fingers down Lennie's body and silenced her gasps of pleasure with a soapy kiss.

NOWHERE CASTLE – THE GUEST WING – WHAT THE BUTLER SAW

The middle-aged man awoke in a strange bedchamber. He would have slept more soundly had his lady-friend been able to make the trip up North with him. The previous night he had partaken in some excellent scotch whisky and a very grand five course banquet, resulting in a particularly nasty bout of heartburn in the wee small hours. How he wished his dear friends would occasionally see beneath the title and treat him more as an ordinary chap. Many was the night he and his darling lady friend had dined upon a tin of Heinz tomato soup, slumped in front of the television set watching the aptly named *Coronation Street*, followed by an energetic romp in his king sized bed. Such nights were unfortunately infrequent but oh so pleasurable, as rare as hen's teeth.

He had long since realised that his life was not his own, but he relaxed when he remembered that perhaps today would not turn out so dreary after all. Once the duties had been performed, the public appeased, the glorious thrill of the Nowhere Hunt awaited him. This thought in turn and the memories it evoked of his darling lady in full red regalia, hunting whip in hand, chasing him around the bedroom awoke the little prince. His mind wandered to the image of her astride a chestnut hunter taking the fence in her own unmistakable style. Looking toward the door, he fully expected Sorell, his butler, to make an appearance but there was no sign of the annoyingly servile manservant. Oh well it looked like he would have to run his own bath that morning. Climbing from the bed the .... made the wise decision that perhaps a cold shower might be more appropriate.

From the doorway, Sorell watched transfixed, unsure of the correct protocol in situations such as this. After taking in the spectacle for a few moments Sorell reluctantly closed the door and left. What the butler saw, he snickered to himself. More like 'I'm a butler, get me out of here.'

GREENHOUSE BISTRO – LADYFINGERS

Elsewhere in Nowhere in rather more salubrious setting the owners of the Bistro were hard at work. Louisa had devised a menu of sorts which promised to be tempting to the taste buds but with ingredients which were easy to procure. She was aware of the limitations of supply in a small market town but wanted to put the Bistro on the map in a gastronomic sense. She described her proposed meals to Joey as being paintings on a plate.

'*An artist's palette to tempt the palate, with a rich infusion of flavours and* textures *to tempt even the most discerning diner.*'

She had included a dish containing okra, even though she knew the difficulties they would face in sourcing the vegetable. As she told Joey, any self respecting lesbian-run restaurant had a basic obligation to include okra or lady fingers on its menu. It was a given, not open to negotiation.

'I think I'll walk Jasper earlier today, if that's ok with you?' Louisa said to Joey in what she hoped was a nonchalant manner. 'He really needs to get used to walking amongst crowds, and according to the local paper Nowhere will be heaving with people today.'

'I only wish we were open today,' said a downcast Joey. 'I bet we'd have made a killing. As it is the only people making a killing today are those '*hooray Henrys*' on that bloody hunt.'

'I heard rumours that that was the real reason for the visit today, overshadowed of course by the big public relations exercise for the Enterprise Scheme.'

'That probably explains the massive police presence; perhaps they are expecting trouble, especially as the Anti-hunt Bill is such a political hot potato at the moment.'

'Well it will serve to get Nowhere on the map if nothing else. Let's just hope the Hunt Saboteurs get to spoil their so called sport.' Louisa remarked as she left the Bistro with a very excited Jasper straining on his lead.

GLOUCESTER COURT – THE OVERZEALOUS POLICEWOMAN

Sooty had just arrived back at Gloucester Court after dropping Jean off at the retreat on Holy Island. She was amused by the fact that she had been frisked by a plain clothes policewoman before being allowed to enter the passageway leading to the courtyard in front of her house. Sooty was convinced her '*frisker*' was a friend of Dorothy's, as her hands had lingered slightly longer than necessary on Sooty's upper thighs. Sooty found it surprising that security proved to be such an issue. Usually on visits such as this security was lax. No doubt the prospect of the Anti-hunting Bill being so emotive prompted such measures. Nonetheless, the impromptu '*laying on of hands*' had whet her appetite for the visit by Louisa later on that day. Now it just remained for her to choose an appropriate outfit for the other slightly more formal visit of the day.

NOWHERE CASTLE

Ten minutes after walking in on the spectacle in the bedchamber, Sorell the butler knocked once again on the bedroom door. His master was now sitting at the desk by the bed in a blue and gold smoking jacket, writing a letter.

'Ah Sorell, have you been knocking at the door for very long?' The ....enquired.

How Sorell wished he could say he'd knocked earlier but his master had been taking a cold shower. But no, such revelations must wait, his diary was growing daily and his day would come. Already he had made discreet enquiries to a more sensationalist publisher and the projected figure had been very pleasing indeed. It was the time for Sorell to play a waiting game. After all it was a jungle out there.

'Shall I run you a bath, Sir,' enquired Sorell. 'If you wish I can have your clothes waiting on the bed for your return.'

'Thank you Sorell but that won't be necessary as I have just showered,' said the ....

Sorell turned his back so the .... would not see his smirk. But the ....was to intent on writing his letter to notice anything. The .... dragged his pen across the paper finishing the letter with a flourish and his usual illegible signature. Sorell watched as he folded the letter into three, placed it in an envelope and sealed it for delivery. Later when his employer was breakfasting Sorell would remove the blotting paper from the writing desk and stuff it in his pocket. There would be plenty of time afterwards, in the privacy of his own room, to rub over the impression his master's fountain pen had made upon the blotting paper. Sorell had already noted that the letter was addressed to a certain lady friend of his master's, and he was sure it would make most interesting reading. He really must invest in one of those new fangled cameras soon, just imagine the prospect of walking in again on a sight such as had greeted him earlier that morning. Now a photograph such as that sent to a certain newspaper abroad would have ensured Sorell a life of luxury, no problem.

THE ALPAHBET GAME

Louisa was strolling through the alleyway which led into Sooty's private courtyard when she was stopped in her tracks by a rather portly policewoman. Above the noise of Jasper barking the officer indicated that she would need to frisk Louisa. Upon hearing the commotion in the courtyard Sooty appeared at the door and took the dog lead from Louisa's grasp.

'Let me put Jasper in the garden my dear,' said Sooty. 'Just come inside once this charming policewoman has finished checking you over.'

Louisa grinned at the older woman before turning again to the policewoman and raising her arms to be frisked. Gosh, she thought, this policewoman is very thorough. The frisking seemed to take forever. Louisa eventually entered the house a short while later and was promptly goosed by an amorous Sooty before being ushered up the stairs towards the bedroom.

'I can pretend that I need to show you the excellent view of the castle from my study window again or be up front and say that I am desperate to take you to bed,' she said, deciding honesty to be the best policy.

'Much prefer the latter scenario,' gasped a breathless Louisa.

QUITE A WHILE LATER ...

Louisa lay enveloped in Sooty's arms beneath the tumbled remains of the bedclothes. The lovemaking had been intoxicating. It reminded Louisa of the song 'Afternoon Delight'. Yes she decided there had definitely been 'sky rockets in sight' at one stage. She was about to voice these thoughts to Sooty when the older woman began to speak.

'I hate to tell you but I could so easily fall in love with you, my dear,' said Sooty deliberately holding Louisa's gaze with her own. This candid statement gave Louisa quite a start, and she hesitated a while as she composed her reply.

'Let's enjoy ourselves before getting into anything too heavy,' she said softly.

'I'm sorry,' said Sooty, quickly backtracking afraid she had said too much. 'I wasn't suggesting we run off into the sunset together,' she added flippantly. 'I just felt the need to put it out there that you would be so easy to fall in love with.'

Louisa averted her eyes but not before Sooty had read the panic in her expression. Despite her better judgement Sooty felt compelled to continue.

'I really must ask you something,' she said.

'Ask away.'

'Do you feel guilty after sleeping with me?'

Louisa pondered on the question for a moment before answering. 'It's complex,' she said. 'I should feel guilty but I don't and that concerns me more.'

'Why does it concern you?'

'What kind of person does it make me, if I can cheat on my partner and not feel guilty?'

Sooty was about to answer 'My kind of person' but sensed that Louisa wanted a more serious answer. 'I think that while loving one person exclusively is an ideal state it's still possible to love another without the second one cancelling out the validity of the first.'

'Isn't that just another way of saying you would like an open relationship?'

'Well yes,' Sooty conceded 'I suppose it is, but what Lennie and I have isn't so much an open relationship. It's more a case of she just turns a blind eye to my indiscretions. We have muddled through like this for many years and the only mistake I have made was to once tell Lennie of an affair. It was selfish of me to try to lessen my guilt by forcing the fact upon her and it achieved nothing.'

'So when you say you could fall in love with me it isn't with the expectation that somewhere down the line I will tell Joey?'

'Well I can't say how I will feel in the future but for the moment I merely meant that you have a place in my heart and I think I am falling in love with you. Have I scared you away? Have I said too much?'

Louisa silenced Sooty with a long lingering kiss. Whispering in her ear, she said 'I think it's healthy to get these things out of the way but let's see how things go.'

As they lay quietly in each other's arms Louisa once again addressed her own motives for starting the affair. It was never meant to be serious but things had changed and she needed to get it back on track.

'I know let's play the alphabet game and lighten the mood.'

'The alphabet game?' said Sooty. 'I've never heard of it. How do you play it?'

'It's easy' said Louisa reaching to touch Sooty's buttocks. 'I'm sure you will pick it up as we go along.'

'*A is for arse*,' playfully she tapped Sooty on the bottom.

'*B is for breast*,' playfully she tweaked Sooty's nipple.

'*C is for caress*', she said as she wrapped Sooty into her embrace.

'Now it's your turn,' she murmured into Sooty's hair as Sooty squirmed beneath her touch.

'*D is for desire*,' Sooty eventually drawled, and '*E is for engorged*.'

'*F is self explanatory*,' Louisa giggled.

'*G is for girth*,' Sooty continued.

'Very funny.' said Louisa. 'Shall I get off you, am I too heavy?

'No I'm only teasing,' Sooty replied, pulling Louisa even closer.

'*H is for heavenly*.'

'*I is for I have eyes only for you*.'

'*J is for joy and K is for kiss*.'

'*L can only be lust*,'

'Or love,' countered Sooty.

'*M is me and you*.' She continued.

'U? Hey, I thought you were a teacher - surely it's N to follow M.'

'Ha ha, *N is for naughty, O is for orgasmic, P is for pure pleasure*.'

'*Q is for cute*.'

'Since when has cute begun with a Q, my dear?' Sooty asked.

'*R is for rules are made to be broken*.' Louisa replied.

'*S is for 'you are a very sexy lady*.'

Ditto said Louisa '*T is for two, you and me together, the perfect combination*.'

'I am flattered, my dear, *U is for you make me tingle*.'

'*V is for Virtuous, which I am not*.'

'*W is for waking up in your arms*.'

'*X is exciting, which you are*.'

'*Y is for why don't we make love again*?'

'Oh dear I've nearly run out of letters but yes that sounds like an excellent idea' said Louisa......and they did....

'I nearly forgot Z' said Sooty, a good while later.

'Z?' said Louisa '*Z is for zonked.*' And saying this she settled down in Sooty's arms and closed her eyes, she was exhausted.

BOB'S CLOSE CALL

Bob the taxi driver was having a quiet day. He had made the decision to accept no fares that would take him into the centre of the town. Rumours were that the Hunt Saboteurs were staging a protest march to coincide with the timing of the visit to the Italian Restaurant. They were hoping this furore would provide maximum publicity for their cause and therefore maximum embarrassment for the Earl and his guest. Bob had seen such protests on the television and was worried about his car being damaged in the fracas that would surely ensue, so he had decided to spend the day at home doing some much needed paperwork. Yvonne had left earlier in the day to go to work at old man Johnson's. She had been in a very strange mood, tactile and affectionate, which fazed Bob somewhat. Their relationship had never been a particularly passionate. They had sort of drifted into marriage coerced by the fact that Yvonne fell pregnant. But they paddled along quite well he supposed, each fulfilling their designated roles of father and husband, mother and wife.

Bob sat in the office staring at the blank forms. He really must make a start on the paperwork '*the VAT man 'calleth*' but spotting his reflection in the mirror above the desk, Bob managed to convince himself that he was in dire need of a shave. A delaying tactic he knew, but he decided it was imperative that he shave straight away. Why panic, he told himself, he had all day to sort the books, Yvonne would be back in a few hours and the paperwork would prove the perfect excuse to keep from under her feet. He made his way towards the bathroom. Yvonne's new negligee hung from a hook behind the bathroom door. Bob stopped and lifted the silk garment to his cheek. It seemed to accentuate the roughness of his skin, catching as it did upon his bristles. Looking towards the bathroom mirror he held the garment up against his body. It was no good he had to try it on. He felt compelled to, almost as if it was not his decision.

Quickly he stripped down to his underwear and delving into the washing basket, he retrieved Yvonne's cream silk panties and 'wonder bra'. Bob stuffed a pair of socks into the cups of the bra, squeezing his chest together as he fastened the hooks at the back to give the desired illusion of a cleavage. Finally, after tucking his penis between his legs, he squeezed his ample frame into Yvonne's tiny panties, and dropped the silken negligee over his head. He draped the matching dressing gown over his shoulders and slinked into the bedroom for some high heeled shoes to complete the 'femme fatale' look. Struggling into the strappy sandals, he decided to apply some makeup and false nails. After all, the house would be empty for hours and it was so rare he had the chance to do the whole look.

Whilst Bob was affecting is transformation Liz was sitting in her car opposite the house. She could make out a lady's figure in the bedroom of no 9. The lady was sitting upon the bed gazing at her reflection in the looking glass and carefully painting her nails. Liz had made the decision to pursue the Yvonne option more diligently. She desperately needed to eliminate her from the enquiries, and her husband Bob seemed the ideal candidate to prime for information. But she was confused. She had seen a lady she believed to be Yvonne going into the Antiques Emporium earlier that day and believed that the coast would be clear for her to question Bob. So who was the lady in the bedroom? Was Bob having an affair too? My God, these market towns were quite a shock to the system. Right little dens of sexual intrigue. She really needed to find out more about Yvonne and Bob but how? Suddenly, the conversation she had shared with Clive the Octopus the previous night sprung to her mind. She could be a working mum enquiring about whether Yvonne could child-mind her imaginary daughter a few evenings a week. It would provide the perfect cover.

Bob felt his stomach lurch as he became aware of the frantic knocking at the front door. Whoever was there must be pretty sure he was in, judging by the persistency of the rapping. Bob ran panic-stricken to the bathroom in order to wash off the makeup he had so meticulously applied minutes earlier and nearly tripping upon the hem of the silk negligee dressing gown in his haste.

'I'm coming, hang on,' he yelled down the stairs in the direction of the front door.

The impatient visitor must have heard his plaintive cry as the annoying knocking stopped as abruptly as it had begun. Once dressed in his workday clothes, Bob swiftly checked his face for any tell tale makeup before hurrying down the stairs, breaking into a clumsy sprint as he reached the hallway. Flinging open the door with a dramatic flourish, he demanded,

'Ok so where's the bloody fire?'

Liz was taken aback at his aggressive attitude but continued with her plan nonetheless. 'Hi, sorry, I heard movement in the house so I knew someone was in, and I am pretty desperate. I had a childminder lined up and she has let me down at the last moment. I hoped to catch your wife and appeal to her good nature. I'm catching the train to London in two hours and need someone to collect my daughter from school. The class teacher said your wife would probably be able to help me out.'

'Bloody childminding!!!!' yelled Bob. 'Are you telling me you've nearly caused me to break my bloody neck on the stairs just to ask me about childminding?'

'Sorry,' repeated Liz, looking, she hoped, suitably contrite. 'I saw a lady at the bedroom window and presumed it was your wife.'

This last statement took the wind quite literally out of Bob's sails. He gestured wildly seemingly lost for words. As he raised his arms to the heavens it was almost as if his eyes and Liz's eyes locked upon his painted nails at the same moment. They both stared at Bobs bright red fingernails, Liz quizzically and Bob in gobsmacked horror. Struggling to compose himself, Bob shoved his hands quickly into his pockets, convincing himself the girl would see nothing untoward about a grown man wearing ruby red false nails.

But the truth dawned on Liz fairly quickly. Oh my God, she thought, the plot thickens. Arthur, Martha or Bob the cross-dressing taxi driver, who would have guessed. At a loss for something to say, she turned away from the doorstep and prepared to leave. She was literally stopped in her tracks by a large flamboyant lady in a bottle green trench coat.

'Excuse me honey,' said the lady in a pronounced American accent. She then addressed her attention to Bob.'Bob, sweetie, is Yvonne at home? I've just been to see my solicitor and she says we can crucify Clive in court for telling these ridiculous lies'

Seeing Bobs' bemused expression Rhonda soon realised that Yvonne hadn't told him anything. Bob moved aside to allow Rhonda to enter the hallway, and without so much as casting another glance in Liz's direction he slammed the front door.

'Gee, you English guys sure have some funny habits,' said Rhonda as she noticed Bob's nails.

Thinking quickly on his feet, Bob replied, 'Just painting them for Yvonne and it was easier to wear them so they dry evenly.'

Rhonda obviously had other things on her mind, as she brushed Bob's explanation aside. 'Whatever. Would you make me a coffee sweetie and I'll fill you in on what my Brief said.'

JOHNSON AND SONS – ANTIQUES EMPORIUM

Yvonne looked up from her desk as a scruffy youth strode past her desk and towards old man Johnson's office at the Antiques Emporium.

'Excuse me young man can I help you?' she enquired to his departing back.

'Looking for old man J,' mumbled the youth as he stopped and turned. Disconcertingly he addressed his statement to her breasts. Pulling her cardigan across her chest in a propriety manner, Yvonne enquired as to the nature of the young man's business with her employer.

'Just say Robbie's here to see him, and I ain't got all day,' he replied, thrusting his face so close to Yvonne's that she physically recoiled.

Yvonne was just about to ask the unsavoury character to leave when George hearing the commotion popped his head around the door and seeing the lad, ushered him quickly into the office.

'What in hell's name do you think you are doing here?' demanded George once the office door had closed.

'Reckoned owing to the nature of the job like, you should bung me a few notes up front,' mumbled the surly youth.

'Could you not have asked me this on the telephone?'

'I kinda thought you might be more willing to pay if I paid you a visit.'

'Well you thought wrong. We agreed on payment once the job was done and not one moment before.'

'I just thought that with all the cops around and me on bail, I would be less likely to get caught if I had a bit of cash in my pocket.'

'I do hope this isn't a clumsy attempt at blackmail boy. Pray remember that I can have you locked up again so quickly your bloody feet won't touch the ground.'

At this timely reminder, the lad's tone of voice changed.

'Ok point taken Mr J. but I would appreciate a few notes,' he whined.

'Alright, alright,' grumbled George satisfied that he had got his point across regarding the pathetic attempt at blackmail. 'I think I have eighty quid in my wallet. Now will you bugger off before I really do lose my temper.'

The lad snatched the eighty pounds, pocketed it quickly in his jeans and turned to leave the office. George promptly pressed his intercom to speak to Yvonne.

'Get me the Earl on the telephone please Yvonne, tell him it's important.'

'Ok Mr Johnson,' replied Yvonne.

A few minutes later and George was speaking on the telephone to his old friend the Earl. He quickly explained how he had averted a possible problem. Let it be known, thought George, that he George Johnson, was a man to rely upon in a crisis. Word would, he was sure, get relayed to certain circles. Blowing his own trumpet had always been a personal attribute which George nurtured. He wanted that job as Town Mayor and his handling of this matter and its successful conclusion would surely pave his way to the robe and chains. It would also get bloody Lillian off his back and give her something new to get her teeth into. She really was starting to irritate him with her constant demands upon his time and intrusion into his privacy. Glancing out of the office window, George saw Raymond crossing the street, newspaper tucked under his arm.

George allowed his mind the luxury of going back in time to the image of Raymond lying upon the Venetian bed, sunlight playing upon the contours of his well-honed chest, the balmy breeze from the open balcony window, the sweat glistening between his bronzed thighs. How George lusted for his young energetic lover. Perhaps he could plan another jaunt abroad, he told himself, once this bloody business of the day was put to bed.

MUCH TOO JOLLY HOCKEY STICKS

'What about this ensemble?' enquired Sooty of her naked lover.

'Oh no,' said Louisa vehemently shaking her head. 'It looks like you're going for tea with a maiden aunt, and I would lose the cravat as well, much too jolly hockey sticks,' she continued in a similar critical vein.

'What do you think I should wear then? And please don't say my birthday suit, we've been through that one before.'

'Will you be angry if I say the first outfit you tried on?'

'Angry? I'll be so angry I may have to come back to bed to scold you,' said Sooty in a mock cross voice.

'Promises, promises,' teased Louisa, leaning back upon the pillows so her breasts stood out pert and proud. 'I have tired you out haven't I? No stamina, you old birds.'

At this statement Sooty grinned, shrugged off her clothes and made a leap towards the bed. Pinning Louisa to the pillow by her arms she said in a husky voice,

'No stamina? I'll show you no stamina. Remember, my darling, I'm as old as the woman I feel.'

Louisa gasped with pleasure as Sooty released her arms and began to make love to her all over again.

THE NEAR RIOT

The crowd outside the Italian Restaurant gave a loud cheer as they saw the Castle gates open, and the cavalcade of black cars revved their engines in anticipation of the signal to drive on. The current Mayor stood poised upon the podium which had been erected in front of the restaurant. Hearing the crowd roar he straightened his Mayoral robes, and his wife by his side adjusted the angle of her new hat. The photographers from the local newspaper opened the lens caps of their cameras and checked the height of their tripods and angle of the sun's rays. The heavy police presence scanned the crowds, easily identifying the Hunt Saboteurs and Pro-Hunt supporters, who they had taken the precaution of positioning on opposite sides of the street.

Outside Gloucester Court, a hastily dressed Sooty (minus the cravat) stood in her courtyard chatting in a good natured way to the large-chested policewoman, who for her part kept stopping the conversation to listen to instructions on her walkie-talkie.

Inside the house at Gloucester Court, Louisa stood in the bathroom facing the large mirror over the bath writing with lipstick upon her bare chest. This gesture was not premeditated in any way, but she had run the idea by Sooty a few minutes previously and the older woman had shrugged her shoulders by way of assent.

In the street, Maggie stood back from the crowd clutching her handbag to her side. It was her first time out-of-doors since the mugging and her good friend Flo had persuaded her to attend the ceremony. She was temporarily alone as Flo had been caught short and had rushed off apologetically to the public toilets in the market-place, assuring her friend she would not be long.

In the alleyway to the left of the restaurant, Robbie reached into the inside pocket of his parka coat and took out a black balaclava. He strode towards a black wheelie bin and opening it he reached in and grabbed a large plastic bag containing an innocuous looking old cricket bat. Taking the bat from the bag he held it aloft before swooping it over his head as if practising the return of a fast ball from an imaginary demon bowler at Lords.

Sorell the butler, held open the door of the black car, standing well aside so his employer could clamber inside. The suited chauffeur glanced in his rear view mirror to check his passenger was seated and belted before putting the engine into first gear and releasing the handbrake.

Maggie was startled to hear the footsteps running behind her. Instinctively, she grabbed her handbag closer to her side. Robbie pushed past her and ran towards the pro-hunt contingent, yelling at the top of his voice 'STOP BLOODY HUNTING,' before pulling the balaclava over his head.

Upon reaching the crowd of pro-hunters, resplendent in their red coats, he let fly with the cricket bat, not caring where and with what ferocity the bat made contact. The hunters, who presumed Robbie to be a part of the Saboteurs, reacted in a predictable way and a few raced across the street to stage a counter-attack upon the Hunt Saboteurs. A large fight ensued. Police officers were thrown upon the ground, the crowd screamed, and the photographers frantically tried to capture the perfect frame to send to the Nationals. In the ensuing chaos Robbie crawled commando-style from the rabble, got to his feet and ran towards the alleyway from which he had emerged. Maggie crouched against the wall in tears as the boy ran towards her. She was even more distressed when she saw Robbie tear the balaclava from his head and she recognised him as the youth who had mugged her. He snarled in her direction and threw the cricket bat against the black wheelie bin where it landed with a resounding clatter.

From his office in the Antiques Emporium, George sat grinning. He had witnessed the event from the safety of his office chair; a very successful mission. Closing his eyes he could sense the Mayoral chains around his neck and feel the fur sable of the cloak about his shoulders.

From the safety of his bullet proof car, the ...... surveyed the near riot scene. Knocking on the glass partition between the chauffeur and himself he attracted the attention of the driver.

'Drive on when the Inspector chappie says the coast is clear,' he added 'I have a job to do and no minor riot is going to stop me in my tracks'.

Take every advantage of a public relations exercise he told himself. After all, it hadn't harmed his grandmother's image when she had remained in London throughout the Blitz.

The crowd again let out a cheer, this time to mark the emergence of the ...... from the black car. He shook hands with a few outstretched palms, posed for an obligatory photograph holding a toddler, then stood upon the hastily re-erected podium next to the Mayor and his insufferable wife to make a brief speech about his hopes for the future of the countryside. After accepting the key to the Town the .... clambered down from the podium. He was directed by the Town Crier towards the passageway leading to the courtyard of Gloucester Court and the entrance to the Italian Restaurant.

The large-chested policewoman stood aside as the ......, flanked by a bodyguard and press photographer, approached a smiling Sooty. Just as Sooty pulled herself up from her curtsey and made to shake the proffered hand, the window above her opened and all eyes looked skywards. Louisa had a starring role in the tableau. She stood, completely naked, surrounded as if on a stage by the velvet curtains of Sooty's bedroom. Her head was obscured by the slightly lowered blind but she had thrust her chest outward. Across her breasts emblazoned in bright red lipstick were the words:

HUNTING IS FOR TITS

Despite himself the ...... laughed out loud, A fact he would later bitterly regret when he was summoned to the family pile in London and berated for his misdemeanour by his angry father. The following day's broadsheets cleverly, with the aid of a photo cropping device, managed to get into the photograph frame both Louisa's substantial chest and the .... appreciative laughter.

The event managed to relegate the earlier riot to almost an afterthought mention in the tabloids. Anti-hunt supporters the country over applauded the 'naked lady'. Her photograph would be reproduced on banners and she would become their mascot. A few reporters from the more tacky tabloids even approached Sooty the next day asking if she would put forward propositions to the 'naked lady'. Their editors had instructed them to offer the 'naked lady' financial incentives for her exclusive interview and centrefold pose. Sooty politely declined to comment, save to again reiterate that she had no idea who the girl had been or how she had gained access to her bedroom.

THE MYSTERIOUS NAKED LADY

Lennie was watching the afternoon news on the television in Wetherby later on that day and gasped as she heard mention of the events in Nowhere that morning.

'Isn't that market town close to where you live?' enquired Tracey.

'Yes,' replied Lennie. 'I think it's strange that when I rang Sooty earlier today she made no mention of this mysterious 'naked lady.'

'Are you sure that it was your friend's bedroom window in the news report?'

'Oh yes I am quite sure, no doubt about it.'

'Well I would hazard a guess that your friend and this naked lady have been making sweet music together. What has upset you? Is it the fact that your ex is having the affair or the fact that she has kept it quiet from you?'

Lennie chose her words carefully, aware that she had stretched the truth slightly regarding her current relationship with Sooty. 'I think it's the fact that she is hiding it from me.'

'Perhaps she thought telling you would be like rubbing your nose in it,' said Tracey quite enjoying her role as Devil's advocate.

'I suppose that might be true,' conceded Lennie, 'but it still hurts that she felt she had to lie.'

'I always find that being friends with an ex is a minefield of omission's and part lies, personally I feel the clean break is best.' Tracey concluded, although this was somewhat hypocritical of her given the complicated relationship she had with her own ex.

'Anyway,' said Lennie, desperate to change the subject. 'Nothing can mar the perfect morning I have spent in your company.'

'Only one thing could possibly make it more perfect.'

'And what would that be?

As way of an answer Tracey raised her eyebrows and grinned.

Understanding straight away Lennie said 'Again?'

Tracey nodded, took her hand and led the way back up the stairs towards the bedroom. Following her lover up the stairs Lennie's mind went back in time to how she and Sooty had been right at the beginning.

Despite herself she found herself wondering how it had all gone so wrong and why she hadn't tried harder to make it work again all those years ago.

NOT ROCKING THE BOAT

Bob sat at the kitchen table of 9 Moss Side Drive waiting for Yvonne to return from work. She finished at old man Johnsons at 1.30 so he anticipated she would be home at 2.00. He hadn't really decided what to say. He had long since suspected Yvonne of an affair but he was angry that it had all become so messy.

Bob did not want to rock any proverbial boats. He wanted an easy life. He only wished to be the best father he could to his children. It would be unfair to say that he had always planned to leave Yvonne when the children were older, but lately that thought had kept him going. At what period during their marriage the thought of escape in the future had first crossed his mind he did not honestly know, but from a distant dream it had become the one thing that helped him carry on. In a way, finding out that Yvonne was as unhappy as he in their marriage was a bonus. It helped him not feel quite such a shit.

But these latest developments had the potential to blow his future plans out of the water. Bob had told Rhonda that he did not wish his wife to be dragged through the courts, and if Clive persisted in his ridiculous claims he could expect a letter from his solicitor for libel. Bob managed to convince Rhonda that he trusted his wife and there was no way she had been conducting an affair with Clive. He told her that Yvonne had told him confidentially of her plans to leave the country with Adam and confessed that he may have inadvertently spilled the beans to Clive. He went on to explain to Rhonda that due to her job as a Registered Childminder Yvonne must be seen to be impartial in cases of custody. She could not show bias in any way. By the time Rhonda left the house Bob had managed to diffuse the situation sufficiently enough to know it would die a natural death.

Bob jumped as he heard Yvonne's key in the door. He had positioned himself so he was at the head of the table looking towards the open doorway. Yvonne walked into the room, and saw Bob sitting patiently awaiting her arrival. She also saw the two empty coffee mugs, one displaying the telltale sign of Rhonda's ruby red lipstick upon its rim. She quickly put two and two together.

Yvonne felt compelled to speak and break the terrible silence that hung in the room. 'Hello sweetheart, have we had visitors?'

'Yes,' said Bob. 'Rhonda called in earlier to chat to you and I made her a coffee.'

Yvonne sat down opposite Bob. She was subdued, as if waiting for him to speak again, as if she wanted him to lead the conversation.

'I think we need to talk, Yvonne. I need you to listen very carefully to what I have to say,' said Bob eventually.

'Ok, go ahead,' said Yvonne, trying to keep her voice from shaking.

'I've handled the Rhonda and Clive situation. I am sure we shall have no more problems from that direction. I only ask that you no longer have any contact with Clive. What's done is done. I have nothing more to say on that subject.'

Yvonne nodded. She started to speak, her kneejerk reaction was to deny everything, but she thought better of it and fell silent.

'Well that's that then do you fancy an Italian meal at the new restaurant tonight?' said Bob. His reaction took the wind from her sails and she reached across the table and squeezed his hand, which was thankfully now devoid of the false nails.

'Yes honey that seems like a good idea, do you want me to book?' she said. Tears were streaming down her cheeks. She took out her handkerchief and quickly dabbed them away.

'It might be a good idea. There has been quite a lot of excitement in the town today,' replied Bob, choosing to ignore his wife's tears, as far as he was concerned the matter was closed. Dredging it up and going over it would do more harm than good.

'Do you fancy a cup of tea,' he continued in a more conciliatory manner 'there's plenty in the pot, and it's still warm.'

JOHNSON AND SONS – THE NEW YEAR GONGS

Later on that same afternoon George had a very welcome call from his friend the Earl.

'George, my good fellow,' the Earl began.

'Your help today has been very much appreciated and duly noted. My guest and I are very grateful. He feels your involvement deserves recognition. Words will be whispered into the appropriate ears regarding the New Year Gongs, but in the meantime, how does the role of Town Mayor sound to you?' George replied in his most ingratiating humble voice. 'Rewards are not necessary. I did what any true English gentleman would to uphold his basic liberty and rights. But I am sure my darling wife will appreciate the role of Lady Mayor. Would you thank your esteemed guest on my behalf and reiterate that it has been a pleasure to be of service?

'Message received loud and clear. Thank you again, my good man.'

After taking a few moments to let the news sink in, George picked up the telephone and relayed the conversation to Lillian. As he had anticipated, she was overjoyed with the news, already planning her outfit for her trip to London. George leaned back on his office chair feeling very smug and pleased with himself. Not a bad day. Not a bad day at all.

Suddenly the door to his office swung open and a young lady stood there looking quizzically in his direction.

'I did knock,' she said, 'but you didn't seem to hear.'

'Not a problem,' said George, climbing up from his seat to usher Liz into the chair facing his desk. He prided himself on being a gentleman. 'Now, my dear, how may I assist you on a fine day such as this?'

'A mutual friend suggested I contact you,' Liz said, 'This friend suggested that you were somewhat of an expert in sourcing antiques.'

George was very open to flattery, and seeing his reaction Liz decided she had hit the right note.

'Well, my dear, it appears my reputation has preceded me. And what, pray tell, is your chosen collective field?'

'Pottery, Deco or Nouveau. The usual names: Cliffe, Shorter, Rhead.'

'Well I do know a man who knows a man, who could be very helpful in this matter. And who did you say had recommended my services to your good self?'

Liz decided to go for the surprise factor and imply that it had been Raymond.

'I don't want to specify a name, but let's say he cuts hair very well.'

If George was taken aback at all he did not show it, he merely replied 'My dear, I really must have a contact name if I am to help you at all.'

'The person concerned told me not to name him. He explained that from the description you would know who he was and that I could be trusted.'

George looked vexed, but tried very hard to hide it. His interlude with Raymond had probably run its course; one thing George insisted on was discretion. Now that he had his new role to fill, discretion mattered even more. He reassured himself with the fleeting thought that young men such as Raymond were ten a penny. Perhaps this girl's revelation had been a godsend. What was that phrase about not doing the deed upon one's own doorstep? Convenient though it had been the risk was now too great. This was probably the opportune time to move onto pastures new. George stood up in order to show Liz to the door.

'My dear, it seems we have got our wires crossed. This is a legitimate antiques business. I am a busy man and have no time for riddles. May I politely ask you to leave?'

Liz was about to attempt to wriggle out of the situation when a youth burst into the office. He began to speak almost before he entered the office. 'We've a big problem, Mr J. That old bird what got me put in the clink clocked me this morning.' He was obviously very agitated as he seemed unaware that Liz was standing behind the door about to leave. George swept across the office to quieten the youth whilst gently pushing Liz towards the exit at the same time. 'Sorry I could not help you, my dear, now if you please take your leave I've this small matter to sort out.'

The door was firmly shut behind Liz but she was going nowhere. The two men were speaking in mumbled tones but by sitting in Yvonne the secretary's chair and pressing her ear against the partition wall Liz could make out the conversation quite clearly.

'Start again in the Queen's English,' snapped George.

'The old bird what I mugged seen me wiv the hat on and wiv the cricket bat.'

'You stupid boy, why were you not more careful?' replied George rapping his fist upon the desk.

'Don't want to get banged up again, Mr J.'

'I'll sort it out,' said George in an exasperated voice. 'The old dear's confused anyway; I will get plod to sort it out.'

'Shall I put the frighteners on her, Mr J?'

'Putting the frighteners on her as you so eloquently put it may not be a bad idea, but other than that leave it in my hands and don't panic.'

'Ok Mr J, thank you Mr J.'

'Stop whining boy. And under no circumstances do I want to see you here again. As you are here you might as well have this now rather than later.'

George reached into his jacket pocket and handed a sealed envelope to the youth. Robbie started to open the envelope with the obvious intention of counting the cash.

'I suggest you trust it is all there and leave or I may be forced to take it back again,' said George, in a very vexed voice. 'Close the door as you leave, I've phone calls to make.'

The youth sped out of the door and left the office without noticing Liz, who had taken the precaution of crouching beneath the old oak office desk. Well, this was most interesting indeed, she thought to herself. What was George Johnson mixed up in?

This was so much more than just a seedy little affair. This had the makings of something really big, so big perhaps it would be her ticket out of the Private Investigator game and into the much more lucrative Investigative Journalist field. The plot thickened. Liz was just making the decision about whether to risk hanging around as George made his phone calls when her left leg went into cramp. She jumped to her feet in pain and in doing so she knocked her elbow on the desk drawer. From his office, George heard the commotion and hastily hung up the telephone to investigate the source of the noise but by the time he had opened the office door, Liz was running from the building and heading towards her car.

She could sense George watching her exit from his vantage point at his office window. She willed herself not to turn around, reminding herself of the pillar of salt story in the bible, but all the time she was aware of his eyes piercing into her back. She was very unnerved. My God, what had she stumbled upon? This was no small-time corruption, a big fish in a little pond. No this was much more serious, and George Johnson was swimming in some very treacherous waters.

George stood at the window, watching Liz's hasty and self-conscious departure. He saw her climb into her car, reach into her handbag and put the key into the ignition. Her posture convinced him that she had overheard his conversation. Although he was not sure exactly what she could have gleaned from the exchange, he nonetheless cursed himself for not being more cautious. There was such a lot at stake and he had been too bloody complacent. As Liz pulled her car away from the kerb and drove away, he took out his diary and made a note of her registration number. Perhaps he needed to have a timely chat with Inspector Plod regarding the strangely inquisitive girl and that stupid boy Robbie who was proving to be somewhat of a loose cannon and liability. As for the Raymond problem he could put that on the back burner for a while. Latest developments were far more pressing.

Liz drove along for quite a while until she was out of George's view before she pulled her car into a side street and checked her car cell phone. The screen flashed that she had a missed call and scrolling down she discovered the caller had been George's wife Lillian. How bizarre. Pressing the voice message symbol, Liz listened carefully to the message.

'Hello my dear, I am pleased to say that the situation regarding my husband's suspected errant ways has changed somewhat, the result of which is that I no longer require your services. I realise that this may leave you out of pocket so I have prepared a golden handshake, so to speak. If you have time this afternoon perhaps you could make your way to Nowhere Manor and collect the aforementioned sum. Sorry for any inconvenience etcetera etcetera.'

This didn't add up at all, thought Liz to herself. But, looking on the bright side, the money would prove very helpful. Making a spur of the moment decision, Liz decided to ring Head Office and book her annual leave. The cash from Lillian would pay for a hotel room and the break would afford her the ideal opportunity to investigate this further.

THE OLD CHAPEL – VIRTUAL LENNIE

Lennie awoke in Tracey's arms just as she had the previous day but this morning was tinged with a slight unhappiness. Lennie had to travel back to Barnacle Beach Cottage as Tracey was catching the train to London for a conference. The last few days had been idyllic and Lennie was afraid the mood would be lost when they parted. They had briefly discussed their next meeting and had exchanged words of endearment and promises of a future shared but in the cold light of day Lennie felt a wave of insecurity. Perhaps, she told herself, it was based upon a disbelief that she had found the lady of her dreams, or perhaps it was a fear that her life would change. She had not yet fully addressed the problem of her relationship with Sooty, which would surely change. Sooty had been her rock, for so long that to lose her would be tantamount to bereavement. Her thoughts were interrupted by Tracey waking up and reaching her arms out towards her lover to engage in a bear hug. A bear hug which inevitably led to a bare hug and more. A while later Tracey was in the dressing area which adjoined the bedroom deciding which outfits to pack for her conference.

'I will miss you terribly my darling,' she called from the ante room.

'Me too,' replied Lennie. 'But I shall call you the second I get home.'

'Still wish you could be here waiting when I get back from London tomorrow, honey.'

'I know, my sweetheart, but I promised to be back to collect my old friend Jean from the retreat. She has been through a most terrible time and I must support her as much as I can.'

'I understand honey, but a girl can dream.'

A horn tooting at the front of the building brought the conversation to an abrupt end. Tracey's taxi had arrived to take her to the train station.

'Must go honey,' said Tracey. 'If you pop the key through the letterbox as you leave I will try to get one cut for when you next stay.'

'Have a safe journey,' said Lennie to Tracey's departing back as she clambered into the back seat of the taxi.

Alone in the house Lennie prepared her own bag for her imminent departure. Finding a pad of post-its on the telephone table in the hallway she wrote out a quick love note and stuck it to the front of the fridge. The note seemed small and insignificant, lost on the vast expanse of fridge door so Lennie scanned the lounge for more inspiration. Her eyes fell upon a sketch pad tucked between the gap formed by the sofa and the bookcase. Lennie crouched on her hands and knees to reach in and retrieve the pad before going to search for a black marker pen. She smiled to herself whilst upon this quest as she had the most wonderful idea of a surprise to leave her lover. After much trawling through drawers, Lennie eventually found a large black felt tip pen. Sketching deftly she drew a life-size portrait of herself, shoulders, breasts and part torso. Hunting once again in the kitchen drawer she found the scissors and set about cutting carefully around the image. She planned to leave the cut out propped up in Tracey's bed as a surprise companion for her return. Turning the image over, she wrote on the back in big letters;

VIRTUAL LENNIE

ACME PATENT PENDING...THIS IS LENNIE YOUR VIRTUAL GIRLFRIEND. AN IDEAL BEDMATE AND CONSIDERABLY QUIETER THAN THE ORIGINAL..... ON THE OTHER HAND THE ORIGINAL IS MORE PLIABLE, SOFTER, CURVIER AND UNBELIEVABLY CUTER.....

NOWHERE CASTLE – CAPABILITY BROWN

Meanwhile, many miles away, in a rather draughty private dwelling in the East Wing of Nowhere Castle, the Earl was sipping his first cup of coffee of the day. His well manicured wife the Countess sat opposite him picking the last segments of fruit from her lightly grilled grapefruit. The Earl had a lot on his mind that morning. The telephone call the previous evening from George Johnson had put the *cat amongst the pigeons* somewhat. His guest had seemed similarly concerned as he had left the castle grounds in the early hours of the morning, his hunting trip put temporarily on hold. A hasty meeting had been organised for later that morning and Inspector Plod had promised to attend. The Earl's thoughts were interrupted by his wife coughing to gain his attention. Reluctantly he lowered his coffee cup to the polished oak table top and addressed his wife.

'How are you this morning my dear? I trust you slept well?'

'Like a proverbial log. It slipped my mind last night but I had that American film director on the telephone yesterday whilst you were entertaining the ....' said the Countess. 'The chap is offering us a considerable sum of money to use the castle ramparts and grounds. Although I would have thought Nottingham to be a more appropriate location,' she added.

'I spoke to the land manager, Mr Summer, about just that yesterday and he suggests we hold out for more. Perhaps I should ask him to telephone this American chappie and sound him out. That is unless you want to handle it yourself, my dear?'

The Countess did not answer her husband straight away as her thoughts were elsewhere. It was only when he repeated the latter part of the sentence that she replied.

'Why have a dog and bark one's self. I shall be quite happy to leave it to Mr Summer. I have rather a lot of gardening to do today and the ladies from the local WTF are calling around for coffee, which as I am sure you will agree is an ordeal in itself.'

Saying this, she wandered across the large dining room towards the arched castle window and gazed out at the vast expanse of unkempt garden. In her mind's eye she imagined a flurry of fountains, wonderful walled gardens and a trio of tree houses high up in the clouds. If only Capability Brown were alive today, she mused to herself. Or perhaps she could contact that red haired girl who was famous for gardening without a bra.

NOWHERE MANOR

In the master bedroom of Nowhere Manor, Lillian was still getting dressed. The local WTF, of which she was a founding member, had been invited for a coffee morning at the castle. Lillian had been introduced to the Countess socially once previously and had found the younger woman quite quite charming and amazingly approachable considering the fortune her husband had inherited. Because it was a coffee morning and knowing the gentry's habit of dressing down during the day, Lillian finally decided upon a casual sweater with matching cardigan.

She had not slept well the previous evening due to George coming home in a spectacularly bad mood. He was a very different George to the euphoric George of earlier that day. After a few brandies he had even gone so far as to say rather cryptically that his dream of becoming Mayor was becoming just that, a dream. He refused to elaborate on the statement but nevertheless it had kept Lillian from sleeping as she sensed the chains of office slipping from her grasp. At least on a positive note she told herself, she had successfully solved the problem of the girl detective. To her surprise, the girl had taken the money and run. Lillian had foreseen that she may have had to think up a lengthy excuse as to why she saw fit to drop the investigation, but the girl had seemed singularly unconcerned and merely thanked Lillian for the envelope and left.

GREENHOUSE BISTRO – LIZ
RENTS THE PENTHOUSE FLAT

While Lillian was dressing for her WTF coffee morning, Liz was knocking at the front door of the Bistro trying to attract the attention of either of the owners. She had spent the previous night in Nowhere's only Hotel, which was exorbitantly overpriced considering it was only a two star. She really needed to sort out alternative accommodation if she was considering staying for a while. Whilst buying a newspaper in the local newsagent's that morning she had heard an elderly lady telling the Postmistress that the Greenhouse Bistro was planning to re-open soon. The lady also went on to say that she had heard that the flat above the Bistro was still vacant and the new owners planned to advertise it as a holiday flat. Thinking on her feet, and aware that the sum of money Lillian gave her would soon run out, Liz decided to be cheeky and to ask if she could rent the flat for a few weeks. Nothing ventured, nothing gained. After much knocking Liz decided to try the back entrance of the Bistro. It was approached through large metal gates which were thankfully unlocked. The kitchen door at the back of the building was ajar and through the fly mesh Liz could see a figure scrubbing the tiled area around a large commercial stove. A radio blared mindlessly in the background which explained why her knocking at the front of the building had not been heard. Suddenly as if aware she was being watched the girl cleaning the tiles looked up from her labour towards the door. Seeing Liz standing there she smiled and removed her rubber gloves.

'Hi there, can I help you?' said Joey.

'I certainly hope so,' replied Liz and proceeded to enquire about the availability of the flat.

Joey pondered the proposition for a while before saying, 'Well, I had better ask my partner first, but personally I see no problem with it. Seems like an ideal solution all around and to be honest we could do with the influx of cash. Would it be possible for you to call around again this afternoon, when I should be more presentable and I can show you the flat?'

Liz beamed, thanked the girl and made to leave. It was then that Joey noticed the newspaper pointing out of Liz's handbag and said, 'Can I be cheeky and have a quick peek at the front of your newspaper.'

Liz slipped the bag from her shoulder and took out the newspaper and handed it to Joey. A large colour photograph adorned the front page. It showed the ...... with a wide open grin staring up at a naked figure at a window. The caption read 'A FINE PAIR OF TITS', obviously referring both to the girl's breasts and the rather gormless looking ....

Joey was at a loss for words. She felt her world was crashing down around her.

'Keep the paper if you like,' said Liz, noticing Joey's crestfallen expression but at a loss as to what had sparked such a reaction. 'I won't have time to read it this morning and can collect it this afternoon.'

LONDON – THE GUTTER PRESS

The jet black Rolls Royce with tinted passenger windows was pulling into the drive of Oxford House, London. The chauffeur had stopped at a petrol station on the motorway and at the request of the ...... he had purchased every newspaper published that day. Without exception, every daily tome, from the gutter sensationalist tabloids to the more worthy broadsheets, all carried the story complete with colour photograph and witty captions. The ...... was a worried man;- he had already had a telephone call from his irate parents berating him for once again letting down the firm. This chastising was very humiliating for a man of the .... age, but he had been taught from a very early age that conformity was the key to an easy life. The family into which he had been born was a complicated hierarchy of birth. Feelings and emotions were to be held in check. He had been carefully schooled in this since the day he took his first faltering steps as a toddler and he in turn must indoctrinate his eldest son.

Now he had his wife to face, a young lady he had married with the sole intention of impregnating and providing his parents with an heir. She had fulfilled her role but now the bloody girl was merely a thorn in his side. From a fluffy young *Sloane Ranger* she had become opinionated and an embarrassment to himself and the family. She was forever threatening to divorce him and spill the beans on their farce of a marriage. But the gutter press loved her and wherever they went as a couple there was the constant clicking of shutter frames. One bloody photographer had even gone so far as to ask him to move out of the frame at one photo call because he was obscuring a view of his wife! On times such as this the .... mind would go back to when he had been a carefree eligible bachelor of thirty. He had run through the Australian surf pursued by the world's press and nubile young bronzed bikini beauties. When one of the beauties had slipped through the net of Security Officers and planted a large kiss upon his lips the photograph had graced the front page of the World's Press. How things had changed, how fickle were the British Public and how bloody judgemental.

Sorell, the .... Butler, climbed out from the passenger seat of the Rolls Royce and began to empty the .... monogrammed luggage from the car boot. The .... wife surveyed the proceedings from the bedroom window, her large *'Bambi'* eyes squinting from beneath her blonde curtain of a fringe. She had long since tired of trying to gain the .... attention and win his love and respect. The .... mistress had put paid to that charade a long time ago. There had been three people in her marriage for as long as the honeymoon glow had taken to wear off, but the worm was turning, she thought to herself.

NOWHERE CASTLE AND
THE NOWHERE GIRLS

The ladies of Nowhere's WTF 'Women turning fifty' were sitting perched on sofas in the Countess's opulent drawing room, china cups of tea balanced upon their rather ample laps. They listened intently as Lillian, their self-appointed spokeswoman, told the Countess of their plans for that year's charity calendar.

'Ideally,' said Lillian, 'we would love your permission to use the castle grounds as a backdrop to this year's calendar.'

'Well, the gardens are rather overgrown, but I'm sure the Earl will have no problem with you using the grounds. Although I must add we are in negotiations with an American chap who wishes to use the grounds for a film shoot, so we must avoid a clash of dates.' replied the Countess.

'This may seem cheeky,' said Lillian, but continued with her request nevertheless. 'Is there any possibility that the Earl and yourself might pose for a few photographs? It would add great credence to the viability of the calendar and the American tourists would just love it.'

Before the Countess had a chance to answer Lillian's request, Sooty intervened.

'May I interject? I'm thinking on my feet here, but Nowhere gained some dubious publicity yesterday with the naked lady photograph. This is just an idea to run by yourself and the other ladies, but would it be wise to cash in on the idea and perhaps run a calendar of tasteful nudes?'

The silence in the room was audible. Sooty continued on regardless. 'As most of you ladies know, a good friend of mine died recently from cancer. As the proceeds from this years' calendar are for the local Hospice, surely our stuffy old-fashioned sensibilities can be put on the back burner for once.' Still the shocked silence dominated the atmosphere of the room.

'By tasteful, I mean photographs with carefully placed objects obscuring the naughty bits. Very tongue in cheek, if you pardon the pun.' said Sooty, laughing at her own joke. 'I'm thinking perhaps we could pose beside a suit of armour with the shield positioned so it blocks a view of our unmentionables. Or we could pose in the conservatory with the potted plants. As long as our modesty is protected surely it would make for a much more saleable product.'

The ladies of the WTF sat motionless. To say the suggestion had shocked them would be an understatement. They were all of an age where they undressed in private, quickly, averting their eyes when accidentally glimpsing their own naked flesh in mirrors. Sex was something to be undertaken under duress, a monthly chore to appease their husbands' fluctuating appetites and fulfil their side of the marriage bargain. Thank god for prostates and temporary time out. Lillian especially could barely remember the last time George had clambered into her bed demanding his conjugal rights. The thought of having to expose her naked body to anyone filled her with terror. But the additional prospect of being photographed magnified the terror threefold. She and the rest of the ladies looked to the Countess for guidance. Surely good sense would prevail. The Countess seemed determined to prolong the agony. She crossed the drawing room towards the tea tray and replenished her tea cup. Choosing a biscuit she bit slowly into it, crumbs floating to the floor. All eyes in the room watched her closely. Eventually, the Countess cleared her throat to speak. Sooty knew that whatever the Countess said would be followed through. Her agreement to the idea was vital to it going ahead; the other ladies would follow suit.

'I think it is an excellent idea. Let me run it by my husband. It's a super and novel way to help a charity, and will no doubt put the town of Nowhere once and for all on the map.'

Lillian, as the spokesperson of the group decided she needed to grab the mantle once again and regain control of the group. Standing up rather grandly, she said,

'Well ladies, I'm sure you will all agree to join me at the local Weightwatchers meeting tonight. If we are going to do this I am sure we all want to look our best.'

The rest of the ladies laughed nervously. The Countess caught Sooty's eyes and winked.

'More tea anyone?' said the Countess, lifting the teapot from the tray. 'I can promise it's virtually calorie free and the milk is skimmed.'

GEORGE GETS A TICKING OFF

In another wing of the castle, the Earl sat at his desk. Facing him were Inspector Plod of the local constabulary (so nicknamed because his surname was Dodd) and George Johnson.

'Gentlemen,' said the Earl. 'It seems we have a problem on our hands. Although I really think that if you George had handed the whole affair more diplomatically we would not be having this conversation.'

'I can hardly be blamed for the turn of events,' protested George, shaking his head in disbelief. 'Yesterday had gone so well up to that point. That stupid idiotic boy is the cause of the problem not my handling of it. I've always ascertained that if you pay peanuts you get monkeys.'

'Let's all calm down and get this problem into proportion', said Plod. 'All is not lost gentlemen. I've had a word in the ear of a bewigged colleague and I assure you that I have the situation in hand and I am equally convinced the young thug will sort out the doddery old dear without the risk of any further participation from us. Following through, my colleague at the Court will see that he is subsequently offered enough rope to hang himself. I have requested that he visit the Station this afternoon, where I shall outline how foolhardy it will be if he speaks of this to anyone. He had a sufficiently bad enough time when he was locked up previously to not want a repeat performance.'

'Thank you so much Plod, well done my good man,' said the Earl. 'Both myself and my guest of last night shall sleep so much more soundly in our beds tonight as a result of your discretion handling this situation.'

'Sorry to *'rain on the parade'* gentlemen,' said George aggrieved that Plod was taking the glory for his hard work. 'But there is still the problem of the young girl who overheard my conversation yesterday.'

'Leading onto the girl,' said Plod implying he had not quite finished. 'More of a sticky problem, I concede, but I assume she is not in possession of the full facts. From what you say she overheard yesterday it would be difficult to piece the jigsaw together. My colleagues in her home town have already paid a visit to her employer who runs the

Private Detective Agency. As you can imagine these chaps often run short of the law and we normally turn a blind eye as they tend make our job easier; doing the groundwork so we need only run in for the kill. Her boss assures me she will receive no encouragement whatsoever and he will discreetly remind her that her job is on the line if she brings his Agency into disrepute and pursues this line of enquiry.'

'The only problem I foresee now,' continued Plod, 'is that she has decided to take annual leave, presumably to sniff around and cause trouble. Her boss offered to decline the request but I decided it would probably look suspicious. She is a 'bit of a loose cannon apparently.'

George shifted uncomfortably in his chair. He had an uncanny feeling that Plod had more to add. And he did.

'I don't know whether George told you.' said Plod. 'The girl was here in Nowhere investigating a case of adultery. It appears, George, that the girl was here at the request of your good lady wife, although she dropped the investigation yesterday, presumably after you told her about the probability of becoming Lady Mayor.'

'May I suggest in future,' said the Earl, addressing George directly, 'that your personal life takes a back seat, at least until this whole sorry mess is forgotten about? May I also remind you that any hint of a scandal will put paid to any recognition of your help in this rather delicate matter. I am hoping that you can assure me that you can curb your appetite until then.'

'By that I assume he alludes to your more dubious appetite.' Plod added placing his hand upon his hip in such a fey manner that George had no doubt of his meaning.

George was shocked. He had been so careful to hide his sexuality. Feeling like a chastened naughty school boy George shot an angry look towards pious Plod then after nodding a farewell to the Earl, collected his overcoat and stick from the coat stand and left the room. Observing his hasty departure, the Earl turned to Plod and enquired, 'I'm confused who is the scarlet woman in question?'

Plod smirked. How he loved to, 'get one up on' the pompous George Johnson.

'It appears Sir'.' he paused for maximum effect before continuing. 'It appears that George prefers the company of gentlemen. A most unsavoury state of affairs I am sure you will agree.'

The Earl coughed, suddenly embarrassed. There had been a chap like that at his Boarding School, a very flamboyant popular boy but most peculiar nonetheless. From what he remembered the young chap had gone on to work in the Civil Service before leaving to seek his fortune in New York. The Earl pictured him striding through the streets his scarf blowing in the Fifth Avenue breeze, a quintessential Englishman abroad.

'Let us hope this will serve as a timely reminder to George that he needs to show more discretion regarding his private life.' said Plod.

'Hear, Hear.' reiterated the Earl. 'What say we have a tot of brandy to put the whole sorry business of the day to bed once and for all.'

TIME TO SAY GOODBYE

Whilst this exchange was taking place, a few miles away in Newton-by-the-sea, Lennie was unpacking her case and putting a load of dirty washing into the washing machine. From her vantage point in the kitchen she saw Sooty's car pull onto the drive so she quickly grabbed her coat and opened the front door. Sooty was picking her up so that they could travel together to collect Jean from the Holistic Retreat she had been staying at. The Retreat was situated on an Island only approachable from the mainland during certain times of the day. Today the tide times allowed a mere two hours to get across the causeway, collect their friend and leave the island. As usual, Sooty was cutting it fine. She almost seemed to flaunt her bad timekeeping with pride and it had always irritated Lennie, who saw bad timekeeping as a lack of respect. It had caused many an argument over the years. Sooty leaned across the passenger seat to click open the car door. 'Next time I buy a car remind me to buy one with central locking,' she said, by way of greeting.

The ladies hugged briefly before Sooty glanced at the clock in the car and said, 'Gosh, is that the time? We must make tracks.'

Lennie had expected a lot of difficult questions regarding her short break in Wetherby, so she was relieved that Sooty was all fired up with the events of that morning and the WTF calendar. 'I'm really looking forward to telling Jean,' she said. 'The WTF ladies have decided to dedicate the calendar to the memory of Lucy, so we need a really nice photograph of Lucy to grace the back cover. That should brighten her spirits and give her something positive to focus on.'

'Would you do me a favour sweetie and check on the map in the glove compartment? I know the turn off to the island is not very clearly marked and it will be a bugger to turn on this dual carriageway if I miss it.'

Lennie leant forward in her seat, grateful for the opportunity of something to do.

HOLY ISLAND RETREAT

Half an hour later Sooty parked the car up against the entrance to the Retreat. It was a rather foreboding place, in the shadow of the Priory and overlooking the narrow pebbled beach. The heavy oak panelled door swung open almost as soon as they approached and they were ushered into a long cool corridor with a row of church type pews adorning one wall. Far away in the distance they could hear rhythmic chimes and a low humming sound; like a million bees searching for their hive. They were still soaking up the tranquil atmosphere when Jean appeared from a door to their left, seeming visibly more at peace and relaxed than when they had last seen her.

'Thank you so much for coming to collect me,' she said, before turning to Sooty and adding, 'Did you get my answer machine message? Have you remembered to bring Lucy? Lennie was taken aback for a few moments before she realised that Jean was referring to Lucy's ashes.

'She's in the car, sweetheart,' said Sooty. 'I've also checked the times of the boats and if we leave now we can catch the 3pm sailing. I've booked the seats. I hope you've got your sea legs, the waves looked quite choppy as we were crossing the causeway.'

Jean smiled.

'That's nice.' said Sooty, and it was; it was so nice to see her smile again.

'Yes, it's so nice to see you smile again, Jean.' Lennie reiterated, hugging her old friend close.

All of a sudden the corridor filled with bodies. Whilst they had been chatting the low humming had stopped as the other people on the retreat had gathered to bid Jean a fond farewell. There was a plethora of hugs, words of encouragement and tears.

They squeezed in the doorway and spilled out onto the pavement, waving and blowing kisses to Jean as Sooty pulled the car away.

SEAHOUSES HARBOUR –
SWEET PARTINGS

Viewed from the harbour, the sea did indeed look choppy, grey and foreboding, but the ladies were undeterred. They were on a mission. Gingerly they clambered into the small fishing boat. It was a rather neglected looking vessel in need of a lick of paint which was transformed during the summer months into a tourist excursion boat. Sooty had spoken discreetly to the skipper whilst buying the tickets and explained why the three ladies were taking the trip. He had agreed on the telephone that the three would be his only passengers and had refused to charge a penalty for making this concession. Sooty once again expressed her gratitude to him as she perched precariously at its helm. As the boat pulled away from the harbour Jeans thoughts were far away as she reflected upon the past. This would be her definitive goodbye to Lucy, and despite all her words and deliberation she had an understandable reluctance to say her final farewell. In her head she understood that it would be healing to do so but in her heart the ache was unbearable. She sat staring out at the cold grey sea, clutching the urn, as if keeping it warm wrapped in the layers of her coat. She stroked its cold varnished ceramic surface as if it were Lucy's soft pliant flesh yielding beneath her touch.

Before long the fishing boat came upon an outcrop of rocks set way out to sea and barely visible from the mainland. Grey seals lay basking upon the surface of the rocks soaking up the last of the afternoon sunshine. Puffins flew overhead hoping to catch an easy tea in the wake of the boat, their bright, tango-orange beaks making them a comical and cartoonlike sight. A flock of arctic terns dive-bombed the gulls upon the rock island, the breeding seabirds reacting with angry squawks protecting their young.

The skipper switched off the boat's engine, and reached into his pocket for a roll up. He cupped his hands and lit the cigarette before turning his gaze towards Sooty. He acknowledged her nod and sat back patiently in his seat. All was silent but for the lapping of the waves against the bow and cries of the birds overhead. Sooty turned to Jean, took her hand and gently said.

'Jean, honey, it's time to say goodbye.'

Jean nodded. She knew it was time, but that didn't stop the tears coursing down her cheeks. 'I need to say a few words,' she said eventually between sobs.

'I was given this by one of the ladies on the retreat and I would like to read it out aloud as I say goodbye.'

Carefully she prised the lid from the urn and began to pour the ashes over the side of the boat. They floated for a few moments forming grey shapes upon the surface of the water, before being washed away behind the rocks. Taking a sheet of paper from her pocket Jean began to read aloud.

> 'Stay, o sweet, and do not rise,
> The light that shines comes from thine eyes,
> The day breaks not, it is my heart,
> Because that you and I must part'

Despite her previous intentions Lennie found herself making the sign of the cross as the ashes whirled and disappeared beneath the waves. The harsh unforgiving wind made the tears coursing down her cheeks sting. The puffins had long since disappeared, but a single gull kept swooping in and out of their vision, as if trying to catch their attention. Suddenly without warning it landed on the edge of the boat by Jean and Sooty, causing them both to flinch. Sooty released her embrace of Jean with the intention of shooing the bird away from the boat, but she was stopped in her tracks as the bird began to caw bizarrely shattering the fragile silence. Jean instinctively reached out her fingers to touch the bird's wing, and surprisingly it allowed her to, not flinching from her fingers at all, its black eyes unblinking, watching her intently.

Suddenly understanding, Jean spoke directly to the bird. 'Goodbye my darling Lucy.'

The bird seemed to hear these words for it dipped its head as Jean continued to stoke its wing, then, just as swiftly as it had landed, it flew away. It flew into the clouds, higher and higher, until it was barely a speck on the far horizon. The skipper, puffing on the stub of his cigarette, watched its flight. He was not a religious man but he felt he had witnessed something beyond his understanding. Sooty reached across and took Lennie's hand and squeezed it tightly. Jean sat serenely, the empty urn at her feet, not saying a word. She was at peace for the moment. Lucy had said her final goodbye.

THE PENTHOUSE FLAT

Joey stood in the living room of the flat above the Bistro leaving Liz to explore the rest of the rooms on her own. The girls had not had a chance to do much with the flat since purchasing the building as the priority had been to get the Bistro up and running, so to gain an income from the flat would be an unexpected windfall. The previous owner had used it as a holiday flat so it was pretty well kitted out with bed linen, towels and kitchen utensils. Liz seemed quite impressed with the surroundings and it only remained for a price to be agreed upon before she could collect her bags from the car.

'I'm really pleased I found out about this flat,' said Liz. 'It's quite perfect. Would it be ok for me to rent it on a week by week basis?'

'Yeah that's fine. Suits us too as we can concentrate on the Bistro,' said Joey. 'I've run the idea by my partner Louisa and she thinks it's a godsend. I'll leave you to get your bearings, come down when you're ready and we can sort out the financial stuff. I'll put the kettle on and we can have a cuppa.'

Joey shut the door of the flat and climbed out onto the wooden steps. A door to her right accessed the Bistro from the first floor and led directly into their makeshift office. Walking through the office, she grabbed the newspaper from beside the filing cabinet. She had pored over the photograph of the naked lady earlier that day. The more she looked at it, the more convinced she was that it was Louisa in the photograph. From this she could draw only one conclusion; that Louisa and Sooty were having an affair. Joey was surprised that this revelation did not hurt more, but the scenario had happened so often in the past she was somewhat numbed by the discovery. She made the decision to follow the usual path of not challenging Louisa. It would surely run its course, as her previous indiscretions had.

A RENDEZVOUS AT THE RENDEZVOUS

Louisa was walking the dog. As usual the beach was full of fellow dog walkers. Louisa threw the ball and Jasper bounded across the sand to retrieve it. In the distance Louisa could see a figure approaching. The figure was conspicuous in that it had no dog bounding alongside. She smiled as the figure grew closer and she realised it was her lover Sooty.

Jasper jumped up to greet Sooty, almost overbalancing the older woman. 'Jasper, get down!' Louisa shouted, reaching out to help Sooty regain her footing.

'You'd think he was still a pup, he gets so overexcited. Are you ok honey?'

'Fine and dandy,' replied Sooty. 'Unless you count the frostbite; it's absolutely freezing out here.'

'Are you sure you are alright?' asked Louisa. 'You look really tired.'

'I'm fine honestly.' Sooty replied. 'I've just had a really emotional day, but therapeutic too in a strange way. I've left Jean and Lennie at the house having a heart to heart so I can't stay for long. I've told them I was popping out for some groceries.'

'Has Lennie said anything about the photograph?' Louisa asked, as the two ladies fell into step.

'No she hasn't mentioned it, which I find rather disconcerting. We are the talk of the town, I could barely make my way through the supermarket aisles without being stopped and questioned.'

'Nor has Joey, which I also find rather strange. Perhaps they've both drawn their own conclusions and decided to let sleeping dogs lie.'

'I think you are probably right my dear. Speaking of which, we must arrange a time to bump into one another again.' said Sooty winking suggestively.

'Tell you what' said Louisa, 'Why don't we consult our diaries over one of Gino's naughty but nice hot chocolates.'

'What a wonderful idea, whipped cream and marshmallows. I'm so glad you suggested meeting today, the other day seemed so surreal I was worried I had just dreamt you.'

'Was it a nice dream?' teased Louisa.

'Oh a very nice dream,' replied Sooty. 'The nightmare would be to awaken and find out it had all been a dream.'

Saying this, Sooty grabbed the younger woman's arm and turned her around on the sand to face the direction of the wind. They both braced themselves for the chilly stroll towards the Rendezvous. Meanwhile, Jasper ran alongside, yapping incessantly until Sooty leant down and threw a piece of driftwood into the waves for him to retrieve.

TIME FOR REGRETS

Lennie and Jean were relaxing in the lounge of Gloucester Court. They had progressed from plain filter coffee onto coffee liqueurs, and the conversation had moved on to their shared past in the convent of St Therese.

'Have you ever had any regrets about leaving the Sisters?' Jean asked her old friend.

'I confess that at times I have missed the security and support of the Sisterhood, but having you in my life all these years has made it easier to cope.' Lennie replied. 'As you know, Sooty and I have been through some tricky times and I have often wondered if I made the right decision all those years ago.'

Jean nodded in agreement. 'I tend to block it out, but Lucy and I had some times where I wondered if we would make it too, but isn't love like that? There are the highs and the lows and perhaps we have to go through the lows to appreciate the highs.'

'Yes I can see your point, but you must have guessed that Sooty and I have just been going through the motions for quite a while now.'

Again Jean nodded. 'Lucy and I sensed it when you last visited, but we presumed that you were just going through a bad patch.'

'It's been a long bad patch Jean and I probably shouldn't tell you this because I would hate you to feel compromised in anyway, but I feel that I shall burst if I don't share it.'

'Carry on.' said Jean. 'I promise to respect your confidence.'

So Lennie proceeded to tell Jean all about Tracey; their dreams, their plans for the future, her fear of change and the damage it would inevitably cause her relationship with Sooty. Jean listened in a non-judgemental way.

'A confidence, for a confidence,' said Jean. 'I once betrayed Lucy'.

'I can't pretend I'm not astounded, who was it and did Lucy ever find out?

'No I am certain she never even suspected as it was only ever one night and it was many years ago.'

Lennie mentally ticked off a list of their mutual friends before finally once again asking who it had been. Jean seemed to hesitate before answering, almost as if it was painful to say the name. 'It was Louisa,' she said eventually. Lennie looked blank and was about to ask 'Louisa who' before it suddenly dawned on her. 'Surely you don't mean Louisa from the orphanage?

'The very same,' replied Jean, unable to look her dear friend in the eyes. 'We met again quite by chance and shared one perfect night. I often think Lucy dying is my punishment for that indiscretion.'

Raising her eyes upward she continued 'Perhaps he thought I didn't deserve Lucy after I showed her so little regard that night. I loved Lucy more than life itself but still I strayed and the price I must pay is to lose both loves.'

Lennie shook her head and in a breaking voice said. 'Surely if he were that vengeful I too would be dammed. I still pray each night for forgiveness. I was so cruel to the girl and it was all unfounded. I know now that my reasons were that I saw in her the traits I had hidden so long in my own character, but that does not excuse my actions.'

'I am just glad I came upon you beating her that day.' Jean reflected.

'I've you to thank for helping me that night, helping me to face my shame and helping me to admit to my sexuality. I like to think I would have come to my senses without you intervening, but I shall never know.'

Jean took her friend's hands in her own. Looking her directly in the eyes, she said. 'You are a good, kind woman Lennie. I believe that being in the convent and denying who you were unfortunately brought out the worst in your character. I would not have befriended you that night if I thought I had witnessed your true self. We are all products of our past. Your parents beat you to cure your unnatural thoughts and in turn you tried to cure Louisa.'

Both women sat back in their chairs reflecting upon how differently their lives would have panned out were it not for that one isolated incident.

'Do you think you will ever meet Louisa again?' said Lennie breaking the silence.

Jean shook her head sadly. 'I see her every night while I sleep. She and Lucy merge into one now. I have loved twice and lost twice. I feel doubly blessed and doubly dammed.

'Had she forgiven me? I wish I could make amends and explain.'

'I confess we did not speak of the incident that night but I am sure Louisa had made peace with her past. She did not seem like the kind of woman to carry a grudge.'

Upon saying this Jean got up from her chair, patting her legs in a 'no nonsense' way. 'Right I've decided that's quite enough melancholy for one night. When Sooty gets back from the shops I am going to treat the pair of you to a meal in this Italian Restaurant the gutter press have been wittering on about.'

At that very moment Sooty walked through the door. 'I heard that.' She said 'I'm starving, let's go. If we hurry we will get there in time for the happy hour.'

OUTSKIRTS OF NOWHERE

Robbie had just left the local Police Station and was strolling up the road towards The *Brits* bar when a car pulled up alongside him. Peering in the windows he recognised George Johnson and upon his bidding Robbie furtively clambered into the passenger seat.

'Just been to see your mate Inspector Plod, but I suppose you know that, don't you Mr J?' Robbie said once he had settled into the car seat. His voice held a slight tremor betraying the fact that he was feigning a bravado that he did not feel.

'My dear boy, I really haven't a clue what you are talking about.' parried George.

'I suggest we go for a drive somewhere quieter as I have a proposition for you.'

'I ain't like that Mr J.' retorted Robbie, suddenly defensive. 'Strictly for the birds me. I ain't no-one's bum boy.'

George looked the boy up and down very slowly before replying. 'You stupid boy, if you think I would touch you with a barge pole you are sorely mistaken.'

'Who's braggin' now Mr J?. Barge pole, geddit?' Robbie guffawed at his own joke, only stopping his braying when he realised Mr Johnson had pulled the car into the entrance of the local graveyard, and switched off the engine.

'If you are quite finished your incessant cackling my proposition is that you do one last job for me, and, if successful, the reward will be substantially more than last time.'

'Ok Mr J, I'm listening,' said Robbie feeling very vulnerable but determined to brazen it out.

'This is strictly between the two of us, and I don't want any mistakes this time.' George's tone was menacing, he was sick of people alluding to his private life and very tempted to take out his anger on this stupid youth.

'Ok, Mr J, point taken.' Robbie's eyes darted towards the locked passenger door.

'I want you to listen carefully. It appears that we were overheard yesterday in my office by a young girl who is a Private Detective hired by my wife to investigate something or other. She is no longer being hired by my wife, but obviously she overheard enough yesterday to convince her there was more to yesterday's anti-hunt demo than met the eye. I've just found out she is staying for a few weeks in the flat above the new Bistro. I want you to put the frighteners on her and convince her to go home. Do you think you can handle it properly this time?'

'For a price, Mr J.' said Robbie who despite his fear was never one to miss an opportunity to make some extra cash.

'Ok, I expected this and I am prepared to pay double what I paid last time.'

'I want more than double.'

'Just be thankful for being paid at all.' said George. 'There comes a time when everyone is expendable.' To emphasise his words George gestured towards the vast army of gravestones.

Robbie raised in hands in defeat he knew when he was beaten. 'Ok Mr J, you've got yourself a deal. Now can we please get the hell out of here, this place gives me the creeps.'

George drove Robbie to a side street near the local bars, checking the road carefully before releasing the passenger door to let him out. Once the boy had left he took his car cell phone from his coat pocket and keyed in Raymond's number. Raymond answered almost immediately. 'Hello stranger, I thought you'd emigrated.'

'No such luck, my dear boy.' George replied, his mood improving at the prospect of seeing Raymond again. 'Warmer climes will have to wait, bit of a cash flow problem at the moment.'

'Well, you're lucky I'm free tonight.' said Raymond, chuckling at his own joke.

The offer was just too tempting for George. What would one last time hurt? It would be quite a while before he could visit Newcastle, and Raymond would prove a welcome distraction to the problem in hand.

'Well, I think Lillian is out with her WTF cronies tonight. Perhaps I can entertain you in style at Nowhere Manor.' said George. 'It's much too cold to meet outside. I'll ring when I'm certain of her plans.'

'Can't wait.' said Raymond. 'I can't stop thinking about all of the entertaining things we did in Venice.'

'Hold that thought dear heart' said George. 'I will ring as soon as the coast is clear.'

So it was with quite a spring in his step that George entered the front door of Nowhere Manor a few minutes later. Lillian was bent over in the hallway tying a lace. George stifled a grin when he saw what she was wearing; a bright pink tracksuit that made her look like a giant strawberry blancmange. She had gone completely overboard on the fitness costume. She wore new white trainers, the sole of which flashed a neon green light whenever she raised her foot. Well, no chance of losing her in the dark, thought George, mores' the pity. A Wimbledon-style sweat bracelet and hair band completed the look. The local sports shop must have done very well out of the WTF that day, if Lillian's outfit was a reflection of what the rest of the ladies were wearing.

'Very Jane Fonda,' said George to his wife.

'Flattery will get you nowhere,' said Lillian, flashing her husband a withering look. 'I'm taking the Jag as I said I'd pick up some of the other ladies so I shall need the larger car.'

'Presumably you will need a smaller car after you leave Weightwatchers,' quipped George.

His wife gave an exasperated sigh as he handed over the car keys.

'When are you expecting to be home, my dear?

'I'm not sure, but it will probably be quite late as I have called an emergency meeting afterwards. I've left your tea in the fridge. Before you complain, it's a salad. If I'm going on this blasted diet to help your career I don't see why you shouldn't suffer to.' With this parting shot, the vision in pink left the house and waddled on flashing green feet towards the Jaguar.

Stupid bloody woman, thought George. If she imagined he was eating rabbit food she had another thing coming. He would ring up for an Indian Takeaway later. Better eat after Raymond's visit, all that exercise on a full stomach couldn't be healthy for a man of his years. Plenty of time to work up an appetite, he decided as he made his way into the bathroom. Raymond had answered his telephone at the first ring and was on his way.

George was just climbing out of the shower and dripping on the bathmat when he heard the doorbell ring. Wrapping a towel around his midriff he contrived to drape it in such a manner that it cleverly concealed his middle-age spread. George crossed the hallway to answer the door. The shock must have shown on his face as he opened the door to a smirking Inspector Plod.

'Expecting someone else, George?' said Plod.

Thinking quickly on his feet, George replied, 'Oh hello there, sorry for my state of undress I thought you were the takeaway I ordered. Lillian's on some bloody diet and there's nothing in the house but rabbit food.'

Plod shook his head in disbelief. He had been on the Force long enough to know when someone was lying. 'Whatever...I just came around to say I spoke to that young thug earlier today and think we shall have no more problems in that area.'

George was just about to say that he had also had a chat with Robbie when a car pulled up onto the drive. Raymond alighted from the car, smiling broadly at George before realising that he was not alone in the doorway and Inspector Plod was standing in the shadow of the porch.

'My my Raymond,' said Plod. 'Moonlighting as a delivery boy now are we?'

Raymond looked totally bemused, until George interjected. 'Have you brought the files around from Yvonne's house, Raymond?' George addressed Raymond before turning to Plod and adding, 'My secretary, Raymond's sister, took some files home from work and I needed them to do my VAT returns.

Raymond continued to look confused and it was a while before he cottoned on to the situation and replied, 'Yes, Mr J. They're in the boot. I'll go and fetch them now.'

Plod still stood grinning at this exchange before saying, 'While the cat's away... remember the chat we had about finding one's pleasures further afield, George. Nowhere's a very small town. I'll say no more. Enjoy your takeaway.'

Nodding and avoiding eye contact, George bid the policeman goodbye. Sanctimonious bugger, thought George. How he wished he could dish the dirt on the 'holier than thou' Plod. Under the pretence of foraging in his boot for the paperwork Raymond waited until the policeman's car had cleared the drive of Nowhere Manor before locking the boot and making for the front door. George stood aside to let him in.

'Perhaps I should try the rear entry next time, might be less crowded,' Raymond joked adding. 'Is that a loofah in your pocket or are you pleased to see me?'

Suddenly recovering his libido George replied, 'I suggest you remove the towel and find out, dear boy.'

Raymond did just that, and was thrilled to find no evidence of a loofah.

WELCOME TO NOWHERE

Liz was strolling down the hill towards the centre of town. She had thoroughly enjoyed her night at Joey and Louisa's home. The drink had flowed, as had the conversation. If the food she had been served tonight was anything to go by, the Bistro was destined to be a rip-roaring gastronomic success. They had chatted throughout the night, brainstorming ideas for the grand opening. Liz promised to try to sort out the celebrity endorsement side of things. She had some great ideas and would enjoy the challenge, she said. They had spent a large amount of the time between courses trawling through veggie publications with amazing results. Liz had managed to find an address for a certain fifties celebrity who was very proactive in animal affairs. She was somewhat of a lesbian icon having appeared in a movie as Jane, a cowgirl. One of the songs from the musical about the pain and pleasure of a 'secret love' was the anthem of many a closeted homosexual. The girls had been thrilled to find a whole page in one magazine which named famous veggies. Searching through, Liz made notes and promised the girls she would use her detection skills to track down contact numbers for as many as possible. Hopefully one famous actor would give his stamp of approval, another Wimbledon-winning tennis player and her ex lesbian lover two more. It was unanimously agreed that to receive an accolade from a particular avenging actress would be absolutely fabulous too. It was a happy and slightly tipsy Liz who stumbled down the bank towards the Bistro flat that night. After weaving across the main high street, she finally reached the iron gates that led to the entrance of the flat. As the security lights flashed overhead to guide her way, they also reflected dazzlingly off the surface of her car, which she had parked behind the restaurant. Liz let out a horrified gasp as she realised that all the tyres on the car had been slashed.

Walking around the car to properly inspect the damage Liz had an uncanny feeling that she was being watched. She peered into the darkness and jumped as a branch scratched against the fence. Her usual calm nerves were in tatters. Who would do such a thing? Was it a random act of hooliganism or a bizarre initiation rite for newcomers to the town? It was only as she got closer to her car that her gaze fell upon a slip of paper carefully tucked beneath the windscreen wiper. Liz removed the note and crossed to the security light to decipher it. It appeared that typeface letters had been torn from a newspaper and pasted onto the notepaper. This was serious stuff indeed. Someone had gone to a lot of effort to avoid detection. This was no indiscriminate act of vandalism.

The note read: 'Welcome to Nowhere. This will teach you not to meddle. We only slashed the tyres this time. Next time it will be acid. Go back to where you belong.'

This was personal. If anything it proved that she had fallen into something very dodgy indeed. Her sensible head told her to flee but her 'private eye' head was intrigued. Liz carefully pocketed the note. After all it could prove to be valuable evidence. A pile of old papers rustled by the bins and Liz was suddenly aware that the courtyard was not overlooked by any other buildings. With trembling steps she made her way up the fire escape stairs towards the front door of the flat. With shaking hands she opened the door and in her haste tumbled inside the hallway, not feeling completely safe until she had dead locked the door and shot the bolt.

THE SINISTER PHONE CALL

Maggie sat in the darkness. She had finally plucked up the courage to attend an early evening service at the local church and was convinced that she had been followed home. A sinister figure in the shadows had darted behind lampposts and parked cars whenever she had stopped to turn and look around. Telling herself this was her overactive imagination, she had just about managed to get back to her flat without bursting into tears.

Since she had come home, the telephone had rung twice. The first time she answered there had been no-one on the line but the second time a muffled voice had spoken to her.

'Hello Maggie' the voice had said, addressing her by her name. 'I am so glad that you are home safe and sound. You really should be more careful going out alone in the evening. There are some very nasty people around.'

Maggie had dropped the telephone receiver with fright. She now sat crouched and shaking in a corner of the lounge. This was where Bob found her when he called around later that evening. Yvonne had been ringing her aunt for the better part of two hours and was concerned that she constantly got the engaged signal from the telephone. Afraid that she had fallen Bob had decided to call around to check on her. He was thankful that he had had the foresight to take the spare key as he was doubtful she would have answered his knocks at the door the state that she was in. When he eventually calmed her down enough to get coherent answers he rang the local Police Station to report the incident.

A short while later PC Plod was driving home after finishing his shift. He came upon a furtive looking Robbie waiting in the queue at the local Fish and Chip shop. Parking his car on the opposite side of the road he tooted his horn and motioned for Robbie to cross the street to talk to him.

'It appears that you have had a busy night, my lad,' he said. 'I trust that you have an alibi set up for when I drag you into the station for questioning tomorrow.'

'No probs, Gov.' Robbie replied in a cocky voice. 'I got a bird lined up to say her and me where doing the business when all this kicked off. Trust me I ain't no amateur.'

'That remains to be seen.' said Plod. Putting his car into gear he pulled away from the pavement adding. 'Enjoy your fish and chips they are so much tastier than porridge.'

THE FOLLY ON THE CRAG

Peter Dodd (Inspector Plod) drove slowly up the driveway towards his home atop Ratcheugh Crag. The castle shaped Folly came into view, dark and menacing in the moonlight, the surrounding trees swaying slightly in the gathering wind.

Peter had lived on the Crag for many years. It was owned by the Earl and Peter paid a peppercorn rent to reside in the desolate building. Indeed the Folly, which was modelled on a ruined castle, had never really been intended for habitation. It was a whimsical building built by a long since deceased ancestor of the Earl who had built it to amuse his young wife, the Countess, who enjoyed riding her horse bareback from the castle. She would picnic upon the Crag before painting in the observatory which adjoined the main body of the folly. The Countess fancied herself a bohemian free spirit and the Folly afforded her the opportunity to indulge in this illusion. Much in the manner of Marie Antoinette who had a peasant cottage built in the grounds of Versailles so she could role play at being a shepherdess. The folly was small and cramped with illogical angles to all of the rooms. It relied heavily on artificial light as the windows were proportionately tiny, narrow and arched. At the entrance of the Folly a carved front door with polished brass lion claw doorknocker led unceremoniously onto a galley kitchen which only just managed to accommodate the white goods necessary for modern living. It had been remarked upon by the present Countess that the Folly was a reverse Tardis, seemingly spacious on the outside but small and cramped within. This barely functional kitchen led onto the main living quarters of the house, namely an X shaped lounge which was dominated by a grand carved fireplace. The fireplace, which now housed a modern gas living flame fire, had been specially commissioned by the old Earl. It was rumoured that he had shipped in Italian carpenters at a great expense, to carve and sculpt the expensive marble with all manner of cherubs and angels. The whole structure and shape of the lounge was a testament to the Earl's devotion to his much younger wife with the unusual x shape of the lounge representing a kiss. A further whimsical detail was found on the faces of the two delicately carved cherubs on the left and right of the fire surround which bore a remarkable likeness to the Earl and his beloved bride.

Peter's vast library of old books and manuscripts now adorned the old oak shelves which lined two entire walls of the lounge, the sheer volume and weight of the tomes causing the shelves to buckle in an alarming manner. Peter had placed a high-backed easy chair in a window recess at the far side of the room, as this faced the largest arched window which had the most excellent views of the surrounding countryside. It was said that the old Earl had placed the Folly on that particular part of the Crag as it afforded him an unbroken vista of his land, which stretched as far as the naked eyes could see. It also gave the Earl the opportunity to spy upon his young bride as she could be seen quite clearly from his vantage point upon the Crag. It was well documented that the Earl was an extremely jealous man and fiercely protective of his nubile new wife.

Rising from the nucleus of the lounge was a rather precarious spiral staircase. This wobbly metal contraption led to the upper floor of the Folly, which was considerably smaller than the ground floor due to the design of the building. It merely housed a very small study containing a desk, chair and yet more groaning shelves of books, a cupboard-sized bathroom with a shower squeezed into an alcove and of course Peter's bedroom. It was the bedroom that was most telling of Peter's particular habits, devoid as it was of any home comforts, save a rather lumpy looking bed. It was reminiscent of a monk's room, sparse and austere. The room had two doors, the door which led from the bedroom into the corridor and another door which led onto a covered bridge formation and from there into the observatory. It was in this room that the Countess had indulged her pastime of watercolour painting.

The observatory consisted of glass panes from floor to ceiling, topped by a large glass domed roof. During the summer the room was like a greenhouse, so intense was the heat which penetrated the panes, but the Countess would set up her easel and watercolours nonetheless. Often so overcome was she with the fierce rays that she would undress and paint in the nude. When the old Earl came upon his young wife painting in this manner, he was so mesmerised by the beauty of the vision that he at once commissioned an artist from Florence to visit the Folly and capture his young bride in oils. The Countess had at first declined to pose in such a manner but upon being introduced to the young Italian artist she had shyly agreed. The artist and model, although always chaperoned by the Countess's handmaid, managed to form a relationship of sorts. The Countess bored with her older husband doglike devotion soon became infatuated by the intense young man and his penetrating chocolate brown eyes. So enraptured was she, that as the painting neared its completion she bribed her handmaid to retire discreetly to the bedroom one balmy afternoon.

And it was there upon the cool tiled floor of the observatory with the sun beating down upon their sweating bodies that the artist and the Countess consummated their love. Although to the Countess's dismay they were to make love only once as the artist disappeared quite abruptly the following day. The Earl informed his wife that the artist had been summoned back to Italy by his patron the Pope to continue the painting of a chapel ceiling. The truth was much more sinister, as below stairs gossip had reached the ears of the Earl and he had fallen into a jealous and vengeful rage. The artist boarded the ship bound for Italy grateful to have escaped with his life. The Earl's men had not been backward in explaining how foolhardy his amorous actions had been. The handmaiden had suffered a far worse fate and was never heard from again.

The Countess distraught upon hearing of the artist's hasty departure sank into such a melancholy that at one stage the Earl's physicians feared for her sanity. She refused to paint, and her easel and paints were left to gather dust in corner of the observatory. Nine months later the Countess died after a long and painful childbirth. The surviving child was a strong robust baby with a distinctive 'Roman' nose, swarthy complexion and dark brown eyes. The Countess's dying words were whispered to her weeping husband as he knelt by her bedside. 'Promise me you name our child Michael, this child is my angel Michael.'

The Earl honoured his deathbed vow and the child was christened in the Chapel which lay in the shadow of the Folly upon the Crag. The Earl, to give him his due, was never unkind to the child in word or deed. Indeed Michael was afforded a life of luxury as befitted the heir to a vast fortune. Any gossip regarding his parentage was swiftly quashed, but the love a father would normally show his son was sadly lacking. It was as if the 'chocolate' brown eyes mocked the Earl and reminded him constantly of his beloved wife's infidelity. To this end the Earl chose to have the boy schooled many miles away from Nowhere Castle and was conveniently away on business whenever the boy returned home. The Earl died, well before Michael reached maturity and he bore his teenage years an orphan. But that's a whole other story and I digress.

When Peter had first taken residence in the folly it had not been inhabited since the grieving Earl locked its front door on the day of his wife's death. Rumours had circulated ever since amongst the locals of Nowhere that the place was haunted by the ghost of the Countess and it had fallen into disrepair, becoming overgrown with ivy. So believable was the folklore that the track leading up to the Folly had not been trod upon for many a year. This isolation suited Peter and he relished the privacy the Folly afforded him. He deliberately kept the track difficult to navigate to deter unwanted visitors, and arranged to have his post left in an oak wooden box at the foot of the Crag. He even fashioned a makeshift pulley contraption so he could collect his newspapers, milk and bread without leaving the Folly.

Peter had arrived in Nowhere a middle aged man swiftly rising through the ranks of the Police Force due to his connection with the Earl. He fell in love with the Folly the moment he had cast his eyes upwards towards the Crag and saw the building rising phoenix like from the trees. The Earl had taken much persuading. Peter had pestered his distant relation to the point of nagging. He had even offered at one stage to undertake the restoration work of the building himself. The Earl reluctantly agreed, washing his hands any repercussions, for although a modern man he was still hampered by the fear of unleashing the curse of the folly. The older residents of Nowhere, who had grown up with the story of the accursed Folly, waited with baited breath for some terrible accident to befall Peter. But nothing untoward happened and the Folly went from being cursed and haunted to just being an odd shaped building upon a rather high hill.

Wearily Peter remembered that tonight was the night he must undertake his weekly discipline of self-flagellation. Stopping only to lay his overcoat upon the bed, Peter made towards his wardrobe and from deep within he extracted a waxed, corded whip.

As a member of secretive cult-like organisation Disciples of God he was encouraged to draw a little blood once a week. Removing all of his clothes he dressed in a white linen hooded robe and a string of bone shaped beads. Standing facing the large wooden cross above his bed and bracing his knees against the mattress, Peter closed his eyes and raised the whip in the air. With a resounding thwack it slashed at the bare skin exposed by the backless robe. Peter winced, eyes smarting, before once again raising the whip high above his shoulders.

LENNIES SURPRISE VISIT

Jean was back at her home in Leeds. Lennie had driven her home earlier that day on the pretext of spending time with her old friend and helping her to settle in again. Although Lennie had the very best of intentions, Jean realised that Lennie was hoping to spend a few days with her new lover. Momentarily Jean was hurt but she reasoned that Lennie would stay if she asked her and perhaps spending some time with Tracey would help her friend make a decision regarding her future.

'It's enough to know you are only a short car journey away, a safety net should I need it,' Jean reassured her.

'Well, if you are really sure.' Lennie said hesitantly.

'Of course I'm sure. Now go, you're cluttering up my hallway,' Jean said in a light hearted manner, ushering her friend out onto the drive towards her car.

During the short drive to Wetherby, Lennie ran through her mind the surprise that Tracey would get when she turned up unannounced at her door. They had been speaking constantly throughout the day so she knew that Tracey had no plans for the evening save a visit to the local supermarket for her weekly shop. When Lennie arrived at the old chapel she was disappointed to see that Tracey's Land-rover was not parked up by the building. Assuming her to be at the shops, Lennie parked some way up the street. She didn't want her lover to spot her and spoil the surprise. She decided to wait until Tracey has unloaded the car and gone into the house before she rang and said 'Pop the wine in the fridge you have a visitor.' Lennie sat patiently in her car, glancing up and down the street waiting for Tracey to return. After a long, cold, boring half hour, she decided to ring Tracey's cell phone to see if she was on her way home. That's strange, she thought to herself as the phone rang and rang before eventually going onto answer phone. But she reminded herself that reception was often non-existent in the large hanger-like constructions that supermarkets where housed in. Lennie was just about to give in to her full bladder and visit the Public House on the corner of the street, when she heard Tracey's Land-rover roaring into the street. Tracey drove her 'four wheel drive' the same way as she drove her motorcycle; with the reckless abandon of a boy racer. Lennie smiled as she saw her lover leap from the vehicle and reach into her handbag for her keys. She was surprised to see that it wasn't her house keys that Tracey extracted from her handbag but her cell phone. Lennie watched as Tracey squinted in the narrow beam of the street light at the screen of her telephone. Putting it to her ear she appeared to be listening to a message then she replaced it back into her handbag and took out her door keys. Lennie's initial curiosity gave way to suspicion as she wondered what the message had been and from whom. She waited a few minutes before ringing Tracey on her house phone. It was a very breathless Tracey who answered the telephone on the fourth ring.

'Hello, it's me,' said Lennie.

'Hello sweetheart,' Tracey replied. 'Sorry I missed your call earlier, I was in the bath. I am dripping water on the hall carpet as we speak.'

'Sorry darling,' said Lennie. 'I'll let you go and get dried off. I'll ring you back in five, shall I?'

'Yes that would be wonderful my sweet, don't want to catch a chill and I'm standing here in all my glory.'

Lennie sat in the car for a few moments, before deciding that whatever Tracey was playing at she would rather know, than always wonder. It was barely a minute before she was knocking on Tracey's front door. The front door swung open almost immediately and the expression on Tracey's face was a picture to behold.

'Lennie,' she managed to splutter 'I thought you were staying at Jean's tonight.'

'Evidently I am not. Are you going to invite me in? I think at the very least I am entitled to an explanation.'

Tracey moved aside and made space so Lennie could squeeze past her into the hallway. Lennie marched into the lounge and perched upon the couch, arms folded, legs crossed, watching and waiting.

Tracey had obviously decided attack was the best form of defence as in an angry accusatory voice she said 'I do think it's terrible of you to lie to me and to imply that you were at Jean's in Leeds, when all the time you were sitting in the street like a stalker.'

'That is by the by,' said Lennie dismissively waving her hand to emphasise her point, 'as I said at the doorway, I think I am entitled to some sort of explanation. Why did you lie to me Tracey?

Tracey took a while to collect her thoughts before replying. She shrugged her shoulders once or twice before saying in a joking manner. 'Ok it's a fair cop, I was visiting my ex Sandra. I would have told you and it was all perfectly innocent but for some stupid reason which I now regret I decided not to. I suppose it's because it's early on in our relationship and I didn't want to rock any boats. I've been to the supermarket that part is true, the bags are in the boot of the car you are welcome to check.' Tracey took the car keys from her handbag and handed them to Lennie. 'After the supermarket I visited Sandra my ex for a quick coffee and a catch up.'

'I still don't understand why you have lied to me,' said Lennie as she was not entirely convinced that Tracey was telling the truth. After years of Sooty's lies and indiscretions Lennie could tell when someone was trying to pull the wool over her eyes. Tracey's body language and darting expression spoke volumes.

'Nor do I to be honest.' Tracey said shrugging again. 'In my defence I was protecting your feelings, I didn't want you to feel compromised or jealous.'

Lennie sat silently and thought it through. On reflection it seemed a plausible explanation and it was true she would have been eaten up by jealousy had she known Tracey had been visiting her ex-girlfriend. It just didn't sit comfortably to be feeling so suspicious so early in a relationship but what choice did she have? She could storm out to save face or choose to give Tracey the benefit of the doubt and trust her. Tracey is not Sooty, she told herself and it is unfair of me to tar them both with the same brush.

'Can I ask you to promise not to lie to me again, whether it is to protect my feelings or for any other reason?'

'Yes, my darling, I promise. Do you forgive me?'

'Of course, as you say, there is nothing to forgive.'

'Then come over here and let's say hello properly,' said Tracey.

THE SWEET LUXURY OF TIME

Meanwhile in Leeds, Jean sat contentedly in the lounge. The leather sofa which had felt so unwieldy before she had gone to Nowhere, felt strangely comforting now. Looking up at the photographs of Lucy, which were absolutely everywhere, Jean spoke out aloud.

'Well, my darling, I'm back in our home. I feel so close to you here. I know you wanted me to move on. So I shall do, I promise you, just give me time to adjust to life without you.'

No sooner had Jean finished her little speech than the telephone rang. She hesitated for a few moments before picking up the telephone and saying 'Hello'.

'Is that Jean, Lucy's partner?' said the disembodied voice on the line.

'Yes, Jean speaking' said Jean in reply to the question.

'Hello, I'm Dianne, you don't know me in fact I don't think we've ever actually met.' The woman's voice had a slight Irish lilt to it. 'I was at the funeral and didn't get the chance to speak to you.'

'Oh yes,' said Jean, suddenly remembering. 'Were you with your parents? I'm so sorry you must think me very rude I should have made more of an effort to speak to you.'

'On the contrary, I'm sorry we didn't coming across and introduce ourselves. You were understandably upset and we were worried about intruding.'

'I'm just glad you managed to make the time to say your goodbyes to Lucy. She often spoke of you and your parents.'

'We were very fond of Lucy and we were wondering if you would like to come and stay with us for the weekend. We would really like to get to know you better. You always seemed to be at work when we visited Lucy and we can only imagine how devastated you must be.'

Jean was about to politely decline, when something had stopped her. What had she just been promising to Lucy's photograph? It was time for her to move on, take on new challenges and make new friends. Perhaps now was the time to start and put this new plan into action.

Jean replied in what she hoped was a confident tone and said she would love to visit.

'That's wonderful,' said Dianne. 'Let me run a few dates by my parents and I will get back to you later tonight.'

'OK. I'm around all night and I look forward to finally getting to know you all at last.' said Jean as she put the telephone down.

After the two women had said their goodbyes, Jean sat for a long while cradling Lucy's photograph on her lap. It was a photograph of their last proper holiday together, taken way back when, in that magical time when Lucy was well. Taken way before the cancer had invaded her body and their lives, like an unwelcome guest stealing their hope cell by precious cell. Jean's thoughts transported her back to Lucca and those balmy nights they had shared sitting in tiny café's overlooking magnificent squares. Just sitting, sharing time, killing time, chilling time, wasting time. Oh, for the sweet luxury of time. How Jean yearned to turn back time to that very moment when they had asked the waiter to take their photograph. Her only concern then had been whether they had enough small change left to order more coffee, or if they would have to wait until morning to exchange the last of their traveller's cheques. Jean remembered they had squabbled briefly, because it had been Lucy's responsibility to ensure they had enough cash left, and she had insisted upon an expensive bottle of wine with the meal they had shared earlier that evening. The Jean all those years ago had been irritated by small things, things which now were so nonsensical and unimportant. Lucy's illness had cured Jean of her pettiness but it had been replaced with an ache that no medicine could ever cure.

Lucy had been so happy-go-lucky, optimistic, often to the most annoying degree. She had seen the good in everyone, snatched her pleasures with the excitement

of a small child. Her happiness and zest for life contagious to all who shared her company. She gathered friends, scooping them up in her warm embrace, collecting them, nurturing them, her loyalty and consistency ensuring they remained equally committed to the friendship. Lucy ensured each friend felt important, her reasoning being that they all enriched her life in different and unique ways. It was ironic that the only similarity and common ground between Lucy's friends was the utter devastation they felt when she died.

Lucy had planned her own funeral to the very smallest detail, stage managed the whole affair. At the time Jean had felt put out that she seemed to play such a little part in the production. It was almost as if their life together was an insignificant passage in Lucy's life. Jean's jealousy reared its ugly head and had fought the urge to scream out her displeasure.

'Hey, look at me!' She wanted to shout,

'Look at me, what about me? I'm here, look at me.

I shared Lucy's life, I shared Lucy's bed.

Hey look at me; I miss her more than you lot could ever imagine.

I cradled her head as she threw up in the toilet, not you lot.

I struggled out of bed every night for the last few months and changed the sheets when the night sweats overtook her.

I lowered her fragile frame into the tepid bath water washing her gently with the softest flannel I could find, her shrunken baby bird's chest wincing beneath my touch. And later when they gave her steroids and she got a sudden surge of energy and her appetite briefly returned. I was the one who went to the kitchen at 3am to make her French toast; because she craved it.

I was the one who sat by encouraging her to eat just one more bite.

I was the one who pleaded with her to give the chemo one last try.

I was the one who was racked with guilt when I saw the effect it had on her and how wretched it made her feel.

I was the selfish one who wanted her to hang on for one more month, one more week, one more day, one more hour.

When the end finally came, I was the one who held her head in the crook of my arm for so long that my arm went numb.

I was the one who whispered in her ear the last goodbye.

I was the one who told her it was time to leave and persuaded her to give up the fight for life.

That was me. I was there for the good times and the bad.

Where were you lot?

At her funeral seeing the vast crowd of Lucy's friends Jean had felt cheated. She wanted to howl, a long loud scream at the unfairness of it all. She still felt like howling even now... Often the urge would come upon her at the most unlikely of places. She could be in the supermarket, trawling the aisles for something for tea and come across a food Lucy had enjoyed in her healthy days. What she now thought of as her BC days; her halcyon 'before cancer' days. Lucy had loved olives especially the big fat green olives, filled with pimento and drenched in olive oil, chillies and garlic. Jean had known Lucy to devour a whole jar, fork in hand, pleasure etched upon her face. Every time Jean saw a jar of olives this memory would come flooding back and with it the reaLouisation that Lucy would never again taste an olive. Some days Jean yearned for a breakdown. She knew it was selfish of her to wish this, but she wished it nonetheless. She longed to escape the pain of losing Lucy and to be allowed to lose control. She wanted to crouch on the shiny supermarket floor amongst the custard creams and the jammy dodgers and curl into a tight foetus like ball,

And howl, and scream, and wail.

Once when Jean had been leafing through some old art books of Lucy's she had come upon a painting entitled *'The Scream'*. A distorted figure alone on a bridge, screaming at the howling wind. That was what Jean needed to do. She needed to stand alone on some distant bridge, rain whistling in her ears as she screamed at the howling wind.

How long Jean sat there on the couch she did not know, but she was awoken from her reverie with a start by the telephone ringing. Composing herself before answering it, she was surprised to find it was the stepmother of Dianne, who had rung earlier. Was it really two hours ago? They wondered if Jean were free this weekend. It was short notice, they knew, but it would be so nice to see her again, and they had promised Lucy to look out for her. Jean pretended to check her empty diary before conceding that she was indeed free that weekend and would look forward to seeing them all then. She then rang Lennie on her cell phone to say she would be going away for the weekend. Lennie did not seem her usual self, and Jean questioned if everything was fine between her and Tracey. Lennie answered quickly, too quickly, saying that yes, everything was wonderful and tickety-boo. Jean bid her goodnight but remained unconvinced, Jean knew Lennie too well, and she had seemed very guarded in her reply.

NUMBER 12 FANNY STREET, SALTAIRE

Tracey had long since been looking for a property to buy. The Chapel she lived in was brilliant and quirky but would never be hers. She had once tentatively asked the owners if they would consider selling it to her, but they had quoted such an off the wall figure she promptly declined. Her Lease was due to expire so rather than commit to a further year it seemed like the ideal opportunity to move on. With Lennie's help she had trawled the local Estate Agents that morning and had three properties to look at. Lennie's favourite was the terraced house in Saltaire, but she freely admitted to Tracey that her opinion was based purely upon its close proximity to the 1863 Hockney Gallery housed in the old Salt Mills.

The village of Saltaire was classed as a World Heritage Site. It comprised of twenty two streets of classic terraced houses named after the Mayor of Bradford's wife, children, family and devoted staff. The entrepreneurial Mayor and Mill owner Sir Titus Salt had been a forward-thinking man so he had created the village to house his staff, who worked at the nearby Mill. Away from the bustle of busy Bradford, the model village was now a centre of the Arts and wonderfully tranquil. Earlier that day, Lennie had managed to convince Tracey to agree to view a house in Fanny Street. The Estate Agent had sniggered as he repeated the name to the ladies, and had been rewarded with a withering look from Tracey. Later on they had laughed at how ingratiatingly servile he had been following his gaffe, and how he could not now do enough to accommodate the ladies.

Number 12 Fanny Street was simply charming. Although a classic two bedroom terraced house, it had been renovated to a very high specification and yet still retained many of its original features. Sunlight shone through the large bay window in the sitting room, highlighting the stripped pine fireplace inlaid with Victorian tiles and the exquisite highly detailed ceiling rose. A panelled hallway led onto the dining room which had been extended to include an open plan kitchen and glass vaulted ceiling. An Aga fitted snugly into the old fireplace cavity and the granite worktops of the kitchens island unit reflected the light and seemed to sparkle. Large bi-folding glass doors allowed the compact courtyard garden to feel as if it were a part of the house. In a sun drenched corner a fountain trickled a tiny stream of water from the mouth of a mosaic fish. It was quite, quite perfect. Tracey stood in the kitchen bathed in the sunlight flooding through the glass skylight.

'What a lovely sunny room,' she said allowing her eyes to take in the view from the patio doors.

'They do say the sun falls on the righteous,' Lennie replied. 'I really think this is an absolutely terrific little house.'

'I agree it has such a fantastic ambience to it.' Tracey mused as way of reply. Then, turning to face Lennie, she added. 'Well, my love, do you think you could be happy living here?'

Lennie was taken aback Tracey and she had never actually discussed re-locating, although it was obvious if their relationship were to continue it was a natural progression. Her surprise and lack of a quick retort were hard to disguise.

'Your silence speaks volumes' said Tracey, her face etched with hurt at what she assumed was a rejection of her suggestion.

She was about to flounce off to look upstairs, when Lennie reached out and stopped her. 'Please wait' she pleaded 'let me have a moment to compose myself, it did come somewhat out of the blue.'

'I thought we were both singing from the same hymn sheet after last night's misunderstanding but if you have to think about it perhaps it is too soon.'

'Be fair sweetheart we should have discussed it first. I feel somewhat ambushed but if you are sure it's what you really want nothing would make me happier. Can we discuss the practicalities when we get back to your house?'

Tracey bent over and kissed her tenderly on the lips. Despite their surroundings Lennie responded with a passion, carried away by the exquisite softness of Tracey's lips upon her own. Pressing her girlfriend up against the cupboard door, she ran her hands deftly across her buttocks. Tracey parted her lips slightly, allowing her tongue to dart teasingly against Lennie's teeth. Bending slightly at the knees Tracey allowed her lips to leave Lennie's and to make the slow agonisingly pleasurable progress towards her cleavage. Lennie reached down and released her breast from the confines of her bra. Tracey cupped it, rubbing the nipple between her fingertips until it grew hard and stood proud against the soft yielding flesh. Tracey was about to encircle the nipple with her lips when she became aware that they were not alone in the room.

Both ladies had completely forgotten the presence of Simon, the Estate Agent. He had left them alone in the house to look around at their leisure, saying he had phone calls to make from his car, but had returned to the house to remind them that the asking price was open to negotiation. His eyes were now fixed upon the two ladies. How much of the lovemaking he had witnessed they did not dare to imagine. They both jumped apart, Lennie averting her eyes, but Tracey staring at him head on as if challenging him to comment. When eventually he spoke his voice was high and shaky. Lennie noticed that he held his briefcase tightly against the front of his trousers.

'Well, we certainly got his 'Calvin Kleins' in a twist this morning!' Tracey said later as they lay in bed cuddling.

'I think he had somewhat of a red letter day,' Lennie giggled, 'He got to walk in on two gay girls sharing a special moment and he got a potential sale into the bargain.'

'Look out, Fanny Street, here we come!' After saying this Tracey pulled slightly away from Lennie's embrace and asked. 'It is we, isn't it my love? I'm sorry I assumed without asking you first.'

'Of course it's we' confirmed Lennie, 'but at first it will be just you. I've got to sell my house, remember?'

Just vocalising this filled Lennie with foreboding, but she decided not to voice her trepidation to Tracey because she might take it as a lack of commitment.

'I wonder if Simon the Estate Agent is lying on his bed right now thinking about us?'

'Now that's a bet I would put a pound on.' replied Lennie, pleased that the mood in the bedroom had lightened. 'I would love to know what odds Ladbrokes would put on that little certainty.'

THE SINGING NUN

Many miles away in Buttercup Close, Upper Wortley, Jean was up bright and early so that she could drive across Yorkshire to spend the weekend with Lucy's friends. Countless times during the previous evening she had picked up the telephone to call Dianne and cancel, but each and every time her gaze would catch Lucy smiling down from the photograph on the mantelpiece and she would stop herself. It was not long before she was packed and on her way. Visiting new people while part of a couple was so much easier than visiting on one's own, Jean decided. It made her realise how much she had relied on Lucy to organise their social life, but she reflected that was probably the case in most relationships. Unless both parties were gregarious social butterflies, there would always be one partner who would be the life and soul whilst the other went along for the ride.

Within the hour Jean was pulling into the village of Clayton West, slowing down just in time to avoid being flashed by a speed camera. She was grateful that Dianne had warned her about it. Jean took a sharp right turn out of the village and headed towards the small hamlet which was perched precariously upon a steep hill. She parked her car in the pub car park at the top of the slope and rang Dianne from her cell phone. This had been Dianne's idea as she had explained that her house and her stepmother's house were set back from the main road and accessible only by a rough muddy lane. Dianne had arranged to stand out on the main road when she arrived so that she could direct Jean towards the lane.

In no time at all Jean was parking her car neatly behind Dianne's rather clapped out Ford Fiesta and clambering from the driver's seat. Dianne rushed towards the car door and engulfed her in a bear hug. Pulling away from the unexpected embrace Jean spied Dianne's parents Betsy and Victor emerging from a house adjacent to where she had just parked. The older couple were much more reserved in their greetings, choosing instead to shake hands and reintroduce themselves. Jean was then ushered into their house for a drink. As she followed her three new acquaintances into the kitchen she noted a look of exasperation cross Dianne's face.

Once the wine was corked and they were seated around the kitchen table the morning was to take a bizarre turn. Jean felt as if Dianne and her stepmother were plying for her attention and approval, rather as two rival lovers trying to impress a potential beau. It was a very strange and disconcerting situation. The first bottle of wine disappeared within minutes and two more were brought from the wine rack and hastily uncorked.

Dianne's father sat quietly in the corner of the room, chain smoking and sipping a glass of wine seemingly oblivious to the whole façade. The air was charged and the freely flowing alcohol seemed to fan the flames. Betsy was a very demonstrative drunk, tactile to the degree of over-familiarity. As a result Jean was very relieved when Dianne eventually took the initiative and insisted that Jean and she cross the square to her house for a spot of lunch. Betsy rose from her chair as if to also invite herself across the square but was stopped by Victor who placed his hand gently on her elbow and guided her towards the couch in the lounge. Jean felt fine until the fresh air hit her face. It was then that she realised exactly how much she had drunk on an empty stomach. As if suddenly aware of her delicate state, Dianne linked arms with her and a woozy Jean half stumbled, half staggered across the square, before flopping gratefully on the sofa in Dianne's living room. That was the last thing that Jean remembered, for she must have flaked out virtually as soon as she was seated. When she finally awoke she was covered in an ancient almost threadbare blanket of brightly crocheted squares which was strangely comforting. Her shoes had been removed and her legs lifted onto the couch. Jean lay quietly and surveyed the room for a few minutes before again closing her eyes as the glare of sunlight shafting through the bay window made her headache worsen. She gingerly opened her eyes again upon hearing a movement from behind the couch. It was Dianne coming into the room from the kitchen, looking very concerned and carrying a pot of what smelt like very strong coffee.

'How are you, Jean?'

'Feeling like a teenager who can't hold her drink,' replied Jean in an apologetic voice.

'To the contrary' countered Dianne, 'I should be apologising to you for letting you get into such a state, the wine was very potent and Betsy kept refilling your glass. My parents can drink the average person under the table, but I am used to pacing myself when I know they are in for a session. That's why I suggested we come back to my house for a spot of lunch, but I fear it may be a case of locking the stable door after the horse has bolted.'

'Talking of horses,' said Jean wryly. 'I think one is galloping on my forehead. Even blinking hurts.'

'I feel really guilty.' Dianne said.

'Please don't,' Jean intoned 'I am an adult and I should have realised how squiffy I was feeling and stopped...I suppose I was just so nervous about meeting you all.'

'We must come across as very full on.' Dianne conceded. 'If it helps I was as nervous about meeting you. I tell you what, if you give me your car keys I will get your case from the boot, and then I suggest that you go upstairs and lie quietly on the bed for a while.'

'If you're sure that's ok,' replied Jean gratefully, 'that sounds like a very good idea.'

'I haven't made up the bed in the spare room yet so lie on mine. It's right next to the bathroom, which will be handy if you feel sickly.'

'Oh I do wish you hadn't mentioned that.' said Jean her hand clasped to her mouth as she rushed upstairs and to what she hoped was the bathroom.

It was dusk when Jean finally awoke and come to her senses. As she remembered that she was in Dianne's bedroom she couldn't help sniggering to herself as she thought of what her good friends Sooty and Lennie would make of the scenario. She had been in Dianne's company a few hours and already she was in her bed. The room was so dark that at first Jean thought perhaps the curtains were drawn, but she soon realised, once her eyes had become accustomed to the lack of light, that they were in fact drawn open. It must therefore be late afternoon.

Oh gosh what a terrible house guest she was, getting drunk and falling asleep. How she wished Lucy was here; how she would have laughed and teased her. Jean heard a shuffling and turned to face the door. She was startled to see a silhouette standing there in the doorway.

A silhouette she presumed to be Dianne. It wasn't until the figure spoke that she realised it was in fact Betsy.

'How's sleeping beauty?' enquired Betsy in a jocular tone of voice.

'To be honest I feel terrible and very embarrassed.' Jean confessed.

'No need, no need. I've have run you a bath so hop in when you're ready. I'll go down and make more coffee. Dianne's popped to the shops to get me some more wine and Victor's at the stables feeding the horse.'

Feeling somewhat like a chastened child and deciding that she much preferred Dianne to her frankly rather scary stepmother, Jean thanked her. The bath looked glorious, so inviting and full of bubbles. Steam filled the bathroom. Jean locked the door behind her, not sure why she felt the need but compelled to nevertheless. She undressed quickly and lowered herself gingerly into the water. No sooner had she settled back into the welcoming warm water and begun to wash her hair than the handle on the door jiggled. Jean held her breath, not sure what to say. Whoever was on the other side of the door was obviously irritated, for Jean heard an exasperated sigh.

'I've brought your coffee up to you,' said a voice tinged with annoyance.

'Sorry I locked the door, force of habit! If you leave the coffee in the bedroom I'll be out soon. Thank-you so much,' replied Jean wondering as she said it why she felt the compulsion to explain. Surely it was common practice to lock a bathroom door in a strange house? Or was she being overly churlish and prudish? Jean felt suddenly vulnerable and very aware of her naked state. She relaxed as she heard the footsteps departing down the stairs. Much later as she was towel drying her hair in the bedroom Jean heard the front door open and Dianne's voice ring out.

'What are you doing here?' said Dianne obviously addressing her stepmother.

'What does it look like I'm doing?' Betsy replied using the same sharp tone she had used earlier on Jean.

They then began to speak in hushed tones. Jean crept to the top of the stairs so she could hear more clearly, hating herself for doing so, but curious nevertheless.

'It seems to me that you are laying claim on our Jean,' Betsy stage whispered.

'Lucy was as much our friend as yours you may care to remember that.'

'I never disputed that fact.'

'Victor thinks you have a crush on Jean.'

'Victor thinks or you think?'

'Don't be clever with me Dianne. You forget I can read you like a well-thumbed book.'

'Ok, you win, yes I find Jean attractive. But if you're implying I invited her across this weekend to lure her into bed, you couldn't be more wrong.'

'I knew it, you are so transparent.'

'Let's not go over this again please.'

'Why not? I'm sure your precious Jean knows all about it anyway.'

'What makes you think Lucy told her?'

'I know, that's how, I can see how she looks at me and then at you. She knows.'

'I personally think she hasn't a clue, but that's by the by. Let's not have this conversation tonight, please. You have had far too much to drink and it does you no favours. For once in your life please consider my father's feelings.'

'Bugger Victor, I'm sick of thinking about Victor.'

'Shush, please, I can hear Jean. Don't spoil this for me.'

'Spoil it my dear? If I have anything to do with it there will be nothing to spoil.'

Jean jumped as she heard the door slam on Betsy's parting words. She quickly scuttled back to the bedroom and resumed drying her hair, thinking all the while about what she had heard. Lucy had mentioned darkly once about the skeletons in her friends' cupboards, but Jean had been too wrapped up in her own affairs to enquire further. Now she wished she had. Jean took her time drying her hair, applying a modest amount of make-up before dressing. When she was finally ready she walked loudly down the stairs to announce her imminent arrival and strolled as nonchalantly as she was able into the kitchen. Dianne was standing by the stove stirring the contents of a saucepan with a large wooden spoon. Without turning she spoke.

'I've made some tomato soup. I thought something easy on the stomach would be our best bet tonight.'

'Are the others joining us?' enquired Jean, although she knew before she asked what the answer would be.

'No,' replied Dianne. 'Betsy had had far too much to drink and she tends to become argumentative. I took the decision that it should just be us tonight. I do hope that's fine with you.'

'Super,' said Jean. 'I must confess that I find your step-mum quite hard work, although your father is really sweet.'

'He is,' replied Dianne, turning at last to face Jean. 'He is such a lovely gentle man. I just wish my blasted step-mum would appreciate him more. She can be so exasperating sometimes, I feel like giving her a shake when she gets like this.'

'I couldn't help overhearing the conversation you were having earlier,' said Jean, deciding that perhaps honesty would be the best policy. She quickly changed her mind when she saw the expression of panic that crossed Dianne's face.

'Which part, did you overhear?' Dianne asked in a quiet voice.

'The part where Betsy assumed Lucy had told me something,' said Jean, deciding to take the bull by the horns.

'And had she, told you something I mean?'

'I think she tried to once, but it probably didn't sink in, or we were interrupted. I'm not sure. It was all so long ago.'

Dianne seemed to relax upon hearing this. She strode towards the fridge and took out a new bottle of wine.

'Hair of the dog?' she enquired holding the bottle aloft.

Jean shook her head. The mere thought of alcohol made her stomach churn.

'Take a seat' said Dianne gesturing towards a chair. 'It's a long story, and one which I admit I take no pleasure in retelling. I'm a great advocate of skeletons being in cupboards for a reason, I think dragging them out is helpful to no one. But it seems my darling step-mum has tried to force my hand yet again.'

Dianne took a large slurp of her wine. 'Dutch courage,' she said smiling wryly.

Sensing her obvious discomfort Jean made an instant decision. Standing up from the table she placed her hands upon Dianne's shoulders and said 'I suggest we leave skeletons where they are for the time being. I'm here to get to know you. Lucy spoke so fondly of you all and I don't want this to get in the way. There will be a time and a place for confidences in the future I am sure.'

Dianne let out an audible sigh of relief. 'Thank you I think you are right. There's a time and place to share a confidence and this is not it. But I do promise to confide in you when the time is right. Did you hear any more of the conversation?'

'If you mean the part where you told Betsy you were attracted to me, then yes, I did.' said Jean, surprising herself at how candid she was being.

'And?' said Dianne peering at Jean from over the brim of the wine glass.

'And, I cannot say I'm not incredibly flattered, because I am. But....'

'I had a feeling there would be a but'

'But, it's much too soon to think of romance. I'm not saying never but just not now. At the moment it takes me most of my energy just to get from day to day without breaking down, everything is so raw.'

At this, Dianne put the wine glass onto the table and reached across to take Jean's hand.

'Ok, please forgive me for being so crass and my step-mum for her lack of sympathy and empathy. My only intention upon inviting you here this weekend was to get to know you as a friend and in my own clumsy way to perhaps help you come to terms with your loss.'

Jean smiled and squeezed Dianne's hand.

'In a strange way this whole episode today has helped me. It's the only time since Lucy died that I have felt that I could have a life without her and if I have gained a good friend from it, well all the better.'

'To new friendships,' said Dianne raising her glass in a toast.

Raising her coffee cup Jean repeated the toast.

THE THRILL OF THE CHASE

Meanwhile in Nowhere, Robbie had been having a very busy time indeed. He was almost certain that the threatening note to Liz had done the trick as George informed him that she had been keeping a very low profile indeed. From enquiries to Plod it also appeared that she had not taken it upon herself to inform the boys in blue or indeed mentioned it to anyone with the exception perhaps of her two new friends at the Bistro.

In retrospect, Robbie found this quite a shame. He had got quite a kick out of his role as tormentor but as compensation there was always Maggie. He had developed a routine of following her throughout the day, letting her catch a glimpse of him shadowing her but remaining tantalisingly out of reach. To see her scuttling into doorways, racing through the shops as fast as her elderly legs could take her, gave him an almost sexual thrill. He knew now the pleasure those posh bods such as the Duke derived from the chase of the hunt. He imagined himself dressed in red, astride a horse, the hounds baying at his feet. His prey, Maggie, dressed in her trademark fox fur hat, almost tripping over her own swollen veined feet in her haste to reach the sanctuary of her front door. The irony of it was not lost on Robbie, despite his lack of formal education.

THE SECRET CEMENT MENAGERIE

Preparations for the grand opening of the Bistro were going very well with 'good luck' letters from vegetarian celebrities arriving with almost every post. Liz in her self-appointed role as 'Head of Public Relations' was hand feeding articles to the local papers to maximise the free publicity.

The girls had decided to have a weekend off before the 'Grand Opening' and the fact that it was Louisa's birthday proved the perfect excuse. They had visited Holy Island earlier that day and then enjoyed a quiet romantic meal by the fireside. It had been, Joey decided, as she drifted off to sleep, quite a perfect day. It was just a shame that the weekend had to be cut short because Louisa had to visit her sister Caro the following day. But even this interruption in the festivities did little to dim Joey's happiness, to such a degree that she even managed to convince herself that Louisa's flirtation with Sooty had run its course. Louisa had been attentive both in and out of bed and convincingly happy to be in Joey's company. Yes, she thought to herself, it had been quite a perfect day.

The next day dawned and Louisa was up bright and early, driving off in the car almost before Joey had a chance to wish her good morning.

'See you later sweetheart' Louisa shouted through to the bathroom as she collected the car keys from the kitchen drawer. Joey was in the shower but popped her head around the curtains to reply.

'I'll miss you,' said Joey.

'I'll be back before you know it,' Louisa replied. 'The sooner I go the sooner I can make my excuses and leave.'

'Give Caro and the kiddies my love.'

'Of course I will.'

Once on the main road, instead of heading towards the city and her sister Caro's house, Louisa turned the car towards the coast and the mainline railway station. She smiled inwardly to herself as she spotted Sooty waiting patiently in the car park, her heart missing the familiar beat as it always did when she saw her lover. There was something infinitely naughty about seducing the formal austere older headmistress, reminiscent of the classic porn scenario of the uptight secretary releasing her long locks from the tight bun and removing the spectacles. Sooty projected the image of a lady but her lovemaking was anything but ladylike.

Driving back out of the station exit, Louisa turned to Sooty and said. 'I think you had better tell me which way I am going on this magical mystery tour my darling. Is it left or right?'

'Turn left out of the station then onto the A1 past Nowhere. Just head towards Edinburgh and I will tell you when to turn off. I've been planning this for days. I wanted to give you the most special birthday ever.'

'Just being with you makes it special,' said Louisa, reaching across the gear stick to squeeze Sooty's hand.

They drove for a while in companionable silence, listening to the car radio, singing off tune to the songs they recognised, each deep in their own contemplations. Sooty directed Louisa off the main road and along quiet country roads before finally telling her to stop at a tiny hamlet called Branxton.

'Just pull up alongside this children's play park.' said Sooty as they drove into what seemed to be the main street.

'What here?' said Louisa, incredulous because the sleepy hamlet seemed absolutely devoid of anything of any interest and it was too small to even warrant a shop or public house.

'It's a secret garden, I've brought you to,' said Sooty. 'It would be a contradiction of the word secret if were easy to find.'

The two women climbed from the car. Sooty linked arms with Louisa and guided her to an ordinary looking house adjacent to the park. Peering closely at the side of the house Louisa made out a rather weather beaten old wooden sign bearing the words 'Cement Menagerie'. Sooty strode purposefully ahead and prised open the creaky metal gate. Once through she motioned for Louisa to follow her. Louisa was reticent as she felt guilty about entering a private garden. Sooty smiled and pulled her by the sleeve. Beyond the gate and sheltered from the road by a dilapidated garage was a sight which made Louisa gasp in amazement. Her gaze was greeted by a riot of colour and a vast garden full of bizarre life-size cement models. The sprawling landscape was filled to the brim with all manner of creatures, both imaginary and real. *Churchill* stood by a moss covered pond, his fingers shaped in the famous victory sign, cigar clasped between his concrete lips. Behind him, a waddle of penguins crossed a makeshift bridge, reminiscent of the cartoon sequence in *Mary Poppins*. An orange striped tiger crouched below a giraffe with a gravity defying neck. *Moby Dick*, considerably smaller than life-size, swam on a sea of weather-smoothed pebbles alongside a turbaned Indian boy high astride an elephant. Looking to her left, Louisa saw a brick built bench on which perched a cement model of *Robbie Burns*. At his feet lay a framed tea towel from a long forgotten holiday destination which bore some lines of his poetry. The rain had soaked into the frame and the edges of the towel were tinged a tea stain brown. This bizarre imperfection added a kitsch element to the tableau.

At the back of the garden a makeshift wooden platform had been erected. Upon Sooty's urging, Louisa joined her on it, the rotting wood creaking alarmingly beneath her feet. The platform overlooked an ordinary looking field with a small flock of sheep grazing by a copse of trees in its far corner. A handwritten plaque nailed upon the fence explained the special significance of the field: Flodden Field, the site of the famous battle where James IV lost his life.

Louisa turned and looked at Sooty. For once she was speechless and tears welled up in her eyes. Sensing this Sooty helped her down from the platform and guided her towards a nearby bench.

'Shall I tell you the story of the garden now? she enquired.

Louisa nodded by way of reply.

"Well I suppose I should start by saying this garden was built as a gift from a father to a son, it became their special project. Whenever I visit I feel humbled and reminded of that deep unselfish love. You get it, don't you my darling?' said Sooty.

'I get it.' Louisa replied, understanding the cryptic question straight away.

'I knew you would. This secret magical place is my birthday gift to you. Not a lot of people know it exists as it's not in any guide books and that's why it's so unspoilt.'

No sooner had she said these words than it began to spit with rain.

'Well that's put paid to my next surprise. I had the most wonderful picnic planned. It's not quite the same eating it in the car.'

'A drop of rain never harmed anyone,' said Louisa, 'let's eat it in the open air, come on, there's benches in that play park next to the garden, let's have it there.'

She was suddenly reckless, nothing but nothing would be allowed to spoil her special birthday. So they sat, rain coursing down their faces, dripping from the tips of their noses, eating their sodden sandwiches. Lifting their plastic beakers of steaming hot tea into the air they toasted each other. Suddenly Louisa let out a gasp of delight, for between the trees, high up in the sky she glimpsed the most perfect rainbow forming.

'Oh look.' she said, pointing towards the arc of multicoloured light.

Sooty's gaze followed the direction of her finger. The rainbow ran from the Flodden Field in a crescent across the sky, diving down into the secret garden.

'If I could, I would bottle today so I could remember it forever and ever.'

'Hopefully I'll be around to remind you,'

Louisa let out a deep sigh, 'Why is it all so complicated? I never planned to fall in love with you. It was never part of the plan and I wonder how it will all end.

Sensing the change in mood, Sooty took Louisa in her arms.

'Let's just enjoy the moment darling. It's your birthday and you shall have cake.'

With a flourish she produced two rather damp cupcakes from the picnic basket.

'I did bring candles but I think the rain has put paid to that little idea.'

'Who needs candles?' said Louisa taking a cupcake and biting into it.

'Delicious,' she stated, her face covered in crumbs. 'This has been the most perfect birthday, with the most perfect picnic ever.'

So we leave the birthday girl and her secret lover and return to Nowhere. In the Town's gym, the ladies of the WTF are frantically trying to lose the extra pounds gained through the many years of complacency and the advent of elasticated waistband trousers in the local *Marks and Spencer*. Lillian, the self-elected leader of the group is vocally encouraging the rest of the ladies. Her new mantra of 'no pain, no gain' struck their gym instructor as ironic since they were not trying to gain the weight but to lose it.

THE CASTLE GARDENS

Meanwhile in the grounds of Nowhere Castle the Earl and Countess are showing a Belgian team of son and father garden designers around the neglected gardens. The Countess has in mind a grandiose scheme to redesign the gardens, much in the style of Versailles. The Earl, for his part, has the more pressing event of the naked WTF calendar on his mind. He keeps switching off from the matter in hand and imagining the very buxom ladies of the WTF naked as cherubs draped across his begonias. What had seemed a totally unlikely idea at the outset has gained a momentum all of its own. The press are now taking a distinct interest in the spectacle and the coverage has spawned an influx of requests to use the grounds for various media events. One of the ladies from the WTF bears an uncanny resemblance to the Earl's own dearly departed nanny, so somewhat in the manner of a naughty schoolboy the Earl fervently hopes to catch a glimpse of her privates amongst the privets.

CHERKASSY, UKRAINE –
TALES OF BABA YAGA

Far far away from Nowhere, indeed far far away from England, a petite woman of fifty-four years sits trying to master the complex intricacies of the English language. Outside in the grey dank street the wind whistles and a steady persistent rain falls onto the pock marked pavement. Years of poverty and hard work have left similar pock marks upon Tania's skin, etching deep furrowed lines intersected by liver spots. After years of struggling to survive as a single parent Tania is no stranger to hard work. She has worked all through Nikolai's life, missing out on significant stages of his babyhood whilst working to provide, secretly jealous that her son spends more time with her Russian born mother, his maternal grandmother, than herself. Yet she is conversely grateful to the old lady for giving her the chance to work her way out of the poor house.

Tania works in a café on the outskirts of town frequented primarily by workers from the nearby factory. These men are not the marrying kind. They either have wives and families or are interested only in a sexual dalliance. This lesson Tania has learned from bitter past experience. Romance, or the notion of it, no longer interests her. She feels old beyond her years, an old woman, a Babushka.

Her son Nikolai jokes with her that she is more like a *Baba Yaga*, the old crone from the nursery tales. *Baba Yaga* is much feared by Russian children, for she lives in a hut which can move on its chicken legs through the forest. The hut has windows which will act as its eyes and its lock is full of children's teeth. It is surrounded by a fence made of human bones topped with skulls whose eye sockets shine and light up the forest at night.

'*Hut move with your front to me and your back to the forest*' orders *Baba Yaga* as the hut spins and races through the birch forest. The other children would gasp with fright but not Nikolai. He was a brave little boy and many a night Tania had sat until late, her precious son on her lap as she told him the story of Baba Yaga.

'Again, Mama, again,' he would plead 'Tell me the story again.'

Nikolai is older now and about to start studying at the local University. He no longer pleads to sit on Tania's lap; he just teases her in his good natured way. *Baba Yaga* he teases, referring to his mother's skinny legs, darting out of range as she flicks her dishcloth towards him. Tania pretends to be upset and Nikolai sidles up to her to give her a bear hug. These are the times which give her most pleasure. These are the moments which make everything worthwhile. Tania loves her son beyond life itself. She sees other boys his age forced to work in factory jobs to supplement the meagre family income. She does not want this future for her son. Mistakes have been made for which Tania blames herself. It was she and only she who chose to fall in love all those years ago with a married man. It was she and only she who chose to have the child and rear him alone. As a consequence it is she and only she who must rectify the situation she has created and give her son the opportunities in life which he deserves, the chance to study and achieve his full potential. If the result is that she herself must do without, then so be it.

Tania has for many years been trudging to night school after a long twelve hour shift at the cafe. She is learning to speak English, the language which she believes will be her son's passport to a better life. Another waitress and she have also laboriously taught themselves to master the intricacies of the English lifestyle. It is on this small island that the two women believe their own salvations lie. Their faith in this new life has already paid dividends. Tania has for quite a while now been conversing with a gentleman in England. She understands him to be a wealthy man. He has sent photographs of his house on a hill, a very English looking castle. This man, whose name is Peter, has told Tania he is a very important man in the town in which he lives. He commands much respect as the Inspector of the local Police Force. The other waitress is envious, for although she too has a gentleman friend in England he is not of English descent and is merely a shopkeeper. He keeps bragging about a shop he owns in the capital city of London but he does not live in a castle on top of a hill.

Tania feels that it will not be long before Peter asks her to join him in England. She has discussed this with her mother and Nikolai. Difficult and heart-wrenching though it will inevitably be, she is certain that this is the only way she can support Nikolai through university.

Peter seems a kind man. He has told her he has never been married and he has never been inappropriate in their conversations. This convinces her that he is looking primarily for a companion in life rather than a lover. Tania knows the time is soon because Peter has asked for a photograph, which she has duly sent, apologising for its grainy quality. She is secretly pleased by the bad lighting on the image as it makes her look far younger than her years. The photograph had been taken at a cousin's wedding. Tania had had her greying hair dyed for the occasion and had borrowed a dress from a neighbour. Nikolai had whistled when he had seen his mother dressed up that night, assuring her she no longer looked like *Baba Yaga*. On that night Tania had felt like a million dollars.

Tania is in the Post Office sending yet another letter to Peter. Tania has paid the money, breaking into her last Markka and the letter has duly been placed in the post box by the counter. She has tried to make her life seem so much more interesting than it actually is. Both she and her friend have agreed that seeming desperate will not endear them to their English gentlemen suitors.

The letter is retrieved a week later by Peter. He smiles as he reads Tania's words. Yes he thinks to himself, perhaps now is the time to get married. It would put paid to the rumours, dispense with the mystery of his lonely life on the Crag. English women were so greedy, expecting and demanding a relationship of equals. Hopefully this Ukranian woman would be so grateful for the chance of an easier life she would not question his religious beliefs or indeed think them odd. The sexual side of marriage held little appeal to Peter. He found it all so messy and degrading but still it was an itch that needed scratching. This Tania was older and since she had made no mention of a romantic yearning he believed it not to be on her agenda either. The more he thought of it, the more it seemed an ideal solution. Someone to cook, clean and see too his every need, Peter wondered why the idea had never crossed his mind before. Checking his watch and putting the letter in the drawer of the desk, Peter crossed the corridor to his bedroom. Tonight was the night for his weekly self-flagellation and it was time to draw a little blood.

OXFORD HOUSE, LONDON – READING BETWEEN THE LINES

In the kitchen of Oxford House, Sorell the butler was preparing a breakfast tray for his mistress. This was much to the annoyance of the head cook, who deemed the task part of her job description. It irked her that Sorell interfered in all aspects of the running of the house. In her opinion he was much too familiar with the mistress of the house.

She knew for a fact that the mistress' dependence upon Sorell was a matter of concern for her husband the ....On more than one occasion he had been heard to mutter as much, seemingly unconcerned that he was being overheard by the chambermaids.

'Doris' said Sorell, addressing the cook by her first name. She was sure he did this to vex her and demean her position of seniority in the kitchen. The young chambermaids sniggered nervously, stopping abruptly when Doris glanced her way. Doris ruled the kitchen with a rolling pin of iron, her tongue sharper than any of the knives on the rack. Sorell was well aware of the kitchen etiquette and aware of Doris' insistence on the use of her title and surname of Bridges. That he chose to address her in so flippant a manner was tantamount to insolence. Doris chose not to rise to the bait and answered Sorell in a civil tongue although she did not trust herself to turn and look at him.

'Is there a problem, Mr Sorell?' she asked.

'Not as such, I merely wondered where you had put the daily newspapers.'

Turning herself around to face Sorell, Doris gave a heavy sigh.

'You were there when the ..... telephoned and asked that we told the mistress that the newspapers had not arrived today.'

'As her right hand man, her rock, I think I have a duty to keep her informed.'

'On your head be it,' said Doris, reaching into a cupboard to extract the pile of newspapers. Secretly she had hoped that Sorell would insist on showing the newspapers to the mistress in direct disobedience to the ...... wishes. Perhaps being sacked would wipe that self-satisfied smug smile from his face. The young man certainly needed taking down a peg or two, and may she be at ringside when it happened.

Arranging the newspapers neatly in a pile by the side of the tray, Sorell motioned with his head for the chambermaid to open the door from the kitchen.

Once upstairs, he laid the tray on the hall table and knocked on the bedroom door. The .... answered almost immediately in her shy hesitant voice and told him to come into the room.

The .... peered from beneath her blonde fringe, silently watching as Sorell crossed the bedroom and placed the tray carefully upon the table by the window.

Clearing his throat, Sorell said.'Madam I have been bold.'

'How so, Sorell?' enquired the ....

'I have gone against the express wishes of the ...... and taken the liberty of allowing you to see today's newspapers.'

'The ...... wished me to not to read the newspapers? Now why should that be?'

pondered the ....

'I suggest you peruse at your leisure and find out madam. I shall be outside in the corridor should you wish to consult with me.'

The .... waited until Sorell had left the room before crossing to the breakfast tray and unfolding the first of the newspapers. The headline read 'Yet another scandal to rock the House of .... The article then transcribed word for embarrassing word a secretly taped telephone conversation between the .... and his lover. From the explicit words and terms of endearment used, it was apparent to all as to the nature of their relationship. But in case there was any doubt, the columnist vindicated the source of the tape, explaining that his mole in royal circles had provided the tape and confirmed its authenticity.

The .... quickly scanned the rest of the newspapers before calling for Sorell. No sooner had she said his name than he seemed to be at her side.

'Well done, Sorell,' she said.

'The pleasure was all mine, madam,' he answered, giving a mock bow.

'How I wish I were a fly on the wall at my in-laws this morning' she giggled. 'I trust you were well compensated by your newspaper friend?'

'Suitably,' said Sorell. 'I can't complain.'

BOOK TWO – A FEW MONTHS LATER

NOWHERE INFANT SCHOOL PLAYGROUND

Yvonne was bored. She had never been so bored in her entire life. She was not bored because she had nothing to do. My God, with children, part-time jobs and a husband there was always some mundane household task to attend to. But that did not change the fundamental fact that she was bored. Nothing she thought of seemed to have the potential to relieve her boredom. Working for old man Johnson was a slight change in the tedium of the day but the rest of the time it was just the constant ferrying of children. Taking them to school and collecting them from school, day after tedious day. The burden of domesticity sat heavily upon her shoulders.

With the Rhonda and Clive scenario a distant memory, life with Bob had reverted back to its mind-numbing normality. Yvonne was aware that her life would not change unless she instigated the change. But the question was how to change it.

Little did Yvonne know that as she stood pondering in the playground, emerging from a rather clapped out Mini elsewhere in Nowhere was her salvation.

Easing her large protruding belly from the confines of her ancient mini, Marina paused to stretch. She rubbed her hands against the small of her back, emitting a cat-like purr of satisfaction as she did so. This pregnancy lark was all well and good for younger women but at her advanced age of forty-two she ached in places she did not know existed. Still she reassured herself with the fact that the end was in sight, thank God. This pregnancy had been something of a mistake, a half-hearted attempt to cling to a younger partner. Why she had imagined that a child would provide a bond of commitment escaped her now. But hindsight was a wonderful thing. Her lover Martin had flown the coop regardless of her advanced state of pregnancy, as in her heart of hearts she had known he would. Perhaps her subconscious body clock had spurred her on, as her chances of bearing a child were diminishing with each menstrual cycle. Regardless of any other reasons, the imminent new arrival coupled with the departure of her errant partner had prompted Marina to seek to leave the hustle and bustle of London behind and to settle in semi-rural Nowhere. Rather meanly she had instructed her friends and old work colleagues to under no circumstances let Martin know where she was. Why should he have the pleasure of knowing a child he had let her carry alone for this long nine months?

She had chosen to move to Nowhere on something of a whim. Her mother, long since deceased, had grown up in the market town and often talked fondly of the area. One day when she was sitting in a smart London coffee shop nursing a semi-skimmed decaf mocha and browsing through the appointments page a University job in Newcastle had seemed to leap from the page. Kismet, fate, call it what you will, Marina had decided there and then to up sticks and move to the sticks.

The University of Newcastle was almost an hour's drive from Nowhere, but the job as Head of Department would offer the challenge that Marina needed. When Marina had visited the University to be interviewed she had taken the opportunity to spend a few days in Nowhere. Finding a place to stay was a doddle compared with the problem of finding someone to look after her baby after it was born, but the taxi driver who had collected Marina from the train station all those weeks ago had mentioned that his wife was a Registered Childminder. Today Marina had gone to the trouble of phoning the taxi firm in order to speak to the driver again and to ask if his wife was willing to take on the job. Bob had rung Yvonne and arranged for Marina to visit her that very afternoon.

Marina knew her hours at the University would be long, as she was enlisted to set up a whole new teaching programme for Religious Studies on top of her own research, but she hoped that having a childminder would ensure that she did not have to disrupt her life too much. The thought of having a small baby to love was very appealing but the day-to-day care was less so. The role of *earth mother* did not lie easily with Marina. She was too used to having the freedom of a child-free life. Hopefully Yvonne would be her fairy godmother.

GREENHOUSE BISTRO – CHUGGING ALONG

Life in the Bistro was chugging along. The great panic over the opening was now a distant memory. Louisa had taken to the role of chef like a duck to water and with Joey front of house the two girls were a formidable team. In the many months since the Bistro had officially opened they were beginning to establish themselves and already had a small posse of regulars.

A mother and daughter dined each lunchtime, holding the fort at their favourite table beside the window whilst watching the world go by. They offered Joey and Louisa an excellent insight into Nowhere as they had lived in the market town their entire adult lives. Over the years the mother and daughter combination had hatched and matched most of Nowhere, their respective jobs being midwife and local registrar. Mr Tears, husband and father, saw to the dispatching as Nowheres undertaker. Joey and Louisa had giggled all night over the appropriate surnames all three shared. Joey likened it to a game of Happy Families she had played as a child. Mr Tears the undertaker, Mrs Tears the midwife, and Miss Tears the registrar.

The local hairdressers, Hair Today Gone Tomorrow, sent their junior over the street every day to collect lunch for their stylists. The Chief Stylist Raymond was especially partial to a cream horn.

Old man Johnson from the antiques emporium sent his secretary Yvonne to collect his lunch and a large slice of chocolate fudge cake under the strict instructions that should his wife Lillian enquire he had only ordered a cottage cheese salad baguette.

Sooty, who was Headmistress at the local Comprehensive, had a regular order, which one of the sixth formers would usually collect if she hadn't the time.

Louisa had the bright idea of a mobile sandwich round and they employed a local retired teacher to drive around the industrial estate outside Nowhere. This proved so popular that they also set up a small kiosk in the old railway station which was now a massive bookshop. This had developed into a barter system and the owners would regularly dine at the Bistro for free rather than taking a commission from the girls.

Yes, business was very good. Profits were not yet going through the roof but the Bistro was slowly becoming a moderate success, a fact which obviously irked Clive the publican from the *Brits*. He had been spotted furtively scanning the menu early one morning under the pretext of walking his dog. The lunchtime trade in the *Brits* had been adversely affected by the opening of the Bistro and Clive was worried he may have to lay off his chef. Joey had been warned by her regulars that Clive would probably try to undercut the Bistro's prices in a last ditch attempt to protect his livelihood. Louisa was under instructions to walk past the *Brits* every time she took Jasper for a walk so she could discreetly check his Specials Board. This suited Louisa as it afforded her the opportunity to visit Sooty, albeit briefly, twice a day during the school holidays, as her house was directly opposite the *Brits* bar.

The affair was still ongoing. They both knew the ground rules and Louisa reasoned that as long as she was discreet it could go on forever. Sooty for her part wanted a more permanent relationship but she knew Louisa was happy with her 'twinned' life and she would far rather have half of her attentions than none at all.

Sooty and her partner Lennie would often dine in the Bistro after work. Lennie was still gloriously unaware of her tempered history with Louisa, seemingly blinkered, as saw Louisa only in the context of her ongoing affair with Sooty. The appearance of Sooty and Lennie at the Bistro would invariably cause Louisa to become jumpy, which proved to Joey the affair was not over. From watching Lennie and her reaction to Louisa, Joey was in no doubt she too was aware of the ongoing relationship. Joey presumed that both she and Lennie had probably taken the same decision to bury their heads in the sand in the hope that the affair would die a natural death.

Liz was still ensconced in the holiday flat above the Bistro now that she had left her job as a private detective. She was presently helping out in the Bistro in exchange for her rent but had grand plans to open her very own Private Eye agency as soon as funds allowed.

Another regular sat hunched by the gas fire in the corner of the Bistro. She would visit every day with her young baby in a pushchair. She drank copious amounts of coffee and wrote furiously in a journal oblivious to her surroundings, emerging from her work only when the baby stirred and the pushchair needed jiggling. Joey tried many times to engage her in conversation but she would release no information save that she was writing a book, an adventure book for children which she hoped would be enjoyed by adults too. When pressed further she told Joey that its main hero was a schoolboy wizard. This struck Joey as a very odd thing to base a novel on, but as long as she continued to buy coffee Joey was happy for her to occupy a table. Joey had quickly gleaned that a semi-full Bistro attracted customers.

Events upon the Crag were moving along at a much headier pace. Peter had been in contact with Tania in Cherkassy many times, finally revealing his true intentions toward her. When he popped the question, so to speak, he worded it as the business transaction they both knew it would be. He was sending money by transfer via the bank so that Tania could purchase the plane ticket, fly to England and upon her arrival they would become husband and wife.

Today Peter had more pressing urgent matters to attend to, as he had been informed that there was a newcomer to the town. It appeared that Marina was well known in the upper echelons of The Disciples of God, *DOG*. She had infiltrated the sect at its grass roots by becoming a fledgling member of the pack even moving for a while into the main *DOG* house. In her damning report, later published as her Doctoral Thesis, she had described in detail the *barking mad's*. These were religious tasks which each member was ordered to carry out each day. These included the 'morning glory' which involved alighting from bed, crawling around in a circle before lying prostrate upon the floor and repeating the mantra 'I am a DOG.' She wrote that she had not been permitted to leave the house without permission from the Master and vividly described how she had been ostracised from her blood family. She declared that sect's aim to 'spread the word of DOG...through everyday life' was a whitewash for a cultist society. She described how she was encouraged to be perpetually cheerful to outsiders so she could recruit the best people of top pedigree. She ended her report by explaining how she had been asked to leave the sect after she failed to satisfactorily increase the pack and had dared to question the need to constantly obey the Top DOG. Her report, which ultimately won her a place on the Board of Directors of a Government Agency researching emerging cults, sent shock waves throughout Rome and prompted Religious leaders throughout the world to renounce and distance themselves publicly from DOG. Marina later unleashed the *hounds of hell* when she went on to co-write the iconic novel Cult Fiction which was later made into an Oscar nominated movie starring the rapper Snoop Dogg and Brad Pittbull.

Marina moving so close had initially sent Peter into spasms of fear, until the Master reminded him of the old adage 'keep your friends close and your enemies closer'. That he had been requested to keep a keen eye upon Marina's comings and goings was a compliment to the extent of trust the pack had in Peter. The Master reiterated that he was aware that Marina had left the Government Agency researching Cultist Societies, but surely her job as Religious Studies Lecturer would touch upon the subject. To this end, Peter was told to keep a discreet eye upon Marina's paperwork and if necessary arrange for her telephone calls to be monitored. Peter had thought it prudent at this stage in the conversation to tell the Master of his intentions to be married to Tania, his transatlantic bride from the Ukraine. Peter half expected to be reminded that, although celibacy was not a pre-requisite of his membership, it was deemed to be an ideal state. But, to the contrary, the Master seemed pleased that Peter would have the foil of a wife who would hopefully prove of assistance to the cause. The Master must have pondered upon Peter's new proposed marital status, because later on during that day he telephoned to say that perhaps Tania could take a job as cleaner for Marina. Obviously Tania would be told the very basics and the fact that she would be given a key to Marina's house could only be looked upon as a bonus. Peter promised to give the idea some thought and to broach the subject to his new bride as soon as she took up residence upon the Crag.

PETERS' PROPOSAL

Many miles away in the Ukraine, Tania sat at the kitchen table in the small flat she shared with her mother and son. She was explaining that her pen friend Peter had proposed marriage to her. Turning to Nicolai she reminded him of her love and that no sacrifice would be too dear as to secure his future. She would go to England, the land of plenty, marry this rich man, and when she had settled she would send for her son and mother. Nicolai would have the opportunity to study in an English university and her mother would receive the medical intervention she needed to cure her chronic condition.

All three were in floods of tears as Tania outlined her plans. Half heartedly Nicolai tried to get his mother to change her mind but even as he spoke he knew his request would fall upon deaf ears. To lighten the mood Tania told the story of her friend at the cafe who had also been courting a man from England. This man she said claimed to be English but had not British citizenship although he owned a large department store in London. A mere shopkeeper, he had hinted to Tania's friend that his son was planning to romance a member of the .... Family, and when this became public upon her divorce his citizenship was guaranteed. Tania, her mother and Nicolai laughed at the silly man in England who expected a Ukrainian woman to believe such a foolish tale. Shrugging her shoulders, Tania said, 'Well, being married to English Peter Dodd and living in castle upon a hill must be better than wearing a head-square and selling apples on the corner of the street.'

At this they all burst into laughter again and toasted the future with the bottle of vodka they kept for very special occasions.

NOWHERE CASTLE – STRANGE GOINGS ON IN THE POTTING SHED

A surprisingly trim looking Lillian stood in a white bathrobe in the Countesses' quarters of the castle, flanked by her fellow comrades from the WTF. For once the ladies were silent. There was no jostling to be heard, no bragging about husband's exploits or grandchildren's university achievements. For once they were silenced, nudity creating an equal and common bond. Like a silent army of white robed soldiers about to enter no-man's land they stood clustered together. All bar one. Sooty stood at the doorway, chatting easily to the Earl and Countess. Sooty had noted the other ladies' discomfort and bore the sight with pleasure.

She remembered the time she had tried to join the WTF a few years ago and been snubbed simply because she had not been married. She recalled how she had argued that the rules did not state that one must be married to join. She had argued persistently, disregarding all barriers they had put in her way. She later learned that Lillian had been the main instigator of the protest. In fact, later on after she had successfully joined the WTF, Lillian had remarked that although the other ladies had no objection to how she lived her life surely there were special clubs that Sooty would perhaps be more comfortable joining. It amused Sooty to hear that Lillian had been recently trying to recruit Joey from the Bistro as the token Asian in the group.

Maggie's niece Yvonne had been very helpful with ideas for the calendar. Sooty had approached her and asked if she was willing to paint an oil painting for the cover. Sooty had visited Yvonne the previous evening to pore over art books and they had settled upon 'Le Bain Turc' by Ingres, an overtly voyeuristic image of a harem of naked women with homosexual overtones. They had decided to superimpose the faces of the ladies from the WTF upon the nude figures. They had both been in agreement that Lillian's face should be centre stage, her figure clasping at her companion's breast. Yvonne warmed to the theme immediately, since she had been at the sharp end of Lillian's tongue many a time when relaying messages from her boss George. People in glass houses should not throw bricks, and both Sooty and Yvonne had good reason to feel malevolent towards Lillian.

Sooty had adhered to Lillian's insistence that the photographer they hired not be male, but as a final nail in the coffin she had chosen the most outwardly butch lesbian photographer she knew. The androgynously named Toni strode confidently into the room to gasps of astonishment from the bath-robed ladies. Lillian being the exception because for reasons of vanity she had omitted to wear her spectacles, stating in a rare moment of jocularity to her husband George that she would be making enough of a spectacle of herself anyway appearing in the calendar. She nudged the lady to her right, saying, 'I thought Susan had agreed that we should hire a female photographer. I intend to exchange some very harsh words with her later.' She was hushed by Sooty crossing towards Toni to introduce her to the group.

'Ladies,' she said, 'I would like to introduce you to Toni, a very good friend of mine. Toni has kindly agreed to produce the photographs free of charge. Toni is an excellent photographer. I've explained the situation regarding nudity and she has come up with some great ideas to preserve our modesty. As the leader of our little group may I suggest that Lillian be first to ceremoniously drop the robe.'

At this the group giggled nervously, all thankful that they were not the first to be photographed. Lillian glowered in the direction of Sooty but, determined not the loose face in front of her peers, she nodded her assent.

'Lillian, if you would just follow me into the gardens, I have some ideas I need to run by you.' said the remarkably softly spoken Toni.

Focusing upon Toni's coat tails as a guide, Lillian did as requested. The Earl made to follow the duo outside but was stopped by an angry glare from his wife.

'Just wanted to check on the petunias my dear,' he spluttered. 'I suppose they can wait till later.' He shrugged, obviously disappointed.

Toni reappeared at the doorway, her slicked back black hair glistening in the sunlight from the window.

'Would you join us for a moment, Sooty? I just want to show you some scenarios I sketched out yesterday.'

Sooty left the room, followed by the Countess, to the obvious envy of her disgruntled husband.

'I thought we could follow through the floral gardening theme of the calendar,' said Toni.

'One of my friends is a bit of a culture vulture and he thought each monthly entry could have a poetic caption along the lines of 'oh my love's like a red, red rose, that's newly sprung in June.'

'I wandered lonely as a cloud amongst a host of golden daffodils,'' said Sooty, warming to the theme.

'Speaking of clouds,' said Toni, 'may I suggest we start in the potting shed as that lonely cloud overhead looks fit to burst.'

'It's yonder to the right of the greenhouses,' said the Countess, pointing into the distance.

Lillian, who had felt overlooked in the earlier discussion of poetry, promptly picked up two potted plants upon entering the shed.

'Gosh,' she said 'it's very bright and warm in here.'

The Countess raced in behind her and quickly turned off the bright lights and heaters.

'These are pretty green plants. I've never seen leaves quite like this before.'

She addressed her question directly to the Countess. Squinting at the lush leafy foliage emerging from the unglazed ceramic pots she continued, 'They really are most unusual. You must give me a cutting.'

Both Toni and Sooty stood back, clutching their sides to stop giggling.

The Countess snatched the pots from Lillian's grasp and deposited them in the depths of the shed.

'Sorry to snatch,' she said after registering the surprise on Lillian's face. 'They prefer the dark. They are rare tropical plants which my husband brought back from a field trip abroad.'

Toni and Sooty were still giggling like schoolgirls.

Toni eventually managed to spurt out, 'we had better not use those plants in the calendar. They could make a hash of the whole thing!'

At this Sooty guffawed so much she had to cross her legs.

'Please don't say anything else,' she pleaded with Toni, 'or I shall spliff my sides.'

'Well we are in the aptly named potting shed,' said the Countess, joining in the jocularity.

Lillian raised her eyes to the heavens before saying crossly 'I really don't understand what is so funny. Would you please let me in on the joke?'

Deciding to take control of the situation, the Countess placed two innocent looking plants in front of Lillian and handed her the gardening gloves and potting trowel.

'Just a suggestion,' she said to Toni 'perhaps the pots could protect Lillian's modesty.'

'An excellent idea" said Toni. Looking through her lens she motioned for Lillian to drop her towelling robe.

A very large heavy breasted Lillian emerged.

'Oh dear, I think we need considerably larger pots.' said a straight faced Countess.

LONELY HEART

Bob sat at desk browsing through the gay 'Pink' newspaper. It was a rare occasion when he had the house to himself in the afternoon and he decided to take full advantage of it. He had been tempted to dress more comfortably but after spending a good half an hour trying on Yvonne's new underwear he had deemed it too risky to apply makeup in case she surprised him by returning early. The chat with Rhonda when she had caught him wearing false nails had really spooked him. He just thanked the fact that Rhonda had been too preoccupied with her own problems regarding Clive to take too much notice of him.

Bob had recently purchased a blonde bobbed wig. It was hidden in the garden shed behind the electric drill and hammer saw. Just knowing it was there gave him a guilty thrill, but wearing it. My God, how good did that feel? Bob skipped the articles and focused on the lonely heart adverts at the back of the paper. Seeing so many made Bob feel slightly less alone.

MARINA'S NEW HOUSE
– LARKSPUR RISE

Whilst Bob was scouring his newspaper, his wife Yvonne was languishing over coffee at Marina's new house. The two had become firm friends very quickly and with Marina's baby due any day the two women were bonding even more. Marina, for the first time in her life, had found a female friend she could open up to, whose opinions she respected. Marina found Yvonne's lack of pretension refreshing. If she were honest with herself she would also admit that she relished the fact that Yvonne was not intellectually her equal. There was a certain Professor Higgins element to their blossoming friendship.

Yvonne played the role of Eliza with Oscar-winning precision. She hung on Marina's every word, soaking up the imparting of social knowledge like a sponge.

When Marina had commented that coloured loo paper was common, Yvonne had instructed Bob to only buy white in future. When Marina had visibly winced at Yvonne describing the front room as a lounge, Yvonne had quickly corrected her terminology, explaining later to a bemused Bob that 'lounges' were found in airports and hotels and not houses. When Bob described an evening meal as tea, Yvonne corrected him by saying that tea was served in the afternoon and dinner after six. Bob found these little nuances of Yvonne's exasperating but indulged his wife, realising that this new friendship lifted the post Clive malaise she had fallen into.

'Do you fancy another Nescaff?' enquired Marina, using another phrase that Yvonne decided to copy when she got home. It sounded so much cooler than asking if a guest wanted a coffee.

'I would love a one, but I should really be getting home. Bob will be back soon.' said Yvonne, instantly regretting her words as she saw the shadow of disapproval cross her new friend's face.

'Do you ever find yourself getting bored with just being a housewife?' enquired Marina.

She asked the question out of the blue and by the sheer unpredictability of it forced Yvonne to think very hard before answering.

'I suppose I do,' she replied eventually. 'If you mean am I sick of being old before my years, well, yes. Bob and I are always so hard up it makes treats out of the question, especially when there is the added cost of a babysitter to consider.'

'Well,' said Marina, clapping her hands at the thought. 'I can help you there. Let me babysit for the pair of you tonight. It will give me some practice for the arrival of this little package.' She patted her large rotund belly and was rewarded with a powerful kick.

'Ouch,' she said, taking Yvonne's hand and placing it on the bump. The baby obliged by kicking Yvonne's open palm.

'Wow,' said Yvonne, laughing, 'you have a regular little *goldenballs* in there.'

'Sorry?' said Marina quizzically.

It was becoming patently obvious to Yvonne that any reference to popular culture held no relevance for Marina. Yvonne tried to explain the joke but it was lost in translation. It appeared that the world of celebrity was as alien to Marina as her world of academia was to Yvonne. Later on that evening Yvonne sat at the bedroom mirror trying to work up the excitement a rare night out should convey but failed miserably. She tried to push to the back of her mind the nagging realisation that given the choice of small talk with Bob or a night chatting to Marina the latter won hands down. The woman had really got under her skin, broadening Yvonne's narrow horizons and liberating her from the chattels of domesticity. Yvonne had a belated wake-up call as to how complacent and comfortable her life had become.

OXFORD HOUSE, LONDON –
DOCTOR FINDLAY'S CASEBOOK

Martin Findlay, or Doctor Findlay as he was known professionally, stood before the vast doorway of Oxford House, the ....'s London residence. He had been summoned by the ...... himself. Apparently Oliver, the .... younger son, had been struggling with a nasty chest infection for over a week. The antibiotics prescribed by the usual Harley Street physician the family visited had seemed to do the trick, but the ...... was still concerned.

Martin was an old chum of the ......, from his school days in Gordonstoun. Many a beau had been impressed by the fact that Martin had mixed in such elitist circles, albeit at such an early age. His last lover, Marina, had been especially enthralled by his boyhood tales of camaraderie, forever pressing him for more information and taking his reluctance as a refreshing lack of pretension. He felt a coolness pervade their relationship when she realised that he and the .... were alas only childhood pals and invitations to garden parties at the Palace would not be forthcoming.

That he and Marina were no longer together saddened him, especially as she had been pregnant when she had abandoned the home they shared. A silly argument had caused him to spend a few days at his parent's house and when he had returned to talk through the problems he discovered that she had gone. It was as if they had never been. Nothing remained, and Martin had no forwarding address to make good the quarrel. This child, his child, was growing daily within the womb of the woman he had loved and would probably never know its father. He had tried to find Marina but her friends had closed ranks. God knows what Marina had told them about their altercation because he had become a social pariah, an outcast. Doors which had previously been open and welcome were firmly closed. That the ..... had contacted him personally surprised Martin. Obviously the news of his tattered reputation had yet to reach the ....'s ears.

Suddenly the double doors swung open and a young butler enquired as to the nature of his visit. When Martin explained he was a doctor making a pre-arranged house call, the butler dipped his head and motioned for Martin to enter.

'The .... is in the drawing room doctor. I believe his is expecting you. Please be so good as to follow me'

Martin struggled to keep up as the butler strode purposefully towards a door at the end of a rather grand corridor. Given a choice, Martin would have dawdled and given himself a chance to take in the opulent surroundings. Glancing quickly as he was ushered into the partially lit room, Martin noted the oil paintings in heavy gilt frames. Martin's father had a print of one of the oil paintings he saw above the door frame. Even under hasty inspection Martin could see this painting was an original Stubbs. My God, how the other half lives, he thought to himself. Many an avid collector would give their eye teeth for such a canvas and there it was, displayed on an inconspicuous wall, badly lit and slightly askew.

Martin entered the room to the dulcet tones of the Three Degrees. The ..... got up from his seat at the far end of the room and hurried across to shake Martin's hand.

'My good fellow,' he said, 'long time no see.'

'It must be a good thirty years,' said Martin nonchalantly.

'Is it really that long?' said the .....

'Must be thereabouts,' replied Martin with a shrug, although he knew almost to a month how long it had been. The ....'s total disregard for their schoolboy friendship had irked Martin for a long time. But, as his father had pointed out at the time, Martin was only at Gordonstoun thanks to a very generous scholarship. It was hardly surprising, given their totally different backgrounds that the friendship had withered and died when the boys went their separate ways. Although Martin had achieved so much, fulfilling his wildest dreams to become a Harley Street practitioner, he would never be the ....'s social equal. Breeding will out.

'You look well, Tricky Dicky,' said the ......, reverting back to Martin's nickname from school.

'And you, Nellie,' replied Martin in turn. The ....'s elephantine ears had been a great source of teasing at Gordonstoun. Such is the cruelty of little boys. This was from the days when bullying was taken as a part of school life and referred to as character-forming. Well, by the ....'s father anyway, who was a great advocate of 'spare the rod, spoil the child'.

'Harley Street obviously agrees with you.'

'It does,' replied Martin. 'I must confess to being surprised at hearing from you after all these years. I always understood that your family used a neighbour of mine, Dr Kildare, for your medical needs.'

'We do, but this matter is of a delicate nature, and I felt he was too close to certain aides to be able to assist confidentially.'

'Delicate?' repeated Martin. 'Ahha.'

He had been a doctor long enough to understand the terminology used for problems occurring down below. Martin sat down and opened his briefcase. He proceeded to take out his stethoscope.

Taking the ....'s silence for embarrassment, he continued. 'If you could just drop your trousers for me, I'll take a quick look. We'll see if the problem is physical before moving on to other possible causes.'

The .... let out a loud guffaw. 'Wrong end of the stick completely, my good fellow. I've no problem rising to any occasion. My crown jewels are in perfect working order.'

Martin looked confused.

'The problem, as such, concerns my youngest son, Oliver.'

'So the story regarding the chest infection is true?' said Martin. He was still terribly confused.

The ...... looked guarded. 'Well no, not as such,' he said. 'That was just a smoke screen to get my wife to agree to Oliver seeing another doctor. What I am asking isn't strictly ethical but I am sure in my shoes any man would do likewise.'

'Carry on.'

'Well it has been brought to my attention that my wife was having a dalliance at the time of Oliver's conception.'

'And?'

'The chap in question had distinctive red hair and freckles.'

'I understand,' said Martin, and he did. Much had been made of the fact at the time by the gutter press.

'So what exactly would you like me to do?'

'I would like you to give Oliver a DNA test under the pretext of taking bloods regarding his ongoing chest infection.'

Martin was quiet for a while he had to weigh this up.

'This is most unethical without the mother's permission. If it were to get out I would risk being struck off.'

'I'm aware of the risks, but I assure you they are minimal. Also may I add that the rewards will far outweigh them.'

'Rewards?' said Martin.

'Well, as you know, Dr Kildare is retiring later this year and the family are looking for a new younger physician.'

'I would be happier to be chosen for my medical merits,' said Martin.

'Still as idealistic as ever,' said the ....

'Idealistic yes, but also realistic,' said Martin realising this was his probably his only chance to climb the slippery pole.

'Thank-you,' said the .... 'My wife is waiting with Oliver in the bedroom. Be gentle the poor little chap is very afraid of needles.'

'I've been told my bedside manner is second to none,' said Martin, smiling.

'So is mine,' said the ....'But I'm not one to brag.'

At this the men both laughed.

'I'll need to take your bloods as well,' said Martin to the ......

The ...... took of his jacket and rolled up his shirt sleeve. 'Don't worry,' he joked, 'It's not really blue, just bog-standard red.'

The Three Degrees played on in the background, the strains of their biggest hit resounding around the room.

'When will I see you again?' said the .... inadvertently echoing the song playing on the tape deck.

'Should be a couple of days,' said Martin, pressing cotton wool onto the crook of the ......'s arm then applying a plaster so the blood did not soak through onto his shirt.

'I'll make an appointment to call as soon as I have the results. May I ask what will happen if Oliver is the fruit of this chap's loins?'

'Nothing at all,' said the ...., going up immediately in Martin's estimation. 'He will still be my son, and my love for him will not alter a jot. The information will merely be a bargaining tool for when I divorce my darling wife. It will never go public and there will be no record of it ever taking place. The information will just ensure that the settlement is fair and the bloody woman disappears off abroad with this latest chap of hers.'

'I understand,' said Martin.

'May I add this conversation never took place? We are merely two old school friends getting reacquainted.'

'Friends reunited,' said the ......, firmly shaking Martin's hand.

Sorell the butler jumped from the doorway as he heard the ...... cross the room.

Taking a duster from his jacket pocket he lifted an ornate silver candlestick from the console table in the hall and began to polish it. He feigned surprise at hearing the .... call his name.

'Yes, sir?' he said carefully replacing the candlestick and shaking the duster.

'Would you please take the doctor to Oliver's bedroom, I believe my wife is sitting in whilst the doctor takes bloods so if you could inform her that he is here I would be most grateful.'

'Yes sir, with haste, sir.' said Sorell in his most ingratiating voice. 'If you would care to follow me, Dr Findlay.'

As Martin followed him up the stairs Sorell allowed himself a little smirk. Whoever said that eavesdropping was wrong? Sorell had no intention of imparting this little gem to his mistress. Nothing would be gained in a monetary sense. No, it was far better to sit tight. The outcome regarding his lucrative book deal was looking better by the minute. The .... should really heed the old adage that walls have ears. Sorell had heard the entire conversation, and would transcribe it into his diary the first chance he had.

NOWHERE HIGH SCHOOL

Sooty was at work overseeing an exam, a mock exam but an exam nonetheless. She sat at her desk surveying a sea of bowed heads. Occasionally a giggle or whisper would erupt from a section of the room. Sooty would clear her throat, glare in the direction of the sound and it would stop immediately.

As headmistress she was often called upon to invigilate. The peace and quiet gave her an excellent opportunity to put some plans into motion. She had an excellent surprise lined up for Louisa, and now it just remained for her to make sure Louisa would be able to join her the following morning.

Saturday 4am

'When you said early, I initially thought you meant six o'clock,' declared a sleepy Louisa as she clambered into Sooty's car the next morning.

'You forget for an insomniac like me this is a normal morning start,' said Sooty apologetically.

'So are you going to tell me where we are going?' said Louisa trying and failing to stifle a yawn.

'My lips are sealed, but I promise to make a clean breast of it when we get closer to our destination.'

'Go on, just a little hint?' pleaded Louisa.

'Let's just say I'm helping out an old friend,' Sooty replied cryptically.

Sooty drove out of Nowhere and onto the main arterial road linking England to Scotland. They drove in silence for a while before Sooty let out an exasperated sigh.

'Bloody hell,' she snarled, 'That Mini has been driving up my backside for the last few miles and now the stupid bugger is trying to overtake!'

Louisa turned and glared at the driver of the Mini. She and her passenger were close enough to be seen quite clearly as dawn was breaking. The driver of the Mini waved her hand, gesturing for Sooty to pull over so she could pass safely.

'She's going to get a gesture of a different kind from me in a minute if she doesn't back off a bit.'

'We'll be ok in a few miles,' said Louisa trying to placate her girlfriend. 'The road becomes a dual carriageway soon, look, there's the sign.'

'I'm fine.' said Sooty. 'I just hate feeling harassed and this is a really bad stretch of road for accidents.'

Both ladies breathed a sigh of relief as the road changed to double lanes and the Mini once again indicated to overtake. Sooty glared at the car as it passed then smiled and let out a whoop as she recognised the girl in the passenger seat.

'Oh my giddy aunt,' she said. 'That's Maggie's niece Yvonne in that mad woman's car! Bet her husband would have something to say about her reckless driving companion. Bob's a taxi driver you know.'

'I thought I recognised her,' said Louisa. 'She works for Mr Johnson, the antique man, doesn't she?'

'Well put, my darling,' said Sooty, grinning. 'He certainly is an antique man. And don't start me off on his dreadful nouveau riche wife Lillian. She has made my life hell at the WTF for many a year now.'

Meanwhile, in the Mini, Yvonne was operating invisible pedals on the passenger side of the car. She kept inadvertently braking and was gripping the edge of her seat so tightly she could feel her fingers going numb. Memo to self, she thought, next time Marina offers to drive, decline and insist on driving myself.

'You're quiet,' said Marina, breaking her reverie. 'Not having second thoughts?

'No, of course not.' lied Yvonne.

The white knuckle drive had pre-occupied her thoughts for the last half an hour but the thing she was about to do still niggled and terrified her. Nevertheless, she trusted her new-found friend and would follow her lemming-like anywhere. If Marina thought this would be a fun adventure then so be it.

Life, said Marina, is all about doing things that scare you.

What Bob would make of this latest adventure Yvonne could only imagine. She could already picture his pursed lips and words of discouragement. As they approached the city quayside Yvonne could see in the distance a crowd of pink bodies. An armadillo-like construction lay in front of them, glinting in the early morning sun. Marina drove at break-neck speed into one of the last remaining parking spaces to the side of the building. The river shimmered in the distance to their left and a newly built bridge, dwarfed by its larger cousin, winked its flashing eye at them.

The quayside had undergone a vast redevelopment programme during the last few years in a desperate bid to grasp the title of European City of Culture. Despite its failure to win, it maintained its fresh innovative outlook and the quayside now boasted an excellent Music Auditorium and modern Art Gallery. The Gallery which was housed in the once derelict but now super trendy flour mill had assigned Toni as its first resident artist. Toni specialised in huge photomontages in which she would strive to make the most ordinary things look extraordinary and, conversely, the most extraordinary ordinary. The idea for this morning's venture had come upon her when she was taking the photographs for the WTF calendar. It had struck her how much more titillating a teasing glimpse of flesh was. The illusion of what lay behind or beneath being the best aphrodisiac. Full frontal nudity somehow took away the mystery as the eye had a tendency to focus only on the taboo areas. From this observation she conceived the idea of a mass of nudes becoming a series of surfaces devoid of individual sexuality.

'Ok sweetie, it's now or never,' said an animated Marina.

'It's a bit chilly,' said Yvonne, grasping at the flimsiest of excuses to remain fully clothed. She was still dithering when she felt a hand grip her shoulder. Yvonne was shocked to find Sooty standing behind her. The girl from the Bistro was standing by her side and they were both stark naked. Yvonne averted her eyes.

Both women were grinning incessantly, apparently at ease in their state of undress. Yvonne was desperately trying to keep her eyes from focusing upon Sooty's pendulous breasts and forest of greying pubic hair but it was proving impossible to keep the shake from her voice. Thankfully the ever confident Sooty took control of the conversation.

'Well, well, my dear,' said Sooty. 'This is something of a surprise, although I confess that when you overtook us earlier on the A1 I was curious as to where you would be going at this ungodly hour.'

Yvonne continued to stand, mouth agape, but Marina leapt to her rescue. To add to Yvonne's further discomfort, whilst this verbal exchange was taking place Marina had also seen fit to shed her clothes. As all eyes focused on Marina's bump it was as if the baby inside sensed the occasion and began to turn somersaults.

'Wow, that is amazing,' said Sooty. 'May I?' she continued, pointing towards Marinas undulating bump to enquire if it was alright to place her hand upon it.

Marina nodded her assent saying, 'I decided why not be photographed nude and pregnant, it may take some of the mystery out of the whole birth mother thing. I must admit I feel quite empowered and junior here is thoroughly enjoying the whole experience.

'There were posters all over the University asking for volunteers,' she continued.

'But I am surprised it reached the distant shores of Nowhere.'

'Actually, Toni, the photographer, is a personal friend of mine. She did the shoot for the calendar that Yvonne so kindly painted the front piece for.'

At this statement Yvonne found her voice, 'I'm really looking forward to meeting her at last,' she said.

'I promise to introduce you the minute I have the chance,' said Sooty. The ageing *lothario* in her could not resist adding, 'I must add that being surrounded by such a bevy of beautiful naked women makes getting up so early on a Sunday morning almost a pleasure.'

Louisa smiled at Yvonne. She seemed to sense her discomfort, a fact that the other two were blissfully unaware of.

'Hi,' said Louisa with her hand outstretched to shake Yvonne's. 'I'm Louisa from the Bistro. It's so nice to meet you at last.'

'Lovely to meet you too,' said Yvonne, reflecting on how bizarre it was to be sharing social niceties with a nude stranger.

Looking around her and seeing naked bodies of every shape and size, Yvonne felt almost embarrassed by the fact that she was the only person dressed. It was the urge to conform and seem less conspicuous that encouraged her to climb into the Mini to undress. No mean feat in such a confined space. Why she felt the need to hide away to undress was something Marina and she would laugh about later in the day.

'I think we need to go and pose in front of the new Gallery,' said Sooty, catching the tail end of the commentary on the loudspeaker.

'How do you feel? Are you ok?' enquired Marina to Yvonne as the other two ladies strode ahead in a confident manner.

'I'm not sure yet how I feel,' said Yvonne. She was struggling to find the words to describe how she felt. 'I feel free from the shackles of domesticity,' she said eventually.

Marina laughed. 'Me too,' she said. 'Very eloquently put, Yvonne.' Marina grabbed Yvonne's hand and together they edged closer and closer towards the pool of naked flesh. A hush fell over the quayside as Toni emerged from the confines of the old Flour Mill. Grasping the microphone, she stood silhouetted against the Art Gallery, the buckles from the braces she wore reflecting the early morning sunshine.

'This will be my most innovative photomontage ever,' she said to the now silent crowd. 'It just falls to me to thank you all from the bottom of my heart for agreeing to leave the comfort of your beds at such an early hour. It proves that despite its many critics, art still plays an important part in our culture. Long live art and originality!'

The crowd cheered at this rallying cry. Toni paused until the cheering had died down.

'I've also just had news from the Guinness Book of Records that we have entered the record books as the largest number of assembled nudes'

Again a cheer erupted from the crowd.

'The naked body is a thing of diverse beauty and there is a fine line between art and pornography. I promise I shall not cross this line. My photographs will not focus on genitals but on shape, light and shade. May I ask that you all lie down on the ground starfish fashion on your backs with your fingertips and toes touching those of your neighbours?'

Sooty turned to Louisa and grinned. Pointing to the glass armadillo building in the distance she said 'Come on let's go and lie on the grass verge, I'm sure it will be warmer than the concrete.'

MOVING DAY

It was very hectic at 12 Fanny Street, Saltaire. Moving days were by nature stressful and this one was proving to be no exception. This was despite the fact that Tracey was remarkably organised. She had colour coded each box to match the room it was to be placed in. But nevertheless the removal men were having a busy morning of it and even endless cups of tea were doing little to tap into their fast diminishing energy reserves. They were climbing the stairs more slowly and placing boxes more precariously in their haste to get the job done. It was time for a well-earned break, Lennie decided.

'I think I should pop out for some fish and chips,' said Lennie. 'Man cannot exist on cups of tea alone.' Lennie had travelled from her bungalow by the beach the previous evening. She wanted to be proactive and help her lover to move into their future home together.

'Your friend sure has a lot of possessions,' the removal men had remarked to Lennie more than once that afternoon.

'What's in this box, a ton of bricks?' intoned his friend. 'More books than bloody Bradford Library in this box.'

'More bloody clothes than Top Shop in this. Opening a boutique is she?'

Sitting in the yard smoking their rollups and munching fish and chips from yesterday's newspapers, they seemed to regain their even temperaments.

'Nice gaff, this.' said one of the men to his workmate.

'Never fancied an old house myself, too much bloody hard work.'

'Me neither, but for an old house it is in pretty good nick.'

'Aye, this yard's a bit of a suntrap too,' said his workmate, stretching back on his chair to soak up the early afternoon sunshine. The removal men were just bringing in the last of the boxes as Tracey welcomed her first visitor. A tall elegant woman strode purposefully into the house as if she owned the place. Lennie knew even before they were introduced this was Sandra, Tracey's ex partner.

Sandra seemed to fill the room with her large personality. She sat down on one of the unopened boxes, confidently crossed her legs and stared at Lennie. Tracey seemed flustered, and a look passed between her and Sandra that was like a dagger through Lennie's heart. Lennie knew then. She knew that they were still lovers and that Sandra had planned that she would know. The question now was how to handle it. A confrontation was out of the question and so undignified. Not Lennie's style, although she imagined that Sandra would relish the chance to fight her corner. This made Lennie even more determined not to give her the satisfaction. The deathly silence was interrupted by the removal men coming through into the lounge to announce that they were leaving and asking if Lennie would please move her car as it was blocking their exit. Grasping the opportunity, Lennie grabbed her handbag, hastily said goodbye to Tracey and made to leave. Tracey seemed about to say something but stopped and averted her eyes.

'I'll ring you later tonight, sweetheart,' she said eventually to Lennie's departing back.

Lennie turned and with a voice that was biting back the tears said, 'Ok, speak later darling. Sorry I have to rush off.'

Driving home, Lennie couldn't resist replaying the scene back in her mind. She rewound it so often she was exhausted. She wrung the emotional sponge until it was bone dry. For a while she managed to convince herself that she had perhaps imagined the whole thing. Nothing had actually been said and perhaps by falling victim to her own jealousy she had played into Sandra's hands. Was this all an elaborate mind game of Sandra's to lure Tracey back into her bed? Was Tracey in fact the innocent pawn, tried and convicted without a hearing? Lennie decided to reserve her judgement until she had the chance to speak properly to Tracey.

OXFORD HOUSE

Martin stood at the now familiar doorway to Oxford House. The blood test results were back from the lab and he had been summoned once more by the .... Sorell the butler once again greeted his entrance but showed no signs of recognition. Martin felt frustrated at having to explain to this young upstart the nature of his business with the ....

'I shall see if the ...... is free to speak to you,' said the haughty Sorell.

'He is expecting me,' reiterated Martin.

'Indeed,' said Sorell, in a disbelieving voice. 'If you care to take a seat, I shall announce your arrival.'

It was at that moment that the ...... made an appearance at the head of the sweeping staircase. Smiling, he approached Martin.

'Martin,' he said. 'I trust you have not been waiting long?'

Turning to Sorell he snapped in an exasperated tone, 'Sorell, I told you I was expecting another visit from my old friend Martin.'

Sorell stood defiantly and replied, 'I am sorry sir it must have slipped my mind. My most humble apologies.'

Bowing in a servile manner, he retreated to the servants' quarters.

'Come, come,' said the ..... to Martin and ushered him once again into his office.

'I must say that Sorell is an annoying ingratiating little man but my wife holds him in such high esteem. If I had my way I would give bloody Uriah Heep his marching orders but she insists he is her rock. I only wish he would crawl back under the bloody rock.'

The ...... laughed at his own little joke.

'Anyway onto matters in hand. Thank you for visiting me in person. I am glad you understand the sensitivity of my request.'

'But of course,' said Martin. 'Is it safe to talk?'

The .... nodded. 'Yes, my wife is out overseeing the boys' riding lessons. Did you know that nasty little red haired man was teaching my eldest son to mount horses whilst he was mounting their darling mother?'

Martin was at a loss as what to reply to this sudden outburst from the ....

'Sorry, sorry,' said the ...... after he had composed himself.

'It's just her bloody liaisons are a becoming a major embarrassment to the family. The sooner this can be sorted out financially the better, and hopefully my trump card lies in your briefcase.'

Taking this as his cue, Martin delved into his briefcase and extracted the lab results. Affording them the reverence they deserved he carefully handed them to the ....

The .... crossed the room, sat at the large oak desk and, retrieving his glasses from his jacket pocket, carefully began to read through the notes. He was silent and obviously deep in thought.

Eventually he said, 'Well I can't say I'm terribly surprised, I suppose I always knew. The ginger hair was a bit of a give-away, but it's a shock nonetheless.'

'I'm just sorry to be the bearer of bad news,' said Martin.

'Mixed bag, really, old chap,' said the ...... 'My father will be thrilled as less of the blasted inheritance goes to my wife, but my mother, if and when I tell her, will be devastated, although scandals such as these have rocked the house of .... for generations. I only hope that once this whole sorry episode is put to bed my soon-to-be-ex-wife chooses more loyal conquests.'

'I think a drink is in order,' said the ...... 'Let me summon Uriah, give the little creep something to do for a change.'

'A drink would be most welcome,' said Martin, grateful for the improvement in the .... mood.

The .... pressed a bell discreetly hidden behind a vast sweep of velvet curtain. Just like last time Sorell appeared almost immediately at the study door. Surely it must have taken more time than that to come through the hall from the servants' quarters, thought Martin, but kept this thought to himself as the .... seemed blissfully unaware of the timescale.

When Sorell had left with instructions to fetch the best oak-aged whisky and two crystal tumblers the ...... continued.

'I have information for you too Martin,' said the ..... as he reached into his desk drawer. He extracted a rather innocuous sheet of paper with a name and address handwritten on it.

This time it was Martin's turn to sit down and compose his thoughts. His face was ashen.

'How did you know?' he said eventually.

'It's my people's job to know,' said the ...... 'anyone who comes into contact with the family, however minor their role, is thoroughly researched by our security chappies.'

'But,' said Martin hesitantly, 'I've explored every avenue to find this information.'

'I have no doubt you have,' said the ......, 'but avenues which are closed to you are open to my people.'

'Ah, at last,' he said as Sorell entered the office carrying a perfectly balanced silver plated tray.

'Just savour the taste of this whisky; it's so much nicer than that cider stuff we drank at Gordonstoun.'

Martin was slightly the worse for wear when he eventually left the ......'s company. The whisky had been of the very best quality and Martin was not used to drinking so early in the afternoon. As he staggered down the driveway temporarily disorientated by the blazing sun, he protectively patted the piece of paper secreted in the breast pocket of his jacket. This information, this address, would hopefully be his passage into active parenthood. His child would get a chance to know his father. Perhaps Marina and he would have a chance to parent together. Hormones were funny things and her actions although hurtful could be explained away by her progressive pregnancy. Smiling to himself he reminded himself that the news that he was to be the official .... medic would probably sway Marina into his arms post-haste anyway. Her desire to climb the social ladder would easily outweigh her need for independence. Of this Martin had little doubt. All in all it had been a very unusual but hopefully productive day.

NOWHERE CRAG – DOING A DELIA

Upon the Crag, Peter was a very busy man. He had been awake at the crack of dawn preparing the house for the imminent arrival of his future bride. Peter was not a natural host. He had lived hermit like in the Folly for many years so it desperately needed a spring clean and de-clutter. Peter had vacuumed and dusted for the better part of the morning then spent a good hour traipsing up and down the aisles at the local supermarket. The kitchen larder heaved with the weight of the tins, dried pulses and fresh vegetables which he had purchased for his future wife to create meals with. A solitary recipe book lay still in its plastic sleeve upon the work surface. Peter was a man of Catholic taste in all things. He liked his food served as he believed God intended; untainted by herbs and spices. Afraid that his bride to be would see fit to prepare his meals laced with flavourings, he had gone to the precaution of buying a simple book of recipes for classic English food. His intention was to present this to Tania upon her arrival at the house. It was to be a combined welcome and wedding gift. It appeared that Peter's love of frugality stretched to all things even the gifting of presents.

Peter had cleared out two drawers in the bedroom for Tania's possessions and the large wooden cross above the bed had been polished and repositioned. The sheets of starched white linen and the counterpane had been tucked tightly into the corners. The wardrobe which held Peter's special clothes had been firmly locked as it was out of bounds to his new bride. The key to the elaborate lock hung on a chain around his neck. All was ready for the arrival of Tania.

It was not without a modicum of apprehension that Peter sat staring at the hands of the clock. It would soon be time for him to leave the Crag and collect his bride to be from the airport. Peter had flirted with the idea of sending Bob the taxi to collect Tania but knowing of his love of gossip he decided to use a day's leave and meet her himself. Peter had no doubt that Tania's presence would forever alter the equilibrium of his life but he was reassured by the thought that even following his proposal of marriage the Ukrainian woman had not issued forth with foolish words of endearment. This was a purely business arrangement from both sides. Purely business but hopefully mutually beneficial.

KIEV, UKRAINE – LEAVING ON A JET PLANE

Many miles away in the Ukraine Tania sat on the hard wooden bench in the Departure Lounge of the Airport. Her weather-beaten brown faux leather case had been handed into the Admissions Desk and she sat nursing a small maroon holdall.

Raising her hand to her cheek she touched the spot where Nicolai and her mother had tenderly kissed her earlier that morning. Nicolai had been bravely holding back the tears for fear of upsetting her but his eyes were swollen and bloodshot. Tania's mother had no such inhibitions and wept so loudly that people in the airport had turned to stare.

Tania's reverie was broken by an announcement to say that her flight was ready to board. Climbing aboard the aeroplane she turned to look back at the Airport Terminal. She convinced herself she could see Nicolai and her mother upon the roof terrace waving frantically. She wished it was them but it was such a distance that it could have been anyone. Tania clasped her hands together in silent prayer as the plane careered across the tarmac gaining the necessary speed for takeoff. She was absolutely petrified as she had never flown before. The island of England seemed so far away from the Ukraine. In Nicolai's school atlas the two countries had been pages apart.

THE FOLLY ON THE CRAG

A very very long time later Tania sat in the kitchen of Peter's Folly upon the Crag. Her introduction to England had been under the cloak of darkness. Her bags had been unceremoniously dumped upon the future marital bed as Peter gave Tania a quick tour of her new home. It was such a tiny house that the tour, such as it was, did not take long. Although it was not particularly cold, Tania shivered. The house had a bad vibe, it lacked warmth. Telling herself that it merely lacked a woman's touch Tania decided to set about preparing an evening meal for her betrothed.

Peter had left soon after she arrived, saying he had urgent Police business to attend to. He had rattled off a list of things that Tania must remember to do before lighting the rather temperamental stove. Ever since he had left Tania had sat sobbing. She sobbed for the better part of an hour before telling herself to buck up. English Peter Dodd had not chosen to marry an old weeping woman, a *Baba Yaga*. No to the contrary, he had chosen her to be his bride after seeing her all dressed up in the photograph at the wedding. Her arrival probably felt as strange to him as it did to her. After all the man was a confirmed bachelor, set in his ways, no doubt he felt uncomfortable at having a strange foreign woman in his home and kitchen. Her feelings probably echoed his own.

Opening a kitchen drawer, she searched for the kitchen utensils she needed for the English meal described in the book. Before he had left Peter had handed her a plastic bag containing the recipe book and instructed her to do a Delia. Tania had to confess she had no idea what the strange word meant, she was sure she had never came across it in any of her advanced English classes. The book was entitled 'How to boil and egg' which insulted Tania's intelligence. Did English Peter Dodd assume that Ukrainian women were so stupid they did not even know how to boil an egg. She would show him. If English Peter Dodd wanted a classic English meal than a classic English meal he would have.

NOWHERE CASTLE – THE EARL'S PRIVATE QUARTERS

'My bride to be has arrived from the Deepest Russia' whispered Peter to his old and trusted friend the Earl.

'From Russia with love,' joked the Earl humming the theme tune to the Bond movie. 'Let's try and 'finish' the game early so that you get home to join your intended.'

Peter had arrived at the Castle a few hours earlier. This was the urgent Police business he had told Tania he must attend to. The Earl had invited him to sit in on a game of poker with a few of his more well-heeled friends. The aptly named Smoking Room was now filled with the fug of cigar fumes. Peter had taken a dive early on in the game to lull his fellow players into a sense of false security. But the Earl knew from way back when he and Peter had been in the Coldstream Guards together that Peter was playing the long game. The trick was to turn from a losing strategy to a winning one without the others guessing. Peter was a former professional gambler. In the old days he had been nicknamed Lucky, a play of words on his surname. Although if his fellow poker players knew his true identity they would say that since that November in 1974 he was still Lucky, lucky to be a free man.

'Well, well my good fellow, I never thought I would see the day when you would take the plunge again.'

The Earl spoke quietly to his friend out of earshot of the other men. They had retreated to the far corner of the room to pour brandies for the assembled group.

'I would not have contemplated this had she been English, but being Ukrainian her grasp of English history is very scant. Nevertheless, I shall be careful.'

'I have no doubt of that,' said the Earl.

'Now tell me do you intend to leave these chaps with a little dignity, or are you planning to strip them of all their assets?'

'I intend to leave them with the shirts on their backs,' said Peter, laughing, 'I'm not quite so malevolent.'

NOWHERE HIGH STREET – THE WAR CRY

Aunt Maggie was delivering copies of the 'War Cry' to the local bars and restaurants on the main street of Nowhere. Dressed in her Sally Army garb, she was a familiar figure on the streets of Nowhere once again.

Time was a great healer and her feelings of paranoia had diminished slightly. She no longer let the phone ring incessantly on the hook while sitting shaking on the sofa afraid to pick up the receiver. Saying that she still peered through her net curtains before opening the front door but no longer felt the need to switch off the lights before doing so. The rocky road to recovery had been a steep one but she felt as if she was reaching the end of it.

Her good friend Flo had offered to help her deliver the latest copies of the 'War Cry' but had called off at the last moment as her 'piles' were playing up again. Maggie had been tempted to leave the task until her friend could escort her but a sense of bravado had taken a hold. Everyone she had encountered had greeted her as a long-lost friend and the coffers of her collection box were bulging. Such was her sense of wellbeing she did not notice a shifty figure sitting quietly in a dark corner of the Brits bar.

Robbie sat hunched over a flat pint of beer which had long since lost its effervescent sparkle. His bird had dumped him for some other Johnny-go-lately with cash to burn and a flashy car. Robbie felt mean and bitter. As bitter as the drink sitting before him.

Clive, the publican of the Brits, rang the bell above the bar to call time.

'Don't panic,' he joked, 'plenty of drinking time left, but the bar is officially closed.'

The regulars laughed at Clive's feeble joke. This was always a good move if a lock-in was on the cards. Clive enjoyed playing to a receptive audience.

'I would like you all to join me in saying how great it is to see our Aunt Sally back on the streets,' he said, raising his glass in Maggie's direction.

'Put your hands deep in your pockets, you bunch of heathens!' he urged before calling across to Maggie, 'usual sweet sherry, is it, Maggie?'

Much later, fuelled by numerous glasses of sweet sherry, Maggie staggered out of the bar and onto the high street. She was followed a few minutes later by a furtive Robbie. Seeing her struggling to carry the collection tin, Robbie had decided to offer to help her carry it, take it from her hands so to speak. With the money in the tin he could probably charm his bird back into his bed. It would be goodbye Johnny-go-lately, welcome back Robbie.

Robbie followed at a distance, chuckling to himself at how easy this would be. It would be like taking candy from a baby, albeit an old frail baby in a weird costume but a baby nonetheless. He planned to wait until they were on a quiet side street before making his move. Maggie staggered up the high street, stumbling over the cobbles, the bright lights from the local playhouse illuminating her briefly as she passed by. Robbie paced himself, so confident was he of catching his prey that he even stopped under a lamp post to light a cigarette. A stray dog sidled up to him and Robbie, thinking it was planning to cock-up its leg against the streetlight, aimed a clumsy kick at its ribs.

The dog yelped and Maggie upon hearing the commotion stopped in her tracks and turned to look behind her. Robbie shifted quickly from the glaring streetlight but he could see from the change in Maggie's gait that she had spotted and possibly recognised him. She scurried off, obviously agitated. Robbie cursed the stupid 'bloody' mutt but decided to follow through his plan regardless. As he had proved in the past, the old lady was no match for him. In a way a chase gave him more of a thrill, it would get him in a good mood for visiting his bird later that night.

Maggie half stumbled half ran towards the corner of the street and the main crossroads. A monument to the First World War stood in the centre where the four roads met and it partially obscured the view of traffic approaching from the right. Maggie was so blinded by fear she ran headlong onto the road. She turned rabbit like, staring into the headlights of an approaching car, suddenly deafened by a loud screeching of brakes. They were the last sound she was to hear. The blinding headlights the last sight she was to see.

Jasper the dog, limping from the kick in his ribs was tangled up by his trailing lead in a bush by the side of the road. Liz was frantically searching for him. She had been entrusted to walk him because Louisa and Joey were hosting a late night party at the Bistro. Jaspers lead had slipped from her grasp almost as soon as they left the house. She had now been scouring the streets calling out his name for the better part of an hour. My god she thought how would she explain this to her new friends. They would probably evict her from the flat and sack her from her part time job. Both girls were hopelessly devoted to the dog; their surrogate child. She was just about to give up and go back and confess to having lost Jasper, when she heard a squeal of brakes around the corner and ran to investigate the noise.

As she ran she desperately hoped that Jasper had not been the cause of some terrible accident. The scene which greeted her was an empty car. Its drivers' door wide open, the engine running and the headlights blazing. An old woman lay sprawled behind the car, a pool of blood seeping from her head. A figure crouched over her prising a tin from her clenched fist. In her peripheral vision Liz sensed a man running down the street towards the Castle, his unusual gait evoking a sense of panic.

Peter had had a few too many brandies at the Castle. He really should have left his car, called a taxi and collected it the next morning. But the Earls' friends had become hostile as he hit his winning streak and he did not want to hang about in case things turned nasty. It was a quiet night, it was very late and there were no other cars about. Peter was belligerent; brandy often had this effect upon him. The Earl recognising this had suggested he cut and run.

As he drove through the Castle gates towards the crossroads he wondered what culinary delights his Ukranian Delia had prepared for their first supper together. Drinking heavily always gave him a massive appetite.

Maggie was under the wheels of car before he had even realised that she had stepped onto the road. He felt his wheels rise and dip as they struck her body. He drove on a few moments before stopping the car. He sat a few minutes before climbing out and apprehensively looking behind the car. An old lady lay crumpled on the roadside, the tarmac a dark red beneath her askew hat. Robbie was clearly recognisable as he crouched over the body prising a tin can from her grasp. Peter ducked out of view before the boy could see him, then with an agility which had served him well many years before he sprinted past the scene of the accident and back towards the Castle gates. A dog tangled up in the bushes snapped at his ankles as he raced by.

NOWHERE CASTLE – THE EARL HATCHES A PLAN

The Earl upon sensing his friends' deranged state quickly stopped the game of cards and ushered his guests away with a promise of a further game the following night. In their drunken states they were unaware that Peter had even left the Castle and refused to leave until he promised them a chance to regain their substantial losses. Eventually after much mumbling and grumbling they disappeared into the night.

The wail of sirens could be heard clearly, the whining sound even permeating the thick Castle walls. They sent shivers through Peter and he started to sweat profusely. The Earl poured Peter a very large brandy and insisted he sat down while they took stock of what had happened.

'You are in shock old man, calm down, take deep breaths.'

Although outwardly in control the Earl himself was in a quandary. He was on the verge of completing a sale of a very valuable work of art and George Johnson was pussyfooting around. Police sniffing around the Castle and interviewing his guests was the last thing he needed. He must concentrate and think of a plausible story which would convince Peter to stick around this time.

Peter was trembling. He was trembling so much he was spilling most of his brandy. He began muttering to himself 'I can't do it again, I can't do it again. I was younger last time, I can't do it again.'

Taking control of the situation the Earl said. 'Calm down John let me think' The Earl lapsed into Peter's old long forgotten name as he struggled to think of a way out for his friend. 'Listen to me and listen carefully' he said eventually.

'I will call for a taxi to take you home. I will say you have had too much to drink and have decided to leave your car at the Castle. When you leave to get into the taxi make a scene as you realise that your car is not where you parked it. Then report it as stolen to your men at the Station. Leave the rest to your 'bobbies' to work out. You say that young thug was rooting around the woman's belongings when you ran past. His prints will be all over her clothes. I'll say I saw him hanging around the Castle grounds earlier today. Get your mates at the Station to plant something in the car which will put Robbie firmly in the driving seat. The evidence is there just convince them that they need to get an arrest this time. I'm sure they will bend the rules as he barely got a rap on the knuckles last year.' Peter sat a while thinking it through, as if by magic the trembling seemed to stop.

'You know it might just work.'

'Trust me this time' said the Earl patting him on the back. 'Promise me no more disappearing acts. Ride this one out. Now stay here and finish that brandy whilst I ring for a taxi.'

Bob the taxi driver tooted his horn twice to alert his fare. He was often called upon to the Castle to ferry guests to and fro as the Earl acknowledged and appreciated his discretion.

'Hello Bob, nice night for it' said a remarkably cheery looking Peter as he swaggered from the Earls private quarters of the Castle. He swayed as he made his way to the cab and struggled with the door handle. Bob jumped from the cab to help Peter into the car.

'Sorry bit worse for wear,' said Peter stating the obvious. 'I've decided to leave the car here and collect it in the morning.' Saying this he waved in the direction of the empty car park alongside the large iron gates.

Bob followed his gaze and let his eyes scan the scene before saying. 'I think you've had way too much to drink Inspector Dodd, either that or you parked your car somewhere else.'

Peter made a big play of raising his head and looking around. In a performance which would have put an Oscar winning actor to shame he bounded out of the car to search for the missing vehicle.

The Earl upon the pretext of hearing the commotion raced outside to help. 'Well I'll be dammed Peter I saw you park it here with my two own eyes, bugger, it must have been stolen. Thinking on, I don't remember seeing it when the other chaps left and there was a young lad from the town hanging around here today.'

'Did you recognise him?' said Peter.

'Yes I'm sure I've seen him in town, shall I pop in the Station tomorrow and look at some mug shots?

'Bloody hooligan.' said Peter striking his fist against the wall in a fit of anger.

'Not much you can do here old chap,' said the Earl. 'I suggest you get home, sober up and report the missing car to your chaps at the Station tomorrow morning.'

'I agree.' said Bob. 'Come on hop in, and we can have a quick scoot around the town on the way back to the Crag, bet the little bugger has taken it for a joy ride and dumped it somewhere.'

Bob led the way back to the cab, followed by Peter who turned to the Earl and winked at his conspirator. For someone who had possibly killed an old woman he seemed unusually cheerful thought the Earl. Momentarily he questioned his own wisdom at getting involved again, Peter seemed to court trouble, but he reminded himself that his kind of people looked after their own, closed ranks against the proletariat. Yes the good old class system was still alive and kicking, albeit underground. He had provided sanctuary for Peter all those years ago in the seventies and he must be prepared to do so again.

As Bob drove down the hill from the Castle he spotted a confusion of lights flashing in the distance.

'I could hear sirens from the Castle,' he said. 'I had no idea they were so close, there must have been an accident, I'll turn the car around and take the country route to the Crag shall I? I'll get on to the lads in the office and put the word out to look out for your car.'

Peter grunted his assent and the two men continued the journey in silence, Peter pretending to be in a drunken slumber on the back seat of the cab.

When they reached the top of the Crag Peter stumbled from the car. 'Keep the change,' he said to Bob.

Bob was about to bid him a peaceful night when he was interrupted by the voice of the radio controller of the cab firm.

'Bob I've just had your wife on the phone. She asked if you can take her to the hospital post haste. Her aunt has been in a bad car crash and apparently it's pretty touch and go.'

Peter made a great performance of looking shocked by the news. 'Bloody hell do you think that was the car crash by the Castle?'

'God only knows,' said Bob as he quickly turned the taxi and sped away back down the dirt track. His wheels sliding slightly as he took the hairpin bends just a little too carelessly.

Peter stood and watched him go. He had temporarily forgotten his Ukrainian bride to be, who was patiently awaiting his arrival home. Crossing towards the Folly he glanced in the kitchen window. He could see a figure stooped over the stove. Her hair shone red in the light from the flickering gas flame. For the briefest of moments Peter was transported back in to 1970's and that night. That dreadful, dreadful night.

Peter's hand gripped the length of lead piping.

It was warm to the touch, wrapped in surgical tape.

It was bent out of shape and heavily bloodstained.

There was a sack. There was blood and mayhem everywhere.

His wife Victoria was screaming hysterically.

He remembered his anger as he thrust three gloved fingers down her throat.

'Shut up, shut up .Let me think. Be quiet woman, blast you I need to think.'

He recalled the agony as she grabbed his testicles. Squeezing, twisting, the excruciating pain forcing his fingers to move from her throat.

Then the sound of Victoria's blood curdling scream as she burst from the house and raced up the street. Screaming, yelling as she ran into the 'Plumbers Arms' Public House. 'Help me, help me. He's murdered the nanny'

Tania turned her head abruptly towards the window. Perhaps Peter had yelled out, his mind was playing tricks on him. He couldn't be sure of anything anymore.

Peter stared into the darkened window. His eyes focused upon her. Not blinking.

Not seeing. She jumped with fright overturning a pan upon the stove.

The motion seemed to kick start Peter back to the present. He clenched his fists so hard the nails drew blood upon the palms. He stared down at his hands.

The stigmata of a marked man. A man forever dammed by his past sins.

He needed to focus, focus and take control. Get a perspective on the whole sorry event. Things were bleak but not as bleak as that night.

Tonight had been an accident, perhaps fatal, but an accident. Peter composed his expression into a lopsided smile and entered the kitchen. Tania flinched as he squeezed his way past her into the lounge. She could smell the alcohol fumes upon his breath and frantically searched his face to gauge his mood. His smile did not fool her and she felt relieved as he made no attempt to touch her. Turning his head as he made to go upstairs Peter said.

'A cooked breakfast would be nice, I rise at eight sharp.'

Tania muttered a tiny goodnight to his departing back. She mopped the contents of the spilled pan from kitchen floor listening to the sounds of Peter fumbling overhead. The bed springs squeaked and groaned as he fell onto the mattress. Tania felt reassured when she heard the steady measured snores of an intoxicated man. He had fallen into a deep drunken sleep almost as soon as his head had hit the pillow. Tania opened the oven door and took out the stew she had prepared for Peters arrival home. Setting it upon the stove top she covered the dish with a tea towel and left it to cool. She switched off the lights in the kitchen. Lying on the sofa she draped her overcoat over herself and closed her eyes. With her eyes closed she imagined that she was safely back within the bosom of her family. Warm and secure in the tiny flat in Cherkassy.

NOWHERE CROSSROADS – THE SCENE OF THE ACCIDENT

Liz sat in the police car, Jasper the dog was at her feet. She was reading over her Police statement before signing it.

The old woman had been on the ground with a young man crouching over her prising a collection tin from her hands. Jasper was barking, his lead was tangled in the bushes. The engine of the car was running and the headlights were so bright and blinding.

For some reason she forgot to mention the man running past her and away from the scene. At the time she had wrongly assumed he was running to call for aid and her subconscious had therefore dismissed his importance in the event.

It is a long time before something prompted her to recall his run and question his relevance to the accident. But that is much later in this story.

For now, Maggie lies in the hospital with little hope of ever waking up. Yvonne sits sobbing at the foot of the bed comforted by Bob her husband. Sooty sits alone in the waiting room sipping tepid coffee. She has tried to ring Lennie but she does not seem to be at home. Robbie bangs on the cell door at the Police Station protesting his innocence and demanding his rights to ring a solicitor. The Duty Sergeant feigns a hearing impairment and continues to write up his reports.

At the crossroads the car is being lifted onto the recovery vehicle. On the passenger seat a glove belonging to Robbie is in full view. The other glove sits in his coat pocket. His coat is locked up at the Police Station with the rest of his personal belongings. A tearful Liz is being driven home to her flat above the Bistro, Jasper barking excitedly on the back seat.

Maggie opens her eyes; in the distance she sees a tunnel and a bright light. At the end of the tunnel she sees her parents. Arms outstretched her mother beckons Maggie to her side. Maggie climbs from her hospital bed and runs towards them. They engulf her in their arms.

The Doctor at the hospital shakes his head as the monitor above Maggie flat-lines. He feels her wrist for a pulse and listens for a heartbeat with his stethoscope. He then nods gravelly to the nurse and she removes the tubes from Maggie's nose and gently closes her eyes.

Yvonne is inconsolable. Bob holds her tightly. He is at a loss at what to say and fighting to hold back his own tears.

NOWHERE TOWN HALL –
THE HAPPY COUPLE

Ten days after the accident Peter and Tania are married. The bride wears her best outfit, the groom his smart Police uniform. The Earl and Countess are witnesses. All in all it is a very happy occasion. Peter has slight reservations that his paperwork might not be in order, but Miss Tears the Registrar is easily talked around and prepared to turn a blind eye to the numerous inconsistencies.

Tania weeps what the Countess wrongly assumes are tears of joy. She misses her family but Peter has promised that once everything has settled down she can send for her son Nicolai. Her new groom had been kindness personified since her first evening in England and she is beginning to think that in time she may even develop feelings for him. Not love, oh no, she is much too long in the tooth for that, but perhaps something more lasting, respect.

Elsewhere in Nowhere, Maggie is lying in the Chapel of Rest overseen by Mr Tears, the Undertaker. His wife Mrs Tears the midwife is helping her husband to make Maggie look more presentable for the grieving relatives. She drags a crimson red lipstick across Maggie's lips and dabs pink blusher onto her pallid cheeks. Later on when Sooty visits she will weep and say 'Maggie never wore makeup' before kissing her cold unyielding forehead for the final time.

The irony of the day is not lost on Peter, he is just grateful to have got away with it once again. He wears plasters to mask the marks on the palms of his hands and a broad smile to mask his moral insensibility.

BETTER THAN CHOCOLATE

Jean and Dianne were sitting quietly upon the uncomfortable leather couch Lucy had chosen before she died. Jean had prepared them both a spicy curry which they had washed down with a dry white wine. They were watching a video entitled 'Better than chocolate.'

'Well do you think it is better than chocolate?' said Dianne breaking the silence.

'It depends upon the quality of the chocolate,' said Jean instantly understanding the question. 'Are we talking Cadbury's?'

'For the sake of argument, yes a good chocolate,' Dianne replied.

'And are we talking a good woman?'

'Yes ok, a good woman or a good chocolate, which would you choose?'

'A bad woman, always more satisfying I find,' said Jean laughing.

Since the ladies had that conversation in Dianne's kitchen a few months previously Jean had often wondered what would have happened had she reacted differently when she first discovered that Dianne was attracted to her. She had often regretted her hasty dismissal of a possible romance now that the lines of friendship seemed to be drawn in stone. Dianne showed no signs of thinking of her as anything but a close friend and to move the goalposts could cause the friendship to waver. So things were left unsaid, and emotions held in check. This was the closest they had come to discussing the double edged sword of sex. An uneasy silence now filled the room.

'Shall I tell you what I think?' said Dianne eventually. 'I think we both need to get out there and test the water'

Jean held her breath and sat waiting for Dianne to make the first move. Dianne shifted by her side. Jean held her breath, suddenly nervous. It had been a long time she had indulged in anything remotely resembling a passionate embrace. To her consternation Dianne merely stretched across the couch and switched off the television with the remote control.

'Let's be proactive,' said Dianne seemingly unaware of Jean's predicament. 'Instead of sitting here thinking of romance let's give it a

head start and write two lonely hearts ads, one for me and one for you.'
Saying this she handed Jean a pen and a piece of paper.

Jean felt a wave of disappointment wash over her as she tried desperately to put on a brave face. 'I'm game if you are,' she said with a jocularity she did not feel.

'Let's wager that whoever writes the best ad gets out of doing the washing-up tomorrow morning,' she added.

'I'll get you the rubber gloves now shall I?' Dianne replied. 'But first,' she said holding aloft a nearly empty bottle of wine, 'I think we need more liquid refreshment don't you?'

Half an hour and many unsuccessful drafts later Dianne put down her pen declaring, 'Well it's not 'War and Peace' but I think that's mine finished.'

Two empty wine bottles now sat on the coffee table.

'Come on then, let's hear it,' said Jean, slightly slurring her words.

'No you go first, I've had more to drink than you and I need to compose myself,' said Dianne.

Jean struggled to her feet and read '*Flirty fly fisherwoman 40s, would like to swim with the mermaids. Tug at my heart and you'll be hooked.*'

Dianne laughed. 'I think trade descriptions will have you for that one Jean,' she said.

'Why?' replied Jean pretending not to understand.

'Think you should put 50's sweetie,' Dianne joked 'although in a certain light I think you.......' she left the sentence unfinished for a while before adding, 'It would be candlelight of course,'

Jean ducked as Dianne aimed the cushion at her head. Dianne tried to get up onto her feet then sat down again clumsily. 'Whoops I think I have had way too much to drink, I may have to read mine from the safety of the couch.'

Do you like pina colada and walking home in the rain? I'm not much good at love songs but I do like champagne.WLM that special woman to make my heart sing.

Jean clapped. 'I notice you omitted your age completely,' she said to Dianne accusingly.

'Yes,' said Dianne 'I thought I would just make sure my first date is a candlelight dinner for two.'

Jean laughed. 'Well, I think that's a draw.'

'So do you think we should both wash up?' said Dianne.

'I think we should both wash up tomorrow,' said Jean. 'I think it's time we hit the sack.'

Dianne made a great play of helping Jean up from the chair, taking her hand as she led her upstairs to the bedrooms. Once on the landing she guided Jean into the main bedroom before turning to go into the spare bedroom where she normally slept.

'Would you stay with me tonight?' said Jean, hating herself for sounding so needy. 'Drink always gives me bad dreams.'

'Alright,' said Dianne, hesitating for just a moment. 'I'll just pop next door and get my nightie and be back in a jiffy.'

Jean undressed, popped between the cool linen sheets and was asleep almost immediately. Dianne climbed in a few minutes later. She lay looking at Jean for a long while before finally wrapping her arms around her sleeping friend and drifting off herself. Jean awoke the next morning aware that someone was stroking her hair. She let herself languish in the feeling for a while before she shifted her position in the bed and turned to face Dianne. Wordlessly she gazed into Dianne's deep brown eyes before greeting her lips in a long lingering kiss.

'This shouldn't be happening,' said Dianne pulling away.

'It shouldn't but it is,' replied Jean before drawing her back into her embrace.

A while later....

Dianne was small breasted but slim of hip not unlike Lucy in her BC (before cancer) days, thought Jean as a sob caught in her throat. Would she ever reach a stage where she could look at another woman without comparing them to Lucy? Telling herself for the umpteenth time that she must try and move on emotionally, she looked again with new eyes at Dianne.

'I had no idea you were quite so lovely,' said Jean suddenly overcome with passion.

Dianne averted her eyes. Suddenly shy she dragged the covers up so they covered her breasts.

'This wasn't supposed to happen,' she said, repeating what she had said earlier.

'No-one needs to know about this but us,' said Jean, 'if that what you are worried about'

'I'm more concerned about how it will affect our friendship,' said Dianne.

'So what's changed?' said Jean. 'Are we no longer friends?'

'Of course we are still friends,' said Dianne. 'It's just that......' her word's tailed off.

'Like I said,' Jean reiterated 'our friendship hasn't changed a jot.' Even as she spoke the words Jean was aware that she was probably lying.

'So,' said Dianne. 'Just to clarify, are we what the youngsters call 'friends with benefits?

'Well I wouldn't phrase it quite as flippantly,' said Jean suddenly aggrieved.

'What would you say if I said one of the benefits was that I get up and make breakfast.' said Dianne desperately trying to inject some levity into the conversation.

'I would say two fried eggs sunny side up.' Jean replied after a while, trying to match her friends' lighter tone.

'About this morning,' said Dianne as they ate their breakfast.

'What about this morning?' said Jean, 'as far as I am concerned nothing happened this morning.'

Dianne stared at her plate for a long time. She started to say something then seemed to think better of it and stopped.

'Have you any stamps?' she said eventually.

'A few in the dresser drawer,' said Jean. 'Why?'

'I think we both have letters to post have we not?' Dianne said. She sounded as if she were issuing a challenge rather than asking a question.

'Indeed we do,' Jean replied. 'If you start writing the envelopes I shall try to find the stamps.'

NOWHERE MANOR – THE
LAUNCH OF THE CALENDER

Nowhere Manor was a hive of activity. It was the official launch of the WTF Calendar and the entire local WTF and their extended families had descended en masse upon Lillian's home. Lillian was in her element. She excelled in social gatherings, relishing the attention which was focused upon the hostess.

George had been called upon to refill glasses and hand out the canapés. He bore the task with bad grace and had spent the day reminding his wife that he was the host and not a 'bloody butler'. Lillian had snapped back that it had been his idea to host the event themselves rather than hire professional caterers. George's penny pinching ways had long been a bone of contention in their marriage.

Upon the arrival of a photographer and journalist from the local Gazette George's surly expression quickly transformed into 'mein host'. The Countess herself was due to arrive for the photo shoot at any moment so George puffed himself up and smoothed back his hair then crossed the room to shake the reporter's hand.

On the vast drawing room table, almost as a centrepiece, a large parcel lay wrapped up in brown paper. It contained the first print of a hundred calendars. The ladies from the WTF were circling the table like lions at a watering hole.

Finally the Countess arrived and an atmosphere of nervous anticipation pervaded the room. The journalist and photographer both made a beeline towards her. They were hoping to have a quick chat, line up a couple of good quotes, take a few photographs, and then beat a hasty retreat to the Brits for opening time.

Lillian stood by the fireplace, her eyes scanning the room searching for George. Her eyes alighted upon him in a corner leaning upon the baby grand. He was talking animatedly to the Countess, who for her part seemed to be desperately trying to feign interest. Lillian tried to catch George's attention by waving her hand in the air but due to the amount of sherry she had drunk earlier she lost her balance. She slumped against the fireplace and knocked a rather valuable ornament to the ground. To her consternation the Meissen porcelain vase broke into hundreds of tiny pieces as it struck the marble hearth. Her companions from WTF raced to her aid followed by a very concerned looking George.

Whispering in her ear he said, 'One too many my dear? Thank goodness it was insured.' His expression held a look of tender concern but his tone of voice was teasing, sarcastic and annoyed.

Biting back a nasty retort she said, 'I was trying to get your attention and stumbled on my high heels. I thought a speech was in order and I remembered how you love the sound of your own voice'

'Next time try calling me my dear, far less dramatic.'

Despite herself Lillian gave an irritable sigh, her husband really was a nasty little man. After making a great show of helping his wife to her feet and guiding her to a nearby chair George cleared his throat in preparation for his speech. But he was piped to the post by Sooty. Standing at a vantage point close to the central table she clapped her hands in the air to gain the rooms attention. The room fell silent as she began to speak.

'Firstly may I thank everyone for coming today. The support this project has received has been second to none. Toni, the photographer sends her good wishes and apologies for not attending. But as I am sure most of you have read in the newspaper she is now commissioned to travel over Europe duplicating the photographs she took in Newcastle. I think it's what is called naked ambition.'

She paused for a laugh, and on cue the room obliged. Once it had subsided she continued.

'On her behalf I would like to thank the ladies of the WTF and of course our generous benefactors the Earl and Countess for their support of this very worthwhile cause. Hopefully the proceeds from this calendar will provide enough revenue to redevelop a wing of our local cottage hospital into a permanent hospice. It only remains for me to ask our dear Countess to open this rather large parcel.'

Sooty took a pair of scissors from the centre of the table and handed them to the Countess. Holding the scissors aloft the Countess paused so the photographer could position the shot. She smiled into the camera then cut the ribbon and eased the package carefully apart.

'I suggest the ladies involved are first to look through these,' she said as she peeled the top twelve calendars from the pile and handed them out to Miss January through to Miss December.

Sooty was thrilled to see how well the oil painting by Yvonne had turned out as the cover. She saw some of the other calendar ladies glancing quickly at it obviously unaware that it was not an original by Ingres but a very good copy with their faces superimposed upon the nude bathers. How they would blush later when this was pointed out to them. Sooty was Miss June and her photograph was based upon the famous image of a nude sitting in a reverse fashion on a chair. Behind the chair were the Earl's bee hives and alluding to Christine Keeler and the infamous Profumo affair the caption read 'The Honey Trap'.

Lennie who was attending the launch as Sooty's guest peered over her shoulder and voiced her approval. 'You look quite stunning Susan' she said 'I really must take a copy to Jean next time I visit, she will be thrilled that you have achieved all this in Lucy's memory'

'It's just a shame that Lucy cannot see it herself,' said Sooty with a note of sadness and regret in her voice.

Lillian had retired to a corner of the room to peruse the calendar at her leisure. She featured in the potting shed holding two clay pots, her more than ample breasts just peeking above their rims. She was surrounded by seed trays of young tender green shoots although her two clay pots appeared empty. On her hands she wore soiled gardening gloves. Lillian was immediately taken with the results and decided there and then to have the photograph enlarged, framed and hung in the hallway of Nowhere Manor. After admiring the image for a while she noticed a caption underneath the photograph. Forsaking vanity she searched in her handbag for her spectacles so that she could read the small print. She was shocked when she realised the caption read 'Gone to seed'. Lillian could not quite believe her eyes and it took a few minutes for the connotation of the phrase to properly sink in. Looking around she saw the other WTF girls smirking in her direction. Sooty even went as far as to let out a loud guffaw.

Lillian held back the tears of indignation, determined to keep a brave face in front of the Countess and her guests.. She felt a hand upon her shoulder and battled inwardly not to recoil from the touch as she realised it was George. He rudely snatched the calendar from his wife's grasp and flicked quickly through the months until he reached hers.

He showed great restraint and support for his wife by acting totally oblivious to the caption under her page. But later on when they got home he said, 'Great touch those gardening gloves.'

The real reason George held such restraint was because he was far more interested in the oil painting on the front cover of the calendar. A look of pure appreciation lapsed into one of joy as he realised that the artist was his very own secretary Yvonne. Well, well he thought to himself, one door closes and another opens. Or in this case one door is firmly locked. The chap who normally helped George out had just been jailed for art forgery. The artist who had a hungry drug addiction to feed had become greedy. He had stopped being careful. The trick was to release a painting a year but he had saturated an already suspicious market and was now paying the price. By gobbling up a healthy profit he was now doing cold turkey.

Now it was just a question of how to broach the subject to Yvonne. George was under no allusions that she was up to the job, her execution appeared flawless, faultless even. If it were not for her clever merging of the faces the painting on the calendar could easily be mistaken for the original. His good friend the Earl would be thrilled. It appeared the castle coffers were rapidly emptying due to his wifes grandiose garden scheme and the Earl had a certain Raphael he wanted to replicate. Finding a new artist so quickly would hopefully put George back in the running for an honour after the Robbie anti-hunt fiasco.

NEWCASTLE UNIVERSITY – FINE ART DEPARTMENT

Yvonne had an itch which she longed to scratch. Trying to focus her mind and thoughts upon the table of still life objects in the corner of the room she managed to temporarily suppress the longing. Oh no, her left leg was going numb. It was no good she would have to move it. Just stretch it slightly from the knee. If she could just rotate her ankle then return her foot quickly to the chalk mark on the floor. She made the tiniest movement hoping it would not be noticed. Alas Yvonne heard an audible sigh from a student to her left who then made a great play of taking his eraser from his art box and rubbing furiously at his charcoal drawing.

'Sorry,' said Yvonne, to the class in general as she resumed her pose.

Glancing at the clock without moving her head she saw she had only eighteen minutes left. Thank God, this was the hardest job she had ever had to do. She was not surprised the pay was so high, it was so mind bogglingly boring.

At the end of the evening Yvonne put on her wrap around robe and wandered through the class looking at the many depictions of herself naked. There were twenty plus easels' of charcoal Yvonne's, some barely recognisable as female or human in form. Trying not to be overly critical she realised that she was probably more gifted and talented than most of the students drawing her. Yes they were first year students, but honestly did they think she looked like that!

This reminded her of the suggestion her boss George Johnson had made to her after the launch of the WTF Calendar. Although he hadn't said so in actual words he had suggested she assist his clients abroad by repainting some of their more valuable works of art. He explained that this was so the actual originals could be protected from any potential damage. He added that they would be stored safely in air tight bank vaults. George finished by saying that for insurance purposes it must be kept secret, which immediately made Yvonne suspicious. She had only last week read of a chap who had been imprisoned for art forgery. She had always had her suspicions that George was not completely honest in his antique transactions but the thought of being implicated in a crime absolutely terrified her. She had decided not to say anything to Bob, because he was invariably hot-headed and she didn't want her job at the solicitors to be in any jeopardy. Bob had not always been so conventional in-fact he had initially wooed her with his infamous Woodstock story.

Many years before they met, Bob had taken a gap year from his job and travelled to a 600 acre farm near New York which was hosting the Woodstock Music and Art Fair. He and his pals had an apparently eventful first day drinking and carousing. During a prolonged performance by Richie Havers they had returned to their tent only to find they had had their clothes stolen. Bob was wearing a beer drenched t-shirt so a boy from an adjoining tent had offered to loan him a crumpled red and white striped top. Later on that evening Bob had got lost in the crowd. After unsuccessful attempts to find him his friends had asked if his name could be announced over the loudspeaker. The announcement coincided with Joan Baez finishing her jaw dropping rendition of *Swing Low, Sweet Chariot*. Joan in a mischievous mood took to the microphone herself to ask the crowd '*Where's Bob?*' Fuelled by alcohol amongst other intoxicating substances the crowd began to chant '*Where's Bob?* A bespectacled Bob in a bobble hat and striped top jumped up in the crowd to make his presence known and the crowd changed the chant to 'Wally, Wally'. Joan herself coined the phrase '*Where's Wally*' and incorporated the ditty into her finishing song '*We shall overcome.*' When his old university friend Martin had written and illustrated his best selling *Where's Wally* book in 1987, Bob mentally kicked himself for not thinking of it first. To give him his due Martin did mention Bob in a later broadsheet interview although Bob thought that share of the royalties would have been a tad more appropriate. Martin had tried many times to buy the tattered red and white shirt from Bob, inadvertently authenticating it in the process. But Bob was not selling. He had it thermostatically sealed in a frame and kept it in his loft, often quoting that it was his future pension. Although ironically and unbeknown to him it wasn't even the original shirt as Yvonne had given the tattered top to a door to door charity collection many years previously.

The carefree Bob of those days seemed like another person and when years later Yvonne had pleaded to go to Glastonbury Bob had steadfastly refused saying why would he want to sleep in a smelly draughty tent when he had a perfectly comfortable bed at home.

THE MIDNIGHT GARDENER

The nights had started closing in. The sky was darkening, a clear almost navy blue sky with a half moon winking in the distance.

Lennie alighted from her car and opening the boot lifted out a small spade and a net bag of daffodil bulbs. The other evening she had had an ingenious idea. Far and away the most romantic idea she had ever had. Tracey's new house had a tiny postage stamp of a garden to the front elevation. It was lawned with a hedgerow boundary, devoid of any colour bar green and so small there was not even room for a narrow border of annuals. Lennie knew that Tracey was away on business so the house would be enveloped in darkness. She had packed a torch, which she now placed on an upturned flowerpot to illuminate a small area of the lawn. Very carefully she dug a small hole into the grass and dropped in a bulb. She did this at regular intervals, twenty five times, until a heart shape of soil circles could be seen on the lawn. After she had finished she wiped her hands on the towel she had brought for just this purpose. Then she stood back for a few minutes to survey the scene before climbing back into her car and driving away. Jean was expecting her and if she put her foot down she would make it to Upper Wortley for an early supper.

Watching from the bedroom window Tracey's ex Sandra dropped the curtain as Lennie drove away from the house. Tracey was lying naked on the bed. They had just made love and she was still basking in the afterglow.

'Was that a car I heard driving away?' Tracey enquired.

'Yes,' said Sandra 'Someone must have been visiting next door.'

'Do you fancy coming back to bed and visiting me?' said Tracey.

'Now where shall I put my calling card?' Sandra joked as she mounted both Tracey and the bed.

NOWHERE COTTAGE HOSPITAL – MATERNITY WING

Yvonne's face was obscured by a gigantic bunch of flowers. In her handbag she had a carefully selected handmade card which she had bought that morning from the retail area of the Greenhouse Bistro. It also held two handmade glitter cards which her children had made the previous evening. The evidence of the glitter was still on the tip of Yvonne's nose which glinted as she walked under the bright fluorescent light of the hospital ward.

Marina was in a bed at the far end of the ward breastfeeding her newly born son. She was the perfect image of a 'Madonna' nursing her child. A stream of light flooded from the window behind Marina giving the illusion of a halo. The religious iconography of the scene was not lost on Yvonne. I've been around bloody art students too long thought Yvonne, now I am seeing every scene as a potential painting.

Baby Prospero was firmly attached to Marina's breast sucking frantically almost as if his tiny life depended upon it. Yvonne thought Prospero a very wordy name for such a small baby but Marina had reasoned that Prospero had entered her life as a tempest, a swirling turbulent wind. Yvonne understood the explanation as she had studied The Tempest at school for her English Literature 'A' Level. Nevertheless she still thought it a very long name for such a sweet wee chap.

Many years previously Yvonne had known a girl who had been addicted to the American soap series Dynasty and called her two children Blake and Alexis after the two main characters. Secretly Yvonne suspected that Marina was doing an upmarket copycat version of just this. When she had told Marina the story of her friend and the embarrassingly named children Marina had assumed Blake referred to the artist and poet of the same name. Although where she thought the name Alexis was gleaned from was anyone's guess. Popular culture and Marina were as Yvonne had discovered a long time ago, estranged bedfellows.

'Hello there you two,' said Yvonne as she peered around a massive bunch of flowers to direct her grin towards Marina and Prospero.

'Hello to you to,' said Marine expertly moving Prospero to the other breast as she did so. 'For a moment there I thought I was being attacked by a bunch of flowers on legs.'

'Very funny,' said Yvonne. 'There's gratitude for you.'

She put the flowers on the bedside cabinet and began rooting around in her cavernous handbag.

'Somewhere in here I do have cards for you from the children.'

'At last, here they are,' she exclaimed holding them aloft.

Cradling her son in her left arm Marina reached out with her right arm to take the cards.

After reading the inscriptions out aloud to an oblivious Prospero Marina said. 'These are very special cards. It seems your children have inherited your artistic talent.'

Yvonne blushed as she had never taken flattery well.

Sensing her embarrassment Marina quickly changed the subject. 'So how did it go at the University on Monday?'

'Absolutely fine.' said Yvonne. 'After posing naked with all those other people on the quayside the other month it was a walk in the park.'

'Did Bob suspect anything?'

'No I told him you had found me a late night cleaning job at the University and he said 'good the cash will come in handy.'

'I still think you should tell him.'

'You don't know Bob like I do. He would be mortified if he knew I had taken my clothes off for a bunch of long haired strangers.'

'It is art. You weren't exactly posing for a centrefold. There is a difference.'

'Not to Bob, you should have heard him ranting on about the naked photographs at the quayside. If he even thought I had been involved he would blow a gasket. The other taxi drivers have taken to calling Newcastle 'Nudecastle' which he thinks it's hilarious.'

'Is Bob so provincial?'

'Yes and narrow-minded but that's enough about Bob.'

Yvonne felt strangely protective towards her husband and his ways. It was ok for her to tease and laugh at them but when Marina did it was somehow different.

'Tell me how does it feel to be a mummy?' Yvonne asked.

'A mother,' said Marina instantly correcting her terminology. 'Mummy's are from Egypt.'

Yvonne felt a flash of irritation. This habit of Marina's to constantly correct was getting tiresome.

'Alright then,' she said trying to keep the tone of exasperation from her voice.

'How does it feel to be a mother?'

'Mother,' repeated Marina, slowly allowing the word to float over her tongue. 'I still can't get used to the word. Other people are mothers. Not me. I've always been the mad favourite aunty who floats in bearing gifts then disappears into the night.'

'Well you are a mother now and the gorgeous evidence is lying right there in your arms.'

As if on cue Prospero shuffled in his blanket and let out a tiny fart. Both women laughed.

'It seems as if he's living up to his Tempest name,' said Yvonne still laughing. 'He's full of hot air just like his mother.'

Meanwhile in the hospital reception area, a smartly dressed man was enquiring about the directions to the maternity ward. Mrs Tears the midwife on duty that evening was walking past the desk, overhearing the enquiry she offered to walk with him as she was heading that way herself.

'I've just been on my break in the canteen' she said as a way to break the silence as they walked along. When the man didn't answer Mrs Tears continued regardless.

'Who are you visiting?'

'My son,' said Martin, his voice breaking slightly as he voiced the words. When he had arrived in Nowhere an hour earlier the taxi driver had told him about the birth. It was quite something when the taxi driver and the general populace of a market town knew about your child before you did!

'Your son?' said Mrs Tears.

There was only one baby boy on the ward. Gosh this would be something to gossip about to the other nurses on duty that night. There they were thinking that Marina was a single mother.

'Yes my son,' repeated Martin. However much he thought about it, he couldn't get his head around the fact that he was a father. Not just a father but a father, who in the next few minutes was about to meet his child for the very first time.

'Well, well, there's a turn up for the books,' said Mrs Tears. 'I'm sure Prospero will be thrilled to meet his daddy.'

'Who's Prospero?

'Prospero is the name of your son.'

'She's called my son Prospero?' Martin tried to keep the note of incredulity from his voice.

'I know it struck us staff as a very unusual name too but in a strange way it suits the little chap.'

'We'll see,' said Martin who had always presumed his first son would be named Martin junior or Victor after his father.

'I said that Marina surely '*Hathaway*' with word's,' chuckled Mrs Tears hoping to impress Martin with her somewhat sketchy knowledge of Shakespeare.

HOLDING MY HEART IN YOUR HANDS

Gino stood gazing out of the large window of the Rendezvous Cafe. The window overlooked the promenade and beyond it a low wall which wrapped around the beach. Trade was intermittent during the week, peaking during school holidays, weekends and sunny days. Today was cold and blustery, not a day for ice-creams but the demand for hot chocolate's and steaming pots of tea would hopefully compensate.

Bob the taxi driver was out of breath. He stopped by the cafe, bending over to alleviate a stitch in his side. Waving to Gino he indicated that he would be back later for a drink and chat.

Bob had run the length of the bay. He chose to run far from the water's edge as it proved more difficult and challenging. He was exhausted but determined to run still further. His feet pounded the sand, a steady rhythm not unlike a mantra. Bob never stopped to think why he was running or what he was running from. The concentration of the running, the sensation of his own heart pumping in his chest deterred all thoughts. What personal demons forced him to cross the pain barrier and still continue to run? He told Yvonne, what he believed to be the truth, which was that he had taken up running to keep fit.

'I'm going to flab, sitting. Sitting and waiting in that blasted taxi. I sometimes feel I have no legs, just four tyres, four spare tyres at that.'

Initially Yvonne had talked Bob into joining the local Nowhere Harriers. Bob had made tentative enquiries, even gone so far as so go on a practice run with some of the chaps. But he soon decided it was not for him. It was much too structured. Bob preferred to run at his own pace, in his own company, dictating his own route.

So Bob ran and ran, and the more Bob ran the more his problems followed him. No matter how fast he ran or how far he travelled his problems still followed in his wake like an annoying relentless shadow.

'I'm sure that's Bob?' said Sooty pointing to a figure in the distance. 'Yvonne told me he had taken up running.'

'He's the taxi driver chap isn't he?' questioned Louisa, she was still constantly astounded at how everyone knew everyone's business in Nowhere.

'Yes that's right,' said Sooty.

'He's running like a man possessed, he must be very dedicated to run in this foul weather.'

'Perhaps he's training for the Great North Run?' said Louisa.

'Perhaps,' Sooty concurred.

Sooty bent over to pick up a piece of green weather-beaten glass. 'I do so love sea glass. I once had a glass frame made out of it, it was so beautiful.' Sooty handed it to Louisa. 'Have you noticed it's shaped like a lopsided heart?'

Louisa turned it over carefully, rubbing her fingertips along its smooth edges.

'Do you realised you are holding my heart in your hands?

Sometimes Sooty would say something so profound it just took Louisa's breath away. Louisa deliberately averted her eyes and looked towards the sea-shore desperately holding back the tears. 'I promise to treat it with care,' she said wrapping it in a paper tissue and placing it in gingerly into her jacket pocket. Jasper gambled into her line of vision, he had a large gnarled piece of driftwood clasped in his mouth. He dropped the wood at Louisa's feet hoping they could play catch. Picking it up Louisa proceeded to draw a big heart shape in the sand. It was pierced by a large arrow. Above the arrow she wrote her initials and below it she wrote Sooty's.

Later on the tide would race in and the heart would wash away. The tide, like Louisa's love for Sooty would ebb and flow. For Louisa had one constant love and it surpassed all others; but for the moment Louisa's heart was on loan to Sooty and Sooty's heart was safely in Louisa's pocket.

'Come along.' said Sooty, taking her lover's arm in the crook of her own. 'I do believe you mentioned treating me to a hot chocolate with all the works.'

'Mmmmm whipped cream and marshmallows, our reward for taking a walk on this cold and windy day.'

'Being in your company is reward enough for me,' said Sooty. Later she would chastise herself for being too serious as she knew that if there was one thing that would scare Louisa off that would be it. Since the beginning of their relationship there had been no promise of it being long standing. It seemed that Louisa and Joey were a couple in the same way that she and Lennie were. Although she presumed that theirs was a more physical coupling than her own. Before embarking upon the affair they had laid out the ground rules. But the heart is a lonely hunter and love is a constantly complicated business.

MY GOODNIGHT KISS

Lennie was grinning from ear to ear. She had just received a good morning fax from Tracey which read simply;

Leonora you are my world.

It was their anniversary in a short while and Lennie had planned a surprise mini break to Robin Hoods Bay. The endless unpacking of boxes in the new house had been getting Tracey down. She had been uncharacteristically quiet and somewhat reticent to talk of their future together which Lennie blamed upon her own tardiness to fully commit. This morning's fax persuaded Lennie that now was the time to bite the proverbial bullet and put her own house on the market. She had dithered for far too long. Now it just remained for her to tell Sooty. She had put it off and put it off but still she hesitated, telling herself that there would be plenty of time to broach the subject to Sooty after the trip to Robin Hoods Bay.

DENBY DALE – SISTER VIRTUOUS

It was mid-day. Jean had arrived at Dianne's house the previous evening for a late liquid supper. As usual they had shared a bed. This had become a regular occurrence since that first time all those weeks ago. They never spoke of it in the cold light of the day but Dianne always expressed some words of regret immediately after they made love. These words never failed to wound Jeans self respect and debase the lovemaking, turning it into a shameful passionless act. The woman that Jean made love to in the dark endless night was always precise in her actions. Perhaps it was this more than the words themselves that made Jean sense that she was after all just a convenient pound of flesh.

Dianne and Jean were at Dianne's step-mum's partaking in a late breakfast. This too had become a regular occurrence, albeit one that was far less pleasurable than the frenetic lovemaking. This journey across the courtyard was something that Jean would happily forego. It had to be said that Betsy, Dianne's step-mum never failed to make Jean feel uncomfortable. Betsy would begin drinking early in the morning and by lunchtime her tongue was vitriolic. Jean still felt as if Betsy and she were stags at bay circling each other, vying for Dianne's attention.

The fact that Dianne had told Jean to say that she slept in the spare bed made Jean feel like a dirty illicit little secret. Although Dianne had tried to sugar the pill by saying that she preferred not to broadcast her personal affairs to her parents. It also made Jean question why Dianne felt the need to be so secretive. She did not hide her sexuality from her father and step-mum and for goodness sake why should she. Which all pointed Jean to the conclusion that Dianne felt their relationship was something that she was not proud of. It was something shameful to hide away.

This particular day Betsy was in an especially ugly mood. Her every comment and observation barbed. Dianne and her father Victor appeared blissfully unaware of the tension in the room. They were both conversing with enthusiasm about Dianne's older brother Martin. Victor had just taken the call from his son to announce the arrival of his first grandson, Prospero. Victor was also telling Dianne that his son had hinted that he had been asked to be the Official ...... Physician. It was quite a coup for an ordinary middle class boy from an unremarkable background. Victor had tears of pride in his eyes.

Betsy was bored with the baby-talk, basically she was bored with any conversation that did not orbit around herself. Grabbing Jean by the arm she half pushed, half dragged her upstairs upon the pretext of asking her opinion regarding a colour scheme for the spare bedroom.

Jean felt it petty to refuse and so she allowed herself be manhandled up the stairs in order to avoid an embarrassing scene. Once they reached the bedroom Betsy ushered Jean into the room and closed the door firmly behind them, effectively trapping Jean in a corner. She then sprawled herself upon the bed and all pretence of home decor went flying out of the window.

An uneasy silence followed. Betsy lay staring at Jean in a most disconcerting way. Jean busied herself with studying the curtain material desperately thinking of a way out of the situation. When eventually Betsy spoke she had a mocking tone to her voice.

'I suppose you imagine that Dianne will fall in love with you if you satisfy her carnal desires.'

Jean was shocked into silence. 'I don't know what you mean,' said Jean eventually, edging her way to the door as she uttered the words.

'Don't lie to me,' barked Betsy 'being coy does not become a woman of your mature years.'

'And being so crude does not become a woman of yours,' said Jean finally finding her tongue.

'Ahah, true colours at last,' said Betsy 'all that prattling on about your dear, dead girlfriend. My god she is not even cold in her grave and here you are sharing Dianne's bed.'

'You really are the most vulgar woman' said Jean in an aggrieved voice. 'Whatever makes you think you have the right to speak to me like this.'

'Hasn't your darling Dianne filled you in on our family history, how terribly remiss of her.'

'I'm leaving now,' said Jean, she was very angry. 'I suggest that you stay up here until you sober up.'

'You do realise that Dianne only wants what she cannot have. Once she gets it she backs off. It's the chase that she loves; once she has caught you she is very easily bored.' Betsy continued in a mock stage whisper. 'Dianne wanted me once. Oh my how she wanted me.'

Jean was shocked to the core, she was speechless.

'Oh have I offended you Sister Virtuous? Have I brought you crashing into the real world? You're a player now, just like the rest of us poor damned souls. Close the door as you leave my dear.'

Jean stormed out of the bedroom slamming the door behind her. As she stumbled down the stairs she ran slap bang into Dianne.

'Hey, where's the fire?' said Dianne catching Jean's arm to stop her missing her step. 'I decided to join you two, Dad's gone out to feed the horse and I was getting lonely on my own downstairs.'

'Then join your blasted step-mum,' said Jean. 'I'm leaving.'

It was quite a while later when Dianne returned to the house. Jean was not in the kitchen or in the lounge. Eventually Dianne found her in the bedroom packing her overnight case.

'Will you please tell me what Betsy has done to upset you?' she said addressing Jean's back.

'Oh I think you can guess.' said Jean in a tight clipped voice. 'I'm too long in the tooth to play mind games Dianne and I have neither the inclination nor the energy to do so.'

'I should have known Betsy couldn't keep her bloody mouth shut.'

'What hurts, what really hurts is that I had to hear about this from her.'

'I'm so sorry.'

'Sorry doesn't cut it. What exactly are you sorry for? Are you sorry I found out your sordid little secret?'

Despite herself Jean felt tears burning her cheeks as she crumpled onto the bed sobbing.

'Jean I am so sorry. I really am. I tried to tell you about Betsy and I that first day we met. But you insisted that we get to know each other properly first.'

'Don't lay the blame for this on me. We have been more than just friends, we've been....' Jean struggled to find the word for the intimacy they had shared.

'I know, but the more I got to know you the harder it became and I was afraid you would find out the truth and reject my friendship, reject me.'

'Ok try me. Please give me some credit.' said Jean sitting up and wiping her eyes.

So Dianne started to try to explain;

'I better begin at the beginning. I was twelve when my parents divorced. My mum had periods of inertia and morose depression and I suppose my father could bear it no longer. I can't blame him really, but I did for a long time, especially after my mum committed suicide. For most of my teenage years I harboured a real anger towards my father. It's only recently that I have been able to forgive him for rejecting my mother when she needed him most. He was a weak man then and he is a weak man now. But saying that he is also a good man and I for one am tired of the way Betsy treats him. That's part of the reason I moved back to Yorkshire and bought a house so close to them both. I hoped to diffuse the anger and resentment she feels towards him but I fear I have only enhanced it.

I was seventeen and at boarding school when he first introduced me to Betsy. She was a young slip of a girl then. She was barely in her twenties, not much older than me. That was part of the problem. I could never look upon her as a maternal figure. She always seemed to be more of a companion or a peer. My father was seduced by her youth and he saw in her a way to start again. He married her on the rebound. I think the death of my mother had knocked him for six. He probably felt guilty for not taking her threats of suicide more seriously.

He foisted a ready-made family upon Betsy, expecting her to take on the role of mother while he carried on with his bachelor lifestyle. Betsy put on such a brave face, but I could tell how hurt she was by his actions. She had fallen in love with a dashing older man. A Mr Rochester with a mad wife locked away in the attic. But she was no plain Jane Eyre, it's hard to believe it now but Betsy was a real beauty in those days. I was at an age where I was questioning my sexuality. I suppose I had always known. When I had crushes they were always on female teachers at boarding school. I was canny enough to not voice my emerging feelings but Betsy must have guessed.

It all kicked off when Martin my eldest brother joined the Navy. After six weeks of basic training he had a passing out parade and Betsy made arrangements for us all to travel to Portsmouth to watch the event. As usual my father had sudden urgent work to attend to. Although I suspect that Betsy guessed the truth. He was cheating on her even in those early days of their marriage. So it transpired that it was only Betsy and I who made the long coach trip to Portsmouth. When we reached the hotel, we realised that the Navy had mixed up the bookings. Instead of cancelling my father and Betsy's double room and booking a single, they had cancelled my single. There were no other empty rooms available so Betsy and I had no choice but to share. I was beside myself with excitement. I could not believe my good fortune. I still remember that night so vividly. I lay beside Betsy in the bed, arms by my side, on my back desperately trying to control my breathing. How long we lay in the dark I don't know, I think we both fell asleep. When I woke I was in her arms and it all seemed so natural and easy.

We carried on the affair right under my father's nose until I left for University. To this day he has never mentioned any knowledge of it, but sometimes I catch him observing Betsy and I, watching our body language, and I get the feeling he knows. Perhaps he has always known, deep down, or at the very least has suspected.

Personally I wish Betsy would just forget the whole thing, but I suppose even all these years later she is racked with guilt. This manifests itself in her drinking. She says it numbs the pain. Yes in retrospect she was wrong as I was a minor in her care. But nothing is black and white. I didn't exactly shy from the act. I wanted it as much as she. No amount of my telling her 'it's in the past, forget it' seems to do. She seems to wallow in it and gets territorial if she suspects I am getting close to anyone.'

Dianne fell silent then. She was waiting for a reaction from Jean.

'Please speak, just say anything,' she begged.

'I'm at a loss at what to say,' said Jean. 'It certainly explains Betsy's animosity towards me.'

'I still can't believe that Lucy never told you.'

'I swear she didn't. My god I would have remembered something like that.'

'Perhaps she was protecting us? Perhaps she didn't want you to judge us before you got to know us properly?'

'Yes,' said Jean. 'That sounds like Lucy. Can I ask you something?'

'Of course you can. That's the very least I owe you after what Betsy put you through today.'

'Does Betsy tell this secret to all of your girlfriends?'

'Only the ones she thinks matter.'

'So I suppose I should take this as a compliment that she thinks I matter.'

'Well, that is one way of looking at it.'

'Of course I am not really your girlfriend am I?' said Jean looking pointedly at Dianne.

Dianne thought a while before replying. 'No you're not my girlfriend, but yes you do matter to me.'

Jean stood up from the bed and began to empty her case.

'Does this mean what I think it means?' said Dianne.

'It means whatever you want it to mean.' Jean replied cryptically.

MARINA'S HOUSE

Tania fumbled in her handbag. She was trying to find the key for Marina's house.

Standing in the rain at her front door, she cursed herself for forgetting to check her handbag before leaving the Folly. Usually Peter would drop her off at her little part time job and return to collect her when she finished. But today he had some urgent business to attend to at the Police Station so she had taken the bus into Nowhere.

Tania had long since realised the necessity of owning a car when living somewhere as remote as the Crag. Peter's house was barely even on a bus route. It was a long trek of fifteen minutes to reach the bus stop and a hard bloody slog to trail back up the Crag laden with shopping. Peter had been known to abseil down the Crag to collect the newspaper and milk in the finer weather so laborious was the track.

Tania was thrilled that Peter had found her this little cleaning job as it gave her some pocket money and enabled her to feel a little more independent. Marina had a beautiful elegant house. Old money bred refinement and grace it must be said. As Tania's mother would say 'you can't make a silk purse from a sow's ear'. Isabella the au-pair peered out of the window when she heard the knocking on the front door. Shifting Prospero further up her hip she hastened to the hallway to open the door for Tania.

'Hello Tania, I did not realise it is you,' she said in broken English.

'I have forgotten my keys,' said Tania miming the motion of opening the door to the young Spanish girl. 'Hello handsome little man,' she said to a gurgling Prospero, tickling him under his chin. He was so like Nicolai at that age, cute as a button. How Marina could leave him each day and go to work in the University Tania did not know.

She Tania had had no choice when Nicolai had been a baby. She had to work to put food on the table and a roof over their heads. But Marina seemed so affluent, and Martin, Prospero's father was a Doctor for goodness sake.

The English were a very strange bunch indeed. Tania she had more in common with the young girl Isabella than English woman her own age. Going into the bathroom to collect the dirty washing from the laundry basket Tania spotted Marina's friend Yvonne busily painting in the spare room. There was another one who left her children in the care of someone else to go out and do their own thing. Unheard of in the Ukraine, Tania shook her head in disbelief.

Life with Peter had improved a little since that first dreadful night when he had come home drunk. He was courteous and polite whilst keeping a distance both in and out of the bedroom. Peter rarely approached her in any way in the marital bed. Most nights he would lay stock still, buttoned up in his flannel pyjamas, keeping firmly to his side of the bed. Tania found this very strange. She had assumed sexual relations would be a pre-requisite of the marriage but Peter seemed to have a very low libido. It was never discussed and on the few occasions they had been intimate Tania had found the lovemaking bizarre to say the very least.

They had been married for such a short while that Tania felt it too soon to broach the subject of bringing Nicolai to England. But she waited and planned for the day. The money she earned today would help. She squirreled most of it away in a bank account. Tania planned to transfer it to her mother in Cherkassy on a monthly basis. What seemed a pittance here was worth so much more in the country of her birth and would afford Nicolai and her mother many meals.

After filling the washing machine with its first load Tania collected the duster and polish from the cupboard in the utility room. Collecting a black bin bag from the drawer above the dishwasher she made her way into the study and towards Marina's desk. The study was a small box room enveloped on all sides by ceiling height bookshelves. Martin joked to Marina that it was a 'womb' like room, but such word play was lost in translation on both Isabella and Tania.

Sifting through Marina's wastepaper bin Tania retrieved the many scraps of paper and placed them in the black bag. Peter was most insistent that she retrieve any scrap paper from Marina's office and bring it back to the Crag. He explained that like most affluent people Marina would have no stock with the practice of recycling paper for the good of the environment. So upon his instructions Tania brought a black bag of old paperwork back to the Crag after every cleaning session. It could not be denied she found Peters request unusual, but if this strange practice pleased her husband then so be it. If she played by his rules he would be more willing to conform to her requests. The day her family would be reunited in a new homeland loomed over the horizon and she could not wait.

PLODINSKI OF THE YARD

Peter sat upon a fallen log in the garden upon the Crag. Between his legs he placed the black plastic bin bag that Tania had brought back from Marina's. He removed each piece of paper, carefully unfolding every sheet and speed reading the script. Scanning through the print he carefully scrutinised it for information he thought would be of interest to the Top Dog.

After the unfortunate Maggie incident Peter had endeavoured to keep a low profile. He was confident that the storm had blown over. The Earl's plan had worked a treat and Robbie was now enjoying a long overdue holiday at his Majesty's pleasure.

Marrying Tania had proved a good move too. It had deflected interest from his bachelor state and it had proved a lot more gossip worthy than his stolen car killing the old woman. Yes the gossipmongers had gone into overdrive regarding his new bride from the Ukraine. He bore the teasing with good grace. He was only too aware of his new nickname of 'Plodinski'. Well aware too of the whispered jokes about how he had joined the KGB and allusions to 'reds' in the bed' due to its close proximity to Russia.

THE CHATTON ART GALLERY, NEWCASTLE

A very nervous Yvonne stood at the rather grand entrance of the Chatton Art Gallery; she was flanked on one side by her children and on the other by Bob, his parents and Marina.

A large poster hanging from a flagpole declared that this was the opening night of the Annual Summer Art Exhibition.

'Come along now,' said Marina, as usual taking control of the situation. She decided that they had dithered at the entrance for long enough. The Chatton Art Gallery was situated in the grounds of the University. It was her turf so to speak. She had already had to stop twice to converse with some students and show off her new baby.

'Let's make a move or there will be no free bubbly and nibbles left.'

Striding ahead she made a formidable leader with Prospero gurgling happily in the papoose like contraption strapped to her chest. Portraying a confidence she did not feel Yvonne followed her into the vast auditorium. Bob straggled behind with his parents and the children. This was not really his kind of thing at all, he felt most uncomfortable as his black lace knickers were chaffing at his groin.

'All this 'arty farty' stuff leaves me cold.' he mumbled to his father.

'Where's mummy's painting? Where's mummy's painting?' the children pestered, pulling at the tails of Bob's jacket.

'Hang on you two, let daddy have a drink first.' said Bob taking the proffered glass of a rather cloudy looking white wine, and thanking the waiter.

'Now let's find mummy,' he said taking the children's hands.

Quickly scanning the room he spotted Yvonne's departing back as she turned the corner into another section of the gallery.

'Look daddy there's Uncle Ray,' said Grace pointing her finger excitedly.

Bob turned to look. Grace was right it did look like Yvonne's brother Raymond but what on earth would he be doing at an event such as this. Bob tried to weave his way across the room to say hello, but Raymond, if it had been Raymond was lost in the crowd.

A few minutes later Raymond stood outside the Gallery cupping his hands as he tried to light a cigarette back against the wind. God that had been close if George hadn't pointed out his sister he would have walked slap bang into Bob and the kids. That would have taken some explaining. Walking briskly out of the University grounds Raymond crossed the main street of the town. Now what was the name of that bar where he had promised to meet George? Looking to his left he saw a pub sign swinging in the breeze 'The Goose.' Of course, there it was. George and he had giggled over the name the other evening, fancy forgetting a name such as that. His George was fond of a goose and he would willingly oblige later that evening with a gander around his nether regions.

Meanwhile in the Gallery Yvonne was in a state of panic. Already she had glimpsed four nude portraits of herself in various mediums obviously executed by the students in the art class she posed for. She kicked herself for not foreseeing this scenario, after all this was the most prestigious Exhibition of the whole year so obviously the kids from University would be desperate to have their work displayed. Standing in front of one such charcoal life size drawing of herself, she realised that the likeness was for once uncanny and only the most blinkered would fail to recognise her. Seeing Bob approach Yvonne hastily crossed the gallery towards her friend Marina. Just before she reached her she felt a tentative tap upon her shoulder. Yvonne was taken aback to see that it was George Johnson her employer.

'What a rare treat indeed. Fancy meeting you here,' drawled a sycophantic George.

'Good evening Mr Johnson. I'm surprised to see you here. I didn't think that this would be your cup of tea at all. I thought you classed all modern art as overpriced untalented rubbish.'

'Oh a little bird told me you were one of the Exhibitors and I decided to surprise you with my patronage.'

'Thank you I'm flattered I but didn't think such amateur work would interest you.'

'Oh to the contrary I am interested in all of your artwork my dear girl. I found that charcoal life drawing especially well executed.'

'That's not my work Mr Johnson. My painting is the large oil in the next room.'

'I wonder?' said George smoothing his hair with the palm of his hand as he spoke. 'I wonder if Bob has noticed that charcoal drawing yet, the likeness to his wife is quite remarkable.'

Yvonne's expression must have displayed the panic she felt.

'Don't worry my dear your secret is safe with me. I shall see you at work on Monday and we must make a point of talking about that business proposition I made to you a while back. You will be well rewarded and I am sure I can pay more than the cash strapped University for your obvious talents.'

With this parting shot and a sly smile he disappeared into the crowd. Yvonne stood shaking, partly with anger and partly with fear. George's veiled threat had not gone unnoticed. She didn't want Bob to find out about her 'new job' and she certainly didn't want her father-in-law to see a drawing of her in her full glory. Her hand shook so much the wine was over spilling the rim. Hearing Marina calling her name she hastily reassembled her face and crossed to the other side of the Gallery.

Marina was grinning. She was really quite enjoying herself and Prospero slept soundly upon her breast lulled by the rhythm of her heartbeat. Seeing her friend approaching, Marina's grin stretched wider. 'I've been watching Bob,' she said. 'He's walked around the room at least twice now, but both times he's only given the charcoal drawing a cursory glance. I'm amazed he hasn't realised it's you.'

Marina turned and pointed at Bob. He stood lost in his own little world staring at a not particularly well executed Picasso inspired oil painting. 'Look at him Yvonne.' said Marina after a few minutes. 'He hasn't got a clue sweetie, he only sees what he wants to see. To be honest I think Martin would be the same. Men do like to compartmentalise their partners.'

Yvonne felt a tug at her handbag strap. It was Grace her youngest daughter.

'Mummy,' she pleaded, 'Daddy said if we were really good tonight we could have an ice-cream. I've been really good haven't I? I've been my very goodest.'

'Yes darling you have been your goodest.' said Yvonne. She was aware that Marina would tell her to correct her daughter's use of the English language, but it was so cute. 'But darling I don't think they have ice-creams here. This is a grown up night and grown up's don't usually have ice-creams at Art Galleries.'

Grace shrugged. 'I know that Mammy, but Daddy said if I asked you and you said yes, we might be able to leave this boring place and go somewhere fun.'

As she said this her older sister Becky nudged her and said. 'Daddy told you not to say that silly, we won't get ice-cream now.'

Marina laughed out loud upon hearing this exchange, causing Prospero to whimper woken by the sudden jolt. Leaning down towards the girls she reached into her handbag and said. 'Here's a fiver. Give this to your dad and tell him I'll stay here and drive your mum home. I really am having the most tremendous time.'

'Are granny and grandpa leaving too?' asked Yvonne.

'Yes granny said that all these naked women were no good for grandpa's blood pressure.' said Grace.

Marina laughed out loud again but this time she took the precaution of putting her hands over Prospero's tiny ears first so as not to startle him like before.

Once everyone had left and the goodbye's had been said, Marina took Yvonne by the arm and said. 'Come on, let's circulate and eavesdrop. I wonder if anyone else will recognise you,' she said winking. 'I had a preview at 'Nudecastle' so I suppose I am at an advantage.'

The charcoal drawing was attracting quite a crowd. Yvonne saw that it already had a red 'sold' sticker on its frame. She felt a momentary flush of pride. Rupert the Director of the Gallery hastened to Yvonne's side.

'That was the very first picture we sold tonight,' he confided. 'The gentleman was very insistent we put the sticker on it straight away.'

'I'm intrigued,' said Marina. 'Did you know the gentleman in question?'

'Not personally.' confessed Rupert. 'But I am given to understand he usually deals in fine art antiques so it is quite a compliment that he chose to buy from a virtual amateur.'

'He obviously saw great potential in both the artist and his model.' said Marina unaware of the change in Yvonne's pallor as she realised the significance of the drawing being sold. She knew who the mysterious buyer had been and that it would be used as the ultimate bargaining tool....

BOB TAKES A TRIP

It was the evening following the opening of the Art Exhibition and Bob was all dressed up in his very best bib and tucker. He was clean shaven with splash of aftershave and wearing the new shirt that Yvonne had bought him for Christmas.

He popped his head into the lounge where Yvonne stood ironing. She had been very subdued since the previous evening and Bob was worried that he had upset her by leaving the Exhibition early. He had been trying to make amends ever since and had even offered to cancel his night out. Yvonne would not hear of it and was most insistent he should go out and enjoy himself. Secretly she was quite looking forward to a nice quiet night in and the chance to gather her thoughts about Mr Johnson's business proposition.

'Ok honey I'm off now. Don't wait up as I'm not sure what the lads have planned for Tom.' Tom was one of the taxi drivers and tonight was his 'stag do'. It was not until after he had left the house that Bob began to panic. The enormity of what he was planning to do and where he was planning to visit suddenly struck him. What in heaven's name was he doing? Firstly he had lied to Yvonne, making up this imaginary friend, a fellow taxi driver who was supposedly getting married. Yvonne had only to talk to any of the lads at the taxi office to pick holes in that daft lie. And secondly he was doing something really stupid and was risking his marriage into the bargain.

Newcastle was heaving. Rowdy crowds of youths spilled from the bars onto the pavements as girls in tottering high heels and very little else staggered arms linked along the cobbled back lanes. A performance at the Royal Theatre had just finished and well dressed middle-aged couples fell into step with the much younger pub crawlers. Bob strode through the crowds mimicking a confidence which he did not feel. The queue at the Inn Cognito stretched the entire length of the Evening Chronicle building. Three of the women at the front of the queue were flirting outrageously with a bouncer. They laughed and joked in their fake shrill voices. To the casual observer the women were just older women on a night out having fun. But even from a distance it was obvious to Bob that the women were not all they seemed to be. With their sexually provocative clothes, over made-up faces and badly fitting wigs Bob could almost be sitting in his shed at home staring into a mirror. Trying to appear inconspicuous and as a result probably appearing the opposite Bob joined the back of the queue waiting nervously for his turn to hand over his cash.

Once inside the club the music was deafening. A repetitive back beat boomed from the loudspeakers. The flashing lights and darkness took a while to adjust to, but Bob finally made out a bar lit up in the distance and made his way towards it. Dutch courage was definitely the order of the day. Reminding himself that this trip was just to test the water Bob stood at the bar waiting for the barman to look his way.

The guy standing in front of him at the bar seemed vaguely familiar to Bob, his stance and build, the cut of his hair at the nape of his neck. It was only when the chap found voice and ordered from the barman that the penny dropped and Bob realised it was Yvonne's kid brother Raymond. What the hell was he doing here? Did he not know it was a gay bar? Bob skulked away into the shadows and watched as Raymond crossed the dance floor and walked towards a table at the far corner of the room. The figure sitting there turned to acknowledge Raymond taking the proffered glass and laying a proprietary hand upon his buttocks. Raymond bent over to kiss his older lover and it was then that Bob recognised the distinctive profile of George Johnson. At once intrigued yet repulsed Bob stared at the couple. He simply could not believe his eyes. Bloody Hell, were George and Raymond a couple? For a brief moment he wondered whether Yvonne knew but he just as quickly dismissed this thought. Yvonne had proved during her affair with Clive that she was not well versed in the art of deception. He had known of that little interlude well before the shit hit the proverbial fan. There was no way Yvonne could have kept this little secret. Darting even further into the shadows Bob fell against a tall elegant woman dressed in a bright siren red dress.

'Sorry love,' Bob apologised.

'Oh the pleasure was all mine,' purred the lady in red as she looked Bob up and down before adding,' but by way of an apology you may buy me a drink.'

Finding it difficult to speak Bob nodded his head motioning towards her glass.

'Vodka martini darling,' said the woman in a very husky voice. 'In the words of the devastatingly handsome James, shaken but not stirred.'

Bob looked blank, he was literally rendered speechless. Running her long false nails down the entire length of Bob's shirt sleeve the woman said. 'The correct response darling is to say I am a cunning linguist and joke about Pussy Galore.'

'Oh James Bond,' said Bob, understanding at last. 'I'm sorry I'm new to all this.'

'You don't say,' she laughed. 'My name is Scarlett by the way.'

'I'm Bert' said Bob, saying the first name with a letter B that sprung to his mind.

Scarlett laughed a deep throaty laugh 'I had a friend had a Prince Albert once, said it hurt like hell'

Bob again looked bemused, this time he did not even try to conceal it. He felt like a drowning man he was so far out of his depth.

'Tell me something Bert?' said Scarlett taking a long sip of her vodka martini, 'Have you ever been here before, something tells me you are a newbie to all this.'

Bob nodded his head. He was puzzled and he had no idea where this conversation was going.

Scarlett smiled. 'Forget the drink Bert, I must be mad, but someone needs to take you under their wing and I reckon I am just the bird for the job.'

'Come with me Bert,' Scarlett said taking him by the hand.

Still bemused and bewildered Bob allowed himself to be led from the darkened room and through a side door. The passageway was a blaze of light and Bob stumbled as he was led down it. Scarlett stopped abruptly in front of two doors. The door to the left had a sign saying '*Ladies*' and the door to the right a sign saying '*Gents*'.

Looking directly at Bob, Scarlett put the question to him. 'Well tell me Bert, are you Arthur or Martha?'

Bob shrugged he was struggling to think coherently let alone speak coherently too. He was stunned into action upon hearing a voice coming from the far end of the corridor. He instantly recognised the fake public school accent of George Johnson. Bob turned quickly and ushered Scarlett through the nearest door.

'My, my we are an impatient boy aren't we?' said Scarlett. 'As I say it is always the quiet ones.'

Once inside the toilets Scarlett again took the lead and dragged a suddenly compliant Bob into the nearest cubicle. Leaning across him she locked the door her breasts brushing against his chest. Lowering the toilet seat she carefully sat down. Without preamble she grabbed Bob's testicles and gave them a quick squeeze. 'Well someone seems very pleased to see me. May I?'

Before Bob had a chance to even form a reply his trousers were around his ankles and Scarlett's ruby red lips were wrapped around his penis. Giving in to the moment Bob grabbed Scarlett by the hair. He was only slightly put off his stride when he found himself holding her wig which had somehow become detached. Scarlett continued on regardless, bald as a coot, her exposed skull shiny with perspiration.

'My my,' said Scarlett dabbing her lips on a piece of toilet roll. 'Care to return the favour Bert?'

Not waiting for an answer she stood up and unbuttoned her straining top to reveal a sexy red lace bra. Pulling the cup down with her long red nails she exposed a plump breast with a dark very pronounced nipple. Seeing Bob staring she said, 'I'm halfway through the whole thing darling.'

Grabbing Bob's hand she encircled her breast with his fingers. 'Touch it,' she encouraged, 'It feels just like a proper tit.'

Bob obliged and Scarlett purred with satisfaction. Leaning back against the toilet cistern she lifted her skirt to reveal stockings, suspenders and a corset style pair of panties. Giving a disparaging laugh Scarlett said, 'Very Bridget Jones I know, but my ops not until next year.'

Shuffling Bob around she pushed him firmly onto the toilet seat. She shrugged the panties from her hips until they lay in a heap upon the floor. Bob watched their descent before raising his eyes to Scarlett's groin. Scarlett's penis sprung to life like a hairy performing snake, one blinking eye stared at Bob, glistening.

'Come on Bert, do the deed,' said Scarlett her voice husky with passion and anticipation. Scarlett pulled his head towards her groin, thrusting outwards to meet his mouth. Bob gagged. He couldn't do it.

The smell of masculine sweat repulsed him. He gagged, choking as if he were a cat with a fur ball. Clumsily he got to his feet and struggled to open the door. 'I'm sorry I can't, I'm not gay,' he mumbled. Bob stumbled from the cubicle and ran towards the sink where he released a torrent of vomit. After heaving out his guts for what seemed like an eternity Bob raised his head to look at his reflection in the mirror. His face was ashen, his hair sleek as a seals and a trace of vomit clung to his chin. At the exact moment Bob raised his hand to remove the vomit George Johnson emerged from the next toilet cubicle. Their eyes met and locked for a second. Bob waited for George to acknowledge him in some way. But George looked straight through him as if he were not there and calmly crossed to wash his hands. As he passed behind Bob, George leant right into him and said. 'We were never here, we never met.' Bob nodded at George's reflection in the mirror. As a parting shot George motioned his head towards Scarlett who was standing in the entrance to the toilet cubicle holding her still erect penis in her hands.

'You really shouldn't keep a lady waiting Bob, it's very bad manners,' George said in a sarcastic voice.

Scarlett intoned. 'Hey Bert your mates right at least give me a hand job, fairs fair.'

When Bob eventually left the nightclub, he was shaking from head to toe and not even trying to conceal it. The crowds were still on the pavement drinking their flat lager and they didn't even give Bob a cursory glance as he stumbled past them tripping up on the cobbles. Sitting on the bus home, Bob closed his eyes. Perhaps, he reasoned, if he closed his eyes he could make believe that the last few hours hadn't happened. Opening them again he stared at his reflection in the glass window. He tried to see if he had changed at all from the Bob earlier that night. He felt an urge to turn to the young lass sitting opposite him and ask, 'Hey do I look strange to you, would you guess that I've just had a blow job from a man in a frock? Do I look queer? Do I look gay? Do I look like a poof? Do I look like a nancy? Call it what you wish. Will my wife know? Will my wife be able to tell? Gripping the edge of the seat he forced himself to read the adverts glued to the side's of the seats, until eventually as they reached the outskirts of Nowhere and he could feel his breathing return to normal.

When many hours later Yvonne eventually tore herself away from the television and made her way up to bed she was shocked to find Bob already there. He was lying sparked out in his pyjamas sleeping soundly. He must have crept in the house while she sat watching the television and gone straight to bed. How strange and disconcerting that she had not heard him come into the house. My God he could have been anyone sneaking into her house and into her bed. As she climbed into bed, she deliberately rested her ice cold feet against the small of his back. Feeling him wince and recoil from her touch she smiled with inner satisfaction. It served the bugger right for giving her a shock like that. If he expected an early morning cuppa tomorrow he was very much mistaken. With this last thought she drifted off into a deep sleep.

Bob lay by her side curled up in the foetal position feigning the long shallow breaths of sleep. He couldn't have faced Yvonne's interrogation tonight. To look her in the eyes and lie earlier that night had been hard enough but to lie about this was so much harder. He kept reminding himself that Yvonne had slept with creepy Clive from the pub but this was much worse. A revelation such as this would blow a marriage apart. It would smatter any illusions of a patch up. Even Relate couldn't relate to something as heinous as this.

LARKSPUR RISE – THE ARTISTS STUDIO

Yvonne was spending the evening at Marina's yet again. Ever since Marina had suggested that Yvonne use her spare room as a makeshift studio she seemed to take every opportunity to 'pop across town for a few hours'. The arrangement suited Yvonne well as she could work so much more productively in the calming atmosphere of Larkspur Rise. Marina would normally be in her study preparing Lectures and they would meet in the kitchen every few hours for a catch up and mug of 'Nescaff.' Whenever she set up the art equipment in the room Yvonne would feel a fire in her belly which she had not felt for such a long time. The sensation of the brush in her hand and the drag of the paint across the canvas was like rediscovering a long lost friend.

For her latest project Yvonne was recreating Raphael's 'Madonna of the Pinks'. This was no mean feat as it was a very complex painting. George had sourced the paints and the fruitwood panel from god knows where. He was very thorough in his planning and insistent that she only use age appropriate paints and materials. The amount of money he had offered her would pay outright for the loft extension she and Bob had planned. George had sworn her to secrecy, a request she was all too happy to comply with. Marina had asked some tricky questions early on but now seemed convinced by Yvonne's story about entering a competition reproducing old masters.

The painting was proving very difficult to replicate. It was very small in scale as it had originally been intended to be held in the hand as an aid to prayer. Yvonne was finding the pink flowers which the young baby Christ was handing to his mother particularly difficult to get just right. She couldn't seem to get the correct tone to indicate the delicate nature of the petals. Yvonne paused for a while and drew back to look long and hard at the painting. At that very moment Marina entered the room with a tiny knock. Marina gasped as she saw the painting taking shape. 'Wow Yvonne that is amazing, I feel as if I am walking into an art gallery.'

Yvonne laughed self consciously, 'I tell you what,' she said. 'I promise to paint you and Prospero next. You two can be my first commission.'

'I can only pay you in cups of 'Nescaff.'

'Suits me fine.....'

'Tell you what I can go one better than that tonight and offer you a glass of wine?

'Oh that sounds so tempting I really shouldn't.'

'But you will.' Marina chuckled.

'Is the Pope a Catholic?

'You've got me there sweetie,' Marina replied. 'But I do believe that like me he was a keen patron of the arts.'

NOWHERE CASTLE – THE EARLS PRIVATE QUARTERS.

The Earl was a happy man. Pouring himself and George Johnson large brandies he raised his glass and allowed himself a smug self-satisfied smile. The day had gone surprisingly well and it seemed the sale of 'Madonna of the Pinks' was in the bag. The Raphael painting which had hung for many years in the castle corridor had finally been authenticated by the experts at the National. The painting had until recently been thought of as a copy dating from the 16th or 17th century but infrared reflectography had revealed an under drawing which was characteristic of Raphael. The painting had been acquired by the old Earl in 1853 having prior to that been a highlight of the Camuccini Collection in Rome. The old Earl had so loved the painting that he had commissioned Giovanni Montiroli to design it a Renaissance revival frame. A chance visit by a curator in the early nineties had convinced the Earl to allow the National Gallery to take the painting away for examination. This had allowed it to be authenticated as a 'lost' Raphael as further tests under a microscope had also identified pigments of paint used in other works by Raphael. The attribution had seen the value of the artwork soar and as a result the Earl had informed the Art World that the painting was for sale. The National had immediately mounted a campaign to raise the funds to purchase it and keep it on English soil. The Earl had just received a phone call to say the reserve had been reached and the two parties had agreed on a collection date the following month.

George Johnson had timed his visit to the castle perfectly as the Earl needed to stress to him the urgency for his artist to complete the copy of the 'pinks'. It needed time to dry sufficiently for it to be installed in the original Renaissance frame and convince the curator that it was in fact the original. George also had the timely news that a private collector abroad was very interested in purchasing the original as soon as the furore had died down.

All in all reflected the Earl it had been a very productive day. Even allowing for George's 'cut' of the profits the coffers of the Earl's bank account would be swollen. If only his darling wife would get off his back about this bloody garden project of hers then life would be perfect.

BUTTING IS FOR NANNY GOATS

Lennie eased her car into the stream of traffic in the fast lane increasing her speed so she could overtake the lorry up ahead. A large bunch of flowers lay on the back seat, purchased this time from a proper florists shop not a bucket in a garage. Lennie's overnight bag was settled comfortably in the boot. She was driving to Tracey's house in Saltaire to take her away for a romantic anniversary weekend at a very exclusive Country House Spa near Robin Hoods Bay.

She had booked the venue; she had bought the flowers, now all she needed was to collect her lady.

Lennie pulled into Fanny Street just as dawn was breaking. She had left Nowhere at some ungodly hour of the morning in order to avoid the worst of the traffic and as a consequence had reached Saltaire in record time. Tracey would be surprised as she hadn't expected Lennie until much later that morning. Lennie carefully parked up her car and leant across the back seat to retrieve the flowers.

Walking up the path towards the front door Lennie peered through the bay window into the lounge and beyond into the kitchen diner. She was taken aback to see the shapes of two figures sitting at the breakfast bar eating breakfast. It's very early to be entertaining visitors she thought to herself.

'Hello, it's only me' she called as she opened the door with the key that Tracey had finally got around to having cut for her.

Tracey was immediately in the hallway.

My god thought Lennie she must have sprinted from the kitchen at breakneck speed. Tracey was wearing a bathrobe which was loosely fastened by the waist. Lennie had the impression that she was naked beneath it.

Giving herself a mental shake to regain her composure Tracey took the proffered flowers from Lennie's hands.

She made a great play of sniffing the flowers before saying. 'Oh Lennie, what lovely flowers, they smell exquisite.'

Lennie released her grip upon the bouquet but didn't say anything.

'We have a visitor. Sandra's here,' Tracey said in a rather breathless voice. Seeing the expression that raced across Lennie's face she continued more quietly. 'The plumbing at her flat has given up the ghost so she stopped the night here.'

Again registering Lennie's expression she added. 'She slept on the couch.'

'That's something you forgot to tell me on the telephone last night, wasn't it?'

Lennie said, hating herself for sounding so petty and jealous.

'I would have told you but I hoped she would be gone before you arrived,' Tracey countered.'

'Apparently.'

'What I mean is that I would have told you but I was trying to avoid a scene.'

'And what makes you think I would have made a scene?'

'You make a scene whenever I mention her name.'

Lennie was about to reply when Sandra's head appeared around the doorway. 'I thought I heard voices, hello Jenny.'

'It's Lennie,' barked Lennie.

'Sorry,' said Sandra barely bothering to mask a smirk. 'I'm terrible with names. Would you like me to put more coffee on the stove, I'm afraid we've drained the pot?'

It was the way that she asked which really got to Lennie. The way she made the assumption that she and Tracey were a 'we' and Lennie was the interloper, the uninvited guest. Determined not to lose face Lennie replied. 'Thanks Miranda that would be very kind of you.'

'It's Sandra,' intoned Sandra.

'I'm sorry,' said Lennie shooting Sandra a self-satisfied smile. 'I'm usually so good with names, this forgetfulness must be catching.'

Turning to Tracey she added. 'I'm going upstairs to freshen up. I didn't even stop off at Scotch Corner I was in such a rush to get here.'

As she reached the top of the stairs she noticed that the door to Tracey's bedroom was tightly shut. Lennie waited a while until she heard the converstion resume in the kitchen then hating herself for being so suspicious but unable to resist, Lennie crossed the passage and swung the door gently ajar. As she had feared the bed was unmade. Two sets of underwear lay in a heap by the chest of drawers.

The room smelt of sex. Sweet and pungent. The unmistakable smell of sex.

She knew then without a doubt. Perhaps she had always known but filed it away in a recess of her mind. She knew that Sandra and Tracey were still lovers. Lennie felt as if her heart would burst. She wanted to run into the kitchen, and confront them but some sense of self-preservation stopped her and instead she walked calmly into the bathroom and washed her face and hands. She never stopped to think of the symbolism of the act.

Sandra left eventually, smiling slyly as she made her goodbyes.

Lennie sat waiting in the lounge as Tracey finished her holiday packing. All the time Lennie adopted a cool exterior, she was determined to play along with the farce that was their relationship. She helped Tracey pile her bags into the boot of the car and opened the passenger door for her to clamber into the front seat. Tracey all the while seemed oblivious to the tension and artificial tone of the atmosphere.

They drove East towards Whitby. Tracey prided herself on her ability to read maps and was obviously enjoying her role as navigator. The subject of Sandra hung between them like a bad smell, the elephant in the room, but Lennie was determined not to mention her name.

It proved to be a much longer journey than either had envisaged due to the Bank Holiday traffic and Lennie suggested they stop off at a Motorway Services for a cup of coffee. Leaving Tracey waiting in the long cafeteria queue she excused herself to nip to the ladies. Instead of going to the toilet she crossed towards the public telephone at the back of the newsagent shop. Carefully checking that she was out of Tracey's line of vision she took the Hotel details from her handbag and telephoned to cancel the booking. When she returned to the queue Tracey had just ordered the coffee and was deliberating whether to have a chocolate brownie or a doughnut.

About an hour later they approached the long tree-lined drive which led to the Country House Hotel and Spa. Tracey was enchanted. 'Oh look darling,' she said pointing to a copse of trees by the imposing glass orangery. 'There's a little pond behind those willow trees.'

'Oh and look,' she continued, 'are those peacocks on that grass verge?'

Lennie stared ahead pretending to concentrate on her driving. Just before she reached the palatial columns marking the entrance to the Hotel she stopped the car. Tracey looked at her quizzically.

'I'll just stop here and let you out with the luggage,' said Lennie, 'then I can park up. It will save us dragging the suitcases across the gravel.'

Putting the car into neutral she climbed out and opened the boot. Tracey had packed enough for a trip up Everest. She had brought five cases in all and numerous make-up bags. Lennie calmly lifted the cases and bags out onto the drive, taking care to leave her own in the boot. She then walked to the side of the car and opened the passenger door to help Tracey out. Tracey was beaming as she alighted from the car. The sun was blazing in the clear blue sky, quite perfect Bank Holiday weather. She grappled in her handbag for her sunglasses as she squinted in the sunshine.

'Shall I go and book us in whilst you park up my darling?' she enquired.

'No need' said Lennie, trying to keep the pitch of her voice as even as possible.

'I rang up and cancelled the booking when we stopped in the Service Station earlier this morning.'

Saying this she turned and walked back to the driver's seat of the car. She calmly climbed in and closed both doors using the central locking system on her fob.

Tracey stood blinking in the sunshine her sunglasses still in her hands. She was astounded. Had she heard correctly? Eventually she made her way over to Lennie and indicated that she wind down the window. Lennie opened the window a tiny jot so she could hear Tracey.

'But, but.' Tracey began.

'My dear Tracey' said Lennie, quite enjoying the moment in a perverse way. 'Butting is for nanny goats.'

'I'm driving back to Nowhere now,' she said opening the window a fraction more to so she could drop Tracey's house keys onto the gravel drive. 'I suggest you ring Sandra and ask her to drive across to collect you. I do hope you will be very happy together, she is welcome to you.'

Then with a wave of her hand she reversed the car slowly down the drive. Her last sighting of Tracey was of a lone figure standing on the gravel surrounded by masses of luggage.

Lennie began to shake uncontrollably. She drove for a few miles then stopped in a lay-by on the main road to collect her thoughts. As she sat there the heavens opened. Bloody typical Bank Holiday she thought to herself. Then a picture formed in her mind of Tracey standing in the rain, surrounded by her belongings, soaking wet. Lennie began to howl with laughter, but the laughter soon turned to tears. Big wet tears of despair. Yet despite the tears she felt a lightness she hadn't felt for a long while. Opening the car door she stepped out into the rain and raising her face to the sky she said.

'Thank you God, as usual your timing is impeccable.'

REACHING FOR THE MOON

Jean had received a reply to her lonely hearts advertisement. She took the letter from the pile upon the doormat and placed it an angle wedged against the butter dish. It was an ordinary looking envelope, plain bog standard white. But what lay within its innocuous folds? Jean sat looking at the envelope as she ate her cereal. She sat looking at it as she drained the dregs of the tea from the pot.

She stood looking at it as she collected the dirty dishes from the table and prepared the wash up. Whilst the dishes drained on the rack the letter still lay unopened leaning against the butter dish. Jean wandered out into the garden and unlocked the rabbit's hutch. Fudge the rabbit hopped out and after sniffing Jean's slippers for a few moments ran off to explore the hedge. Still the letter lay unopened.

Jean wandered back into the kitchen, boiled the kettle to make more tea all the while averting her eyes from where the letter lay. As the kettle boiled she tried to analyse her fear of opening the letter.

Was she afraid of getting hurt?

Was she afraid of embarking upon another relationship?

Was it too soon after Lucy's death?

Or was she just still hoping the situation with Dianne would change?

Her reverie was broken by a tune playing upon her telephone indicating that she had received a telephone message. Her heart skipped a beat when she realised the message was from Dianne. Her euphoria was short lived when she discovered that Dianne was ringing to say she had received three replies to her advertisement and had made dates with all three ladies the following week.

Refusing to allow herself to sink any further into a melancholy Jean made her way across the kitchen and opened the envelope.

The caption read 'Reach for the moon.'

The card made Jean smile for the first time for days. The message inside was brief but to the point.

'Hi, I've got the record by Rupert Holmes. Ring me and we can give it a spin. Ruby 0191 2587902.'

Jean laughed out loud, this Ruby seemed to share her sense of humour. Impulsively she decided to ring her straight away. The call went to voicemail and Jean nearly lost her nerve and hung up but she had promised herself she would speak to Ruby and speak to her she would.

'Hi Ruby, thank you for the card it made me smile. Yes, let's escape... it sounds like fun. Oh this is Jean. Bye then.'

Then Jean sat on the uncomfortable leather couch, her telephone on the table by the side of the couch and willed it to ring.

LARKSPUR RISE – FIST SHAPED DOORS

Marina was rushing around; she was late or would be if she didn't get a wriggle on. She had a new class of students starting her classes that very morning and was ill-prepared. She was no stranger to academia but this mothering lark was proving one big spanner in the works.

Marina had planned to spend the previous evening preparing her lecture notes. Martin who had promised to babysit had been called away to London on urgent business and had handed Prospero over to Isabella the au-pair. Normally this scenario would have been fine but Prospero had other ideas. He wanted Marina and no-one else would do. Marina's every attempt to hand him over to Isabella was met with a heart wrenching wail. For such a tiny baby he had a very powerful set of lungs. The only thing that seemed to calm him was being nursed. She was aware that he was using her breast as a human dummy but none of the artificial ones would do the trick. They had tried several brands from the chemist but none would suffice. Martin joked that his son took after his father a, purist and connoisseur. His joke had been met with a withering look from Marina as timing had never been his strong point.

Marina and Isabelle had arranged cushions upon Marinas' lap in the study which had enabled her to nurse a fractious Prospero and work on her notes. But it was a far from ideal solution. The tot of whisky that Isabella had brought her employer had helped to numb the pain produced by the constant suckling, but by the time Prospero had eventually gone to sleep Marinas eyelids were so heavy a matchstick would have buckled under the strain.

This morning Prospero lay grizzling in his cot, intermittently letting out a whimper.

'It is his tooth which is paining him,' stated the suddenly wise Isabella.

She was the eldest of six siblings and knew the language of cries.

'I know that' snapped Marina, instantly regretting her irritability. My god without Isabella the previous evening would have been so much worse.

'I'm sorry for being so grumpy,' she said 'Prospero has been fractious all night but it is wrong of me to take it out on you.'

She turned towards the cot and caught the calf of her leg on the side of the drawers.

'Miss Marina,' said Isabella addressing her employer. 'I think you have a step ladder in your stocking.'

'Bloody hell,' Marina mumbled, not raising her voice for fear of disturbing Prospero, 'a ladder that's all I need and these are my last clean pair.'

Going into the bathroom she grappled in the washing basket trying to resurrect a half decent once worn pair of tights to wear until she could get to the shops after work. God the things she was reduced to, her once ordered life a confusion of half completed tasks. To think that such a sweet tiny creature could so alter the equilibrium of her day.

At that moment Tania walked into the bathroom, duster in hand and mop tucked under her arm. 'I'm sorry,' she said. 'I would have knocked but I have no hands free.'

She lowered the mop onto the tiled floor and began to dust the mirror above the sink. At that moment Prospero let out a long loud wail. Tania dropped the duster to the ground and raced across the passage to his side. Murmuring quietly she carefully rubbed her digit finger across his red inflamed gums applying a slight pressure. Prospero let out a long sigh of contentment.

'Miss Marina have you any vodka?' Tania called across the landing. Marina was sitting on the toilet seat trying to ease her foot into the slightly damp pair of stockings. She had eventually located a half decent pair under a pile of damp towels. She would need pints of Chanel No 5 to mask the damp dog smell.

'Don't you think it's a bit early to be drinking?' said Marina, wondering what on earth this strange Ukrainian woman was talking about.

Tania laughed. 'It is not for me, Miss Marina, it is for Prospero.'

'Well I certainly think it's too early for him to be drinking,' said Marina in an incredulous voice.

Again Tania laughed. 'It is not for drinking Miss Marina it is to rub on his gums, it is an old Russian trick my mother taught me when my Nicolai was making the baby teeth.'

Marina was unconvinced but she hated seeing her baby in such discomfort. If Tania had suggested that she dress up in lime green leggings and stick a straw up her nose she would have been tempted to try it.

Marina poured a small amount of vodka into an egg cup and handed it to Tania. Tania rubbed the alcohol onto Prospero's gums. It seemed to do the trick almost instantaneously and Prospero snuggled down into his cot blanket. He was soon drifting off into a deep pain free sleep.

'I have a spare pair of stockings in my bag if you wish,' said Tania.

'I suppose that's an old Russian trick too, I certainly don't think Prospero is old enough to wear stockings,' joked Marina.

'No,' said Tania, the joke going over her head. 'I just always carry a spare pair for emergencies and noticed you had a hole in yours.'

Damn thought Marina, I must have snagged them taking them from the washing basket.

It was as Tania was searching in her handbag for the stockings that Marina first noticed the deep bruising and swelling under her eyes. She had cleverly concealed the purple black blemishes with foundation but no amount of make-up could hide them when seen at such close quarters. Tania's sleeve ruffled up as she reached into her bag revealing a matching set of bruises upon her wrist.

'Tania however did you get those dreadful bruises?' Marina exclaimed.

Tania shrugged saying, '*Old Russian proverb, I am the woman who walks into doors.*'

'Must be fist shaped doors on that Crag of yours then,' said Marina. 'I'll get Martin to check them over when he gets back, and we'll talk about this later.'

'There is nothing to talk about,' said Tania defensively. 'I am clumsy old woman that is all. I am foolish Baba Yaga.'

Much later after Marina had left for the University, Tania turned towards the light and inspected the bruises beneath her eyes. 'Bloody things' she thought to herself. She had tried so hard to hide them earlier that morning. She could never tell Marina how they had been inflicted. Things between a husband and wife were personal and to talk of them would be a betrayal of a trust.

Her new husband was a deeply troubled man of that she had no doubt. His infrequent visits upon her body to exercise his conjugal rights were an ordeal of degradation for Tania. They followed a strict pattern. He would watch her go up to bed, feigning a great interest in some television programme. Then appear ten minutes later at her side dressed in a dog collar and lead. Without speaking he would unclip the lead and motion for her to raise her arms above her head. He would then tie her wrists tightly to the bedposts and blindfold her with the dog collar.

She would sense him standing at the foot of the bed, his breathing becoming increasingly laboured. He would start to bark strange words in an unfamiliar tongue, unlike any language she had heard before. The bizarre ordeal would end as he lumbered upon her upturned body and forced his way into her tender flesh, thrusting and grinding against her buttocks.

After he was spent Peter would immediately leave the room, giving her a chance to wriggle free from the restraints, rearrange her clothing and remove the dog collar blindfold. Tania would then lie cowering in the bed covering her ears with the pillow. For despite the fact her husband had inflicted pain upon her she could not bear the sounds of him inflicting pain upon himself. The swish of the whip had an unmistakeable sound and the blood splattered towel in the washing basket the next morning would bear witness to the previous night's events. She had once came upon her husband in the shower and let out a cry of horror as she saw the ugly bleeding welts upon his torso.

When she returned from work at the University later that afternoon Isabella informed her Tania had made an excuse to leave work early. Marina was well aware of her cleaning lady's reluctance to speak of her marriage and she decided there and then to take matters into her own hands and make discreet enquiries regarding the elusive Peter Dodd. For if there was one thing that Marina could not stand it was a bully and surely only a bully would inflict such injuries upon his wife.

RUBY TUESDAY

The loud trilling sound broke Jean's concentration. She let the telephone ring on the hook for a few seconds before she picking it up and answering it. She was expecting a call from Ruby and was ridiculously nervous.

'Hello,' she said.

A strange voice answered.

'Hi, is that Jean?' enquired the voice.

'Speaking,' said Jean,

'Hi this is Ruby.'

'Hello Ruby, it's nice to put a voice to the name at last,' said Jean trying to inject in her tone a confidence that she did not feel.

'I'm incredibly nervous' said Ruby, with a slight tremor to her voice.

'Well that makes two of us' Jean replied, relieved that she was not alone in finding the situation incredibly unusual.

'You sound nice,' said Ruby. 'I like your accent, is it Yorkshire?'

'Yes,' Jean conceded, 'it's a Yorkshire accent. I was born and bred in Pontefract.'

'Is that where the famous cakes come from?' said Ruby with a laugh to her voice.

'That's right.'

'Is it true that early in the morning the whole town smells of liquorice?'

'It's true,' said Jean. 'I can't stand the stuff. I think I was sickened of it being brought up so close to the factories.'

Ruby laughed. 'I heard that some politician declared that they couldn't be called cakes as they were actually sweets.'

'Don't get me started on politics,' said Jean.

The tension had lifted and before long the two women were chatting away like long-lost friends.

'I must get a coffee I'm hoarse from all this laughing,' said Jean eventually.

'Me too,' said Ruby. 'Give me five minutes and I'll ring you back.'

'Ok will do,' said Jean, hanging up the telephone and going into the kitchen. Walking past the kettle she took a bottle of red wine from the rack below the kitchen unit. She quickly uncorked it and poured herself an extremely large glass. This getting to know people was great fun, such an adventure, but bloody nerve racking too.

NOWHERE CASTLE – A DARK AND DANK CELLAR

The Countess was dusty, cold and exhausted. She had been rooting around in the Castle cellars for the better part of an hour. So far her search had gleaned a few artefacts which would be perfect for the WTF Charity Auction later that month. The stack of old ornaments and picture frames were now piled in a haphazard heap by the stone stairs of the cellar.

What had at first appeared to be something of an adventure was rapidly turning into a thankless chore. Not for the first time the Countess wished that she had accepted Lillian Johnson's offer of help. Had it not been for the fact that Lillian was so infuriatingly servile in her presence the Countess would have snapped her hands off?

How the Countess had ended up being patron of the WTF she was at a loss to say. She had been railroaded into it by a very persistent Lillian and her reasons were not as altruistic as they appeared because she hoped to gain interest in her garden project as a knock on effect of the auction.

To this end she found herself spending her weekend rooting like a latter day 'Steptoe' amongst her husband's ancestors cast-off possessions. Spying an interesting looking bundle of clothes in a deep recess of the cellar the Countess rolled up her sleeves and waded in. Beneath the clothes she could found an old wooden trunk. Intrigued she swept the dusty pile of clothes away and prised the clasp of the trunk open. Reaching gingerly into its depths her fingers grazed something cold with deep grooves embedded into it. It seemed to be the edge of an ornately carved frame, possibly an old family photograph or mirror. Only a small section of it was visible to the eye as the main body was swathed in a type of sacking material which was remarkable primarily for the fact that it was clean and dust free.

Carefully peeling the layers of sacking away the Countess gazed upon the deep almost translucent lustre of an oil painting. Removing it completely from the trunk she held it up to the light which streamed in from the tiny skylight at the front of the cellar. The Countess gasped as she recognised the image of 'Madonna of the Pinks'. The recognition had been instant because the painting had hung for so long in the castle corridor at the entrance of the castles banqueting hall. It had been sold to the National Gallery earlier that week and had left such a gaping hole on the wall that her husband the Earl had filled it almost immediately with a Constable from their own private quarters.

But hold on this couldn't be the original because she had seen the curators van collect it. Staring at it more intently she decided that whilst she was no expert if this was not the original it was a very good copy. With a reverence not normally afforded to a fake she placed the painting amongst the other things she had earmarked for the Charity Auction. Suddenly she recalled how she had always ran her fingers against the frame of the original. It was a habitual thing she had done for good luck whenever she entered the Banqueting Hall for a formal occasion. Many was the time that she had grazed her finger on a knot in the wood and dined with a plaster on her digit finger. Once much to her husband's consternation she had been forced to change her pale pink evening dress as a trickle of blood had trickled upon its bodice.

Bending onto her knees to face the painting she traced her fingers once more along its frame. The Countess winced as her finger caught on the familiar knot in the wood. But how was the painting hidden here in the cellar when she had seen it packed and taken away with her own eyes? Only that morning a representative from the Gallery had been waxing lyrical on the News about the amazing generosity of the art loving public and what a fantastic coup it was to have secured the painting in England. And why had her husband hung a Constable in the corridor when the original was sitting here hidden in the cellar? Surely he had known of its existence. She crossed to where the discarded sacking lay and dragged it across towards the light. As she did so an envelope slipped from its layers. The envelope was ripped open and its contents removed but it was addressed to her husband and the postmark was recent. This proved if nothing else that the Earl knew of the existence of the 'fake' painting.

Sitting back upon her haunches the Countess cast her mind back to the last few months. On numerous occasions she had walked into a room surprising her husband and heard him hastily hanging up the telephone. At the time she presumed he had been organising one of his 'gambling nights' and knowing of her disapproval had hidden it from her. But perhaps her husband was a far wilier chap than she gave him credit for. She had long since realised that the bumbling eccentric exterior he presented to guests was as fake as the painting she suspected he had just sold. What if this painting actually was the original and the 'National Gallery' painting a fake? The question now was, if her suspicions were right, what was the best way of using this to her advantage?

LARKSPUR RISE – A SENIOR MOMENT

Liz knocked gingerly upon the door of Marina's house. Joey had been at pains to remind her that there was a baby in the house and she was afraid of disturbing it and incurring the wrath of its parents. Liz was thrilled to have this chance to do some Private 'Eyeing' again and determined not to scupper her chances of a job before she even had a chance to start it.

When Marina had enquired if she would like to tackle the job she had tripped over her reply in her haste to agree. She was still living in the flat above the Bistro, but despite helping out as a waitress as often as she could, her funds were seriously depleted. Recently she had contemplated going cap in hand to her parents or returning to her old job with the Detective Agency. But as both instances would mean a move from Nowhere and more importantly Joey, she was reluctant to consider either.

In a last ditch attempt to acquire some jobs she had hastily pasted up some adverts and leaflet dropped throughout the town. She based her illustrations upon the advertising campaign of 1925 by the most famous Private Detective Agency in the world. The American Pinkerton Agency had used a large picture of an eye and the slogan 'we never sleep'. It was said that it was as a direct result of this campaign that private detectives became known as private eyes. Liz wasn't sure if this was an urban myth but she was thrilled at getting a result so quickly to her own much smaller campaign.

As there was no answer to her first tentative knock so she tried again this time using slightly more force. Eventually the door was opened by a rather flustered looking Marina.

'I'm so sorry for being so tardy,' she explained. 'I was just putting Prospero down for his morning nap.'

She motioned for Liz to follow her into the kitchen and once there presented her with a large mug of coffee and a file marked 'PC Plod'.

It took Liz a few moments to realise to whom the file referred but as Peter was a well known figure in the town she soon recognised the nickname.

'Isn't this the chap who lives on the Crag?' questioned Liz. 'I heard that he had recently married a lady from the Ukraine.'

Marina nodded. She was reaching up for the biscuit tin and was perched precariously with one knee on a stool.

'His bride is Tania my cleaner,' said Marina handing Liz the now opened tin.

'So is it Tania who wants her husband investigated? Liz was confused.

'No definitely not, in fact I would stress that you say nothing to her,' said Marina. 'Let me explain my concerns.'

And she proceeded to describe to Liz how afraid Tania seemed to be of her bully of a husband and of the frequency of her bruises.

'I've been making discreet enquiries myself,' Marina continued. 'Unfortunately I have come to a bit of a dead end. Prior to his arriving here in the seventies Peter seems to have no history at all. I find that most bizarre. I know of his involvement in the DOG and my ex-colleagues in London are delving into that for me but that involvement seems to have begun in the seventies too.'

'The plot thickens,' said Liz. 'Leave this with me for a few days. I shall call in a few favours and see what I can find out.'

It was just at that moment that Martin walked into the room. Martin tightened the belt of his bathrobe as he noticed Liz sitting at the breakfast bar.

'Good morning,' said Martin as he crossed the room to shake Liz by the hand. 'I must apologise for my state of undress I hadn't realised we had visitors. I woke up and smelled the coffee.'

'Took you long enough,' said Marina with a smile to her voice, it was their own private joke. 'Would you like me to brew a fresh pot?'

'Let me darling' said Martin kissing the top of her head 'I had more sleep than you last night, that son of ours would wake the dead.'

Waking the dead!!

Liz had a 'Eureka' moment. Just a thought, but an idea was forming in her head.

She had heard of people who changed identity to escape something in their past and took on a name of someone who had just died. Wow that was definitely something to investigate. Her inquisitive juices were starting to flow. Making an excuse, she hastily left.

Martin remained at the breakfast table, nursing his coffee. 'I'm sure I recognised that young girl,' he said to Marina. 'What did you say her name was?'

'Liz Bell,' said Marina reading the name from the advert she had on the fridge door.

'Even the name rings a bell,' Martin was blissfully unaware of the wordplay. 'I must be having a senior moment. Normally I'm great with faces.'

'What time do you have to leave for London?' said Marina changing the subject.

'An hour tops,' replied Martin.

'Fancy having a senior moment with me?' said Marina.

'Do I ever,' said Martin shrugging off his bathrobe as he pulled a most compliant Marina into his arms.

THE PENTHOUSE – A FITFUL SLEEP

Liz was having a terrible time sleeping. She rarely dreamed but that night she was dipping in and out of a most disturbing nightmare. It revolved around the accident she had witnessed all those months ago.

She kept hearing a crash.

Flashing lights,

Broken glass,

Maggie's twisted body lying on the road,

Jasper the dog barking frantically,

The young lad rifling through Maggie's handbag,

Then footsteps,

Running steps,

The running man turned.

He stared at her.

But his face was a blur.

She tried to focus.

Then she woke up.

Every time she drifted off, she would awake at the same point in the dream. She was getting quite spooked. Eventually she got up out of bed, switched on the light and made herself a hot drink. Insomnia had won yet again.

WEARING HER HEART ON HER SLEEVE

Jean had a spring in her step and a constant smile upon her face. Things with Ruby were progressing very well, very well indeed. They had talked often and were discovering a common bond. It only remained for them to meet. Jean was postponing this moment. Sub-consciously she was worried that either or both of them would be disappointed. The chemistry was certainly there over the telephone, but in the flesh who knew?

She had finally decided to bite the bullet and arranged to meet Ruby that Tuesday but had completely forgotten that she had already promised to help Dianne lay her new kitchen floor. Whilst the urge to meet Ruby had grown in magnitude Jean did not want to let a close friend down. She had not seen Dianne in such a long time. Dianne had been dating her three lady friends so there was a lot of gossip to catch up on. She finally settled upon meeting Ruby en route to Dianne's house suggesting they meet at the service station and share a coffee.

The day arrived. Jean deposited her hastily packed bag into the boot of her car. As she did she reflected upon how different it felt to when she had first visited Dianne. She recalled the blind fear she had felt then at the prospect of meeting a stranger. The Jean of today was a different Jean. Staying at Dianne's house now, evoked the sensation of visiting an old and trusted friend.

As she pulled the car into the Motorway Service Station car park Jean scanned the parking bays for a car meeting Ruby's description. There was only one red car in the entire car park so Jean reasoned that this must be Ruby's and pulled carefully alongside it. The occupant of the red car seemed blissfully unaware of Jeans arrival. Jean switched off her engine, sat back in her seat and willed Ruby to glance her way and break the ice.

After a few minutes Ruby relaxed into her seat, glanced at her watch and looked around her. Jean smiled in her direction and raised her hand to give a tiny wave. Ruby returned the wave and gesticulated for Jean to join her in the car.

Jean clambered from her own car and crossed in front of Ruby's car holding in her stomach as she walked. She opened the car door and climbed in. Initially, neither woman seemed to find voice and the few moments silence was deafening. When eventually they did speak, they spoke in unison, stopped, started, stopped and then fell into fits of nervous giggles

'I have an idea,' suggested Ruby. 'I think we are both finding this strange, recognising the voice but not the face. Why don't we both close our eyes and talk for a while. It will help us get used to each other slowly.'

'I think that's an excellent idea,' said Jean.

That's what they did.

'I really must go,' said Jean during a momentary lull in the conversation.

'Me too,' said Ruby checking her watch for the first time since Jean had climbed into the car. 'Gosh I can't believe that's the time, I must collect my daughter from the child-minders'

Jean's lips brushed Ruby's neck as they said their goodbyes and she felt a frisson of excitement. Perhaps, she thought to herself, this is the start of something wonderful. During her journey to Dianne's Jean switched off the car radio and drove in silence, allowing her train of thought to replay the earlier conversation in her head. She smiled inwardly as she recalled the amusing things that Ruby had said.

'Well, well, you look one very smitten kitten,' Dianne declared as she opened the door an hour later.

'I have loads to tell you sweetie,' said Jean hugging her friend.

'Sit down and while I fetch you a large vodka and orange,' said Dianne. 'I want to hear all the gory details.'

Dianne seemed genuinely pleased for Jean, encouraging her to talk and express her joy at meeting Ruby for the first time. This reaction was a relief for Jean as she had been worried that it would encroach upon their friendship. Thankfully this did not seem to be the case.

Much, much later as they climbed the stairs to bed, Jean made her way into the spare bedroom. Dianne giggled, grabbing her friend by the hand in a clumsy gesture.

'Oh come on don't be so churlish Jean,' she chastised.

'We always sleep together, I need a cuddle I've not met my Ruby yet.'

302 A TOWN CALLED NOWHERE

Despite her better intentions Jean undressed and wearing a nightdress climbed into bed beside Dianne. It was still quite early, barely nine o'clock but a combination of tiredness and drink ensured that Jean fell promptly asleep as soon as her head touched the pillow. She awoke from a very inappropriate dream about Ruby to discover that Dianne's arm had snaked across her midriff. Dianne nuzzled deep into Jean's neck. She was very gentle and hesitant obviously fearing a rebuff. Despite herself Jean felt her body responding to the familiar touch. The movements so predictable and comfortable like a well worn pair of slippers on a frosty night.

'Tell me if you want me to stop.' Dianne murmured into the nape of her neck.

'Don't stop,' Jean replied her voice husky with passion. Turning to meet Dianne in a kiss she rolled over so Dianne was lying on her back.

Pinning her gently with her hands Jean gazed down at Dianne before saying, 'Oh Dianne, you are so lovely.'

Time for regrets later she told herself.

Jean was just enjoying the warm glow coursing through her body when her cell phone began to ring from the depths of her handbag. Jean studiously ignored the incessant tone, surely if it was anything important they would ring her back. Dianne shuffled from Jeans embrace and glared towards the offending handbag.

'Don't you think you better get that?' she snapped. 'It might be lover girl checking up on you.'

Shooting her a concerned look Jean got out of bed and retrieved her cell phone. Ruby had left a voicemail. Deliberately not looking in Dianne's direction Jean left the bedroom to call her back in the privacy of the downstairs lounge.

'You sound sleepy, have I woken you,' Ruby enquired.

'Yes,' said Jean. 'I was having such a lovely dream too. I was dreaming of you, do you mind?'

'Mind,' said Ruby. 'I'm thrilled that I have I made such an impression upon you.'

'I've been waxing lyrical about your qualities all night long.'

The conversation continued in this manner deep into the night.

Jean kept having flashbacks from an hour ago of Dianne and herself in each other's arms. But she kept on reminding herself that because

Ruby and she were not yet in an actual relationship, her fidelity was not in question. But in her heart of hearts she knew that morally she had been wrong. It was inexcusable that she had slept with Dianne. My God, what type of person was she turning into? When had it all become so complicated and messy?

It had been a long while since Dianne had been so pro-active and Jean could also say it was probably the only time that Dianne had seemed to really enjoy the lovemaking. This confused Jean, until she recalled Betsy's words during that awful argument. Dianne would always want what was unattainable. Once it was hers she would cast it aside. She stole Betsy from the arms of her father, and tried to steal Jean from the arms of Ruby. Had Jean suddenly became attractive solely due to her budding romance? Surely Dianne could not be so Machiavellian.

Jean hung about downstairs for as long as she possibly could, but she was very chilly as she had left the bedroom in haste without her nightdress or dressing gown. She held back downstairs for fear of provoking more bad feeling and a potential argument. When she did eventually venture upstairs she was relieved to find Dianne's bedroom door firmly closed. Her overnight bag had been unceremoniously dumped on the spare bed with her nightdress draped over a chair. The message was very clear. The next morning Dianne knocked twice and waited for an invitation before entering the spare room.

'I've brought you breakfast,' she said averting her eyes as Jean straightened her nightdress. 'I trust you have slept well, I'm just popping out the DIY shop for more tile cement. I noticed you had left your cell phone on the table last night. You had run out of battery so I've charged it for you.'

'Thanks sweetie that was kind of you.' Jean replied. Dianne left the room nonchalantly as if the previous night had not happened. Well thought Jean, if that's how she wants to play it, so be it. It was not worth risking a friendship over.

THE CHARITY AUCTION – NOWHERE CASTLE – GOING FOR A SONG

'Ladies and gentlemen may I have your attention please.' said Michael Mickelson as he took his place behind the podium in the Banqueting Hall of Nowhere Castle. His orange fake tan and dandy clothes made him easily recognisable from the landed gentry who flanked him either side.

'I'm just back from my rumble in the jungle,' he continued. 'Let's get ready for a bargain hunt that's as cheap as chips.

The Countess had scored quite a coup arranging for Michael to be the Celebrity Guest Auctioneer. The promise of free publicity had been the only financial inducement needed as the WTF calendar had brought Nowhere very much into the media spotlight and Michael was hoping it would help persuade Channel 4 to commission his latest TV offering. It seemed that the majority of the main participants in the Charity Auction had ulterior motives coming into play.

The Countess for her part had included the 'Madonna of the Pinks' painting in the Charity Auction for one reason and one reason only. Although still unsure of the provenance of the oil painting the Countess had her suspicions and decided to bluff her husband into showing his hand. She had slyly included the oil painting in the Auction listing it as a fake. She had then informed her husband the Earl that she was onto his little game and she would ensure that the painting was kept in the family hands if he agreed to her proposition. Her grand plans for the gardens had hit a snag. Although they had gained Lottery Funding the proviso had been that the amount of the fund was to be matched by the Earl's own money. Her husband had been reluctant to agree to this, quoting poor till receipts at the castle gates and a bad run of luck with some investments he had made but the mere suggestion that the painting was to be included in the Charity Auction Catalogue had suddenly changed his mind.

'I'm thinking Versailles,' declared his wife the previous night. 'I'm thinking fountains that cascade into to a musical light show. I'm thinking of the largest tree house in England.'

'To sugar the pill,' she added, 'those exotic plants you have growing in the potting shed will still have a place in my garden. I'm thinking of incorporating a Poison Garden growing those particular varieties. We will claim they are being cultivated for educational purposes, although obviously you can harvest discreetly at will.'

George Johnson, the newly appointed Mayor of Nowhere was also attending the Auction. The chains of office weighed heavily upon Georges shoulders as he stooped slightly to one side and shuffled from leg to leg obviously in some degree of pain. Way back in the audience Raymond noticed Georges discomfort and allowed himself an inward smile. He was recollecting the very energetic sex he and George had partaken in the previous evening. He was not surprised that George was in some degree of discomfort. Raymond still had the marks upon his back from where the chains and medals that George insisted upon wearing had rubbed and chaffed.

Jean stood near the front, with Lennie to her left and Sooty to her right. Sooty had thought it wise that Louisa not attend. It was one thing to have an affair but another to rub Lennie's nose in it. Louisa was only too happy to comply. Joey and she hoped that the crowd leaving the Auction would be in need of liquid refreshment. Sooty had seen that a discount voucher to dine at the Bistro be inserted in every Auction Programme and the Bistro had tendered a signed photograph of Doris Day to be included in the auction. With the large gay following the Auction had attracted due to Toni the photographer it was sure to far exceed its reserve price.

Toni the photographer stood behind Raymond. She had flown in from New York earlier that morning so she could add her support to the Charity. She had donated the original proofs of the Calendar stills which she hoped would prove popular. There were rumours that a certain movie company was thinking of making a film about the production of the calendar and it would surely push up the price of the negatives. Toni's latest project was her most ambitious yet and she hoped that releasing information on it to the news hungry journalists would result in some rich benefactor willing to underwrite the trip. Toni's idea was to lay nudes head to toe along the entire length of the Great Wall of China then arrange for a shuttle to blast her into space so she could take photographs. One bearded entrepreneur had offered Toni the use of a hot air balloon, but Toni's plans were far more adventurous than that.

'Let the auction begin,' declared Michael striking his gavel to the block in an attempt to gain the attention of the crowd. A hush fell over the room and all eyes were on Michael, all ears hanging on his every word. The Countess stood to Michael's right alternatively holding the various items up in the air or pointing to them in the manner of a game show hostess.

As expected the Doris Day autograph far exceeded its reserve as did the Calendar stills. The final item to be auctioned was the 'Madonna of the Pinks'. The Countess placed it carefully on the easel at the front of the hall before retreating gracefully behind the curtain backdrop.

'And now,' said Michael. 'Our final item of the evening is one of breathtaking beauty. This fine reproduction replicates the iconic 'Madonna of the Pinks' which once graced the walls of this very castle. Its age is unknown although our dear Earl thinks it may have been painted in the last century or even before. Who is going to start me off on the bidding? Remember guys all proceeds from tonight's Auction are going to a very good cause.'

The reserve placed upon it was one thousand pounds.

The Earl was happy. His wife had adhered to his wishes and set the price ridiculously low. What was one thousand pounds when one took into account the painting's true worth. The Earl raised his hand to start the bidding. He was confident that he would be the only bidder, after all who would pay over one thousand pounds for a fake painting when an excellent print would cost a fraction of that cost. He allowed himself a pompous self-satisfied smile as Michael raised the gavel for the third and final time. Suddenly from the back of the room came a rival bid. Peering into the distance he could see a rather tall lady with striking auburn hair and dark glasses. Cursing inwardly he upped his bid. To his horror the woman again raised her hand. The price was creeping up, bloody Michael Mickleson was adding on one thousand pounds with every new bid. But the Earl had to carry on as he knew the paintings true worth. Again and again the bloody woman raised the stakes.

The crowd were getting very excited and were now craning their necks to see the rival bidder. Cool as a cucumber she matched the Earls every bid. The Earl was beginning to sweat. His bloody wife had insisted he wear a dress shirt. Running his fingers around the collar he struggled to appear outwardly calm.

Still the bids increased.

At one stage the woman waited till the last descent of the gavel to raise her bid. The Earl felt trapped, like a fly in that bloody Venus flytrap plant his wife so loved.

The price was now fifty thousand pounds.

The entire crowd looked towards the Earl.

Was he prepared to offer fifty one?

He hesitated but had no choice, reluctantly he raised his hand.

All eyes turned to the corner where the mysterious woman stood.

The crowd gasped, she was no longer there.

It was as if she had never been.

Michael raised the gavel then slowly let it drop onto the block.

Upon its descent Michael turned and congratulated the Earl upon his purchase.

The crowd clapped.

It had been pure theatre.

'Wow' said Michael.

'I bet Raphael will be turning in his grave at that one.'

The Earl inclined his head. Any more bids and he would have joined bloody Raphael. Feigning a lack of concern he mumbled 'all for a good cause my dear man and it is an excellent reproduction.'

The crowd cheered. At that point the Countess emerged from behind the curtain.

She expressed regret at missing out on all the excitement discreetly reminding her husband that the call of nature was not to be taken lightly at her age.

Much later that night the Earl sat despondently in his private quarters in the East Wing of the Castle. Financially he was much worse off but at least the bloody painting was still his and the profit although reduced would still be substantial. He just had to sit on it for a while before George could courier it abroad.

Much later still in her private quarters in the West Wing of the Castle the Countess carefully placed an auburn wig and sunglasses into the trunk at the foot of her bed. Yes her husband was a wily fox but she had outfoxed him this time. Her dear mother had died of cancer and it was a cause that was very close to her heart.

PENTHOUSE FLAT

Liz had reached a proverbial dead end. She was frustratingly no further forward in her search into Peter Dodd's past. All avenues had ended in a cul-de-sac. Somerset House had drawn a blank. Church Parish Records had drawn a blank.

Questioning locals, who had been around in the seventies when Peter had first moved into the Folly on the Crag had drawn a blank.

Liz still had an inkling that the answer lay with the Earl. But to question him was unthinkable, they didn't exactly socialise in the same circles. The local paper lay on the kitchen worktop. Flicking through it Liz almost dropped her mug of coffee. The answer was staring her in the face.

The headline read;

'Grave concern for St Michael's church graveyard'

Quickly scanning it Liz realised that it referred to the church which stood upon a hill adjacent to the Folly on the Crag. The burial plots of the present Earls ancestors were all housed within its consecrated grounds.

The article described how ghostly goings on had been reported by a member of the public who had been walking his dog in the nearby wood. The previous Friday had been the Summer Solstice so the article left the reader to 'read into that fact what they will'. The Earl was quick to distance himself from such 'goings on' and had declared that he would immediately commission a stone mason to re-erect and repair the collapsed gravestones. Liz experienced a similar 'Eureka' moment to one she had felt at Marina's house.

She knew the answer lay within the grounds of the church. She wasn't sure how she knew, couldn't explain how she knew but she did, she just knew. She could see from the photograph that the burial plots lay secreted behind large iron railings. She really needed to get inside the railings. Short of scaling them in the dead of night, a much too scary proposition how was she to gain access?

THE QUEEN OF TARTS

'Guess who? said Martin placing his hands over Marina's eyes in the manner of a human blindfold.

'Are you tall dark and handsome?' said Marina playing along with the game.

'So my girlfriend tells me.'

'Oh so you have a girlfriend?'

'Oh yes, I have a very beautiful girlfriend,' said Martin placing a kiss upon the top of her head.

'Go on then,' said Marina. 'I'll let you have your evil way with me, but we better be quick as my boyfriend will be back from London soon.'

She raised her head and turned to meet Martin's lips.

'Hello darling how are you back so soon?'

'False alarm, I'm sure the bloody woman didn't fall at all. I'm convinced she threw herself down the stairs to get the .... attention.'

'Well it worked he was on the telephone to you fairly quickly.'

As they spoke the .... image flashed up on the TV screen.

'Bloody hell,' Martin exclaimed 'What's she up to now? This could put the cat amongst the pigeons.'

The opening shots showed the .... walking sedately into a dimly lit room. Head bowed she crossed towards the reporter, shook his hand and lowered herself gingerly into a chair.

'Not a hint of a limp,' said Martin. 'I knew she was faking it this morning. What did I tell you darling.'

'There were always three of us in this marriage.'

'Only three,' said Martin. From what the .... had told him she had enjoyed quite a few dalliances herself yet here she was on the screen a picture of innocence, coyly peeking from behind her fringe of blonde hair.

'I like to think of myself as the Queen of hearts.'

'Queen of bloody hearts,' said Martin, 'more like the queen of bloody tarts.'

'Calm down darling' said Marina placing her hand upon his knee. His constant asides were getting annoying and despite herself she was really quite enjoying the unfolding drama.

THE PALACE - LONDON

The .... sat staring open mouthed at the television in the corner of the room. As luck or bad luck would have it he had been visiting his parents as the so-called impromptu interview flashed up on the screen. This was all he needed. His mother had left the room in disgust after the first few moments but his father sat stone-faced glaring intermittently at the .... then at the unfolding scenes on the TV.

'Why couldn't you be more damn discreet you stupid, stupid boy,' he barked.

'I love ......' insisted the ....,'if you had allowed me to marry her in the first place all this would never had happened.'

'She was tarnished goods even then so you knew it would never be acceptable,' snapped his father.

The .... rose clumsily from his chair and stormed from the room with one of the blasted corgi's snapping at his ankles. He respected his father but this time he had gone too far.

His father's words followed in his wake, 'You should have just mounted that old mare and left it at that. You had that gorgeous young filly waiting at home. You have broken your mother's heart. We should have just stuck to breeding bloody corgis.'

RENDEZVOUS CAFE

Louisa sat at a table near the large plate window staring beyond the promenade and onto the beach. It was a weekend, the busiest time in the Bistro and normally not a time she would be able to engineer an assignation with her lover but she had awoken that morning with an urgent need to see Sooty. Sooty for her part was thrilled at having this extra time to spend together and had hastily cancelled her lunch plans so she could meet Louisa.

Sooty entered the cafè and gave a quick wave in the direction of Gino as her eyes alighted upon Louisa. She cut quite a comical figure sitting at a table for four holding Jaspers lead in one hand and a scruffy teddy bear in the other.

'Who's your friend,' said Sooty moving her chair so she could sit alongside Louisa rather than opposite her.

Louisa picked up the tattered teddy and presented him to Sooty saying, 'This furry chap has seen me through some scrapes. I've had him since I was a child at the orphanage.'

Sooty leant across and took Louisa's hand in hers. 'Oh darling,' she said.

'You never told me you were brought up in an orphanage. I've never pestered you for stories of your background because you seemed so reluctant to discuss them. I feel terrible for not being more persistent now.'

'That's why I asked you here today. It was one of things I wanted to talk to you about. I also figured everyone should have a teddy bear. It will give you something to cuddle when I'm not there.'

'I wish you were,' said Sooty in a dreamy voice. 'I mean, I wish you were there beside me every night,' she continued as if to clarify her meaning.

'That's another thing I wanted to talk to you about,' said Louisa.

Sooty held her breath. It was what she had hoped to hear for so long. It was what she had hinted to Louisa so many times. Not allowing herself to pressurise her into making the decision but letting it be known it was out there on the table. Was she finally at the stage of leaving Joey?

'Are you lost for words?' said Louisa teasingly. 'This must be a first.'

'I think I need to pinch myself I'm so sure I'm dreaming. If you knew how often I had hoped you would choose me.'

'I know,' said Louisa. 'It wasn't a case of choosing it was always just timing. But first I need to tell you something.'

'Don't look so worried darling,' said Sooty. 'Whatever it is it can't be so bad or change how elated I feel.'

'I've wanted to tell you this for so long.' said Louisa haltingly. 'But I kept telling myself you would never know or find out so why rock the boat.'

'Ok' said Sooty, she was starting to get worried now. Louisa looked so anxious and nervous.

'I didn't want our life together to be underpinned by secrets or lies because that's what destroys a relationship.'

Sooty squeezed Louisa's hand for reassurance. 'Whatever the big dark secret is,' she said 'we can face it together, fire away, I'm a big girl I can take it.'

So Louisa began to tell her of the reasons she began their affair. She described her childhood in the orphanage and her feelings for Bernadette. Not going so far as to describe her as the love of her life but the meaning was clear to Sooty. Sooty felt her body jolt as she realised that Lemon lips was in fact Lennie. Lennie rarely spoke of her life at the convent and evidently this was why. But she and Jean had often alluded to it in conversations. Suddenly a thought struck her and with it a realisation that Bernadette was Jeans given name at the convent. There was no mistaking the description of the voice and Lucy being ill with cancer. It all fitted into place like a very complicated jigsaw.

Louisa abruptly stopped talking and stood up to leave the table.

'Where are you going?' said Sooty anxiously.

'I'm going to take Jasper for a walk on the beach.'

Sooty made to join her but was halted by Louisa's hand upon her shoulder.

'I want you to sit here with Fred Bear and think over what I have told you, it is a lot to take in. But in my defence all I can say is I've grown to love you more than I ever dreamt would be possible, and I would like us to make a life together. I know all this won't be easy and telling Joey will be so difficult but I feel I must follow my heart.'

Two espressos later and Sooty was still confused about what to do. One the one hand it would mean she would need to lie, possibly forever, but on the other hand the risk of Louisa still loving Jean was too great to contemplate. She was stuck between a rock and a hard place with no evident escape route. Deciding not to make a decision straight away Sooty left the cafe and strode purposefully out onto the sand to search for Louisa.

Seeing Louisa in the distance, she forced a smile upon her lips and waved in her direction. It would take an Oscar winning performance but she must convince Louisa that everything was fine and dandy. Sooty loved Louisa with her whole being and if it took a lie to keep that love alive then so be it.

RATCHEUGH CRAG – LETTER FROM HOME

Tania was in a quandary. She had just received a letter from her mother in Cherkassy and was certainly not a letter she had ever expected to receive. It was a letter that broke her heart. Her mother, the person she should trust above all others had deceived her.

Tania had finally talked Peter around to agreeing that Nicholai could come and stay in England for a while. Before he changed his mind she had hastily sent a cheque to her mother to buy the plane ticket. Tania had opened the letter expecting it to contain confirmation that the ticket had been purchased and details of the flight. Instead the letter contained a heartrending apology and plea for forgiveness. It appeared that the money Tania had been steadily sending month by month had not been saved at all, instead it had been given to Tania's brother to support his failing business. All of it, every penny she had sent, every penny she had earned cleaning Marina's house, every single penny. All of it was gone.

What was worse was that her brother had coerced Nicholai into taking a loan from a local moneylender. This loan too was also lost in his company accounts. Nicholai upon his grandmother's advice had handed the entire loan to his uncle, and from the tone of the letter there was little chance of him ever seeing it again. As the debt was in his name, it was to be Nicholai's responsibility to repay it and if he did not the 'moneylender' in question would use dubious means to achieve this.

Tania decided it could not possibly get any worse. She had travelled so far to secure a future for her son and in doing so had left him vulnerable and at prey from the very people she had entrusted with his wellbeing. Here she was in a strange country all alone married to a husband who barely gave her the time of day. A man who abused her body and destroyed her soul. What use was she to her beloved son so far away? What use was a foolish Baba Yaga?

UPPER WORTLEY, LEEDS –
SUSPICIOUS MINDS

Jean was also in a quandary and annoyed at herself for being so suspicious and insecure. She kept telling herself everything was fine and it was her mind playing tricks. Ruby and she had been getting on very well. In fact Ruby had spent the night at Jeans the previous week. She had slept in the spare room, all very proper and above board but the promise of a loving relationship hung in the air.

It seemed that both ladies were reluctant to rush into anything and for her part Jean was pleased. For despite what had happened with Dianne she was an old fashioned girl at heart. The best things in life were worth waiting for.

Ruby was on a residential course for work and had explained to Jean that the Hall the course was being held was surrounded by fields and the team had been warned that the telephone reception was very touch and go. Jean had been cradling her phone for the better part of the day delaying going out in case she missed a call. They normally communicated numerous times throughout the day and she missed the warm reassurance this gave her.

Suddenly her telephone began to ring. She fought the feeling of disappointment as she realised the call was from Dianne. Dianne had rang to say that Ruby had not been able to reach Jean and had telephoned her instead. Ruby had asked her to relay the message that the course was expected to drag on another day so they may need to rain check on their dinner date.

Whilst pleased that Ruby was well and thinking of her, Jean was also irked that Dianne had muscled in on her relationship. Also she had never given Dianne Ruby's telephone number or vice versa. This gave rise to the conclusion that Dianne must have rooted about in her handbag to find Ruby's number. The only time it had been out of her sight was after that argument at Dianne's when she had left her handbag in the lounge. Could Dianne have taken the number from her cell phone then? Jean recalled that she had charged her cell phone for her. This thought sent a chill through Jean and she tried to put it to the back of her mind. But it was an unsuccessful endeavour and her imagination went into overtime.

She recalled a time the previous week when she had been trying to ring Ruby and the line had been constantly engaged. She had decided to while away the time speaking to Dianne and had been exasperated to find that she too was engaged. She had dismissed it as coincidence at the time but now it appeared more sinister.

Had Ruby been chatting to Dianne? Were they conducting a friendship unbeknownst to her? Were they perhaps cultivating a potential relationship?

Had it gone further and were they actually having a relationship?

Jean's imagination went into overdrive. Jealousy was an emotion alien to Jean. But once jealousy reared its ugly head, it could not be ignored.

ST MICHAELS CHURCH GRAVEYARD

Mr Summer the Earl's Land Manager was waiting at the gates of Grizzly Tower. He had been informed by telephone earlier that day that the stonemason's apprentice would be arriving at mid-day to price up the job. He could not contain his astonishment when Liz drove up. Firstly he was taken aback that she was female and secondly she looked much too feeble to hack away and repair stonework. But putting his sexist attitudes to one side he smiled in her direction before unlocking the heavy metal gates.

'I may be quite a while,' said Liz. 'My boss has very exact measurements he wants me to take. If you like I can ring you when I finish so you can pop back and lock up.'

'How long do you think it will take?' said Mr Summer.

'How long is a piece of string?' Liz answered most unhelpfully.

Mr Summer weighed it up. Yes he was responsible for the site, but it was a cold blustery morning and he could slip home for a hot drink. It would prove a most welcome break in his otherwise busy day.

'Alright,' he said eventually. 'I'll be back in two hours unless I hear from you otherwise'

Liz watched him drive off slowly down the muddy track.

Clapping her gloved hands together in an attempt to keep warm Liz made a great show of studying the brickwork until Mr Summer was out of sight. Despite it being daylight the tower had an eerie feel to it. It was surrounded on all sides by long forgotten graves covered in moss. Taking out the flat knife she had brought for the purpose Liz began the arduous task of scraping away the years of neglect. She wasn't exactly sure what she was looking for, a name, a date, a clue?

Some of the gravestones were elaborate with carved angels and grand columns. Others were small, almost an afterthought. Liz was shocked at the evidence of infant mortality, she had assumed this was the blight of the poor but it seemed the nobility suffered equally. After an hour's hard slog her eyes alighted upon a small grave, obviously of a child. It was the child's name that caught her attention, Henry Wilfred Peter Dodd. The child had died aged two weeks in December 1934.

Taking a pencil from her pocket Liz took a rubbing of the inscription upon the grave. It was too much of a coincidence to overlook. Quickly calculating in her head she worked out that it if the child had lived he would have been 52 last birthday. She suspected PC Plod to be a similar age, or in his mid fifties at least.

The plot thickened. But she now needed to find out Peter's birthday. That would really give her something to work on. Coincidences regarding names were everyday, often a particular surname was prevalent to a particular area of England. But a date of birth that also matched. Now that would be more than just a coincidence. As coincidences go that would be pretty hard to explain away. The question now was how to find out Peter's birth date without causing him to suspect anything. Liz was well aware that owing to his high position in the police force he could make life very difficult indeed for her and perhaps even scupper her fledgling business plans. She must tread lightly, use what contacts she had and think outside the box.

LARKSPUR RISE – HAPPY BIRTHDAYS

Marina jumped from her car and raced up the driveway of Larkspur Rise. She had left work early in the hope of catching Tania still busy at the house. Approaching the front door she was pleased to see Tania at the bay window methodically polishing the stained glass insert. Not for the first time Marina marvelled at how judging by Tania's expression she seemed to be actually enjoying her work. Tania took a pride and satisfaction in a job well done and the house was shiny as a new pin as a result. How difficult it would have been to find a worker of her calibre in London. For a 'lady that did' Tania was certainly a diamond, a gem beyond compare.

'Hello Tania I'm so glad I've caught you, I hardly seem to see you these days, have you have time for a coffee and a chat?' Marina enquired after she had taken off her coat and said a quick hello to baby Prospero.

Tania was worried. Was Miss Marina unhappy with the quality of her work, had she been lacking in some way? She dearly loved her job at Larkspur Rise. She relished the time spent watching Prospero growing up. It almost compensated for all those years she had missed with Nicholai. Her mother had heard Nicholai's first tentative words and witnessed his first hesitant steps. But through Prospero Tania had a chance to imagine how magical that must have felt. She missed her son now more than ever before. Especially because it now seemed it would be an intolerably long time until she saw him again.

'Don't look so worried Tania, it's just a friendly chat nothing serious.' said Marina when she saw the look of panic race across Tania's face.

'Oh Miss Marina you had me thinking anxious thoughts, l will be finishing this window then I will be for joining you in the kitchen.'

Much later they were both sitting at the kitchen table sipping coffee.

'I need your help Tania,' said Marina, using the approach that Liz had told her to use.

'Anything I can do Miss Marina I willingly do.'

'I need some ideas regarding a gift for Mr Martin's birthday, men are so difficult to buy for I find.'

'Surely you have given him the greatest gift of all in baby Prospero.'

'Yes, yes,' said Marina waving the sentimentality aside. 'What did you get Peter for his last birthday? That may give me some ideas.'

'Miss Marina, I can be off no help to you. Mr Dodd birthday is not until December, we have yet to share a birthday as married persons.'

'In December,' Marina mused 'It isn't by any chance the 19th of December is it? That was my father's birthday.'

'No Miss Marina it is the 13th.'

'More coffee?' said Marina lifting the pot, she had her answer, Liz had been right it had been as easy as taking candy from a baby.

'No Miss Marina' said Tania, putting her hand over the top of the mug to empathise the point 'I must be for going. Mr Dodd will be waiting for me at the gate. I hope you manage to find a most suitable gift for Mr Martin.'

'Thank you Tania you have been very helpful, I've left your wages in an envelope by the front door.'

Marina watched as Tania left the house. The Ukrainian woman nearly tripping over her own feet as she realised that her husband was already waiting at the gate. Marina watched as Peter raised his hand to his approaching wife. For one terrible moment Marina feared he was planning to strike his wife as a punishment for her tardiness. She breathed a sigh of relief when she realised he was merely making a point of displaying his watch to her. It did not escape Marina's attention that Tania had visibly flinched at her husband's gesture. If anything it proved to Marina that she was doing the right thing in enlisting the help of Liz the private eye. Peter Dodd really was a most disagreeable bullying little man. Putting him in his place would be such a pleasure. Now it only remained for her to ring Liz to tell her the result of her successful sleuthing.

FLEET STREET – LONDON

Placing the telephone back upon the receiver Court Reporter Penny Bond allowed herself a self congratulatory whoop of delight. Sorell her mole at Oxford House, had come good yet again. This was the scoop to end all scoops. It would knock Watergate out of the water. Sorell had taped a secret conversation between the .... and his ladylove, where the ....described his wish to be a feminine hygiene product so he could be even closer to her. Thinking on her feet Penny decided to run with 'Tampaxgate' as the headline.

She raced across the crowded office much to the amusement of the younger reporters, as she had neither the figure nor the aptitude for such an energetic sprint. 'It's like someone making butter' joked one of the sports writers, prompting a large raucous laugh to spread like wildfire around the room. 'It must be something important to make her break into a sweat, probably the .... breaking a fingernail.'

Let them laugh Penny thought, a pack of hyenas at the zoo had more decorum. She had this illusion that owing to the nature of the reporting she did, she was a cut above the rest. Had she not been Oxford educated. Was she not at the forefront of every major event. Granted the .... himself when skiing had once been heard to refer to her as 'that annoying reporter woman'. But hey at least he recognised her.

Bursting into the Editors office without her usual well mannered knock she slapped her notebook upon his desk saying the words she had waited her entire career to say.

'HOLD THE FRONT PAGE'

Meanwhile, the .... strode purposefully across the crest of a hill, far below him lay a crofters cottage and to his side a clear blue loch. As if on cue the sun decided to peek its head around the clouds and cast a striking light upon the scene. The cameraman was almost beside himself with glee, perfect, absolutely perfect. The scene played out before him was cinema like in its quality. Surely that Bafta was now within his reach.

The .... was dressed in hiking clothes and a rather ridiculous deer stalker hat.

He smiled his little boy lost smile into the lens of the camera and began to drone on about how painful the break-up of his marriage had been. How his sons were his priority and he pleaded that the press would not intrude in their lives and make the transition as painless as possible. It was all very regrettable but hindsight was a wonderful thing. The ...... even managed to squeeze a tear from his eye. Albeit this was only achieved by staring directly at the sun, but the cameraman gave him the thumbs up so it must have looked good for the camera. As public relations events went it was a blinder, but unfortunately many miles away all this good work would be undone with a whirr of a printing press...such is the irony of life.

THE GREENHOUSE BISTRO
– BORROWED TIME

Joey was troubled about her relationship with Louisa. Recently they had lost all the intimacy they had once shared. Working together had been a bad idea for it seemed that in the evenings they had nothing to talk about as they had exhausted all conversation during the day. Even on the rare occasions they were both at home together and sparked up a conversation it would inevitably lead to being about work.

Joey's old friend from the local Labour Party had invited her to an impromptu party at her house in Jesmond, a small suburb near Newcastle. The friend was most insistent that Joey attend, citing the reason as being a 'special mutual friend' they had both not seen for a great many years. Joey deliberately did not extend the invitation to Louisa. Not so much out of malice but more a pettiness for all the times she had been excluded from events in Louisa's social calendar. Louisa seemed unconcerned and said it would give her an opportunity to catch up on the accounts. Although Joey suspected she would use the night of 'freedom' to visit her lover Sooty.

They still had not discussed Louisa's affair but it often felt as if Louisa were leaving obvious clues to force it out in the open. A casual mention of something amusing Sooty had told her, the careless receipts left lying around for outings they had not shared. But Joey would not be drawn. Although her mindset had realised that they were living on borrowed time she was reluctant to give up on what had been the defining relationship in her life. She kept hoping the affair would fizzle out but the longer it continued the less likely that seemed.

PENTHOUSE FLAT
– THE PLOT THICKENS

Liz had just received the telephone call from Marina with the information regarding Peter's birthday. As she had suspected PC Dodd and the dead baby shared not only the same forename and surname but also the same birthday. Surely as coincidences go that was a big one. Liz was aware that it did not actually prove anything. But Liz had a feeling she had only scratched the surface. She needed to find out why Peter had taken the name and birth date of a dead child, claiming it as his own. What would make a man so desperate to change identity? What would give someone cause to reinvent themselves?

He was either hiding from someone or something, which would make him the victim. Or he had committed some crime so heinous that he had been forced to hide to evade justice, which would make him the perpetrator.

Liz pondered the problem until her head ached from the effort of concentrating. She knew the answer was there but how to get at it. It was if it were filed away in a big locked cabinet and she could not find the key.

She decided to try her luck in the 'Yearbooks' in the library. They claimed to have all the answers. Now was their chance to prove it. She enlisted the help of the index and turned to the date 13th December, 1934.

The Yearbook index broke the date up into chapters. From the grandly titled 'Celebrity Linked Birthdays' which proudly proclaimed the birth of Martin P Zanuck on the said date, and the fact that 'Dick Tracey and the Boris Arson Gang' had been reprinted on the 13th December. The latter Liz mused was quite apt given her chosen profession but of no real help bar its novelty value.

Whilst she researched she doodled on a piece of paper that lay by the table. She doodled flowers, a square house, interlinked hearts, all the while searching for the illusive flash of inspiration. Then she doodled upon the date changing the 3 of the 13 to an 8. On a whim she turned to this date in the Yearbook.

To her amazement an array of far more interesting chapters were alluded to this date. Most of the pages focused upon the Lord Lucan mystery, it appeared that his birthday fell upon 18th December 1934. One chapter was along the lines of the various conspiracy stories of the time which claimed amongst other things to have sightings of Elvis Presley working on the tills at the local K Mart. But turning the page she was shocked to see a full page photograph of Lord Lucan. Seeing his eyes made her gasp out aloud. A cold shiver raced down her spine and Liz was transported back to that night that fateful night and the crash scene which fuelled her nightmares.

Those eyes.

That man.

It was the same man she had seen running from the dreadful accident.

Oh my God could it be possible that PC Dodd and Lord Lucan were one and the same man. Liz tried desperately to focus on the facts and not let her imagination run away with itself.

She knew that PC Dodd had not been driving his own car the night of the fatal crash. She knew that a local 'thug' had been incarcerated for the 'accident.' But she also knew that the running man had some strong significance. Was it possible that the police had arrested the wrong man? And if they had was it possible that the actual perpetrator was in actual fact PC Dodd? More importantly was PC Dodd really Lord Lucan? Was it really conceivable that that Lord Lucan was living upon Ratcheugh Crag.

Yes he was older, the hair greyer, the eye colour changed. But that stare was unmistakable. The arrogance of posture. The piercing look.

Fear gave way to realisation that she was perhaps sitting upon the greatest story to break in the last twenty years. The question now was how to handle the information. Ringing the police was unthinkable, she would be labelled a scaremongerer and anyway how could she trust a police force which had Peter Dodd at its helm. The newspapers were a possibility, but again proving it was the problem. How many calls along the 'my mother was abducted by aliens' theme did they get each day? Eventually Liz deduced that she should talk to Marina first and then together they could find a way exposing Peter Dodd for the murderer he so obviously was.

It was a rather desperate Liz who raced through Nowhere's streets that evening. The photocopy from the book secreted in the pocket of her jacket. It was dusk and the streets felt sinister and foreboding. Liz realised she was hyperventilating from the adrenaline rush and forced herself to steady her pace so as not to draw unwanted attention to herself. Nevertheless by the time she reached Marinas front door she was sweating and virtually incoherent. She stumbled into the porch and it took a tot of whisky administered by a concerned Marina to help her regain some power of speech.

Marina listened intently, shaking her head in disbelief at one stage but agreeing the likeness was uncanny. She agreed with Liz that the eyes held the proof. The colour was changed, but as Liz said that could be easily achieved with the aid of contact lenses. Peter's face held more wrinkles but heavens above given the passing of the years that was only to be expected.

How clever Marina concluded. How clever of Peter to take a high profile job, to become a member of a community. It was quite the perfect way to detract attention from ones past crimes by becoming a part of the posse who would strive to hunt him down.

But for now her immediate concern was for her cleaner Tania. She must be warned in some way and time was of the essence. If she happened to relay the day's events to her husband and mention that she had been questioned about his birth date. All hell could break loose. Peter could prove to be a dangerous man and if their suspicions were correct he had already extinguished two lives a third would cause him little regret. Rushing to the Crag was not an option so therefore Tania's salvation lay in the telephone. Marina just hoped and prayed that it would be Tania rather than Peter who answered her call.

The phone rang, and rang, and rang. Marina was getting very nervous indeed. Imagining the very worst scenario and blaming herself for being the catalyst. Eventually on about the twelfth ring the phone was answered, thankfully by Tania. She enquired in her halting English

'Hello who is calling? How I can I assist you?

'Thank God,' said Marina.

'Hello, hello,' said Tania, unsure of the voice and hoping the person on the other end of the line would enlighten her.

'Tania, it's me Marina.'

'Oh Miss Marina,' said Tania. 'Is it Mr Dodd you want? He is in the showering room. I shall call him for you.'

'*NO DON'T DO THAT*,' said Marina, in a far louder tone of voice than she had planned. She was supposed to be keeping calm and not alarming Tania for goodness sake.

'No,' she said in a quieter voice, desperately trying to contain her anxiety. 'It's you I wish to speak to Tania, I would prefer if Mr Dodd did not hear our conversation.'

'As you wish Miss Marina, I am enquiring why?'

'Why...........' said Marina stalling for time, trying to choose her words carefully. 'It's because I must warn you to be wary of Mr Dodd.'

'I am confused,' said Tania. 'Mr Dodd is my husband, why must I be wary?'

'Mr Dodd is not who he says he is. He is a very dangerous man wanted by the police.'

'I'm still not understanding Miss Marina are you forgetting my Mr Dodd is a policeman.'

Marina stopped for a few moments to collect her thoughts. She really needed to explain this is words Tania would understand without causing her to fly into a panic.

'Mr Dodd is a very bad man Tania. He has done some wicked things. I want you to leave the house as soon as possible. I will be waiting at the bottom of the Crag in the car. Please Tania I will explain everything when I see you. Do you trust me Tania?'

'Yes Miss Marina you are nice lady, I trust you.'

'Ok then please do as I say. Hang up the telephone. If you see Mr Dodd tell him you are going to the shop for some groceries.'

'Are you sure I should do this Miss Marina, Mr Dodd will be very angry.'

'I know Tania, do as I say and I promise no harm will come to you. Hang up now Tania.'

'Ok Miss Marina I am making to hang up.'

Tania replaced the receiver. She peered up the spiral stairs. If she listened very carefully she could still hear the shower running in the bathroom so Peter must still be getting washed. She turned to collect her handbag from the cupboard but froze to the spot as she heard Peter's heavy footsteps on the stairs. He appeared with damp hair but fully dressed. He moved deftly towards the door effectively blocking her exit from the lounge.

'Are you going out?' he enquired in his usual bullying tone.

'Yes Peter,' said Tania, fighting to keep the quiver out of her voice.

'And why are you going out?

'I have forgotten some groceries. I am foolish Baba Yaga.'

Peter stood aside as if to let her pass but as she scuttled past he grabbed her by the neck with such ferocity that she slumped against the doorframe. The shock of the attack took her breath away. She was gasping for air, her eyes felt as if they were popping from her sockets. Slowly Peter loosened his grip upon her throat. His fingers still pressed into her flesh but her airways were free.

'Who may I enquire were you talking to on the telephone?'

'My mother,' said Tania, her voice coming as a croak.

'Your mother?' said Peter very slowly, enunciating each vowel very carefully 'Don't lie to me wife, I listened in on the extension upstairs I know very well who you were talking to.'

Tania stared open mouthed, she was petrified. This man, her husband, had changed before her eyes. She saw in his eyes the desire to kill, Marina had been right her husband was an evil man. Tania's instinct for survival took over. She raised her right knee and pummelled it into Peter's groin. Screaming in agony he released her, his hands instinctively moving to between his legs. Tania staggered against the chair to catch her breath as Peter dropped to the floor. He sat slumped like a marionette with its strings sliced through. Suddenly he didn't seem so manic. He seemed more like a man who had given up all hope, lost and alone.

He began to sob, his shoulders heaving and his head dipped between his knees.

'I didn't mean to kill her. I didn't mean to kill her.'

He kept repeating the words like a mantra. It was as if he thought if he said them often enough they would become the truth.

'Who didn't you mean to kill?' Tania asked hesitantly.

'My children's nanny, Sandra, I didn't mean to kill her. I panicked, went too far. I never meant to kill her. I swear Tania I am not a bad man just an unlucky man. My God has forgiven me but the British public would have me lynched.'

Tania was repulsed. This man, this man who had shared her bed who had touched her intimately, this man had killed. The blood of his children's nanny stained his hands. Her blood ran cold and her flesh recoiled at the thought. Instinctively she knew she had to hide these feelings from her husband. Her reaction could send him over the edge. My god he was so close. If he thought he had nothing left to lose who knew what he was capable of.

'I know you are a good man at heart,' said Tania, not because she believed it but because she wanted to pacify him. She desperately wanted to get away from him and away from the house but she knew he was more agile and could easily catch her. Her words had the desired effect. Pity was the key to her escape, pity and the illusion of forgiveness.

'Would you help me Tania,' he pleaded pathetically. 'You are my only hope. I have money, lots of money. Will you help me? Will you help your husband.'

At this stage Peter had risen to his knees and he was begging her. How pitiable he looks, this strong husband of mine Tania thought to herself. Despite what had happened she could no longer think of him as a murderous man. Surely a murderous man would have taken his chance and strangled her. He was far stronger and larger than she. No this was not a dangerous man this was a frightened man. A man trapped who had reacted by attacking He was a cornered rat. His words played upon her mind. Well one word really if she were honest, the word 'money'. Money which would help her son out of his situation. Surely something good should come from something bad.

'I know you are not really evil man' she reasoned, crossing to his side, forcing herself to lay her hand upon his shoulder. 'I will help you, but only if you help me in return.'

'Anything, anything, please Tania. See me I am begging.'

'I want you to give me twenty thousand English pounds and I will ask my mother to provide a safe house for you in Cherkassy.'

'Twenty thousand?' said Peter trying to keep the note of incredulity from his voice. Stupid Ukrainian woman, he would have paid so much more. He had twenty times that amount hidden behind the fireplace, more than enough to secure a good life anywhere abroad.

'But Peter you must leave immediately.'

Even as she uttered these words Peter was foraging behind the fireplace for the cash he had hidden. Taking care that she did not see the full amount he counted out twenty thousand into her hands. Then he collected the rest of the cash and grabbed his passport from the bureau. The fake passport had cost a trip to Newcastle and an exorbitant amount of used twenty pound notes but Peter was glad he had seen fit to have a contingency plan in place for an event such as this. It would ensure his safe passage to pastures new.

'I will ring my mother, she will be expecting you,' said Tania.

'Thank you Tania, thank you my wife.'

'Go, go,' said Tania ushering him out of the door not fully relaxing until she heard his car tyres sliding on the gravel as he sped down the Crag.

Tania raced upstairs and hid the money in her overnight case before going back into the lounge to wait for Marina. Whilst she sat waiting she quickly formulated a plan. She would tell Marina and the police almost everything, with any luck Peter would be arrested before he set foot on Ukrainian soil. About the money she would say nothing. The money, the blood money was hers, her divorce settlement. It would be enough to pay off Nicholai's debt and hopefully secure a future for her son and herself in England.

ASHLEIGH GROVE – JESMOND
– A TOUCH OF CLASS

Joey had just arrived at the party. It was in full swing with the usual Labour Party supporters already slumped worse for wear upon the floral sofa's in the lounge. Joey made her way through to the kitchen hoping to find the host there. A throng of people were surrounding a tall woman. From the back she looked well dressed with a 'touch of class' about her. Maria the host let out a cry of welcome as she saw Joey enter the room and 'the woman' and the rest of the crowd turned. Oh my God thought Joey as her eyes met the eyes of 'the woman', it was her, older yes, but her. How many years had it been since they shared that brief dalliance and secret tryst? Suddenly she remembered that the local newspaper had hinted that she may visit the area in her capacity as newly elected Minister for ....

'The woman' raced to Joey's side and 'air kissed' her on both cheeks. As her lips grazed Joey's cheek for a fraction longer than socially acceptable Joey felt a frisson of excitement course through her. Yes there was no question that .... was still in the closet but her eyes told another story. Once they had been very nearly 'women in love'. Discreet as always, once they were joined by the others the talk again returned to politics and the probability of having the A1 from Nowhere to Edinburgh widened. But looks were exchanged between the two and Joey reasoned that perhaps the day would not be the 'Sunday Bloody Sunday' it had initially started out to be.

JEAN TAKES A TRIP

Jean was perplexed. This feeling, this jealousy was taking over her life. She had been through enough during the last year and she was afraid that coping with duplicity in a potential lover could just tip her over the edge. She needed to get a fresh unbiased insight upon the dilemma. Who better than her old dear friends Sooty and Lennie? Making a positive decision for the first time that morning Jean threw some fresh underwear into her overnight bag and reversed her car out of the driveway and onto the motorway.

It was only when she reached the junction to Nowhere that she realised it may have been prudent to have checked if either woman were at home first. But as she told herself, if Lennie were not at home Sooty was sure to be and either woman would provide a welcoming shoulder to cry on and a calm voice of reason.

HAPPY EVER AFTER

Louisa lay in Sooty's arms. The three legged cat sprawled upon the chair at the foot of the bed lazily cleaning its paws. Sooty looked down at Louisa and revelled in her good fortune. I love this woman more than life itself she told herself and if I could bottle this moment forever I would. All that I hold dear is in my arms. She craned her neck and kissed Louisa upon the forehead.

'Bit lower,' Louisa mumbled shuffling from Sooty's arms until she lay alongside her. Sooty raised herself up onto her elbows and took Louisa's nipple tenderly into her mouth flicking it with her tongue.

'Very nice,' said Louisa 'but lower still.'

'Lower?' teased Sooty.

'Yes lower.'

Sooty ran her tongue down Louisa's stomach and came to rest upon her navel. Her tongue snaked into the tiny folds of flesh.

'Is this low enough?' she asked raising her eyes questioningly.

'No lower,' Louisa whispered her eyes masked with pleasure.

'Shush darling, you'll disturb the neighbours,' joked Sooty.

Suddenly there was a knock on the front door. Both women jumped apart.

'Shush let's pretend we're out,' Sooty whispered raising her digit finger to her lips before adding, 'I do hope it isn't the neighbours.'

Again there was a knock at the door, but this time louder and more sustained. 'Bugger, I shall have to answer it,' said Sooty. 'Just lie there I will be straight back.'

'I'm not going anywhere darling,' said Louisa. 'My legs are like jelly, what have you done to me?' she teased.

Sooty could see the silhouette of a figure through the patterned glass of the front door. Whoever it was knew that she was in, they were not going anywhere. Wrapping her dressing gown tightly around her middle she struggled to tie the belt. Sooty opened the door a sentence forming in her mind to explain how she was in such a state of undress at such a time in the afternoon.

'I'm sorry I've been so long,' she started. 'But you've just caught me getting out of the b.....' the end of the explanation trailed away as she realised she was speaking to her old friend Jean.

Desperately trying to regain her composure she continued. 'Hello Jean, this is a surprise.'

'I'm sorry to drop in unawares,' said Jean. 'I was desperately hoping either you or Lennie would be at home. I've already been to Lennie's, no joy there, and I'm desperate for a pee.'

Sooty moved aside so Jean could enter the house.

'You know where the little girl's room is,' Sooty said, silently thanking the fact that she had a downstairs loo.

Now her only problem was how to get Louisa out of the house without her walking slap bang into Jean. Jean came out of the loo a few minutes later drying her hands on the legs of her trousers.

'Typical Sooty,' she joked. 'No hand towel. You really do need a wife.'

Suddenly there was a muffled noise from above. Both women looked towards the stairs. Footsteps could be heard walking from the bedroom into the bathroom then the sound of running water.

'Is Lennie here?' asked Jean.

When Sooty didn't answer Jean persevered in her questioning.

'So, if it isn't Lennie who is the mystery woman upstairs?

'Just a woman,' answered Sooty enigmatically.

'Just a random woman,' Jean teased. 'Come on Sooty spill the beans.'

But before Sooty had a chance to answer Louisa appeared like a vision at the top of the stairs. The sunlight streaming in from the window in the hallway framed the tableau. Louisa held the stair rail to steady herself. She stood stock still as if she had seen a ghost. Jean raised her eyes upwards. She lifted her hand to her mouth, a gasp escaping from between her fingers. Their eyes locked and time stood still. No-one uttered a word. Jean gazed at Louisa. Louisa gazed at Jean.

Then Louisa half tripped, half tumbled down the stairs and they met in a wonderful forever embrace. Words were not necessary, words were just audible sounds. This moment needed no words. It was if the rest of the world had ceased to exist and it was at that precise moment that Sooty realised that she had lost Louisa forever. For true love never dies, the flame never goes out. It flickers, it dims, but it never goes out. One glance, one look and it reignites.

Well Jean and so our story ends.

We walk away arm in arm. We walk away with waves lapping at our toes.

Beyond us is a glorious orange blazing sunset. The happy ever after I promised you when I held you in my arms all those years ago. Write our story, you said to me and I have.

AFTERWORD

Meanwhile life in Nowhere and beyond goes on.

Bob the taxi driver returns home after a long day at work. Yvonne his wife hands him his reheated tea. Her fingers are stained with oil paint and she carries a constant aroma of white spirit about her. She has had a promise of an Exhibition, her first real Exhibition despite 'Madonna of the Pinks' still hanging in the National. She is frantically trying to complete her debut solo collection using the events of the past year as her inspiration. Bob still spends an inexplicably large amount of time in his shed at the bottom of the garden. Hidden in a suitcase is a complete wardrobe of ladies clothes. One day, but not yet, he will be brave enough to speak to Yvonne. One day, but not yet, he may even complete the transformation and become the woman he feels he was cheated of by a quirk of fate.

George still has regular dates with Raymond his much younger lover. He tells himself that he is safe. He tells himself that no-one else will guess his secret. But George is getting older and Raymond wants more. George cannot give more. George is so far into the closet that even a wire coat hanger cannot prise him out. Lillian is his foil, his beard, his mask of normality. She plays the game for the rewards it affords her. One day George will stumble from his closet into Narnia and be devoured by the lion and the witch.

Sooty and Lennie are back together. Lennie is even considering moving back into Gloucester Court. Their latest failed relationships apparently just a hiccup in their life journey together. As Lennie has said and Sooty confirms 'the grass is not always greener'. But words left unsaid also ring true. I feel it won't be long before one or both ladies spread their wings again. The yearning to feel the wind whip their feathers is a powerful one. They will both soon fly again. Solo.

Joey still runs the Greenhouse Bistro with Louisa. It's complicated they tell people. Liz has moved into the house with Joey, and Louisa is currently living in the Penthouse flat with Jean. Liz is still riding high on solving the Lord Lucan Mystery. The movie company who are producing the WTF calendar story are considering making a Lord

Lucan expose. Liz is secretly in love with Joey, always has been, but the transition from friend to lover is a tricky one. At the moment she is providing a shoulder to cry on, all the while wishing that Joey would see her, really see her. Joey meanwhile is enjoying secret assignations with her closeted lover but her visits to the House have been remarked upon and it will not be long before the Press starts sniffing around again.

Martin and Marina are engaged to be married. Marina finds it a very bourgeois thing to do. She still likes to think of herself as a bohemian, a nonconformist but Martin insists that now that she has given birth to their second child Miranda, it is the proper thing to do. Ferdinand and Ariel the cats complete the happy family. The tempest has blown over their lives and all is calm for the time being.

Tania still lives upon the Crag. Her mother and Nicholai her son moved in a while ago. Tania has been offered a permanent job as housekeeper for Larkspur Rise, she is beside herself with joy at the prospect of working in a house with two young children. Her marriage to Peter has been annulled. As a special dispensation the government have allowed her to stay in England. Nicholai is studying for a degree in Politics, one day perhaps Downing Street? Tania's mother has an appointment to see a Bupa specialist who claims a simple operation can control her chronic condition.

Ruby is driving across Yorkshire to spend the weekend with her lover Dianne. She's feeling insecure. Dianne doesn't seem as enamoured as she once was. She is certainly not as romantic as she had been when Ruby was in her brief relationship with Jean. Ruby does not enjoy being dragged across the road to spend time with Dianne's parents, Victor is a sweetie but Betsy is hostile. The lovemaking too has changed. Ruby sometimes feels that she is an itch that Dianne feels compelled to scratch. Ruby often thinks of Jean, her honesty, her gentle sense of humour, and wishes she hadn't allowed Dianne to sweep her of her feet, but hey she's made her bed and it's a tough old world out there in the dating scene.

Tracey still sleeps with Sandra, occasionally but more out of habit than lust. She still tries to contact Lennie, but to no avail as Lennie refuses to acknowledge or return her calls. Tracey realises what she had and what she has thrown away, but also realises that it is too late now.

Peter lies basking in the brilliant Brazilian sunshine. He often laughs as he thinks of the wild goose chase his wife Tania sent the British Police on. To think he would be so stupid to trust her promise of a safe house. He had seen the fear in her eyes. His friend the Earl has already been to visit. He travelled alone to fully enjoy the 'entertainment' that his friend Lucky had laid on. He was relieved to find his libido intact although the little blue pill did help. His wife the Countess seems to be super glued to her gardening gloves these days, constantly overseeing the creation of her dream. Marie Antoinette had her Versailles so the Countess will have her Nowhere Garden.

Mrs Tears, Miss Tears and Mr Tears are still living in Nowhere, hatching, matching and despatching its inhabitant's.

Many miles away from Nowhere and Brazil the .... is also basking in the sunshine on a yacht. She has decided to ditch her older heart surgeon lover for the much more fun loving son of a department store empire. He has told her of his plans to whisk her to Paris for a romantic break. She smiles as she thinks of how much it will disgruntle her ex husband the .... and the bloody firm. She strikes a pose, languishing in the warm rays as she dips her toes into the clear blue sea, remembering to hold in her well toned stomach. The telescopic lenses glisten in the sun from their positions far away on the distant beach. Tomorrow's tabloid exclusive and next week's fish and chip paper.